THE FLY KING

By

Karling Abbeygate

STORY MERCHANT BOOKS
LOS ANGELES
2016

STORY MERCHANT BOOKS

Copyright © 2016 by Karling Abbeygate. All rights reserved.

No part of this book may be reproduced or transmitted in any form or by any means, electronic or mechanical, including photocopying, recording, or by any information storage and retrieval system, without the express written permission
of the author.

ISBN: 978-0-9981628-2-9

www.facebook.com/theflykingnovel

Story Merchant Books
400 S. Burnside Avenue #11B
Los Angeles, CA 90036

www.storymerchantbooks.com

TABLE OF CONTENTS

Prologue 5
Chapter 1 11
Chapter 2 19
Chapter 3 23
Chapter 4 26
Chapter 5 30
Chapter 6 38
Chapter 7 45
Chapter 8 50
Chapter 9 54
Chapter 10 57
Chapter 11 67
Chapter 12 68
Chapter 13 75
Chapter 14 78
Chapter 15 88
Chapter 16 97
Chapter 17 103
Chapter 18 108
Chapter 19 114
Chapter 20 119
Chapter 21 124
Chapter 22 128
Chapter 23 131
Chapter 24 137

Chapter 25	144
Chapter 26	152
Chapter 27	161
Chapter 28	166
Chapter 29	172
Chapter 30	181
Chapter 31	184
Chapter 32	191
Chapter 33	195
Chapter 34	198
Chapter 35	206
Chapter 36	213
Chapter 37	221
Chapter 38	223
Chapter 39	236
Chapter 40	241
Chapter 41	246
Chapter 42	250
Chapter 43	256
Chapter 44	266
Chapter 45	296
Chapter 46	301
Chapter 47	317
Chapter 48	323
Chapter 49	328
Chapter 50	332
Epilogue	358
Reader note	362

PROLOGUE

Chief Lumberman's Cottage.

Iddlesvein, Black Forest, Germany

27 Years Ago.

In the tiny clearing, smoke pig-tailed from chimney to sky, curling and picturesque.

Inside the cottage, the silver-haired midwife battled to keep Sara Günter and her unborn baby alive. Years later, with her dying breath, she would ask God's forgiveness for this.

Kneeling next to the bed, holding the patient's hand, was Jakob Günter. And behind, watching from the shadows, their five-year-old son, Delroy. Everyone knew the boy wasn't as the good Lord had intended. His exterior deformities were not the whole of it, either. There was something else. She'd felt it the first time she laid eyes on him.

"Jakob..." The midwife handed the man a towel, indicating he wipe some of the blood away. But Jakob was useless. He was shaking all over like a small dog.

Sara's death-white face peered anxiously down the bed. Then came the screaming.

Slick skin began emerging from between the woman's bloody thighs.

"Now, push...just a little more. You can do it. Push."

The midwife supported the baby's head in her hands. But there was something else. Within a moment she understood. It was a second baby.

"Oh, Jesus Christ!" This was bad.

"What? What's wrong?" Jakob asked.

"It's twins," she whispered. "If we don't open her--"

Before she could finish, Jakob's face crumpled and fell into his hands. He nodded slowly, whining like a broken machine.

Thirty minutes later the midwife was holding the twin girls in her arms. But this was not real. She felt disorientated. Shocked at what she saw before her.

The babies weren't deformed in the same way as the boy. They were conjoined, attached to each other from their little pink ribcages to their tiny hips. They wriggled independently, and somehow that made it worse.

Sara murmured. She was too weak to lift her head.

The midwife held the twins close to their mother, keeping the blanket tightly around them, hiding the truth.

"Twins, Sara. Beautiful little girls."

As the midwife tucked the babies into the crib she heard the boy's scratchy breath behind her. She turned. He met her eyes with a questioning look then dropped his gaze into the crib. These are his sisters, she thought. The idea shot panic through her heart. She sighed deeply and turned toward the dying mother.

Sweat had pasted Sara's hair in dark wet strings onto the pillow. She beckoned the midwife to come closer and on dry lips she whispered, "Fraulein, there is something...you must take."

The midwife felt suddenly as bloodless as the woman lying before her. She knew in her heart this moment had been coming. It was as if her whole life had been leading up to this. It was the reason she had sent her own child away all those years ago. Her own precious Magdalena who was now a middle-aged woman. Sent to America. Sent far away from this cursed place.

Sara reached her pale hand underneath the pillow. She paused, then brought out the thing that was hidden there.

A crudely forged iron dagger. Sides pitted and scabbed like wounds that never heal.

The midwife stared at it. Her breath stopped.

Everything stopped.

Except the sound of the fire, which seemed to grow louder.

"Take it...I'm sorry..." The woman held out the dagger, her thin arm shaking under the weight.

The midwife hesitated, Sara's grip loosened, and the dagger fell as if in slow motion, hitting the side of the mattress and dropping downward. Its point stabbed solid and hard into the wooden floor.

The midwife looked around for the boy.

He had fallen to his knees and was scuttling towards her.

Frightened, she moved back.

Grabbing the dagger, he pulled it easily from the wood. Then, sitting on his haunches he held the dagger high above his head. The midwife watched as a strange energy surged through his buckled little form. His wispy hair lifted around his head, charged with unnatural power. The seconds slowed to a deathly crawl, the scene scorching itself into her senses.

Was she slipping into a faint?

No! She blinked hard and slapped her hands over her powdery cheeks. *You must take it from him before it's too late.*

She reached down she clasped her hands around his.

Deroy's grip was strong. With difficulty, she pried his fingers from the handle one by one, his gray eyes blazing as she finally freed the dagger from his grip.

"Get over there!" She screamed.

He looked at her pitifully. The strange energy now gone, he slunk back into the corner.

She placed the dagger in her apron pocket. So heavy, she thought. Already weighing me down like an anchor to hell.

The midwife pressed her fingers on Sara's motionless neck. She was dead. A moment later, in grim punctuation, a gunshot punched off somewhere in the forest.

She had noticed Jakob edging toward the door but hadn't heard him leave. She didn't need to check to know he was dead, too.

She allowed herself to disengage for a second. Her eyes became glassy and she felt herself drift away, up above the cabin, where the smoke still curled in a calm little thread. Suddenly, she snapped back.

Her hands flew over her mouth, stifling a scream.

Somehow worse than the loss of life, than the little pink babies joined cruelly together, was *this*. His face frozen in a silent wail, the boy was smearing himself in his dead mother's blood.

Worse still, the thing in her pocket.

* * *

Translated excerpt from the notes of Frau Heiniger. Freiburg Social Service Agent.

5 year old Delroy Günter. Mother and father both recently deceased. Delroy has severe deformities and is socially inept. He may have some learning disabilities too but, otherwise is fit for special schooling.

The mother is originally from England and has a brother who still lives in London. She also has a sister who now lives in the USA.

I have just returned from escorting Delroy to London to live with his uncle. Personally, I am not comfortable allowing Delroy to be left in the care of this man. He showed no remorse for his sister's death or any warmth for the boy. He seemed like a foul man. Honestly I think an institution would have been better for Delroy under these circumstances. However, gut feelings are not facts, and unfortunately it's out of my hands.

The newborn twin girls are also afflicted. They are

conjoined. When old enough to travel, they will be adopted by their Aunt and taken to live with her and her husband in Chicago. I have spoken to the Aunt over the phone and she seems very nice indeed. However, she is eager for confidentiality. She wants the twins to know nothing of their beginnings. She wants to raise them as her own. She is not going to tell them about their brother, Delroy. I am not sure if I agree with this decision but, again, it's out of my hands.

CHAPTER 1

Hancock Real Estate.

Chicago, Illinois

27 years later.

The lady sitting opposite was the real estate agent in charge of vacation rentals. Rachel looked into her face and tried to get a sense of the woman: late fifties, tightly woven blue-sequined sweater with shoulder pads. She sipped black coffee and left startling pink lipstick smudges around the edge of her cup.

Gavin sat next to Rachel in the big soft armchair. Since he had come here under protest, she'd let him have the comfy one.

It had all started four months ago with a timid knocking at their front door. Rachel had opened it onto a crisp evening and two matronly volunteers from St. Anthony's standing either side of a wicker collection basket. Both women looked tired. They delivered an overworked yet heartfelt spiel about the poor unfortunate kids they were trying to help. Rachel melted and made a hefty donation, then invited the ladies in and offered them tea. They accepted gratefully.

Carefully moving a pile of sheet music from the couch, one of the ladies asked Rachel what line of work she was in. She told them that she and Gavin, her boyfriend, were musicians, and they had just released an album that was doing quite well in Japan.

Both ladies were impressed by her seemingly glamorous profession, and the short, fat younger one had gotten red-faced, as if she was in the presence of a superstar.

Not wanting to spoil their illusion, Rachel didn't tell them she could never have children of her own, that it was God's way of punishing her for what she had done. She also failed to mention that her life was like a watercolor painting washed with gray. As usual, she put up a good front because she would never quit hoping, never stop trying to rid herself of the shadows. *Pinks, blues, and bright music!* That's what she told herself. And she had Gavin to be thankful for. Even if she manipulated him from time to time, even if he was widely misunderstood and under-appreciated by her family and friends, he was, nonetheless, the love of her life.

Then, Rachel beamed with a sudden revelation, and before she knew it there was a plan in the works. She would write an album's worth of songs--children's songs--for their organization to raise money with. Another stab at redemption.

Gavin balked at the plan, but Rachel had gone ahead regardless, until she reached the stage where his audio mixing skills were needed to complete the album, which required full commitment from him.

After thinking about it, she came up with a solution. Convert the tour bus into a portable mixing studio, rent a vacation home, and park the bus alongside it. She would have her own space, and Gavin would have an inspiring change of scenery. It was a good *plan*. Unfortunately, Gavin still seemed irritated by the whole idea.

Now, he tapped his fingers on the tired velvet armrests while

Rachel rifled through a binder stuffed full of photos. All the properties were beginning to look the same. A reflection from the window bounced and glared on the plastic protectors, and by now she'd stopped angling the book to avoid it. Gavin sighed. Rachel wanted to sigh too.

"Anything more isolated?" she asked the agent.

Gavin crossed and uncrossed his legs, rat-tat-tatted his fingers.

"Well...I do have another book of rentals. Not on the East coast, though," the agent warned. Standing, smoothing out her sweater, she walked over to the metal filing cabinet.

"Please, Rachel, *please,* just pick a place."

"It has to be *right,* Gavin. Don't be so impatient."

He didn't want to get into a fight, so he kept his mouth shut. The things you do for love. That's what his mother always said, and she should know.

But Rachel had become so passionate about this *project.* Passionate, yes, but he feared this particular passion was fueled by her deep reservoir of guilt. And although her enthusiasm could be contagious, it was sometimes misguided. Now she'd involved *him* in this project of hers, and he was going to be stuck for two months--he didn't care how fucking lovely the scenery was--for *two fucking months* listening to kids songs. Over and over and over and over. He had much more important goals, musically. "Make a phenomenal, ground-breaking record," he'd told her, "money flows like water, and you give a big 'ole chunk to the kids." He'd argued his case to a deaf ear. And so, as usual, he'd given in. He smiled, despite himself.

He'd first met Rachel seven years ago at Chicago Sound Studio.

Gavin had been the house recording engineer, waiting for his 6:00 P.M. session. Some girl wanting a backing track. Rachel.

For him, meeting a new client was always nerve-wracking, especially when it was a beautiful female. Gavin was somewhat of a geek; his mother said he lacked tact and was awkward in company. But because of his rare musical talent, he'd become a successful recording engineer, despite his dubious people skills.

"Your world would be more pleasant," his mother told him, "if you were a little more outgoing." So he made the effort, but it was a square-peg/round-hole kind of effort. He'd figured out a few one-liners to break the ice, but too often they were followed by silence. Regardless of all the people he came into contact with, his world was lonely.

Only music transcended this feeling. When he was lost in the creation or admiration of music, he truly came alive with unquarantined excitement and wonder. Like a kid.

But from the moment he first laid eyes on Rachel, he somehow knew she had the capability of understanding him. She was gorgeous, yes. But that wasn't it. There was a sadness about her, a vulnerability, a loneliness. This *thing* cried out; he heard it like music as it reached inside him and grabbed his heart. All this before even a word had passed between them.

When the session was over, he told her she wouldn't have to pay, *if* he could take her out for dinner. It was the first thing that popped into his head. She took it all wrong, spat out a curt *"No thanks,"* paid, and left. Afterwards, the same *head* came up with infinite better ways he could have asked her out.

A month later, he was at the Brick Palace nightclub; he'd been invited to help judge the Chicago Songwriters Competition. The place was crowded. He sat stage front, sipping beer, avoiding people, and counting the seconds.

Contestant Number 3: The curtains pulled open and out came Rachel, singing to the track he'd produced for her, a sweet ballad about lost love.

He'd been mesmerized.

She won, of course.

He spoke to her at the bar afterwards and told her he had voted for her. "Only because you were the best," he added. She looked at him smiling, eyes squinting doubtfully. It was true, she had been the best, but he still felt like a big old liar because he would have voted for her regardless.

When she said she had to go, he wanted to ask if he could see her again. Perhaps they could listen to CDs or check out a concert together. Maybe she'd tell him what it was that sang so sadly from inside her.

Instead, he said, "Well, good-bye then," and watched her leave.

But after she'd gone and he'd had another couple of beers, he did something completely out of character. He snuck backstage, riffled through the contestants' papers, and got her phone number. The next day, after a restless night of mental rehearsing, he called.

She accepted his offer of dinner, and even told him that she'd planned on paying him a visit at the studio. The smile nearly ripped his face in two.

It had gone on from there. Seven years later, it was still the same. Even though he was grumpy, fussing and complaining, he always gave in to her. When she praised him, when she looked at him that certain way--which was *any* way--it was just the same. He was glad to orbit her sun.

Gavin watched the agent get another really thick folder from the filing cabinet and tried his best not to sigh.

The agent laid the folder on the edge of the desk, sat back down, and put her cup to her lips again.

"Your grandchildren?" Rachel asked, pointing to the framed photo on the woman's desk.

"No, those are my husband's grandchildren."

"Please. Rachel..." Gavin said, handing her the folder.

She began turning the pages. "Don't you want to look, too?"

He shook his head.

Now, Rachel did sigh. She rested her eyes on the pictures, looking *through* rather than *at* them. Perhaps she'd made a mistake. Distractedly, she turned the page.

She saw the cabin.

The plastic protector began rattling slightly between her fingers as her eyes fixed on the picture. The photo was blurry and faded, but something in her corrected, adjusted, and brought the scene to life.

But it wasn't the cabin drawing her in. It was the forest surrounding it. And how far back did the forest go? A good distance, she thought, nodding as she looked. A good distance back there.

As she stared, she began rubbing her side.

"What are you doing?" Gavin asked, sounding alarmed.

"Nothing." Rachel dropped her hand, but the feeling remained. Creeping up and down the scar, as if it were coming undone.

Damp pine air, the faint rustling of a bird landing high in a treetop, the hypnotic drone of the river running alongside. The water would be cold--really cold. The skin on her arms puckered as if splashed by it.

"Where is this?" she managed to ask, although it didn't matter. Gavin would handle the details; he'd figure out how to get them there, which roads to take, what time to leave, where to stay on the way. Gavin would talk about the cost and the keys and the conditions. All she knew was that this was it.

"What you're looking at there is the Black Woods of Klickitat, Washington. About seventy miles east of Portland. "It's a lovely cabin, isn't it?"

"Too far," Gavin said.

Rachel heard them peripherally, like two little sparrows tick-ticking at each other. Yet it all seemed strangely familiar, as though she were perched on some gateway between past and future. Gavin and the agent--actors, puppets spinning lines that had been written an eternity ago.

"Wake up, Rachel." Gavin tugged at her arm, but she didn't care to come back.

"How much?" he asked the agent.

"For three months? That would be..."

Little sparrows chirp, chirp, chirping, fighting over the crumbs. That was fine. This was the place.

"Would you like to hear the history of the Black Woods?"

Rachel could hear an extra chirp in the agent's voice; things must be going well.

Her side was still itching, but she didn't rub it. Wouldn't help to let Gavin see that.

"Back in the 1800s, German immigrants from a tiny village called Iddlesvein in the Black Forest took a ship over to America." The agent paused and sipped. "They brought seeds from the Black Forest along with them, settled in Klickitat, Washington, planted the seeds and...voilà! The Black Woods." She held her hands open like a magician, as if the trees had grown overnight purely to assist her in renting the cabin.

"Anyway, the saw mill closed ten years ago. Very quiet town. Your cabin and...I believe, one other cottage are the only structures that were built in the forest itself. Perfect for your...your...*thing*." The woman waited, but neither Rachel nor Gavin spoke.

"Well, then..." She clapped her hands together. "Should we start the paper work?"

Half an hour later, the sky had clouded over, and Gavin held Rachel's hand as they hurried to the car.

"You satisfied?"

"Yes, I'm satisfied."

A melody had begun circling around in her head. At first, it felt so familiar that she thought it must be one of the children's songs she'd written. But it was older. She kept thinking *Greensleeves,* but this tune wasn't nearly as pretty. She felt it had words too, but they escaped her. She wanted to hum it, but something told her not to.

Rachel put her hand in her coat pocket and, after a few seconds, brought out a Kleenex. She didn't really need it; her hand had been in the pocket scratching at the scar.

CHAPTER 2

Wapping, East London

It was dark inside the oven. Delroy turned his head a little. The pain in his neck was un-fucking-real.

As he breathed in more gas, the space in the oven became even darker. His neck began to go numb, and he could feel his tongue starting to prickle. *Peter piper pricked a peck of prickled pickle*...then the hissing stopped. He blinked, and waited.

"Ah, fuck me!" He pulled his head out, the pain bolting up his neck and into his skull. "Fucking gas meter." He fished though his pockets, already knowing there was nothing in them. God would never oblige him with one last fifty-pence piece for the meter. No fucking way. Shit, this was so typical of his luck. What a wanker he was. *Pathetic* was actually the word that came to mind.

Delroy walked through his filthy basement flat and up the unfinished wooden steps to the door. The flat was an old converted basement-storage area. No shower or bath, just a twelve-foot-square room, a doorless closet with a toilet and a sink rigged up in it, and a poky little kitchen full of mouse shit and bugs. Like bleedin' Buckingham Palace. The jerk-off who'd lived here before him had left an old armchair, a black-and-white TV, and a piss-stained mattress. That was all the furniture Delroy owned. The place was obviously a shit-hole, but the way Landlord Bill complained, you'd think it was the Taj-Ma-fucking-hal.

He opened the door and took in a big lungful of back-alley air. The gas had made him feel sick. He wanted to die, not feel sick--he'd already had enough of that. Every day was a fucking miserable pain-filled lifetime. Unless of course he scored pain killers.

What a moron. He couldn't even manage to kill himself without fucking it up. He'd killed Uncle Ross, though, hadn't he? Seventeen years ago. It still seemed like this morning. Uncle Ross had deserved it, and Delroy was still paying the price. No doubt, God's punishment would last a lifetime and beyond. *Fuck you, God. Okay, I take it back, take it back. Yeah, yeah, yeah.* He coughed and spat phlegm on the ground, watching the cockroaches scuttle toward the dumpster.

Uncle Ross. What a sweetheart. He'd hooked Delroy out to perverts, even put him in a couple of porn flicks. Right fuckin' movie star he'd been. Delroy had never been able to get a hard-on, no matter what they did. Still couldn't, his equipment didn't work. Another one of God's little jokes.

He couldn't stand mirrors either, then or now. First thing he'd done when he moved into this place was smash the one in the bathroom with his fist. He looked okay in a broken mirror, like a jigsaw puzzle. Still, pieces never fit together, not unless you force them to.

Uncle Ross was always on his mind. Cocksucker. And Uncle James. 'Course, Uncle James wasn't a real uncle, he was a nasty fat-bellied little prick who liked to jerk off while Delroy undressed. Had him turn around so he could see the way his shoulder blades stuck

THE FLY KING

out to the moon. "Look at those," he'd say as the bed squeaked and rocked. "Can ya fly, Del? Can ya bark for me?" Then he would inspect Delroy's tiny little *thing*, gloating and insulting till the tears streamed from Delroy's bulby eyes, down his lumpy cheeks. Then the inevitable butt-fuck. The old cunt wasn't the only one, either. Uncle Ross knew where to find all the pervies. For an orphan, Delroy had never been short of uncles.

Delroy stood in the doorway of his flat, smoking and thinking. He couldn't decide if God was a cruel child who toyed with him like an ant on the pavement, crippling him with a magnifying glass, making his life unbearable while the other ants moved happily around unnoticed, or if it was the reverse, and God simply cared for the others and not for him. Booted him off the conveyor belt with a giant *REJECT* stamped on his head.

Uncle Ross had finally gotten what was coming to him. Delroy had planned it every moment of every day, but when it actually happened, it wasn't planned at all. But God knew everything, and now Delroy was paying for his sins. *Yep, God knows everything. Except mercy.*

Leaving Uncle Ross dead in his stinky old recliner--head crushed in, Aunt Gracy's cast-iron frying pan lying on the floor next to him-- Delroy had run away to the underbelly of the East End.

He was fifteen at the time, and he'd been an outlaw for seventeen years now, getting no help from anyone, hiding in the shadows like a beast. Aunt Gracy was a total cunt. He'd been glad to see the last of her, too. Although, occasionally, he regretted the whole thing. At least back then he'd had a family.

Sometimes at night, after he'd snatched some poor old bird's handbag and scored painkillers, he'd lie in bed and his mind would just kinda go away. It would float around for a while, and then all of a sudden he'd be in this other body, one that didn't hurt. He'd be in America, and there would be his sisters. He and his sisters. He'd be a well-dressed bloke with nice hair and a nice smile, and his sisters would be beautiful. Separated, so as they were two instead of one.

"Delroy, we're so proud of you," they'd say. "We love you so much." Bittersweet fucking dream it was. *What would they really say, I wonder. If they even knew I existed.*

He closed the door and hobbled back down the stairs into his room. The gas smell was fading. Not even fifty fuckin' pence. He was broke.

Lying on the mattress, he stared up at the ceiling. He couldn't see it, the lights were out, but he could picture it in his head; stained yellow with smoke and damp, riddled with cracks that spelled out words in a language he didn't understand. Chinese, he supposed. Then there was Landlord Bill. He'd have to talk to that wanker tomorrow about the rent, but that was another story. He closed his eyes and sighed. *Fuck You very much, God. Take it back. Okay, okay, I take it back.*

God, if only you'd given me some lovable trait. But God hadn't. Delroy's soul was stuck in this stinkin' cage, while others around him flourished in shining palaces. And the more those fuckers sparkled, the more tarnished he felt.

He pulled the thin blanket up around his chin. As he relaxed, he began to hum. A strange little tune, a lullaby or a nursery rhyme, something he might have heard as a lad. Didn't know the words, but he thought maybe he had once, a long, long time ago.

CHAPTER 3

Klickitat, Washington

As they drove, the October cottonwoods provided a vivid canopy above them. Gavin kept his eyes on the road ahead, which was narrower and steeper than he'd imagined.

He shifted into a lower gear as they continued to climb, still paying close attention to the road. Every so often, when the trees thinned away, he caught a glimpse of the wide and wonderful Klickitat River.

Already, they were on the backside of the day. The sun cast its golden light through the leaves onto Rachel, dappling her skin and hair with a beautiful orange shimmer.

Gradually, a few miles up the road, evidence of a town started to appear. First, the altitude leveled off, then the road widened and the canopy of trees gave way to a clear view of the river. In this perfect light, it traveled like honey, glistening and rich. But Gavin knew that up close a river like this was bound to be cold and cruel.

An abandoned car, complete with bullet holes, turned over by the side of the road came next. A field, a dilapidated barn, a yellowed yard-sale poster nailed to a tree. Finally, side roads. Fluss Lane, Schwarz Forest Pass, Wald Peak...

Gavin saw a short wooden pier in the river and someone, the first person they'd seen in hours, sitting at the end fishing.

He'd had reservations about this trip, but now that it was happening, he was excited. And he liked driving the bus. The constant roar of it made him feel as if they were in the belly of a giant beast.

"Rachel, would you get Kiki off me, please?" He had tried to convince Rachel to leave the cat with friends, but she wouldn't hear of it. Damned thing looked at him with those saucer eyes as though it knew what he was thinking. He tried to be nice to it, he really did.

"Kiki, come here, sweetie. Come to Mommy. Leave Daddy alone."

Gavin cringed. The worst part was that the cat adored him and didn't give a shit about her. Selfish animal. He petted it as she lifted it from his lap.

"We must be getting close," Rachel said.

"Yeah." He looked at her. The sun was even lower now, and her face glowed a warm pink. Her eyes were dark, like two black bees on a pretty wild rose. He cleared his throat and slid his new Calstrani CD into the player. To Gavin, musical tones were like colors, like the splashes of rose on Rachel's face.

"You should get a job as a lumberjack, Rachel. Give you something to do while I'm working on your album."

She smirked. "Should I wear my blue plastic mini-skirt?"

They bantered back and forth, chattering nervously the way people do when unknown adventures lay ahead. Rachel rolled down the window, leaned out and shouted, "Tim--ber!"

She was happy, and that was good. "Really, though," he said, taking his eyes off the road to look at her again in the fading rosy light, "we'd better watch out for the locals. They'll be the inbred mongoloid relatives of those German pilgrims Coffee-Breath told us about." He squeezed an *um-pa-pa um-pa-pa* out the side of his mouth.

Rachel laughed. "Well, if I'm going to be a bratwurst-eating lumberjack, then..." She fell silent as they passed a sandwich-board sign sitting close to the edge of the road. *Candles and Magick.*

Back farther was a house nestled in the trees.

"Uh, oh, watch out...witches in the woods." He creased his brow for her, but she wasn't looking at him. She didn't appear to hear him, either.

Sometime in the last second or two, the sun had lost its strength. Rachel sat in thin blue light, pale shadows hanging from her cheeks. He saw her reach for the scar, but she hesitated, resisted, gripped her armrest instead--hard enough for him to see white knuckles, like a row of tightly shaved monk heads, poking out from the skin.

Gavin turned back to the road. She could be peculiar sometimes.

CHAPTER 4

Magdalena held the curtain out of her view as she watched the tour bus go by. The rings on her fingers tatted on the glass. *Stop shaking, you old fool. It's just a bus.*

It took five seconds for it to pass by and disappear around the bend in the Klickitat Road, which was about normal, she noted. Normal? Then why had she gotten up in the first place, fifteen minutes ago, and raised the goddamn curtain? Why had she been expecting it?

She looked behind her. The bedroom lay in shadows. Those gloomy shapes edging up on her back, those didn't frighten her. But that red tour bus, gleaming and new...

This was insane. She had, as they used to say in high school, the heebie jeebies. But she'd been out of high school for over forty years. Twenty of those had been spent as a world-renowned psychic and parapsychologist. *Hardly the type of career that lends one to random bouts of nonsense, huh?* She chuckled slightly but it was true. At least for her. Some psychics got off track, started believing that no rules applied. Her mother most definitely had. But not her. Until now.

Knowing her mother had gone crazy didn't help at all. It was a hereditary complaint, like alcoholism or arthritis. It wasn't a given, of course, but it certainly left her feeling vulnerable.

She tried not to ponder on her mother and the reasons why a woman, a respectable mid wife, would send her thirteen-year-old girl thousands of miles away to live in a country full of strangers.

It had come right after her birthday. Had Mother been crazy way back then? She didn't seem it, but her actions said yes. The whole thing seemed more than crazy to her thirteen-year-old daughter. It seemed cruel.

Magdalena let her eyes drift across the road and rest on the river. Dusk had fallen. The arm-wrestle between day and night had already begun. They'd battle it out for a while, until day inevitably surrendered, leaving darkness to bow and take the stage. She felt a cold stone in her stomach turn slowly with the strange tide that had come in. She waited.

Waited for the bus to come back past her window.

Ever since Mother died (was it ten years ago already?), Magdalena had refused to entertain the spirit world. That's how she saw it, too. A hostess, a babysitter, a Kiss-O-Gram. A strange ability, for sure, but it didn't seem to serve any higher purpose. In the end, something of a sideshow act. Instead of an extra limb hanging off her torso, she had an invisible one hanging off her brain.

Having psychic powers wasn't at all how people imagined. There was nothing different about the dead. If they had been mean in life, they usually continued to be mean afterwards. And anyhow, she had only been a peon at the crossover point. Dealing with tearful relatives, showing grumpy passengers to their assigned seating, making sure baggage was checked (and most had plenty). Then she'd disembark, wave good-bye from the terminal, and off you go. Destination unknown.

Magdalena had sensed Mother's passing. She remembered exactly where she was when it happened. Rain beating down on the windshield of her Volkswagen. Sometime between the beginning of St. John's Bridge, Portland, Oregon, and the end. Mother died somewhere in the middle of the Willamette River. Magdalena had known, and right then, she quit. Closed the door and let that extra limb hang unused. She still felt her mother trying to get in at times, but it was too late for that. She'd see her on the other side. If they had tickets for the same place, if they really did, they could talk about it then.

Magdalena had arrived at almost three o'clock in the morning. She'd driven clear across the country to say good-bye. All the way from Lye, Connecticut, to her mother's cottage in Klickitat, Washington.

The rain had finally stopped, and she remembered walking for the first time down the little dirt path that led to the cottage, the sky as black as newly laid asphalt. And the stars seemed in disarray, clustered in strange configurations. It made her feel somehow, uncertain, about the future.

The house was set back twenty feet into the trees and looked like a fairy-tale cottage. Honeysuckle quaint. But she knew that somewhere in there, up there behind those closed curtains maybe, was her dead mother.

There's usually a serenity about the newly deceased, but the old woman had looked troubled. Her eyes were open and staring up, almost through the ceiling, her mouth stuck wide in a terrible last-breath gasp. She lay ridged on top of the blanket. Her legs were

THE FLY KING

covered in fresh dirt all the way up to her knees, and her pink nightgown was damp, ripped and filthy. What had she been doing? Magdalena stroked her mother's thin white hair and cried.

She sat next to her, stroking her hair for the longest time. It was so soft, like a little child's.

Eventually, hours later, a weak dawn light arrived, and the birds nesting in the oak tree outside the window began to sing. She left Mother's side and brought her bags in from the car.

Magdalena's youthful dream had been to help people with her talents. To make a difference, use her gifts for the betterment of mankind, perhaps even in some profound way. But in the end, she couldn't even help her own mother.

Finally, Magdalena let the curtain down. She'd been watching the empty Klickitat road for over an hour.

It was dark.

The light had lost again.

CHAPTER 5

Gavin pulled the bus into the tiny parking lot, filling most of it.

Jack's Shack was the name of the market. A sign, hand painted on wood, hung above the door, the words flaking off in black crispy shreds. He didn't suppose Jack's Shack would have much in the way of nutrition. He and Rachel would have to do their grocery shopping thirty miles away, in Hoodriver.

"You stay here, I'll go ask directions."

Gavin took the piece of paper Coffee-Breath had given him and jumped from the bus.

A heavyset Indian man was sitting cross-legged in front of the store. Gavin looked away to avoid eye contact.

"Got any change?"

"Sorry, I don't," Gavin said, tapping his pockets, which jangled a little.

Inside, he went directly to the counter help, whom he presumed was Jack or at least a close relative, since this man couldn't possibly be employed by anyone other than himself or family. He wore a limp, colorless Harley Davidson T-shirt and oily jeans. Gavin thought he could actually see the man's skin oozing toxins.

"Hey, there. Can you tell me how to get to this cabin?" Gavin handed him the paper.

"Ah, yeah, the old Jenkins place. What, are you renting it? Buying it?"

"Just renting it is all." Gavin looked around the store. One full wall was refrigerated rows of cheap beer. Boxes of it, bottles of it, cans of it, every form of it imaginable. The place was almost a specialty shop.

"Uh, what are ya gonna be doing? Fishing? That's a big bus. What kinda bus is that?"

Gavin looked around toward the bus and saw that Rachel was outside talking to the guy, giving him money.

"Uh, looks like she's fallin' for old Zak's bull. That your wife? Girlfriend?"

Gavin didn't reply.

"So what ya gonna be doin' in the woods, little lady?" Jack asked as Rachel opened the door.

"We're mixing a children's album," she said.

Gavin scratched the side of his neck, pulling a pained expression that she wouldn't have liked.

"Ah, so that's what the bus is for, then."

"How do you get to the cabin?" Gavin asked, throwing some sprouting potatoes and a bag of onions on the counter.

"Want some steak to go with those?" Jack smiled, showing them his bad teeth. "Got some in the freezer over there."

"I'm a vegetarian," Rachel said.

"Ah, I couldn't do without meat."

"Kid's album, eh?" He looked at Gavin. "I like good old rock 'n' roll myself. Pink Floyd..." He started thrashing air guitar, using his mouth as distortion.

Gavin took a step back then explained that the children's album was an isolated incident, they were actually *serious* musicians.

"Ah? Got any demos?"

Before Gavin could stop her, Rachel was back in the bus, getting both Zak and Jack CDs and promo photos.

Before they left, Jack gave them a red plastic fly swatter. "Trade ya," he said, holding the CD in one hand and the fly swatter in the other. Gavin took the damned thing and threw it in the bag with the food. Once outside, they laughed pretty hard.

* * *

Jack watched them pull away in their big expensive bus. *What's a cute chick doin' with a dork like that?*

Zak came in the store as soon as the strangers had left.

"What do *you* want?" Jack asked him, with an easy contempt.

Zak took his promo picture and rubbed it over his crotch.

"I wouldn't kick her out of bed for eating cookies." His voice was hoarse and his laugh sounded like an old dog barking. "I gotta get this for my little 'uns." He slapped the six-pack on the counter.

Jack didn't answer. He was examining the picture on the front of the CD.

"*Glory Girl*. What kinda fucking dipshit title is that?" He looked out at the expensive vehicle disappearing down deserted Main Street, stirring up the dust.

* * *

The toilet bowl spoke for the cabin at large, filthy. A ring of rust grew about halfway down, and the water level was low. Rachel tried the handle. No resistance, it was floppy and loose. Great, she'd be crouching behind trees until Gavin fixed it. Just perfect.

The swatter hadn't been such a bad trade after all. The cabin was alive with flies. Right now, one was buzzing and thudding unpleasantly against the kitchen window. She slapped at it with the red plastic flyswatter, but her timing was a hesitant fraction off and the fly escaped.

She could see the bus, which was parked alongside the cabin, out the window. It was much more comfortable in there than in here. Gavin was probably laughing his ass off. She couldn't blame him. He hadn't liked the scraping of the trees as they'd edged it in, though. Neither had she. An amplified screech, like skeletal fingers dragging down a blackboard.

A dirt trail led from the cabin out of the woods, and then another dirt trail led back up to Main Street. The cabin was isolated all right. Coffee-Breath hadn't lied about that.

Rachel walked into the bedroom. A glaring, orange, junk-shop print of Paris hung opposite the bed, and the moth-eaten curtains were drawn closed. The carpet was filthy, greasy, suspiciously darker in some places than others. *Shit, so many flies.* She should check beneath the bed, make sure something hadn't died under there. She got down on her knees and cautiously looked underneath. The air wafted out cool and musty. Dark, but no dead bodies. At least none that she could see. The hairs on her neck pricked awake.

Rachel returned to the living room and looked out the window at the Klickitat River, roughly twenty feet from the cabin. What might've been an awesome view was obscured by high bulrushes and a giant boulder covered in aging graffiti. The little she could see of the river under the darkening sky looked gray and cold. But then, she already knew it would be.

A queer sense of *deja vu* drifted over her, and she felt a tickle on her arm. A fly. She brushed it off, but it was slow and sleepy and her hand made unpleasantly long contact with it. She felt its solidness, its wings opening, its body vibrating as it took off. Shouldn't flies be gone by this time of year, she wondered. Sleeping wherever flies sleep? Not on me, though, not on me, she thought, looking up at the ceiling. It was peppered with them. Her eyes moved back to the window, then over to the doors. *Ah, yes, no fly screens. Perfect.*

Gavin had been right about this place; he'd told her not to get her hopes up. He was usually right about stuff like that. He had good instincts.

It had taken them ages to get into the cabin. Rust had damaged the lock. When they finally got the key to turn, Gavin pushed the creaky door open, pulling apart dusty cobwebs. He went in first and turned on the kitchen light. After taking a brief look around, he held his hand up to his mouth and faked a cough--a cough Rachel suspected was hiding a smirk. "Well, then..." he'd said. "I'll start getting the bus set up." Then he had gone, leaving her with this.

It was growing steadily darker, so she flicked on the overhead light, half expecting no response, but a sickly yellow glow, like turned butter, came over the room. It became a sepia-toned murder scene, all but the yellow tape and the anxious detective. Oddly illuminated household objects seemed somehow sinister, as if they had been used for something despicable.

She spent about half an hour complaining to herself before beginning the clean-up process. She had brought some supplies, and there was a half-empty, dried-up box of Ajax under the sink, which she could rehydrate into a scrubbing paste. In the kitchen, she lit an incense stick and jabbed it into the soft wood around the window frame. Mildew, dirty paint, and a dead fly fell onto the counter.

The kitchen taps were mute for a second or two. Finally, they coughed, gagged, and puked up brown water.

By the time the moon was fully out, she had the place looking better. Tomorrow, she would find some flowers to brighten it up. She unpacked the candles and set them over the fireplace, lit them and turned off the ugly overhead light. She gave Kiki fresh water and dry cat food and placed her litter box by the side of the toilet. Gavin would hate it there.

"Okay, let's see if the gas works." She looked at Kiki. The cat frowned. Her primary concern seemed to be the unreasonable omission of soft food. Dry stuff was for the birds.

Rachel pushed open the cabin door and stepped outside with a cup of hot cocoa.

The trees, huge spruce pines, towered about her. The scent was overwhelming and heady, and when she looked up high into the treetops, up there on the cusp, she almost felt as if she were in a dream. As if anything might happen. As she continued to stare upwards, the slight ache in her neck was suddenly gone-- the awkward position suddenly, inexplicably comfortable. She'd been so annoyed by the state of the cabin, and the flies. But this place was theirs, not hers. *Perhaps she should just ask them to leave her alone.* A strange little laugh gurgled up from nowhere, and the treetops seemed to bend in slightly. Rachel's sleepy eyes stayed on them. She stood still, neck craned back, drifting away into the sounds of the forest. Then, like an image coming forth from seemingly random dots, it was there, filling her mind, the wind in the pine needles, the *ahhhshhhh* of the river--they were singing to her. Quite clearly she heard it.

"Ahhhshhhhh...Sleep my baby sleep

Sleep my baby sleep, Ahhhshhhh...

Time to close thy tired eyes

Shhhhhhh... Mother bring a sweet surprise..."

Were these the children's lyrics she had come to create?

The treetops darkened as her eyelids relaxed themselves shut.

Then, quickly, they snapped open. She stumbled, disorientated, bumping her back against a scratchy tree trunk. A wave of hot cocoa sloshed over the side of her cup and landed with a strange *whomp* on the forest bed.

Blinking and looking around now, she noticed the woods were grotto dark, the trees standing guard in every direction. But didn't the grottos in fairy tales always hold court to some terrible ogre? Rachel held the cup tightly and listened for footsteps coming through the forest. She laughed nervously. Whatever was she thinking?

But she couldn't help it. Her eyes traveled to the river and she wondered why it seemed to be escaping rather than flowing. Why did she feel as if the trees formed a cage, had her trapped, like a rabbit? No, not a rabbit, something else. Something rare. Something worth keeping.

She sipped at the remaining cocoa and tried to smell the chocolate over the pine but couldn't.

She walked farther away from the cabin and glanced at the roof. Those needles would *bury* this place if they didn't get cleaned off soon. The thought struck something deep.

Her mind turned away, refusing to look.

She laughed. Boy, was she doing a number on herself. It was fatigue, of course, blended with disappointment over the cabin. Tomorrow would be a new and beautiful day, and all this nonsense buzzing around in her head would be gone. And she bet the disturbing itch on her side would be gone, too.

Gavin had already started working. She could see his silhouette moving around inside the bus. Moments later, she was hearing "Never Be Afraid of the Dark." He was tweaking the vocal track, so it was her voice alone she heard, singing out into the forest night. A chill slipped like a snake from a branch down the back of her neck. I'd better get a jacket, she thought, but instead found herself walking deeper into the trees and onto a rutted track that was lit softly by the glow from the bus and candlelight from the cabin.

Gradually, the sound became lovely, the night sweet. She walked without looking down into the comforting dark blanket of the forest.

She found she was following her own voice. But it was an echo, perhaps, since it wasn't coming from back there but from ahead, somewhere deep in the belly of the woods. And the melody, the words...they were quite changed.

But it was certainly her song. She knew that.

CHAPTER 6

Wapping, East London

Delroy could only spare the money for one cheap beer. The last gal he'd snatched from was as broke as he was. Sometimes he scored big, fifty quid, a hundred. One time he'd nicked a purse with three hundred smackers in it. Not tonight, though, when he really needed it. It pissed him off.

"What the fuck are you looking at?" he said under his breath. His silent remark was pointed at a tall leggy blonde standing at the bar, but her back was turned to him, and so were her friends'.

As Delroy drank, his bottom lip stuck to the glass, limp and fleshy, like a slug shot up with Novocain. He was alone, of course, and the two tables either side of him were empty, even though the pub was packed.

The King Edward Inn was all low ceiling, white plaster and black beams. He'd never been in here before. Socializing wasn't his *thing*. He chugged his beer and thought about the half hour just gone, the half hour that ended with him sitting here at this fucking tray-sized table with a bunch of wankers as scenery.

He'd gone down to work the dock area. He needed another fifty

THE FLY KING

quid to make the rent money. It had been two nights since he tried to gas himself, the morning after which Bill had shown up with a sarcastic grin and an ultimatum. Delroy had been out busting arse ever since. *Two days to get the cash or you're out.* It was like a game show for Bill; he owned the fucking building, the whole row. It had been in his family for years. Bernard's furniture store, which sat above Delroy's flat, had been thriving there since 1864. That's how much Bill needed money. Wanker.

So, already tired, Delroy had made himself go out. The moon was full and the rain had slicked Dockside Road till it glistened, warping and reflecting the old Victorian streetlights, making it look as if he could walk down into it, like some gateway to a demented fairytale.

A ground fog sulked in low streaks, sometimes cutting Delroy off at the knees. Fucking fine by him. His knees where shit anyway, puffy and soft like cotton balls.

About five years ago, the wank-for-brains government started renewing Wapping, south of the Fenchurch Street railway line, doing up some of the old historical buildings that housed the pubs, cleaning up the docks--stealing it away from the locals and turning it trendy. But quite a few well-off tarts came around here now. The improvements had been good for business. Still, Landlord Bill and Delroy's wanker fence Weaz always seemed to have him by the balls.

It was quiet and late, the restaurants preparing to close. Soon, the last few customers would be spewing out the door like the vomit they were. Swanky fuckers.

In the beginning, stealing from people had made Delroy sick. But he'd had no choice. It was them who'd made him do it. If people weren't such heartless fuckers, maybe he could have gotten a job somewhere. Maybe the doctors could've helped him. Maybe he wouldn't have killed his uncle. Maybe, maybe, maybe. God has no mercy.

God had put him here to make the swanky bastards feel better about themselves. And so Delroy made them pay. A few quid here and there. Small price to be reminded of what you could've turned out like.

The Thames, dirty and still, sat behind the warehouse he hid in. The ground by the doorway was littered with crisp bags and fish 'n' chip papers, and kids had sprayed the few remaining windows blue, tagged the whole place up with obscenities. He sighed, pulled out a smoke. Kids were the worst. Cruel bastards. He'd attended school for less than a year when he was seven. Aunt Gracy was a drunk and a Catholic. One day, after a slurred conversation with God, she'd enrolled him into St. Mary's.

She'd given him a shirt three sizes too big so that his shoulders would fit in. He couldn't wear the jacket, so he carried it over his arm. The headmaster immediately informed Social Services, who made an appointment for him to see a specialist and a shrink. But Uncle Ross, scared Del would blurt something about his extended family, soon put a stop to that by pulling him out of school and moving them to the other end of Barking. Over the years, Delroy's condition got progressively worse.

He could see his breath pluming in the air as he peeked out of the warehouse. Across the street, a rich-looking couple pushed open the door of the French place and strutted onto the pavement. It looked ritzy in there, the candlelight and all. Delroy watched them, his attention fluctuating between bursts of laughter bouncing off the empty cobbled street and the rats scuttling behind him in the darkness. He preferred the rats.

The wanker kissed her goodnight and sped off in his brand new shiny Porsche, left her standing there digging around for her keys.

Some fucking gentleman. He drove right by Delroy, splashing water up from the puddles and potholes; there were still lots of potholes in the streets of Wapping, even with all the crappy re-modernizing.

Delroy came out of the warehouse, hunching through the ground fog, and crossed the road. He came up pretty fast. He planned to swipe her purse and take off down the alley left of the French place, get behind a dumpster and wait. Women never chased after him; they were scared of him. That's why he stuck to purses instead of wallets.

Un-fucking-fortunately, the bitch had one of those rape whistles, and before he even got close, she blew it. *Just at the sight of me?*

He ended up down the alley with nothing, crouched behind the dumpster waiting for her to leave in her white Mercedes. Still shy fifty quid.

And fuck, his shoulders hurt. Sometimes it felt as if he were carrying a sack of spuds around on his back.

He sat in the alley for ten more minutes, took a leak, then discovered, as if all that weren't bad enough, that he didn't have any cigs left. And it started to rain again. So he walked to the King Edward, opened the door like a surprise turd at a party, bought his cigs, eyed the pussy at the bar and thought, why the fuck not have a beer and a look. Free fuckin' country.

Now he was sorry he did.

The bitch with the long legs and blonde hair had looked at him briefly, then nudged her friend to move over, giggling and pulling a "yuk" face. People thought he was stupid. One day he'd show them who was fucking stupid.

He glanced at the fireplace. It was done up with farm stuff. A plow, horseshoes, a bridle, and a bunch of phony blokes sitting around it on bar stools talking and laughing like girls. The air, thick with cigarette smoke, made Delroy think of a gas chamber. He wouldn't be sorry if someone gassed these morons. He'd even be a little fly on the wall, a little fly that was immune, and watch these fuckers start going spastic, their laughter turning to screams. Mass extermination of God's pretty butterflies, and it could start right here, in the fucking King Edward Inn.

Blondie sat her drink down on the bar, tossed her hair, and came his way. She wiggled through the crowd and opened the door to the ladies room. The door closed, and he imagined her pulling her knickers down to piss. He'd never fucked a woman, or anything else for that matter, but he got urges just the same. *Thanks, God.*

Delroy noticed the barman staring at him--bet he'd seen him ogling the blonde bitch. The cocksucker was drying a glass and eyeballing him, a fucking threat if ever there was one.

Delroy stood. "What you fuckin' lookin' at?" He clenched his fist and shook it at the barman. Smoke plumed from the cigarette, the effect oddly mystical, as if he had a handful of dragon's breath. *Yeah, Puff-the-Magic-fucking-Dragon.*

"That's right, you cocksuckers, here I am. Take a good look. Pretty, ain't I?"

"Easy, mister, we don't want any trouble in here."

Delroy bristled at the voice. The barman was a faggot. A fuckin' poofter.

Just then, Blondie sauntered back from the ladies room, adjusting her skirt. Delroy grabbed his faggy little table and tipped it over. It wasn't much of a show. There was no beer left to spill, and the glass didn't smash when it hit the carpet, but he had their attention. He scanned looks, tried to make as much eye contact with *the other side* as he could. Blondie's lip curled as if she'd stepped in dog shit, and she turned and whispered to the dark-haired bitch with the little tits. He felt a glimmer of satisfaction.

He kicked the table, ignoring the pain that bolted through his knee, and started moving through the crowds of people to the back exit. They parted Moses-style. His leaving was plainly a relief, as though he'd been the turd clogging their fucking toilet.

He walked through the beer garden and into the back parking lot. The air was snippy and the ground wet. The light from the parking lot shone an oily rainbow on a puddle, and he was startled by his own reflection. That's why he smashed mirrors. He kicked the puddle, and his face broke into ripples.

He hadn't been able to score any painkillers, and by the look of things, he would be thrown out of his flat tomorrow morning. Just couldn't scrape up that last fifty quid to make the four hundred rent. Fucking extortion it was, anyway, for that shit-hole.

As he maneuvered between the cars, he took the keys from his pocket and started scratching as much paint as he could. Fucking cunts.

Crow Street was dead, nothing but Jack-the-Ripper-fog skulking low around the lampposts. But as he approached Doreen's Cafe-- blinds pulled down, closed sign hanging in the window--he heard a noise coming from the tiny doorway jammed alongside the cafe. He stood and waited in the shadows. An old woman with a cane and a big white handbag came out onto the pavement. Favoring a bad leg, she snailed over to a three-wheeler invalid car parked at the curb. Delroy shook his head and looked down at the pavement. He didn't have much choice. *She's a purse. Just see her as one giant purse.*

He walked up swiftly behind her. She dropped her car keys, sucking air in a small *'oh'* sound, and Delroy grabbed her handbag. In a sudden quick motion, she brought the stick up and whacked him across the back. He yelped, and she whacked him again.

"Stop it, stop it!" he cried.

She whacked him again, this time over the head. The stick caught his ear.

"Ouch, stop it!" He managed to grab the end of the cane. He heard her gasp. She pulled, he pulled.

"Let go, you bastard!" she said, her falsetto voice shimmying through the quiet night. He pulled and jerked the cane. She fell backwards, tripping down the curb and bashing her head on the door of her car.

"Fuck! *Fuck*!" Delroy turned around twice, holding his head in one hand, her purse in the other. "Fuck. Lady?"

The old woman groaned, opened her eyes and looked at him. "Monster!" she hissed.

"*Fuck, fuck, fuck.*" Delroy took off down Crow Street, slowing only when he turned onto Brenton Avenue. He checked through her purse as he walked. Cash *and* painkillers. There were only four in the bottle. He swallowed them, stopped at the next phone box, and called Emergency.

"Yeah, an old lady outside Doreen's cafe on Crow Street. Dunno, she was lying on the ground. Huh? Sorry, gotta go." He hung up and started the long walk home.

At least he still had a home. The old gal had a fifty-pound note and change in her purse. The *monster* had made his rent. She'd be all right. She was a tough old bird.

CHAPTER 7

Klickitat, Washington

After clumsily skipping out on a 10:00 P.M. appointment with Bertha Klaus, Magdalena decided to put her mind at rest by taking the thirty-minute walk into town. The bus would be easy to spot; Klickitat only claimed about three hundred souls.

She grabbed the flashlight she kept by the door next to the coat stand. The stand had been her mother's, like most of the furniture in the place. It always cast the strangest shadows, turning the fuzzy inside of her parka into Bigfoot, or her raincoat into a thin, headless, medieval lady-in-waiting. She laughed silently, although it wasn't funny. Quite possibly she was going crazy. Living in these woods was hard. They had never felt welcoming to her like the forests of Connecticut. Still, she stayed. And the question only surfaced once in a while. *Why do I stay here?* Then she'd push the thought away and get on with cleaning the cupboards or sweeping off the constant litter of slick pine needles that collected on her doorstep like never ending hate mail.

Magdalena didn't take a coat, enjoying the cooler nights. Autumn was finally here. The leaves on the oak trees lining the Klickitat Road had turned every shade of orange and yellow. Soon, they would fall like lovely copper pennies. But the forest, it never changed.

There were no streetlights on the outskirts of town, only reflectors in the road, but Magdalena knew the walk so well that she could do it without the flashlight. She wouldn't want to, though. Especially not tonight.

The moon was large, and the stars were scruffy and numerous, like ash spilled on black carpet. Which reminded her again of Mother. After the funeral, she had kept the urn in the house for a few days, wondering what to do with it. She didn't want Mother sitting on the mantel; she didn't want to keep her cooped up or, quite frankly, be cooped up with her. So she had taken the ashes outside and thrown them in the Klickitat River. She never told anyone, and she kept the empty urn on the mantel for her mother's old acquaintances to admire. But whenever she saw Zak or one of the other Indian men who fished nearby, a fresh salmon hanging over his back, she always thought of Mother. The thought made her smile.

She rounded the bend and caught sight of the town lights. From here, it all looked storybook perfect. From this distance, there were no drunks or wife-beaters or derelicts working the system. From here, the town was just a cluster of stars, like the ones in the sky. Stars that blinked, then turned to ash and blew off into the night or headed downstream with the salmon.

Magdalena turned the corner onto Main Street and found it empty. Jack's Shack had been closed since six. By now, Jack would be holed-up with his flea-bitten dogs and dirty movies in the house his parents had left him out on Pullman Road. She always felt uneasy walking past that house, as if it might tumble down on top of her. Maybe it was the lack of paint, or the three lopsided cars half on blocks, or maybe it was just Jack himself. Magdalena didn't care too much for Jack, and she suspected the feeling was mutual.

A fluorescent beer sign buzzed behind the grimy store window, a red and blue reminder to buy your beer before six o'clock or pay double at Huntington's Bar.

She looked over at Huntington's.

The only two cars in the lot were Bill Howard's Jeep and Hans Finklef's old green pick-up. No red tour bus. She had already looked down each street branching off from Main. If the bus wasn't here in town, then it had to have left when she'd stepped away from the window. She *had* spent about two minutes in hiding, when Bertha showed up.

As Magdalena walked across the road, she glanced up at the sky. The wind breezed smoke down from Huntington's chimney and the stars seemed to fall on her like poison powder.

She peered in the window. Several faces looked back. She smiled and quickly turned away. She knew what they thought about her. Her mother however, who was referred to by the locals simply as 'the midwife' had been quite well liked. Some of the older folks had known each other in Germany, and met up again after retiring to be with family over here.

Magdalena looked back up at the sky and thought, same sky, no matter where you are.

Mother had finally immigrated to Klickitat, Washington to be near her cronies, not her flesh and blood. Magdalena, thirty years old at the time, and living in Lye, Connecticut, was still willing to make amends. But it hadn't worked out that way. Her mother had made it clear, *forbidding* Magdalena to visit. Magdalena would get cards from her at Christmas and on her birthday, little notes scratched on the back, but they were hard to understand. What little she did decipher sounded like crazy talk.

After the funeral, Magdalena decided to stay in Klickitat. But just lately, she'd begun to question that decision. It was too late to leave, though.

Then, there was the matter of the spells. She always felt a little trill of distaste thinking about it. Hatty, an old friend of Mother's, had started it off about eight years ago by asking Magdalena if she would do the protection spell on her granddaughter. The old woman had heard of Magdalena's career as a psychic and thought perhaps she would follow in her mother's footsteps and perform the well-respected duties of town witch. Magdalena had graciously declined, and laughed for a week. But after making friends with Hatty, she started to value the company, the friendly face on the street, so she finally gave in and performed the spell. Pure silliness, but it didn't hurt anyone, so when Annie Kaufman asked her to do the same for her youngest, Lilly, Magdalena agreed. After a while, there was no turning back.

Suddenly, Magdalena saw a dark shape stumble out of the alley next to the bar. She stepped backwards into the street, almost tripping.

"Hey, Mag, got any change?" It was Zak.

"Oh, Zak." She paused long enough to steady her voice. "I didn't bring my purse. Maybe there's something in here..." She reached into her skirt pocket. "Zak, did you happen to see a big red bus today?"

Zak scratched his stubbly chin, eyes glistening with moisture. He seemed to be calculating, wondering if the information could somehow be parlayed into some extra benefit for him. Thoughts screened across his face like an old-time movie, and then he said, a little slyly, "New people, a couple. Stayin' in the woods. Stayin' in the old Jenkins place."

Magdalena gave him the coins and lint from her pocket.

"God bless ya." His usual response.

Tonight, though, the words left his mouth with an unaccountable weight. And they repeated themselves in a sober and sickening round in Magdalena's head as she started down the dirt trail that led to the woods and the old Jenkins cabin.

CHAPTER 8

Gavin pointed the flashlight up the forty-foot pine, his neck tilted back so far that his Adam's apple felt tight and ready to pop out of his throat. Thank Christ the stupid cat hadn't gone all the way to the top.

"Gavin, how are we going to get her?"

"Well...she wants to climb trees, I say let's leave her. She'll come down when she's ready." The remark was half irritation, half threat, aimed at the cat. Not that the cat ever cared.

"No!" she cried. "There might be coyotes. You're going to have to climb up there."

He already knew that. But still, he felt an evil gleam of satisfaction at the panic in her voice.

Rachel had come running into the bus about half an hour earlier in hysterics. She told him she had stepped outside to walk a little and drink her cocoa. When she went back in, she noticed the front door was open. Naturally, the cat was gone.

He sighed. Why couldn't she have left the damn cat with Jeff and Paula? They liked cats; maybe some unbreakable bond would have been struck between them. His neck was about ripping open. Stupid cat. He trained the flashlight on it, and its eyes caught red. Damned animal, she treated it like a child.

Suddenly ashamed, he lowered the light, grabbed Rachel's hand, and squeezed it. "It's all right. I'll get her down."

He took in a deep breath, the smell of pine cloying. He felt as if he'd walked into one of those miniature Christmas scenes, a train going through the forest and little people waving from tiny mushroom houses, trapped forever inside their Winter Wonderland.

Twigs snapped underneath them as they paced around the tree. Kiki looked down at them curiously, the moon resting on her shoulder.

"Please don't let this happen again Rachel. If you want this album done right, I've got to concentrate on it."

"It won't happen again, Gavin. I promise."

He could tell she was sorry. He handed her the flashlight, his tone softening. "Okay, keep this on me so I can see the branches."

Rachel nodded and took the flashlight, examining and testing the switches as if they were space shuttle controls. He smiled to himself. She *is* cute, no getting around that.

Kiki sat huddled about halfway up, just a shadow until the light hit her. Her green eyes, big as saucers, turned red and seemed to glare down at him.

Dry bark scratched his hands. He wished he'd brought his gloves. Damned cat must've seen something, a possum or a raccoon.

Coming down proved harder. Kiki insisted on digging her claws into Gavin's chest, and he had to bite his lip and let the pain ripple through him. Finally, he felt pine needles crunching under his boots.

"Here she is!"

"Oh, Kiki, you're *so* naughty." But there was no scolding in that voice, only relief. "Thank you." Rachel gave Gavin a big kiss that almost knocked him over.

She makes it all worth it, he thought. Everything.

He took the lead, making the way back with her and her cat close behind, or so he thought.

"Rachel?"

Flashlight aimed, he turned, lighthouse style, bringing the nearest trees into gnarly brightness, creating hideous stunted shadows.

He did this four times before Rachel finally answered. He judged she was only about twenty feet away.

"I'm over here," was all she said, but there was a tone, a flatness to her voice that made the skin pucker up on Gavin's arms. The sound of a person caught for long hours in a bear trap. Dying yet calm. No emotion, no fear, just an eerie resignation.

He walked in the direction of her voice, branches cracking under his feet like the bones of small animals.

"Rachel, you okay?"

A pause--too long, as if time had no meaning.

"Yes. I'm over here."

The light shone straight ahead, although all he could see was the bark of the next giant spruce. He could even see the sap bleeding shiny tears from crusty wooden eyes.

Then he came on the clearing. He shone his light on Rachel. She was sitting on the corpse of a toppled pine, its greenness long gone, roots huge and tangled and clumped with dirt. She had Kiki in her arms.

"What the hell are you doing?" It was his turn to fake anger, when relief was what he really felt.

He moved the light over the rest of the clearing, a circle roughly twenty feet around. Several stumps covered in moss and toadstools pushed up through the earth's gum like broken teeth. He thought briefly of Jack at the store. *I can't do without meat.*

"Look...those are *flowers*." She pointed off to the side without moving her head.

He supposed she meant the spindly green plants growing close to the ugly stumps. They were ropey looking things with bulb heads, he'd seen them in forests before. But they didn't scream *flowers*, at least not to him. This was really strange. She seemed to be in a daze. Maybe she'd hurt herself.

"Are you all right?" He sat down on the trunk next to her. She nodded but continued looking straight ahead.

"Must be the light..." she said, in the same monotone voice. "They get sunlight here in the clearing."

Fuck, this is weird. "Rachel, you okay? Can we go?"

She stood. He put his arm around her, his mind racing as to what could have happened, but as soon as they got back on the tiny rutted track, she seemed almost normal again.

"Can you believe Kiki climbed that tree? Kiki, you are such a bad girl." It was a predictable Rachel-style thing to say, but he noted her timing was off, as if she spoke only surface words her brain could fish for easily.

CHAPTER 9

Wapping, East London

Bill Johnson, otherwise known as Landlord Bill, had found the two runaways outside the Old Nag off-license. They'd asked him if he had a smoke, and if he could spare any change.

They claimed to be from Manchester, but both had Scottish accents. Silly tarts. They didn't seem to be strung out on drugs, which was good. He didn't fancy a bout of anything nasty. They were, in his expert estimation, no more than fifteen. Into all that punky-goth shit, safety pins, short spiky hair, pierced tongues. That was all right though, he'd never gotten a blowjob from a bird with tongue ornamentation. Okay, Bill, he told himself, you're getting too far ahead of yourself, mate. *One step at a time.*

He turned the lock and opened the door to Delroy's flat. "Well, ladies, this is it."

The girls went jumping down the stairs like little lambs. For all their bravado and weird make-up, they were green as the soft highland meadows. He smiled and flicked away his cig before going in behind them.

"Achh, it's no very clean," the girl who looked like a young Angelina Jolie minus twenty percent said. The other girl gave her a don't-blow-it nudge. "I mean, we can clean it for ya. What kinda loser lives here, anyway? Take a wee look at that mattress, Lindy. Give ya ten quid if ya get naked on it."

"I'll give ya twenty," Bill said, laughing but meaning it.

"So, ya said he's weird...how'd ya mean?" Angelina-minus-twenty's-friend asked, hands on hips.

These chicks would dig it, skanky little fucks. He wished he had a picture of Del. "Well, his name is Delroy. And when I say he's ugly, I mean like horror-movie ugly. See his shoulders are all..." Bill stooped over, smooshed his face for effect, and came after the Angelina chick. They both screamed brightly the way young excitable girls do, and urged him to *stop it, stop it.*

He straightened up. "Yeah, so, poor bastard, he's got some deformity...ya know, like the elephant man. They looked at him blankly. "Like, err...Quasimodo."

They continued to look. *Fucking kids don't know nothin' nowadays.* "The Hunchback of Notre Dame?"

"Oh, right..." The carrot-topped floppy-titted one said, still unsure.

"He's like a throwback from the Middle Ages, I'm tellin' ya."

Bill turned the light on in the kitchen. The sink was filled with trash, roaches scuttling in a city of chip papers and empty baked-bean cans.

The girls giggled and made disgusted noises, thoroughly enjoying themselves. He went back into Del's living area and had a sincere snoop. Fucking tosspot. The guy gave him the creeps.

Bill saw something poking out from the side of the mattress. He bent down and pulled out Delroy's wad of money, then glanced behind him quickly and stuffed the cash into his pocket.

"All right, girls, we gotta go. The boogie man could be home any time." Bill hurried them up the stairs and locked the door. "So, what do ya think?"

"Well, we don't have any money yet..." Carrot-top looked at eighty-percent-Angelina, her eyebrows high and clueless. "And anyways, how do ya know this Quazi bloke won't have his rent money? We don't like to be fucked around, do we, Sue?"

Sue shrugged.

"Take my word for it, he won't have the rent money. And as for you lovely ladies, you're new in town...I'm a good guy, like to help when I can. I'm sure we'll work something out."

* * *

Forty minutes later, Delroy turned into the alley. Boy, he was fucking knackered. He hadn't gotten but a couple of hours sleep in the last two days. He stripped and collapsed onto his mattress.

CHAPTER 10

Klickitat, Washington

Normally, at one-thirty in the morning, Magdalena was fast asleep. But tonight, tired as she was, she was sitting in the shop area tinkering with the display cabinet's lock. It had been faulty for months. She could have been in the den reading a book, but here in the shop area--originally the living room--she was used to keeping her mind on the surface of things. Informing wayward tourists of the therapeutic effects of lavender oil, what year the mill had closed down, steering them away from Huntington's infamously bad cuisine. Tonight, she preferred this headspace.

Really, she should go to bed. She was tired as hell. What an evening. She smiled thinly at the old plaster wizard by the door. The shelf of crystals above him glimmered fluid shapes on the wall as he stared back with his painted eyes.

She'd found the bus, but so much for a casual "hello." She shook her head and yawned.

After Zak told her about seeing the couple who'd rented the old Jenkins cabin, she'd quickly decided--perhaps a little too quickly--to pay them a visit. It was 11:00 P.M. when she headed down the trail, only two and a half hours ago. It felt like an eternity.

Her flashlight showed thick tire marks in the dirt. She stopped for a second and watched dust dancing in the beam of light.

The trail curved. A black awning of cottonwoods on either side, wasteland behind them. It would remain like this for another quarter mile, Magdalena knew, then the towering pines would appear and she would be in the forest.

She walked deeper into the tunnel of cottonwoods, listening to the sound of crickets and the crunch of her feet on the fine gravelly dirt. The thick woody trunks were crowding in on her, seeming to lean. *Too close--claustrophobic.* She forced herself to think about how beautiful they would look in the crisp autumn sunlight. Friendly cottonwoods, she told herself, just like the ones along Klickitat Road. She lifted her flashlight high to illuminate the golden leaves as proof, but was struck instead by how red they were. Crimson, just like...

Then she heard a voice.

Magdalena froze. She caught a quick breath, snapped the light off and hurried to the side of the trail. From there, she listened.

Someone crying.

No, someone *singing*. A lone voice. A woman's voice. Adrenaline shot through Magdalena's body, giving her a sudden weightlessness. She felt like running but didn't.

Magdalena switched the flashlight on and continued down the trail. It must be the girl from the bus, and the cabin door is open. That had to be it. Still, her mind insisted on conjuring an image straight from the easel of Botticelli. A cherub-faced nymph, dancing naked around a fallen pine tree, arms swirling out by her side, serenading the gods above. *Or below*, the voice in Magdalena's head reminded her. *Don't forget the ones below.*

Magdalena continued on, deeper and deeper down the trail, only patches of moon and her plastic flashlight to light the way. The soft eerie singing, like a beacon in the night, guiding her in.

What are you doing, old girl? Have you finally gone insane?

The trail curved sharply. She took it holding her breath, half expecting to find someone standing there, waiting for her around the corner. Instead, she saw the light from the cabin, and there--she could just make out its dark cave-like behind--was the bus, pulled up beside it. *Don't get involved, Magdalena. This isn't your problem. But what if it is,* another part of her asked.

She was close now. The bus was softly illuminated too, and, no surprise, the source of the ghostly voice she'd pictured wandering naked out in the woods.

Although seeing the bus didn't evoke the knee-buckling sensation she'd expected, the original sense of uneasiness remained. She put her hand on it--no change.

She shone her light on the back of the vehicle, its huge red doors, the stickers--some new, some older. *Q101 Chicago's Alternative. WZZN the Zone.*

"A young couple," she whispered. What was she sensing? Was it precognition, something that hadn't yet happened, like the Clamberty case? Or had her psychic abilities been locked up so long, they'd finally rebelled? Like Mother's had.

It must have been more than 30 years ago now. It was Spring and

Magdalena was a regular speaker at the Philtech University in New York.

She remembered that particular Tuesday night vividly. The evening news, the picture of the missing girl Samantha. Magdalena had gotten a *feeling*. Strong, but pale in comparison to what she felt now. If that was the needle, then this was the whole bloomin' hayfield. She had forced herself to eat dinner but ended up vomiting. So she got into her car and began to drive, slower than usual. So slow, there was a bewildering sense that it wasn't really her who was driving at all.

She stopped at the old Farmland Ranch outside town on the Crigleford Road. She'd never heard of it before that night. It was horse land, private, except for the ditch that ran alongside.

She pulled over and got out of her car. The ditch was four-foot deep, gnarly with blackberry bushes and wild roses, the kind that would cut your eyes out sooner than be plucked. She almost broke her leg getting down there, and she was instantly scratched to pieces by the spiteful bushes.

She stepped over an old twisted bicycle, plastic bags, soda bottles full of urine--a real off-road collect-all. Then, she found the spot. But nothing was there. No signs of a struggle, no pieces of pink ribbon, no freshly dug grave. But the feeling was there. A stable harmonic, resonating through her in an unknown key. Precognition, she thought. Perhaps they could still save the little girl.

She rushed home and called Detective Belinda Jose, whom Magdalena had assisted on a case three years before. She explained what had happened, what she felt. Detective Jose was excited. Magdalena spoke with the detective several more times, even held the little girl's favorite teddy bear, but she couldn't come up with anything more useful.

Two weeks later, Peter Denning dumped seven-year-old Samantha Clamberty into that ditch. Fifty pounds of body parts stuffed into black trash bags.

Magdalena turned the flashlight off. She could hear the words, *"Close your eyes and see with your heart, and you'll never be afraid of the dark..."* That's not true, she thought, that's not true at all.

The voice stopped, and then started again. A recording.

What was she going to say to these people?

Candlelight glowed in the cabin, so she would knock on that door first, see if someone was in there. The bus was too intimidating.

She knocked and waited, hoping sensible words would fill her mouth when someone opened up.

But no one did.

She knocked, harder this time, and the door moved inwards. Then, in an instant, she felt something brush her leg.

She took a sharp breath and shot the flashlight down at the ground. A cat. She'd let their cat out.

It had already scampered off and was scratching on the trunk of a pine about fifteen feet from the cabin.

"Here, kitty. Here, kitty."

She knocked on the door again. Desperate now, she pushed her head inside. "Hello?" No reply.

She turned to see the cat wandering into the trees. *Damn it.* Magdalena began to follow.

"Here, kitty, kitty."

The cat seemed happy to be out. Its tail was high, and it was sniffing around inquisitively. It moved deeper into the woods, checking behind frequently to see if Magdalena was keeping up. It had no plans on being caught but apparently didn't mind the company.

Magdalena trained the light on the cat as it stayed a tantalizing four feet ahead of her. Finally, she got close enough and grabbed its tail. It screeched at her, bolted, and the tail slithered out of her grasp. From that moment on, Magdalena was the enemy. She continued to follow. "Here, kitty. Come on, kitty, let's go home now."

But the cat was getting braver, its pace quickening, little pads slapping confidently over the bed of needles.

It must have been fifteen minutes she spent under the animal's infuriating thumb before she finally came to her senses.

Magdalena turned, immediately startled at how far into the forest she'd gone, suddenly and acutely aware of activity. Branches breaking somewhere out of sight, a restless bird causing pinecones to fall up high and over to the left, scuttling around that tree over there. And although she couldn't see them, she sensed red nocturnal eyes high and low, watching her every move.

By the time Magdalena got back to the old Jenkins cabin, the singing had stopped and the door was standing wide open. "Hello? Hello?" She sounded ridiculous to herself.

She walked over to the bus door. "Hello?" *Shit. Now what?* The people were probably out searching for their cat.

The only thing she could think to do was walk all the way to Huntington's, write a note explaining what had happened, walk all the way back and put it on their doorstep. They might be home by then with the annoying animal under arm, and she could apologize in person. The thought wasn't appetizing, but it would serve her right.

But at the bar, things got worse.

She didn't look before going in, and there, right at the first table, sat Bertha Klaus.

"Magdalena! Where were you? We had an appointment today."

Bad enough that Magdalena had *hidden* when Mrs. Klaus, along with offspring, had knocked, but the middle child Sara had *seen* her. She'd pulled at her mother's coat and pointed through the window into the far corner of the kitchen, where Magdalena was pressed against the wall. Mrs. Klaus was sparing her the embarrassment of voicing it, but both women knew good and well what she'd been doing.

"I'm so sorry, Mrs. Klaus. You know, I really wasn't feeling well. It's my heart..." She did have a bad heart, but using it as an excuse... She felt shame burning her cheeks in little red nubs. "It makes me very...uh...makes me seem--"

"It's okay." Mrs. Klaus waved her short.

Magdalena borrowed a pen from Bertha and took it over to an empty table, acutely aware that the eyes of the patrons were on her. She had nothing in common with them, but even so, she had a certain place in their lives; they needed someone to pinpoint as the outsider--every little town has one. In effect, it made her an integral part of the community.

She took a drink-special flyer from the small plastic holder on the table, turned it over and began to write. *Great, they'll think I'm a lush.* "A lush came down from the bar and let our cat out." She'd fold it in half. Maybe they wouldn't look inside.

"Dear neighbors,

I apologize, it seems I have let your cat out.

I tried to catch it, but no luck. It headed into

the woods, due south. I'm deeply sorry.

Only wanted to say hello, not be such a nuisance.

Magdalena

Candles and Magick Store 509 369-6976"

She returned the pen. Bertha nodded as she chased her drink around the glass with a thin red straw. It was unusual to see Bertha on her own, since she normally had a trailing of kids behind her.

"So, can we make it for tomorrow instead?" Magdalena asked.

"I can if you can!" She sucked the last of the pale amber liquid off the ice and plunked her glass down on the table. But there was nothing malicious about Bertha. She simply said it the way it was. She was also one of the few townspeople who actually treated Magdalena like a friend. Certainly, she must think her rather kooky, especially after spotting her hiding against the kitchen wall. But Bertha believed in the spells, the old wives' tales, the stories brought over from the homeland. To her, Magdalena was a shaman. So she could get away with being a little kooky.

She thanked Bertha for the pen, promised to see her tomorrow, and walked out onto empty Main Street. She hit the dirt trail again, flashlight in one hand, apology note in the other.

The night had come alive in the few minutes she'd spent inside the bar. Crickets whirred like fallen power lines, and owls, who seemed to prefer this side of the woods, swooped alarmingly low overhead. Could an owl pick up a cat? God, she hoped not.

The cabin remained deserted, so she laid the note in the open doorway and placed a stone on top of it.

She started on the trail for the fourth time that evening, her flashlight catching dust, her ears attuned to the sounds of the night, waiting for the singing to return, perhaps, or the scream of a cat caught in the slobbering jaws of a coyote.

Then, she heard someone calling. She recognized it instantly as the voice in the woods.

She turned to see two people standing outside the cabin door. Magdalena smiled, waved awkwardly in their direction, and began walking toward them. As she got closer, she saw a young woman who looked to be in her mid-twenties--although it was hard to tell nowadays--and a man about the same age.

They introduced themselves, and Magdalena apologized.

She was drawn to the girl Rachel. She had an overwhelming sadness about her. It was enough to make Magdalena dizzy. But she couldn't sense any more than that. Sadness. The man was quiet and uncomfortable, a genius type, she guessed.

They talked for a while, and she took a look at their studio on wheels. Magdalena had been on a few radio chat shows after her book came out, this reminded her of those days.

She wondered a couple of times if she should say something, pry a little, see if there was any easy answer to explain her feeling, but the meeting was cut short by the boyfriend. She did find out one thing. The feeling was about the girl, about Rachel, not the bus or the man. She prayed the girl wasn't in danger, hoped it was all in her crazy old head. She'd rather see herself insane than think something dreadful was about to happen to this poor child. *So much sorrow around her.*

"Oh, Magdalena, here's a thought. Got any spells to get rid of those damned flies?"

Magdalena went rigid. Those words, those innocent words had iced her heart to a standstill. *Why? What is it?* She didn't know, but she had the horrible notion she'd soon find out. Thankfully, the feeling passed quickly, although it left her weak-kneed and somehow exhausted. She made her good-byes and left, headed home along the embankment and beside the river, which ran black and silver as it chased itself out of town.

As she walked, she stared up at the silent moon and its dirty sky. She must clear her mind for a while. Maybe she'd try and fix that display cabinet door, have a little glass of brandy, go to bed as tired as possible. Things would look different tomorrow. A new day brings a new way.

Back home, she decided against the brandy. It helped her sleep, but it also helped her mind cut loose, and she wanted to avoid that, at least for a while. She made one of her special teas instead, a blend of various herbs and spices. She'd discovered the recipe in a kitchen drawer the morning after she found Mother.

CHAPTER 11

Wapping, East London

The knocking at the door woke Delroy. He felt strangely disorientated, lightheaded, as if he'd suddenly been called back from somewhere. Somewhere far away. He stood up and staggered like a drunkard toward the door, putting his hand on the wall to steady himself.

"What the fuck..."

* * *

Five thousand miles away, in Klickitat, Washington, it was still the middle of the night. Delroy's sister Rachel, whose name he'd never been told, was roaming naked through the forest.

Searching unknowingly for the thing that would bring them together.

CHAPTER 12

Klickitat, Washington

Rachel's eyes shot open. She stared wildly at the dark unfamiliar wall, remembering nothing. Didn't know where she was, or even *who* she was. The feeling was primal, animalistic. But within seconds, her mind began filling up with information. Memories trucking back, one by one, pulling in and parking. It reminded her of a bedtime story Rosemarie the babysitter had once told her:

"*When the lights go out, and you're fast asleep, the garage door opens and the family automobile goes cruisin', checkin' out the scenery, racing down the country lanes and picnicking on moonlit beaches. But it makes a point of getting back before you wake up. Unless you're awake when you shouldn't be, then you'll see, then you'll start to know, that just 'cos something ain't made of flesh and blood, don't mean it ain't alive.*" Then she'd tickled Rachel's ribs and made a *'MAW-HA-HA'* sound.

Rosemarie had only told the tale once--thought better of it, maybe--but it had stuck with Rachel all these years.

There would always be a hole inside of her, she knew it. She wished she'd been normal like the other children, but she wasn't. Not even when she appeared to be. Part of her was missing, gone. *Greedy, wicked girl, that she should bite off her nose to spite her face.* "Not your fault," the doctors said a million times. *"Still, there's a big hole to fill,"* they'd added. And how she yearned to fill it. But it was insatiable. Nothing could undo what had already been done.

Rachel breathed in and tilted her head toward heaven, "Please, God," she said, "don't let it be the nightmare."

But as she raised her hands to her face, she smelled the sweet musty soil on them. She rubbed her fingers together; they were sore and gritty. *It had been.*

Her feet touched the carpet, and crumb-sized bits of forest crunched between her toes and under her soles. Suddenly, she was seven years old again. Back in that volatile time--the countless hospital rooms, the soft smelly couches of the shrinks she'd seen. Standard therapy had gone on for over two years, then finally, they'd signed a bunch of papers and declared her okay. But the nightmare started after that. She hadn't seen anyone about the nightmare. But wait...yes, she had. Mother had taken her to a psychiatrist on Glen Street. His name was...Dr. Johansson. God, she'd totally forgotten about him. She'd seen him for probably a year or more. How could she not have remembered? She could even see his face right now, his silly ginger moustache that always had some type of food or beverage hinged to its edge. Then, around her tenth birthday, the nightmare suddenly stopped.

But had it really gone, or simply sunk back into its hole to bide its time? Because here it was again, ready to take her on midnight rides down dark, winding country roads--no driver, no brakes. *No picnicking for you, little lady. Wicked little girl.*

Her stomach tensed into a knot, and she began to cry. She wept silently, tears finally swimming up into her eyes, fracturing the moonlight from the window into glistening starbursts. She held her position, choking back any sounds that tried to escape.

She felt better after a few moments. She hadn't cried much when Ani died; maybe she should have. Maybe that hole was filled with tears. *Get'em out, and it might heal up.* Geez, what was she thinking? She'd better snap out of it. She wasn't ten years old anymore, she was a grown woman. A grown woman with a career, a boyfriend, and a cat.

Body still folded, she made her way to the bathroom, watching her dirty feet move across the carpet, those sore traitors.

The moonlight helped her make out the geography of her new and disturbingly quiet surroundings. Not like Chicago at all. Other than Gavin's soft snore, the only sound was the intermittent chirp of a cricket that was so close it might well be trapped with them here in the cabin.

Rachel had been a pampered child, anything she wanted she had. Well, except the thing she really wanted; no one could give her that. But camping hadn't been part of her childhood experience. She'd always been a city girl, and this silence was new to her. Obviously, it wasn't sitting well. Must be what had brought on the nightmare after so long. A cold shudder ran through her body, and she got the distinct feeling that someone was watching her. She looked around quickly at the windows, the bed. Nothing seemed to be amiss. Just her own heartbeat pounding in her ears, and the whirring cricket searching for a way out.

The bathroom doorknob was icy cold. She went inside without turning the light on, no need to wake Gavin. But when she closed the door, the room went completely black. Instantly helpless, she fumbled for the light switch. She couldn't find it and began to panic. With sudden clarity, she knew that something was behind the shower curtain, laughing at her blindness, *her wickedness*, watching with night-vision eyes, readying for the attack. Her hands scrabbled across the walls and the door, searching for the doorknob or light switch. Finally, her fingers brushed across the protruding plastic switch, and she sighed with relief as the room filled with artificial light.

Rachel looked at her reflection. Her eyes were startled and teary, her hair ratted. *Out in those woods, naked, unconscious of my actions. As if governed by some other entity. A body snatcher.* The notion was terrifying. It meant that something in her was so disturbed, it was willing to wait patiently for the opportunity to take over. God, she hoped it was just this once. She pulled several pine needles from her knotted hair, handling them by the edges like moldy toothpicks, and tossed them into the trashcan.

The nightmare itself was a mystery. Dr. Johansson hadn't been able to bring it to the surface, not even with hypnosis. The nightmare was, and still remained, completely unremembered. But, uncovering and demystifying the dream, he assured her parents, would be the solution to the *real* problem. The sleepwalking.

This is what had her parents scared. They couldn't see what was in her head, only the physical ramifications of it: Rachel huddled and shaking in the back of a closet with a strip of packing tape over her mouth, Rachel behind the shed sitting in a hole she'd dug with her bare fingers, Rachel in bed, as she'd found herself this evening, with dirty feet and cuts, having no idea where she'd been.

She lifted her foot into the bathroom sink and turned on the tap. First, she'd rinse the dirt off, then take a bath. Afterwards, she'd put ointment on the cuts and scratches.

As she lay in the tub, she thought about Dr Johansson. He'd been picked more for his friendly office furniture than his skills. She'd even overheard her parents talking about a different shrink with extra qualifications versus Dr. Johansson and his fun-fur footstool. Rachel's fear of hospitals or anything remotely connected to them had driven her parents to choose a shrink for his interior design talents over his psychiatric credentials.

She smiled a narrow little smile, then let the water in the bathtub rise up over her chin and drown it.

But should she tell Gavin about tonight? She looked at the swirls of dried dirt above the taps. She had tried to clean that area earlier, but with her lack of supplies, she hadn't done a good job. Thought she'd gotten rid of it, but she hadn't, it was back again.

I don't want to scare him, but maybe it'd be safer if he locked the doors at night and hid the keys.

After she got out of the bath, she dried off and attended the injuries. They were minor superficial cuts and scratches. She had been lucky. Yeah, real lucky, she thought, and laughed humorlessly at herself in the foggy mirror.

As Rachel put away the tea-tree oil and the Band-Aids, she suddenly became intensely tired. Her arms dropped to her sides, as if weighted, and her eyelids were quickly turning to lead. The monster laced the room with morphine; he's getting ready to turn off the light and rip me apart--for good, this time. But she was too tired to be scared. Bring it on, she thought, and opened the bathroom door. She needed to get back into bed before she fell to the floor like sleeping beauty.

Whatever she'd been doing out in the woods had been exhausting. And her chafed fingertips were a dead giveaway. She believed she knew *exactly* what she'd been doing.

But as she walked, something--a voice, instinct perhaps, nothing she could hold or analyze--peeked a terrified eye through the surface of her mind and whispered, *"No, Rachel, you* don't *know. And Rachel? Take my advice. Leave this place. Right now!"*

Dr. Johansson would have had no problem either. He would have said she was out there in the woods, in the dead of night, digging up her sister's grave. But the whisper wasn't into Jung or fun-fur footstools, it was only into hiding, as deep down and as far away as possible. And it suggested, in no uncertain terms, that she do the same.

* * *

Magdalena stopped fiddling with the display cabinet, finished her tea and went to bed. Sleep came within minutes. She slept soundly until three o'clock, when she was suddenly shocked awake, sitting upright in bed, sweating, hands screwed into bony fists.

Her heart was kicking like a jackrabbit.

She reached into the drawer beside her bed and pulled out her pills. After fumbling with the lid, she finally got one out and slipped it under her tongue.

Jesus, a nightmare!

Must have been bad.

She was no dream analyst, and even if she had been, it would have done her no good. It must have been terrible, too terrible to bring home. But there was one thing left of it. A slow monotonous melody, singing itself inside her head. She knew it, of course; it went along with the old nursery rhyme the kids around here sang about the Fly King. But now she knew something else. It was also the missing melody to the protection spell. No question about it.

Magdalena had no idea how she knew this, but she was as sure of it as her own heartbeat thumping unpleasantly in her chest.

CHAPTER 13

Wapping, East London

Delroy sat in Wapping Park, with the rain and the winos, a wet bench, and a wet arse. The pond, stagnant and green, smelled of dead fish. He could see himself in it looking up from the bottom, covered in slime and weeds. The ducks were skinny diseased things with growths on their beaks and patches of feathers gone. Ugly pigeons limped around like lepers.

He lit a smoke, inhaled, and coughed. The match crackled in the rain and went out. He dropped it on the ground, and a pigeon hobbled in closer to inspect. The headache he'd had all day was a real champ. His brain pulsated against his skull, beating harder than his heart. *Squeeze and release, squeeze and release.* The pain was shocking bad. *Fuck it.* With any luck he'd keel over and die, be done with it.

He shifted around on the bench, pants catching on its old wood. He ran his hand over two names gouged deeply into the wet seat, so deeply they had splintered into one. *To know such love.* He picked at the wood, took a big drag on his cig, closed his eyes, and let the pain flow. Even though he tried to absorb it, he couldn't help but gasp.

Delroy heard shuffling behind him. He turned and looked at the bums sleeping around the toilets, half in the doorway, half out. Happily resting their numb heads on the urine-stinking floor.

It's cold in London in October, blustery and threatening with winter looming on its coattails. Not a good time to be homeless. Is that what he was now--homeless? He laughed silently. Sometimes he had a roof over his head, but he was always homeless.

Bill had stolen his dough. Did that fucker think he was completely stupid? How bleedin' obvious can you be? Plus, the kitchen light was on when he got in last night. He hadn't thought much of it, except it being odd because he hardly ever went in the kitchen. Then, he'd taken his clothes off and slumped onto his mattress. At about ten o'clock this morning, he was awakened by Bill knocking. Delroy remembered the strange dizzy spell he'd experienced, during which he'd managed to climb up the steps in his skivvies and open the door.

"Jesus Christ, put some clothes on." Bill's disgust at Delroy's partially naked body had been complete and undisguised. Delroy was so sleepy and woozy, he hadn't realized. He grunted, looked down ashamed, and hurried back in to throw on his shirt and jeans.

"Fuck, Del, can't you get any help? Man, you oughta be in a home or something." Bill followed him down the steps.

"I am in a home. My home," Delroy said. He wiped his mouth, suddenly aware of the drool that had wetted his cheek while sleeping. He only had limited control of the muscles in his face, which was why his speech came loose and spitty sounding.

"I got the money." He pulled out the fifty-quid note from his pocket, then bent down, groaning, as he reached under the mattress for the rest. He slid his hand up and down the edge.

"You're not stringing me along again, are ya, Del?" Bill was standing behind him.

Delroy grunted. "It's here. It just got pushed under, that's all. Help me lift it, will ya?"

"Jesus. All right." They lifted the mattress clean up on its side. No money. Delroy noticed a little glimmer of amusement in Bill's voice.

"Sorry, Del. Gonna have to ask ya to leave. Hate to do it, mate, but ya know how it is. Business is business. No can pay, no can stay."

"But it was here! Right here under the mattress. I swear to God."

"Right, you look like the religious type, Del."

"Fuck. It was right here." Delroy scratched his head and stared blankly at Bill. It wasn't until later, after he'd packed his few possessions into a rucksack and sat on this park bench for six miserable hours did he finally realize that Bill had taken the money.

Then he'd gotten angry and cussed, kicked out at the pigeons and threw a fifteen-pound rock in the pond. Even the bums heaved up their heads to see what the commotion was about. After that, he settled back down and sank into a depression.

Delroy flicked away the remains of his cigarette, causing commotion among the pigeons, who were convinced it must be edible. The rain was starting to get serious, but Delroy didn't attempt to find cover or even wipe the stream of water running off his nose. *What's the point?* Nothing would ever change for him. It would only get worse. But he did have fifty quid and two credit cards he'd found in the feisty old gal's purse. What best to do with his stolen wealth?

The sky exploded in a downpour. He sat for another ten minutes, then finally stood and moved on.

CHAPTER 14

Klickitat, Washington

Rachel walked the trail leading to Main Street. The trees were beautiful, and when she looked up, she could catch glimpses of the vivid blue sky through the leaves. She examined the scrape on her forearm. *From last night*. She took a lung full of crisp October air, held it, then let it out.

Hardly ever did she sleep in late, but she had today. A fly buzzing around her face had finally awakened her. She'd pulled herself up in bed, squinted away from the orange Paris scene--she'd have to move that--and saw the place was full of them: silly little fool flies that waltz around in the middle of the room. She lashed out at the one that had buzzed her face. A big fat thing with a toxic-green sheen to it.

For a second, everything--excluding the initial shock of awakening in new surroundings--seemed pretty much as expected, but then she remembered last night and the sleepwalking.

By the time she'd showered and dressed, it was one o'clock. Gavin was already up and in the bus making music. She went out there with two cups of tea and told him about last night. She had to. Lying would only make things worse. He was wearing headphones when she climbed into the bus but had quickly ripped them off his head on seeing her, stopped everything, even slapped his monitor off. He was probably working on something other than the children's album, hence the headphones, hence not waking her up at a decent hour.

He was very concerned, as she knew he would be, but there was something else. He went pale and quiet, and was lost in thought for a while.

"Gavin?" she said. "It's okay. I doubt it will happen again. It's just being in a new place and everything..."

"Yeah." He stared into his teacup as if trying to find some leaves in there to read.

"Gavin?"

"Sorry. Yes, you're right, probably it's okay. I agree. I'll lock the doors before we go to bed and put the key somewhere..."

He clearly felt uncomfortable saying it, so she said it for him. "*Hide* it from me."

He nodded.

"Gavin, it's not that serious. I'm not really worried about it." She sounded convincing.

At least last night's mystery of Kiki's escape had been solved. After rescuing her from the tree, they had walked back to the cabin-- *via the clearing, Rachel, don't forget the clearing*--and found a note lying in the doorway.

Rachel had read the note, looked up toward the trail, and seen a figure walking away from them.

"Hey! Excuse me, er..." She quickly read the name at the bottom of the note. "Magdalena?"

The woman turned and began walking back toward them. She gestured with her hands and shook her head slowly, preparing for an in-person apology.

"I am so, so sorry. I see you found the cat. Is he, she, okay?"

"Oh, she's all right," Gavin said, taking Kiki from Rachel and throwing her in the cabin, closing the door firmly.

"I just wanted to come by and say hello, and then..."

Rachel extended her hand. "Oh, don't worry about it. Thanks for stopping by."

"For being a real pain in the behind!"

"No, not at all." Rachel smiled at Magdalena. She liked her instantly. She didn't seem to belong in Klickitat, Washington, out here in the middle of nowhere. She was obviously well educated. Rachel's mind immediately started forming theories as to what had brought her here. And a magic shop. How interesting.

They had given each other a brief history. Rachel told her about the children's album, even showed her inside the bus. Gavin trailed behind a little awkwardly. He didn't do too well around strangers. Magdalena told them about her career as a psychic, how she had retired after her mother died, how she'd taken over the little shop her mother ran from the cottage. She also told them about her reluctant duties as town witch. Rachel found it all quite fascinating, but after ten minutes of chitchat, Gavin had begun to make subtle gestures, sighing noises. Rachel took the cue and told Magdalena it was very nice meeting her and they should talk again sometime. The woman seemed reluctant to go, as if there was something else she wanted to say. But instead, she apologized about the cat one more time, and left.

Rachel was almost there now. She was going to the payphone outside Jack's Shack. Mother would be waiting for a call to say they had arrived safely. And maybe she would call Magdalena, too. The note was in her pocket, just in case. Supposedly, Magdalena was a psychic. Rachel wasn't sure if that stuff was real or not, but maybe she knew something about sleepwalking. And while Rachel had mostly been joking when she asked about a spell to get rid of the flies, she'd certainly try anything since she was allergic to fly spray. But was Magdalena's expertise legitimate? How could it be? In all likelihood, it was just another can of worms.

Rachel looked down at her feet, which were puffing up little clouds of fine white dirt as she walked. She noticed animal prints in the shade of the trees. Evidently, she hadn't been the only one out last night.

* * *

Gavin found himself staring into the empty teacup. Poor Rachel. And the melody that had slapped into his mind last night-- that's how it came, like a big hand slap--was it because he'd subconsciously known she wasn't in bed next to him, that she was out wandering around in the woods? God, what if she'd fallen in the river? But that would have woken her. Wouldn't it?

Before sleeping, they had christened their new bed. She was responsive enough, but also distant. Made all the right noises, said all the right things. But he'd felt that she was on cruise control, programmed to stay on course while she, the real *she*, went somewhere else. Afterwards, they must have drifted off to sleep. Then this crazy melody.

He'd gotten up at five o'clock this morning to set it down on tape. Over and over it had played in his mind. All night long, even though he supposed he'd been sleeping. It was Rachel's voice *la la la-ing* at times, but then it had morphed into others. The effect was horrible, made him nauseous. The melody itself was none too pretty, either. It sounded old, choral, midrange--chanting range. Over and over in his head. *"La la la la la la la."* He didn't remember falling asleep, or waking up, just finally making the decision to go out to the bus and exorcise himself of it by laying it on tape. But then he'd started adding things, slow chords underneath the chorus of *la la la la la las*; he'd found a spinet-piano sound that almost perfectly matched the tone. Next, he added a slow drumbeat. It was haunting--unpleasant and haunting. He kept thinking about hitting the erase button and getting rid of the damned thing, but he couldn't. When Rachel came in, he felt guilty, as if she'd caught him jerking off to porn. But then she told him about the sleepwalking.

He pulled his eyes away from the empty teacup and looked at the erase button. I'll give it just one more listen, he thought, as he put the headphones back over his ears.

* * *

Rachel set her purse down on the shelf area beside the telephone, watching out for wads of chewing gum and other distasteful things that lurk around such places, and called her mother. There was a weird echo on the line, so she made it short and promised to call her again in a day or two.

She took the note from her pocket and inspected it, then slipped in a quarter and dialed Magdalena's number.

The phone rang three times, and an old style answering machine picked up. Rachel let out her breath. Good. Mid-dial, she'd decided it was a bad idea. Plus, Jack had noticed her there and left his post. He was outside now, smoking a cigarette and eavesdropping. Rachel turned her back toward him. Ignoring or oblivious to the body language, he walked around to the other side of the phone to get within good listening range again.

Magdalena's recorded voice said, "Thank you for calling Candles and Magick, please leave a message at the tone."

Rachel cleared her throat. "Hi, this is Rachel. It was very nice meeting you, and please don't worry about letting Kiki out, she's an opportunist." She paused, wondered for a second, changed her mind and said, "Anyway, I hope you have a nice day. I'll stop by your shop sometime." She hung up, grabbed her purse.

"Who was it let your cat out?" Jack offered up his empty gums and laughed, lowered his head and spat beside the base of the pay phone.

"Magdalena. The lady who owns the shop on the edge of town."

"Ah, that old nutcase. Typical. Nosing around, was she?"

Rachel wasn't really sure *what* had brought Magdalena over.

"Just being polite, I suppose. Saying hello to the newcomers."

Jack sucked hard on his cigarette, cheeks collapsing inward with the effort, then said, "She's crazy. Know what she does?"

"No," Rachel replied, but her focus had drifted across the street to a little boy who had fallen off his tricycle. His mother was picking him up by the back of his T-shirt and brushing him off like a dirty old rag, dusting and slapping at the same time. *If I had a child,* Rachel thought, I'd love him so much, I'd never let him fall. I'd never let anything hurt him.

"She puts curses on people."

"What?" Rachel looked back at Jack, confused.

"Magdalena," he said, taking another long drag on his tiny cigarette, "is a witch. She puts *curses* on people."

"*Curses?* Really? She did tell me she does spell casting." He was just trying to be dramatic, she supposed, pull her into the local gossip. But still, what a disturbing accusation.

"Oh, uh...yeah. She does good spells, too. Probably as a front, though," he said off to the side. "Does 'em for all the old women around here. Say, for instance, their man isn't, ya know..." Jack thrust his pelvis back and forth, holding onto imaginary hips, "givin' it too 'em like he should, then old Mag puts a spell on 'em. Better then Viagra, they say." He laughed and spat again. "'Course, I ain't never had any complaints in that department." He showed her his winning smile as proof.

"You don't believe in all that, do you?" Rachel frowned.

"Well, no, as a rule I think all that stuff is crap. But this woman is damned creepy. And I mean...damned creepy. Gotta watch out for her, I'm tellin' ya."

Rachel nodded. "Well, it's good the town has you to keep the nasty old witch at bay, huh?"

His chest expanded a good five inches. "Well, I don't know about that. I suppose if she got real out of hand, I might step in."

"I bet you would," Rachel said, and showed him *her* winning smile--a mouth full of nicely capped big city pearlies.

"Uh, if you need any help with that old cabin, just let me know.

Your boyfriend don't seem like he's got much *woodsman* in him."

Jack watched Rachel walk down Main Street. Last time he'd gotten some ass was with a hooker from the Dalles, a fat bitch with sweat stains under her armpits and a face like a Shar-Pei. She'd seemed passable, until the morning came around, then he'd seen the error of his ways. She was even uglier than Zak, and Zak's face was like a bucket full of night crawlers. Now, this girl Rachel...now, she was a fox. *I wonder just how close she is with her asshole boyfriend.* They weren't married, that was a good sign.

Rachel walked back down the trail, glad to have Jack's eyes off of her. She wondered how much truth was in his story about Magdalena.

She watched the dust plume up, and a bird chirped in the tree above her head. It made her sad, it sounded as though it had lost someone.

They say no smoke without fire. Why had Magdalena been snooping around? The more Rachel thought about it, the more peculiar it seemed. How did this woman even know they were there? Why not wait until daylight to come over and say hello?

She stared ahead at the darkness of the woods looming closer with every step. Then the scar came awake. A second later, it was inflamed with a maddening itch. Suddenly, Rachel was angry. Her hand shot up the side of her T-shirt and scratched the hell out of it. She dug her fingers into the scar, clawing at it till all she could feel was pain.

"What do you want? What do you want, Ani?"

Ani had been dead for twenty years.

The operation had never happened, at least not until after the fact. Ani and Rachel were conjoined twins, the fusion associated with a very rare form of Osteochondromatosis, a debilitating bone disease. Males with the condition, whose likenesses were well documented in medieval literature, can be considerably deformed. Female babies are sometimes conjoined.

Rachel tried hard not to think about Ani, or the details of her death, but it all remained so vivid. Some memories were like brightly colored photos, others like old paintings, watching her from the walls wherever she went.

Both she and her sister had been lucky enough to be born with their own legs, but being joined at the hip made walking a real art. It seemed natural to them, though, never having known any different.

Their movements flowed like a well-choreographed dance. Mother said seeing Ani and Rachel walk to the sink for a glass of water was like watching a strange ballet.

Their arms were also their own, but it wasn't that simple. Even though there was a certain independence, Rachel would know beforehand when Ani made a move. Perhaps it was the subtle muscle movements, the readying required for action of any kind. But Rachel knew it wasn't that alone, there was also some type of pre-perception. She was reminded of the sensation in the real estate agency when she first saw the cabin.

Around Christmas of their seventh year, Ani started to pale. She ate, even more than normal, but her face became thin and the doctors grew nervous. They said an operation would be necessary. But then they waited, waited for Ani to pick up a little. But she didn't. Rachel remembered feeling stronger; the stronger she felt, the weaker Ani became. Later, when Rachel was old enough to understand, she realized her body had been sucking the nutrients from her sister's--she had been sucking the life out of her. Within five months, Rachel had grown considerably larger than Ani. Ani's feet no longer touched the floor when they tried to stand. They couldn't play anymore. Ani would just sit there, her thin face and dark eyes staring into Rachel's.

Rachel would ask, "What's wrong, Ani?"

Ani would smile weakly. "Nothing."

Mother had to feed Ani with a spoon; her arms weren't strong enough for her to do it herself. Rachel remembered very clearly how her sister had continued to eat, continued to try and hold on, but every day the fat cuckoo pushed her closer and closer to the edge of the nest. And then Rachel woke up one day and knew that something was different. She felt somehow loose, released. She nudged Ani, but Ani didn't move. The small withered face looked up at her from the pillow. Ani was dead. Rachel touched Ani's shoulder. It was cold.

Rachel stopped scratching the scar and wiped the tears from her cheeks.

Her dead sister had felt like an extra arm whose circulation is cut off in the night. Except no pins and needles came to bring the life back. Ani only got colder.

Rachel had screamed. Mother and Father had come running.

The operation was long and intricate. Ani's dead blood had flowed through hers. The black shadow that visited Ani visited Rachel too.

Rachel had lived with death. It had been stuck to her for twenty-four hours. Gone now, surgically removed, as if that were possible.

CHAPTER 15

As promised, Mrs. Klaus showed up at Magdalena's house at three o'clock, towing three kids. Sara was the one who'd just hit puberty, and the lucky recipient of today's spell--the protection spell. And, of course, Magdalena would be performing said spell very differently today. Today, she was miraculously in possession of the missing melody.

She was quite aware that the spell was intended to be sung. The only one in her mother's extensive collection that called for such a thing. But Magdalena hadn't bothered to ask the old cronies about it. She wondered why they hadn't mentioned anything. Perhaps they thought it was optional, or trusted her to know what she was doing. Her lips rested in a flat smile. This would be a first in her book.

The protection spell, as far as she understood, was a guard against unwanted pregnancies. She'd never taken it seriously, but performed with enough pomp and circumstance, it seemed to satisfy the natives, although judging by some of the fat bellies in town, it hadn't worked too well. Perhaps she should drop it--possible lawsuits. She shook her head slowly, smiling. God, what a joke.

Magdalena opened the drawer and pulled out the book of spells. They had been winnowed down considerably by her own hand. She'd found them far too long and repetitive. She had started off innocently enough, making slight tweaks here and there, but over the years she had revised practically every one of them. She had removed whole phrases, shortened lines, crossed out passages, even ripped some of the spells clean out of the book. She refused to do the libido spell, for instance, because it could be performed without the consent of the other party concerned, i.e., the woman's husband. And any self-respecting witch, even one who wasn't, knew you shouldn't cast spells on people without their consent. Not that it would have mattered, since it was all just wishful thinking anyway, but still, she had to draw the line somewhere; and one less spell offered was one less she had to perform. But the protection spell...that one remained pretty much intact. And now, even more than before, it was fully complete and ready to go. Like a loaded gun under her pillow. She felt the hairs on her arms spring to attention. What was going on? Either something very wrong was happening, or she was chasing her mother's tail down the road of madness. And why not?

She took a deep breath and looked at Bertha sitting patiently at the kitchen table, her big bottom spilling over the sides of the chair. Her children were running around the room with abandon, oblivious to the antique china cups that sat on the counter and the carefully painted cupboard doors they were bashing against.

"Well, should we go outside and start?" Magdalena said, standing.

The family followed Magdalena baby-duck style through her neat kitchen and out the back door into the woods.

She pointed at a clear patch of ground next to the dead rose bushes. "Okay, Sara, kneel down and close your eyes."

The melody had mercifully faded from her mind, but she'd heard it so many times before, it would be easy to call back. In the

Iddlesvein Kindergarten, it had been a playground favorite; and the phrasing for the spell would all fall together. She knew it. She knew something else, too. Mother hadn't written this spell. It was old, much older than Mother--much older than the nursery rhyme.

"Now, my dear, as I sing these words, let them sink into your heart. Don't resist them. Allow them to work their magic inside you. Do you understand, Sara?"

Sara nodded solemnly. The unaccustomed attention reddened her cheeks but was clearly not unwelcome.

Magdalena began to sing, at first in only a whisper. She breathed the words slowly, finding that the dull, stark melody fit them perfectly.

Safe...safe...safe...

The blood that fills her veins

    Keep it safe...keep it safe...keep it safe

The blood that spills away,

Keep it safe...keep it safe...keep it safe

Let no baby fill this space

    When'st out of time and out of grace

Gods of all, be true, be light

Protect her blood through day and night

Safe...safe...safe

Safe...safe...safe

Safe...safe...safe...

Magdalena repeated the spell twice, her voice a little stronger each time. Bertha was smiling. The two younger children stopped playing and listened.

Sara sat still and silent, but her breath was rapid and her eyes were moving wildly under their closed lids.

Magdalena finished the spell and put her hand on Sara's head. She could feel the heat from it rising up her arm. Sara had just started her first menstruation. Most likely, she'd be getting married a few years from now. A ceremony at St. Joseph's on Bridgewater Road, a few kids already at her heel. One more fleeting day in the spotlight.

"Okay, Sara, open your eyes."

"Thank the Goddess Tauret for your womanhood and ask her to watch over you at all times."

"Thank you, Goddess Tauret. Please watch over me at all times."

Bertha was wiping her eye with the corner of a little flowered handkerchief.

Magdalena took the silver chalice, which she otherwise used as a sugar bowl, and sprinkled herbs over Sara's head. She'd made this part up herself. She'd always liked it because it signified the spell was done and also because she would secretly envision herself seasoning a Sunday roast. Sometimes pork, sometimes salmon. It was her childish revenge. But today, it was only the head of a vulnerable human being crouched before her that she saw.

As the broken-up pieces of sage and hyssop fell into Sara's hair, an overwhelming sense of pity rose up within Magdalena. She almost choked on it as she stared down at Sara's crooked part, her thin mousy hair. But it wasn't Sara she was feeling it for, it was someone else. The girl whose voice sang lonely in the woods--Rachel. Magdalena had heard that voice again this morning on the answering machine.

Magdalena laid both hands on the girl's head, mostly to steady herself, and said underneath her breath, "Please, dear God, let this pass. And God, if this isn't going to pass, please let the storm be guided by Your hand and not..." She stopped and opened her eyes. They were bleary with emotion.

"Stand up, Sara." Magdalena's voice was weak, her throat constricted, as if she'd been crying for hours.

"That was beautiful," Bertha said. "Thank you so much." Then she opened the small square of cotton and blew her nose into it. Sara looked away, disgusted her moment should be tainted so.

Then Becca, Bertha's youngest, came running out of the woods and began skipping around in a large circle.

As she did so, she sang:

"The Fly King, The Fly King

Come to take another

His son is his father

His daughter is his mother."

Magdalena felt her face drain of blood. She became lightheaded, and her hands began to tremble.

The girl's voice was sweet and thin, and her face was serious as she skipped the circle, jumping each time over the small pot of dead

THE FLY KING

rhododendrons Magdalena had set outside to be emptied into the compost heap.

"The Fly King, The Fly King

Come to take another

His son is his father

His daughter is his mother--better watch out or..."

The girl stopped skipping, spun around alarmingly fast with her eyes closed and her arm extended out. *"You'll* be his lover." She stopped, her finger pointing at Magdalena. The girl looked puzzled, then added, "No, not you. You're too old!"

Magdalena smiled, but her stomach had become a terrible quivering hollow.

"Becca, don't be rude!" Bertha pulled the girl's arm down. "You apologize, right now."

"Sor--ry." Becca muttered, looking at the ground and kicking the toe of her shoe into a pile of pine needles.

"That's all right." Magdalena was still smiling, but there were no smiles inside, just a frantic race to understand.

She'd played the answering machine message four times. The feeling was getting stronger. Perhaps she would pay Rachel another visit this afternoon, get some answers. Because if things didn't change for the better soon, she was beginning to fear she would have to do it, she would have to open the door. If someone was trying to tell her something, she'd have to open herself up again, *if* she wanted to see it.

This was the thing she had spent ten years hiding from. Her heart was beating erratically and her throat was tight and sticky, like a kid's hand around a candy cane. She'd better take a pill.

The noisy Klaus family left, thanking Magdalena the whole time. "The midwife would be proud of you, Mag," Mrs. Klaus told her.

Magdalena smiled, but she barely heard a thing they said. Becca was forced to apologize again, and Sara was forced into exuberant thank-yous. But all Magdalena heard were their sounds.

As soon as they were down the path, she raced into the living room and played the message again.

And again.

* * *

It was early evening when Delroy hurried past Shepherd Of the Flock All Denomination Church on the corner of Hancock Street and Belmont Avenue--cars buzzing by, headlights glaring like the eyes of anxious animals.

The sky was cloudy and drizzling, and there was a cold mean wind. Church lights shone through the arched windows, and the sounds of distorted organ and fifty bad singers trying to impress a god who could care less rang through the night. *Pitiful. Don't they know God has no mercy?* He looked down at his feet dragging through the puddles.

Something else besides the physical deformities made Delroy different than most. His belief in the existence of God. He didn't know where it came from. Aunt Gracy was a drunk, a Catholic through association and guilt. Nothing God-fearing about her. Just another fucked up old cunt. And Uncle Ross was as far away from *believing* as a person could get. He wondered where Uncle Ross was now. No, he didn't really wonder, he knew. The old fucker was frying in Hell with his underpants 'round his ankles and a hot hellfire poker shoved up his arse. For eternity too, Delroy hoped.

Delroy huffed and watched his feet splashing along. *Where we goin', feet?* The old fucker might be in Hell, but that made Delroy a murderer. He thought he knew where he was going, too.

He concentrated on getting past the church. Something about churches repelled him. Physically. He felt the cells in his body turn, as if he'd been hit with a reverse magnet. Guilt, probably. *Yep, what else.* But then his mind struck on a memory from before that, of running from church when he was five and just over from Germany. His aunt racing after him down the street, holding onto her hat, yelling in that raspy used-up way she had, telling him to *"come back here, you little freak."*

"*Pssst*...hey, man, over this way." The voice was coming from one of the decorative alcoves built around the church, convenient cubbyholes for crack dealers, whores, and bums. Delroy peered uselessly into the darkness, not approaching the voice.

"Man, it's me...Wiggy." A small black man, all skin and bones, skittered out of an alcove. "Hey, how ya doin', man?" His hands were jammed into his pockets, and he jumped from foot to foot as if he needed to piss really bad. His face and head were skull-like, and his eyes darted side to side as any good observant tweaker's might.

"Oh, you." Delroy started to move on. This fucking wanker had ripped him off a couple of months ago. Delroy was trying to score painkillers, and the little rat had taken his money and disappeared.

"Hey, where ya goin', man?"

"To hell." Delroy continued walking.

"Man, what about your landlord, what a gas. Fuckin' tosspot."

"Waddya mean?" Delroy looked back, mildly interested.

"Man, didn't you hear about what happened earlier? Don't you live in that place no more?"

"Nope!"

"Yeah, well, I was over behind Chan's when the cops pulled into his alley. Shit, man."

"What happened?" Now Delroy stopped and looked at him.

"Ah, man, yer gonna love this...you got a fiver you can lend me?"

CHAPTER 16

Klickitat, Washington

"So close your eyes and see with your heart, and you'll never be afraid of the dark..."

Rachel smiled as the song breezed past her and into the woods, blending with the ghostly *ahhhssshhhh* of the river along the way, like a hundred pale-faced choirboys accompanying from below.

She had planned on making some lunch for Gavin when she got back from making her calls. She thought she would take it out to him, let him play her the songs he'd been working on. Instead, she found herself walking past the cabin and down the trail, deeper into the cavern of trees. She stopped and looked up.

So high. What's it like up there? Silent, she supposed, up there on the pointed treetops.

The song became distorted as it traveled to her through the ever-thickening filter of spruce. The forest had a way of soothing her. Nature was supposed to be calming, but this...this was almost intoxicating.

She could still make Gavin his lunch, but first she'd get the flowers, the ones she'd seen in the clearing. She didn't question the uncanny certainty she had in knowing the way, her feet led her, unthinking.

She breathed the darkness and the sweet overpowering smell of pine. She might even have closed her eyes, but she didn't recall if she had or not. Such a pleasant, floating sense of familiarity. When she came upon the clearing it was as if she'd come home.

The scar began itching numbly. She scratched it without fanfare, her fingers working the area with a type of automatic claw.

She was here. She floated, although there was the crunch of the pine needles beneath her, into the center of the circle. The stumps looked like long lost friends. She felt as if she knew each one personally. Up, up, in the sky she gazed. She was a speck down here in her narrow forest-green tube with its bright blue lid. A spike of fear jabbed her belly. She suddenly felt enclosed. But within a second a wave of comfort drifted over her. *But isn't it wonderful to belong, to be wanted? Doesn't it feel good to have purpose, even if you don't know what it is?* And surely that wasn't true. She knew, she just didn't have the words or thoughts one needed to explain.

The flowers were waiting--little enticing blossoms. She smelled one, and it smelled of nothing. On this, she stirred slightly. She thought of empty promises, but the thought was lifted away. Here, in her forest-green tube with its bright blue lid, there were no empty promises, only things that needed seeing to. She'd started last night. In the middle of the circle, close to the fallen tree and its muck-thick roots, were five holes in the ground. Mounds of dirt by each one; fresh, black dirt. A busy worm wriggled through the pile nearest her foot, his heavy red end swollen, and again, just for a second, she felt unease. Again, it was wafted away by the perfume of the woods and a soothing, numbing vibration that registered only as a comfortable sense of well-being.

Then there was the hole underneath the large branch that reached out like a dead arm from the tree. She noticed a clump of hair snagged on the end of the branch. The sight of it unraveled a chill that tamed itself before she could act upon it.

This is the one. Look how deep it is. The others were only dug about four inches down. This was over half a foot deep and two-feet wide.

She stared at it.

It stared back.

She took six of the flowers that smelled like nothing, smelled them again, and started out of the clearing. She walked back down the trail. At least she supposed she did. And she heard bird song echoing from up high. She must have.

And the sound of the river; it came upon her suddenly, but she'd heard it far back in the forest, hadn't she? Certainly she had. And anyway, what did it matter?

As she got closer to the cabin, she noticed Gavin standing in the doorway, staring at her.

He greeted her coldly, seemed nervous, asking her where the hell she'd been. It was six o'clock, he said, and he'd been worried. He'd made his own lunch, gone back out and worked some more, and she'd still been nowhere around when he'd come out hours later.

"Oh." She didn't know why he was so concerned. Look at the flowers she'd brought back. "Smell them," she said. "Aren't they lovely?"

He smelled them, then looked at her.

Gavin didn't like the way she was acting, not one little bit. He'd had a terrible day. She had no idea what he'd been through. It was as if he couldn't think straight. Probably because he hadn't slept well last night. His day was one big blur.

"The lady who let Kiki out came over again. Said she wants to talk to you about something. Asked if you would call her."

Rachel shrugged it off. "Yeah? Did she say what she wanted?"

"*No*. She said she wanted you to call her." His voice was tight.

Rachel made a soft snorting sound at him and raised her eyebrows. He supposed he was being edgy, but Jesus, she'd been missing all day. He'd been worried. Christ, only this morning she tells him she sleepwalked again, then she disappears!

Gavin pointed to the envelope on the table. Maybe this would snap her out of it. "Here, this came. I see you didn't waste any time letting *them* know where you'd be."

She picked the envelope up and smiled at it.

Gavin watched her curiously. He'd spent a fortune on that little venture: sponsoring a child from Africa. It was the same face on the goddamn envelope as the one fifteen years ago when he was in school. The first kid she'd--they'd--sponsored died. Jesus, that had been an overwhelmingly hard thing for her to handle. She took it personally, as if she'd killed the kid herself. He hoped the new one was healthier. She'd made him the official sponsor this time because she believed that having her name on the paperwork would kill the kid just as surely as if she stuck it in the belly with a butcher's knife. So, here he was, adopted parent of little Advik. That was okay, he didn't mind. He didn't even mind doing this album, even if he couldn't think straight out here in this fucking wilderness. But he did mind her wandering off, and the sleepwalking. He minded that a lot. Didn't she realize he was worried about her?

"Rachel, do you think this was such a good idea? Coming out here?"

She was looking at the envelope. Totally ignoring him. When she looked up, her eyes were shiny with tears. Her face revealed nothing. Only her eyes.

"It's okay, honey. Whatever you want. I like it here..." He paused after the lie. "But if you feel it's too...I don't know...Don't worry about the money." He put his hand over hers, but she slid hers away and placed it in her lap.

He was left with his hand on little Advik's face. Wouldn't she ever realize that she didn't murder her sister, for chrissakes? It was nature, survival of the fittest. He didn't know what the fuck it was, but it wasn't intentional, people don't do those things intentionally.

Before they went to bed, while she was taking her bath, he locked the doors and hid the key in the bottom of his boot, under the innersole. She was a clever girl--who knew just how clever in that strange land of the sleepers.

Rachel got out of the bath and dried herself. She almost regretted telling Gavin anything. He was such an overreacter. You would think his mind would be on those songs--those sweet songs that the choirboys sing so well.

As she lay there, she noticed the slight buzzing in her body--very faint, very relaxing, dreamy. She closed her eyes and drifted into sleep.

"Stop it! Stop humming that!" Gavin screamed, suddenly sitting upright.

"What?" Her heart raced at the abrupt awakening. "What the hell are you talking about?"

He was quiet for a second. "Oh." He took in a huge breath. "Sorry." He slid back down the bed, pumped his pillow and cuddled in beside her. "Bad dream."

As she started to fall asleep again, she found she was already living what her morning would be. She was up bright and early, with the first birds and the fresh smell of dew on the witch grass, walking up the trail to Jack's Shack.

Thinking surely a bright young man like Jack could help her locate a shovel.

CHAPTER 17

Jack held the soft fabric up to his nose, then caught a glimpse of himself in the mirror across from the bed. *Fuck it, so what?* Wasn't every day a hot chick came to visit his house.

The sky had been dark all day, as though a storm was heading in. Long shadows sprawled across the bedroom floor and stretched halfway up the wall. Even though it wasn't late enough to put the light on, the room needed it.

Gladys, his mother, used to get real moody when a storm was on its way. She died in this bed. He didn't tell Rachel that, of course.

Driving to the Shack earlier today, it could have still been dusk. The streets were dead quiet--even checked his watch to make sure he hadn't made a mistake.

He passed Harry Drenich coming out of his house with Myrtle, who was all dressed up. Jack supposed she'd conned him into taking her to church. Old Harry must be paying penance for something. Jack hooted and waved. Harry looked but didn't wave back, he was just about to ease fat-ass Myrtle into the car.

At 9:00 A.M., Jack pulled his pickup into the parking lot, got out and unlocked the store. It was cold, so he'd worn his big shaggy sheepskin. He was glad he did, he looked good in it, like Davey

Crocket.

As he pushed open the door, someone tapped him on the shoulder. He tensed and almost yelled out. Now, *that* would have been dumb. He wasn't normally jumpy, but she'd come up so quietly. And those clouds, threatening rain, threatening *something*. And the empty street...

But holy shit, she looked fine. And he'd thought Jessica Tussle was cute. Jessica lived out on the Ballfork Road. Her dad, Fran Tussle, and his partner Josh Pennig owned the gravel pit out there. Jessica had a nice figure, nice face, but couldn't hold a candle to his Rachel.

Of all things, Rachel had ended up over here at his house. Jack inhaled her scent from the fluffy blue sweater.

"Get down, Rufus." The dog whimpered and jumped off the bed. The dogs stank of piss and that other eye-watering dog smell. He should bathe them, but not yet, though, Cookie was still nursing.

Boy, she'd dug petting the puppies. That is, until Barry started driving her nuts, sniffing at her crotch. Stupid mutt. Should've left him in the pound.

Jack picked up the remote and rewound the movie to his favorite part, where the two blonde chicks start getting it on. He wished one of them was a brunette, like Rachel. The other one could be Jessica from the gravel pit. He laughed, grabbed his can of beer, and took a swig. Now that would be hot.

"Don't you fuckin' dare, Rufus!" The dog looked up at him with dopey, mongrel eyes.

"All right, get up here, come on..."

Rufus panted, tail wagging. He backed up a few paces and projected his solid weight onto the bed.

Jack turned his face, complaining as the dog slathered his cheek. "Come on, now. I'm missing the best part."

The dog whined, staring dejectedly in Jack's face, moved to the bottom of the bed and slumped down at his feet.

Lucky he even had a shovel. He wasn't much into gardening. Out front needed cleaning up still--his cars and the old refrigerator lying on its side. The rotten old boat didn't help much, either. Zak's cousin Bello had asked if he could store it there for a couple of months. That had been eight years ago. Cookie had had three litters of pups in the thing, and that stupid orange cat had had kittens in there, too. He'd dumped the whole litter out at the gravel pit. He would never tell Rachel that, she seemed to be a cat lover. He was a dog man. Perfect match.

The back was mostly a tangle of weeds. *Should wait a couple of weeks till the weather settles before starting on that mess.* He had a linen line out there. Thank God he didn't have his skivvies on it today. He needed new ones, should probably invest in some. Did the girl really need a shovel? He doubted it. Sounded more like an excuse to get to know each other. She hadn't objected when he said come back to the house with him. Well, maybe she had, a little, but then she was one of those city girls. They like to play their games. He chuckled and took another swig of beer. The two blonde chicks were getting it on pretty good now. This was the best part, when the guy comes in to fix the plumbing. That would be him. Rachel and Jessica go nuts, can't keep their hands off.

About two years ago, he was out in the woods hunting deer. Walking back to the truck, he'd suddenly found himself flat on the ground. His hat had gone flying and Rufus got a fat stinky lick in before he could turn his face. "Fuck." He'd stood up and brushed off the leaves and pine needles. Fucking things got all over him. Then he saw the wooden handle sticking out from the side of a bush. He kicked the dirt away with his feet. The shovel was practically buried. It must have been there a while because the varnish had weathered off, but it looked in pretty good shape. A decent shovel costs a shit-load at Garden Center, so he'd taken it home, put it in the shed next to the old lawnmower Zak's cousin had conned him into buying, and it had remained there ever since. Until today.

One hand held the feminine blue cardigan up to his nose as he inhaled the tantalizing odor. The other rewound the tape to his favorite spot.

Rachel had enjoyed the puppies, but she got real antsy when his truck wouldn't start. Fucking thing. He had to spend hours underneath it. The shop was losing money with him gone, and Rachel was getting pissed. Women. It was past three when they headed back to town.

"So, what's the hurry, anyway?" he'd asked.

"I need to get back while there's still daylight," she said, looking out the window.

"Oh, yeah? You gotta start planting those veggies right this minute, do ya? It's gonna rain soon, ya know." He guessed she was getting nervous about having made the first move and all. He played along with the vegetable garden thing, but she acted way too anxious about getting back. Obviously, she had the hots for him, and she felt like a slut for coming over to his house. Fucking vegetarians, no one needs vegetables that bad. He hoped she could cook a good venison stew.

At one point, she was ready to *walk* back into town. "You're crazy," he'd told her. "You can't walk all that way, especially not with that shovel." Women. Sometimes they just don't think right.

So she'd hung out with the puppies while he fucked around with the truck some more.

Finally, the truck fired up. He went in to get her, and as she walked to the front door, he touched her ass. She about jumped through the ceiling. But she didn't say anything, and she left her sweater. That was a good sign.

He turned the video off and looked out the window, wondering if she'd really started digging a garden. It had been an awfully bleak day today.

CHAPTER 18

Klickitat, Washington

Father Liebermann held the ice pack on his head. The water dripping down his arm was more annoying than he could say, worse than the injury itself somehow.

"Bertha, really, I'm fine."

The woman was hovering around him like a big bothersome bee. Finally, thankfully, he got her to leave.

Excluding his six-month stint in Vietnam, Father Liebermann had been resident priest at St. Joseph's for nigh on forty years. The church was constructed back in 1857 from 5,000 square feet of musty pine lumbered at infancy from the surrounding forest. And so it sat, high on Bridgewater Hill, God's complacent eye looking down on the town.

At night, Father Liebermann mostly holed up in his on-grounds cottage, although occasionally, like last night, he felt the urge to field-trip, spread God's word and test out God's whiskey at Huntington's Bar. He did more testing than spreading. Everyone knew that, but he was an old man, and life itself had been a test, one he'd only passed by a margin, he suspected.

His sermons were empty shells of what they'd once been; he didn't like to think about the connection, but the patronage had dwindled to almost nothing over the years. People still showed up for Easter and Christmas Mass, weddings and funerals, but regular Sunday service? He kept on serving, but the town had lost its appetite.

Except today. Today, they had shown up. And today, he'd let them down.

He had left his cottage as usual, at 8:45 A.M., tired and feeling a little low. They call it a hangover, he reminded himself.

Bertha Klaus would be there; she was his regular. Maybe Fran, Julie, and Jessica Tussle. Possibly a few others, he wasn't holding his breath.

But before he even reached the east side of the church, he heard them. A stream of cars coming up the steep dirt lane, pulling into the hedge-trimmed parking lot.

He hurried to the front and quickly unlocked the doors where a silent crowd was already gathering. He watched, speechless, as they began shuffling into his church.

He stood dazed for a second, unable to fathom it, then realized with a biting certainty that he had forgotten an important occasion. A wedding or a baptism, maybe. He ran, quite swiftly for an old man into the rectory office and pulled the calendar out of his drawer.

There were no red marks on Sunday, the square was empty. Just regular Mass. He double-checked his dates, put the calendar back in the drawer, and made off to welcome his congregation.

He stood in the pinewood doorway smiling and shaking hands.

Between the welcomes, he glanced out at the graveyard. It circled the entire church. The ring of dead.

He looked up. The clouds moved with an eerie purpose across the sky, as if hurrying to some event--his service, maybe. He half smiled, until his eyes settled on the one unmoving cloud that hung black and solid, smothering out the sun.

Like a mother holding a pillow over her baby's face.

He greeted Felicity and George Braintree with a stiff hand and skin-deep smile. Embracing such dark thoughts wasn't his nature. It must be the sudden change in weather, or the shock of this unexpected turnout. Maybe the hangover.

A blackbird sat on the Grover family tomb and watched him fake his way through the line of welcomes. Even from here, he could see its beady yellow eye, quietly assessing him.

He looked up again at the black pillow-cloud hiding his congregation from the sun. The silver-white rays reaching out from behind it looked like the arms of a desperate child. It made him wonder if the Lord's heart was broken to see His children so indifferent toward Him. Not indifferent today, he thought, shaking Phyllis Haffshien's hand. He glanced once more at the black cloud, then got back to work.

Here comes Bertha with two of her kids. He watched her counting the cars. And here come the Wilsons. Kathy, their eldest, hiding the child in her belly with a long loose sweater.

Then the biggest surprise of all. Magdalena Baum. Now, there was a strange bird. She looked older than last time he'd seen her. He liked Magdalena, she was clearly touched by the Lord. Maybe she'd never quite understood that, but God works in mysterious ways. Even still, it unnerved him to see her in his church. She was supposedly an atheist, but she'd bought into the local Pagan superstitions and rituals. Even his most devout church goers were guilty of it. Magdalena had only attended service at St. Joseph's once--her mother's funeral. She was the stranger in town back then. Still was, to some degree, although she always helped out with the annual bake-a-cake at St. Joseph High School. She manned the cherry pie table along with Bertha. The thought brought a welcome smile to his lips. He'd better get a move on.

As he squeezed politely around Myrtle, he noticed Bertha over to the front left-hand side of the church, shaking her head. Someone had taken her usual place by the marble statue of St. Francis of Assisi. Pinning on his fatherly demeanor, he walked over to her. "Good morning, Mrs. Klaus. Good morning, children." He couldn't remember their names.

"Good morning, Father," they said back quietly, as if they'd just been scolded.

"What do you think brought everyone out today, Bertha?" If anyone knew, it would be her.

Bertha looked at him, her eyes red-rimmed and tired. Her skin, he noticed with some alarm, was not its normal ruddy complexion, but pale and yellow, the color of buttermilk.

"Are you feeling well, Bertha?"

"Father," she paused, looking him in the eye, "there's something in the air." Holding his gaze with unnerving intensity, she continued. "Couldn't say what, Father, but it's there. Don't you feel it?"

He smiled and laughed lightly, but her words sent a black ribbon of doubt, fluttering his insides like a flag at a funeral.

He spoke calmer than he felt. "Well, Bertha, I'm sure it is *God* who is in the air. *God* has brought these good people to Mass."

Bertha looked at him with those solemn eyes. "Maybe."

He moved away. The woman had given him the chills.

He forced himself to shake it off. He had a full house, for whatever reason, and he was going to make the most of it.

Damn, there wouldn't be enough Bibles to go around. The spares were in the cellar, beneath the stage. The thought of going down there made him think of the black cloud again, and he noticed his hands had begun to tremble. *Goodness. Thank you, Mrs. Klaus!*

Father Liebermann took the keys from around his waist and unlocked the pinewood door to the cellar. The hinges creaked--laughed almost--as they swung open. *Stop it, man. You're a seventy-year-old priest, not a seven-year-old schoolboy, and there's a church full of people waiting for those Bibles.*

He walked blindly down the steps into the dark cellar and found the light's pull-string dangling at the bottom of the stairs. He tugged it a tad harder than needed and sent the bulb swinging madly; lunatic shadows danced over the boxes and the floor. And his eyes seemed inexplicably drawn to the dusty cobwebs, which stretched to every corner, giving the cellar a tomb-like roundness.

Most of the boxes were crammed full of old books, curtains the school had asked him to store for them, and ancient velvet pew cushions that had finally been replaced last year, thanks to proceeds from the bake-a-cake.

The extra Bibles should be right...

How long had it been since he'd needed the spare Bibles? Ten years? Yes, at the old midwife Helga Baum's funeral. Magdalena had arrived a few days before. Evidently, she hadn't seen her mother since she was a child. She was the one who'd found the old lady dead in her spooky little shop out on the Klickitat Road.

The body was cremated. He had, of course, conducted the funeral Service, even though Magdalena had declined to bury the remains in his graveyard. His church had seen a full house that day. Like today.

He pulled a cardboard flap open and reached in to check if it was the right one. His fingers searched around. Something was wrong, he felt softness and movement. He screamed, dropped the box, and the Bibles tumbled out.

He held his hand up at the light. It was covered, boxing-glove thick, with filthy black flies. "Oh, Jesus..." He ran toward the stairs, shaking his hand violently. His body was jolted with adrenaline.

By the time Father Liebermann reached the first step, his bladder had deceived him. The flies swarmed close behind, their terrible sound loud and dirty.

Grabbing onto the banister with one hand, shielding his face with the other, he bolted up the wooden steps, tripped on his cassock, fell and smashed his cheek against the unfinished wood step. Whimpering, he dragged himself the rest of the way up, rolled out of the cellar and kicked the door shut.

Jesus Christ Almighty...it's the den of Beelzebub!

His face was bleeding, and the congregation, initially stunned, was beginning to react.

Service was canceled.

CHAPTER 19

Wapping, East London

The sound of her own footsteps reminded her of the shire horses she'd seen at the Queen's Jubilee. Yeah, that was her--lone bloody Shire horse clompin' down dirty wet Crow Street. She even looked like a bloody horse, too. Thank God Teenieweenie preferred women in their late forties, with that certain *hard* look. Bless his fat little soul.

Crow Street was cobbled stone, both the road and the pavement. Awkward it was, for someone in heels. The street ran parallel to the dock, and the smell of rotting fish was a constant. During the day, seagulls squawked overhead. But it was late already, they would be sleeping on poles around the back of the cannery and on the unkempt boats over at Victoria's Wharf. The docklands were deserted.

Denise was careful not to stand in too many puddles. These boots had cost her fifty quid. She'd needed them, though. A lot of blokes had a *thing* for shoes and boots, the higher the better. Bleedin' things were a real pain in the arse to get on and off, all those bloody laces.

The gloominess of Burkes Breaker Yard came up on her the way it always did. She was glad it was well fenced in. Giant metal corpses towering up from rusty graves, broken jagged limbs reaching out to the moon. Like the modern-art crap they slung outside the library, she told herself, trying to make a joke of it. She always got a little nervous passing Burkes.

Delroy was relieved. His plan might not seem like much but to him it was perfect. Bill would be able to see this was a statement, that Delroy had broken into the flat and done it there just to show him what a cocksucker he'd been. He could've rented a room, but after what Wiggy the Tweaker told him, Delroy was glad he'd held onto his money. He'd gone to see Weaz this morning at the pawnshop. Things had gone smooth as clockwork. Obviously, it was meant to be.

Delroy lit a cig and marched down Crow Street, the drizzle oddly refreshing, as if it were the first time he'd ever felt it.

The other night, after handing over five quid to Wiggy, he'd gotten the story. Bill had been arrested for interfering with two under-age runaways. Wiggy didn't know the details, except that the cops had handcuffed Bill and he'd called the female officer a fucking whore pig as she pushed his head down into the patrol car. Chan, from next door to the furniture shop, said that Bill had been planning on keeping the runaways in one of his flats, having them pay rent by way of sexual favors. Yeah, and Delroy knew whose place he'd been planning on giving them. Wiggy said Chan thought the rich fucker would be out in a day or two with a slap on the wrist. That night, Delroy had gone back to Wapping Park. He was lying on the bench, staring up at stars misted through rain and tears, when he came up with his plan. It was simple enough. He was on his way over to the flat right now.

Who was that on the other side of the street? The steps seemed to be quickening. Denise looked over, tilting her umbrella. Oh, him. Couldn't quite remember his name. Poor ugly bastard. Probably some kind of bone disease caused that hunch, or whatever it was, although his face looked a right mess too. *Delroy*, that was it. She noticed he was smoking. God, she could use one of those.

She let her bag slip off her shoulder, then swung it over the other one. Heavy bleedin' thing. The fellas loved *stuff*. The more *stuff* you could shove up their arses, or dress them up in, the more they liked it. One of her friends had turned her basement into a dungeon, stayed home and worked. But Denise wasn't as pretty as her friend. Like a bloody Shire horse, 'cept skinny. She had to do house calls.

"Delroy...isn't it?" she called over, slowing down a little.

"Yeah, that's right."

She thought she detected a note of defensiveness, as if he wanted to finish off with, "What's it to ya?" Funny bugger, he was.

"Can I have one of yer ciggys, love?" She flashed him a motherly wink. He wouldn't be able to resist. Even though she wasn't a babe, she was bleedin' Bridget Bardot compared to him. She *was* dressed skimpy underneath her mac, and she'd left it undone despite the cold, just in case. Not that she needed another session tonight. She'd left old Teenieweenie with more than two grand in her purse. He was her best client. Without him, she'd be...well, she didn't want to think about that.

She saw Delroy coming across the empty road. God, he was an ugly bastard. Sad, it was. Poor bloody thing.

He pulled the cigs out of his pocket, took one out and handed it to her. She took it from his fingers, suddenly not wanting it anymore.

Then he spoke again. She didn't watch while he did, she'd already noticed the horrible spitty stuff 'round the corners of his mouth. He smelled, too.

"Seen your brother lately?" he asked, as he fished around for matches.

Poor sod didn't look very well. "Nah, not for a while." *Bloody weasel*, she wanted to add but didn't. She wasn't sure how friendly ugly-mug was with that tosspot brother of hers.

As they walked silently past Doreen's café, she caught her scrawny reflection in the window. Shit, she looked like a scraggly old chicken walking with the hunchback of Notre Dame. What a pair.

"Can I get a little?" he asked, in a pathetic attempt at playfulness. They were passing an empty bus shelter.

"A little *what?*"

"You know..."

She snorted loudly through her nose. "You gotta be jokin'!" She realized her tactlessness, paused, and said, "I mean, I ain't a hooker, Delroy, I'm a dominatrix. I don't fuck for money."

He was quiet, and she thought she might have upset him, although she wasn't sure. He was probably a bit retarded.

"I know that," he said, after a while. "I just wondered if you'd come over to my flat. Stay and talk for a bit?"

She sighed. "It's sixty quid an hour. But I'm sorta tired tonight." She felt sorry for the poor bastard, but she wasn't cutting no deals. No way.

"I've got money at the flat."

Simple bastard, she thought. She'd stay for an hour. Even for a quid a minute, she didn't want to stay longer than that. "All right, love. I'm sorta tired, so only for a little bit. Just talkin', right? You sure ya got the money?"

Delroy nodded.

"Where d'ya live?"

He didn't suppose it was fair, having the bird come along. But fuck it. If he knew anything, it was that life ain't fair. He'd gotten scared all of a sudden. He didn't want to be alone, not until he had to. Because this time there would be no gas running out, no mistakes or turning backs. He touched the hard object in his pocket. He thought the feisty old lady with the walking stick would have gladly given up her fifty quid plus change, her pills, and her two credit cards to buy a wanker like him a gun to kill himself with.

CHAPTER 20

Klickitat, Washington

The shovel was heavy, but as Rachel started on the oddly familiar journey, the weight of it seemed to lessen. She was still aware of it, but her muscles were so relaxed, they simply held the weight with no complaints. And her breathing, steady and rhythmic. She felt as though the whole woods breathed, and she had somehow fallen into unison with it. She could almost hear the trees sigh, and she sighed along with them. *Good girl, Rachel, breathe deeply.*

That's what the nurse had said twenty years ago, when they put her under.

Ani was buried at Mount Hope Cemetery. Sometime later, Rachel was enrolled in a regular school. She became normal except, for years afterwards, she would stay awake at night staring out of her bedroom window, haunted by her oneness and the strange cold scar on her left side.

She attended Granger Elementary School. After graduating, she became a student of Granger High. Every day, for eight years, she took the same street to school.

The Avenues.

It was a thin, quiet street. The bulk of the children walked along Habernash, or took the bus. The Avenues was *her* street, and every crack in the sidewalk, every streetlight, every tree, became engraved in her mind over the years.

She felt the same sense of familiarity as she walked through the woods toward the clearing.

The forest seemed dark for only a little after five o'clock, but then the sky had been gray all day. She'd kept looking at it through Jack's dirty living-room window. It hadn't bothered her. She felt inexplicably bonded to the elements right then. Except the one *dark* cloud, which had settled in front of the sun. That one bothered her.

All of a sudden, the scream of an animal ripped through the woods, a long and agonized cry. Normally she would have panicked, searched around hoping to find the creature, taking on the responsibility and joy of rescuing its life, and if she failed, the sadness and guilt of its death. The animal screamed one last time, then stopped, a scream so pitiful, so final, a listener's heart could seem to stop too. But today, hers neither quickened nor slowed.

Next came whimpering and a scuffling that sounded like back legs dragging through the undergrowth.

She smiled vacantly. Everything dies, she thought. She knew that. She'd known that for a long time.

The wind brushed past her arms, urging her along.

As she walked farther, the sound of the river hushed to a whisper. She hadn't seen Gavin on her return from Jack's. He'd taken the shuttle bus into the Dalles for supplies. She vaguely remembered insisting on this, and that he'd objected, said he was in the middle of a song. Finally, she'd persuaded him to go. But he must be back now, working again, because she could hear angelic singing somewhere in the distance. *Maybe it's the choir boys at the bottom of the river. Sweet, pale-faced choir boys with dainty black wings.*

A squirrel darted across the trail and up a tree to her left. She smiled giddily. Silly thing, it acted so scared. Its eyes were pinned on her as it scuttled up the trunk and out of sight. Wild, frightened eyes--just trying to survive. Is that what I am, she thought, a survivor?

She suddenly felt the hollowness inside, it was palpable, physical. Why hadn't the doctors spotted it on the X-rays and filled the damned thing up?

A survivor?

Ask Ani. Maybe she could answer that one.

The sun was going down. Its silver rays shot out from behind the cloud like flares from a sinking ship. Night would be here soon.

A child would fill the hollow place. To create a living, breathing life. The thoughts slipped into her head. Not new thoughts. She had these thoughts every day, but now they were strangely defined, purposeful, as though she might have some choice in the matter. But that was only wishful thinking. The doctors had been quite adamant, she could never become pregnant. But if only she could...

Creating a life. Isn't that the opposite of taking one away? Could I be redeemed by it?

Yes, yes, the voices whispered. *Redemption, Rachel. Redemption.*

Unaware that her feet had been moving steadily for twenty minutes, she found herself upon the clearing.

She glided into the center. Back in her butterfly jar. She'd kept butterflies as a child. *Such beautiful wings.* She looked up at the sky. She had seen it this way before. She'd seen the tips of the surrounding trees bending in the wind. She'd seen the raven, the one that just flew across the black cloud and landed on the tip of a tree to her right. Something about a circle...no, a cycle... The thought wouldn't quite blow in, even though the wind twisted and turned the tips of the trees, even though the poor raven could barely hang on, flapping his wings for balance. Was he waiting? Waiting for her to get on with it? Maybe. She looked down at the earth, where her fingers had already begun the job, and started to dig.

As the sky darkened, the pile of dirt by her side grew. Her arms were chilled, but she never noticed. A thin layer of sweat dried on her skin as the sharp breeze whipped it, but she didn't feel it, and she didn't hear herself singing softly, forgotten words.

Her breath labored as the hole became deeper, and the pile of dirt continued to grow. I'm digging a grave, she thought, a slight unease finally penetrating the thick hypnotic state. *No, no, saving someone from the grave, right?*

Yes, Rachel, yes...yes...yes... Just a little more. Shhh, dig, dig, dig...

She caught sight of the white flowers; they had closed their blooms in tight cones of green. Empty promises, she thought, and then she laughed for no apparent reason, laughed loud into the chill air, and continued to dig.

She found she couldn't rest. It was a race. Against what or whom she didn't know, but she knew her place, so did it really matter? The raven *cawed* out...she took it as a *no*, regardless. And it's best to keep certain things stashed in dark corners where the light never touches them, because there are some things you cannot make go away. You can only hide them for a while. But in the end, everything has its day.

The raven *cawed* again, frantically flapping its wings against the wind, trying to hang on.

"See?" she said out loud, then her spade hit something hard. This time, she didn't look away. Time to dig it up.

She pushed the black dirt aside and saw a clear plastic bag. She pulled the parcel out of the ground and saw that it had been wrapped with several rubber bands. They were rotten and broken away in pieces like dead worms. It was heavy. It weighed...what did it matter? Weight is felt in your heart, not your hands, and if that weight can be taken away, then let the hands do it. Isn't that right, she thought, looking up. The sky was now the gray-blue of dirty dishwater. She waited for the raven to answer, but he had left with the last strain of sunlight.

Through the plastic she could see white cotton material, which appeared gray under the weakening light. It was an old-fashioned handkerchief.

Embroidered on it in faded pink silk were the initials "*HB*".

CHAPTER 21

Klickitat, Washington

The last few hours of Helga Baum's life.

10 years earlier.

Must work fast, Magdalena will be here soon. Mustn't let her see it. Must keep it away from her. Take it out into the woods. Give it back.

The midwife had woken in the middle of the night, her brow on fire, sweat running down her cheeks like salty tears.

She got out of bed, taking shallow breaths because it pained her to take deep ones, and walked over to the dresser. She sat down on a chair opposite the mirror and removed the key from the velvet ring-box. The wind, suddenly enraged, screamed through the eaves, and rain slashed sharp nails on her bedroom window. Her weak muscles tensed, but she continued.

She unlocked the drawer for only the second time in twenty years, smelling old coffin wood as she pulled it open. The midwife snatched a painful breath at the sight of her prisoner.

Still there, then.

THE FLY KING

Over the years, often for months at a time, she'd make believe it was her insanity, that the crazy brain in her snow-white head had made it all up. But there it was--the dagger--its ugly wicked metal staring back at her.

Then, in a calm ritualistic manner, she sat and assessed herself in the mirror. The years had been far less than kind to her, her face was gnarled as an old pine. She took the large ivory-handled brush off the dresser top and began stroking it through her thin hair. As she did, she hummed the old tune, as always these final days, unknowingly. "Hmm hmm la la la, hmm hmm la la la..."

She had become crazy over time, her sanity sucked out and spat aside, but her soul had never given in. She stopped brushing her hair, tilted her head, watery blue eyes questioning like a child's. *But how can I be sure?* Perhaps she had been doing its will all along, without even knowing.

She began brushing again. The one thing she did know, it wasn't her it wanted.

The other time she had opened the drawer was eight years ago. She had gotten up in the middle of the night, taken the evil one from its locked place and put it in an envelope--had it ready to mail, for heaven's sake. She knew where the surviving girl was, she'd been able to keep tabs on her. Not the boy, though. She prayed to Almighty God he was dead.

The midwife brushed her hair one last time, then, without thinking, stood up.

The rain threatened with icy fingers at the window, and the wind warned, *Stay put old lady, it's not your business anymore. Let the young ones take care of it.*

"Liar!" she yelled. Her hand grabbed at the pains riding through her chest. "Liar!"

She ran down the stairs to the kitchen, easily for an old woman on the brink of death. Cancer had feasted on her insides, eaten the best stuff and poisoned the leftovers, but her only thoughts were getting this done before her daughter arrived. How she would love to see Magdalena again, but she couldn't trust her own feverish tongue, couldn't trust herself to keep the secret.

She wrapped the dagger in a handkerchief and a plastic bag, while age-old images of the boy raged in red colors through her mind. Her bony white hands bound the parcel with rubber bands, then she walked, feet already cold, to the back door and opened it.

The wind punched her body, blowing her nightgown tight against her skin. The slanting rain shot Helga Baum head to foot with silvery ice bullets.

Eyes squinted, face pummeled, hair whipping in sad white strands behind her, she walked calmly out to the preserve shed, where she kept the shovel.

She coughed hard, her sick lungs shocked by the cold rain. She blew water away from her mouth, looked up at the blank eye of the moon, and laughed, the laugh of a young woman. Coming from rotten lungs, it was somehow worse than whispers from the dead. It scared her too, but fear was no stranger to her world.

Her arms shook with the weight of the shovel, and she stopped many times to cough, grip her chest, and laugh hysterically at the frozen moon. Three times she fell to the ground like a drunkard, hardly noticing, using a tree trunk to hoist herself back up; and using the shovel Jack would find sometime later as a crutch.

Delirium had woken her up that night, had laid her sick and dying mind open to it. Finally, the voices made sense. *Bury it.* The voices were strong in the woods. She could hear angels. *Listen to them.* They sang her name and pulled her like a nymph into the darkness. Dead babies, sweet little cherubs with black wings, showed her the way.

CHAPTER 22

Wapping, East London

At the same moment Rachel reached into the hole and grabbed the object from the dirt, Delroy and Denise turned the corner into the alley. It was past one in the morning. Denise hadn't realized it would be so far.

If he couldn't even afford a taxi, how the hell was he going to have money for her services? She was sick of the whole deal, and needed to pee almost bad enough to crouch behind one of those bleedin' trash cans. If she was ever going to be able to afford her own dungeon, and not rely totally on the kindness of Teenieweenie, she would have to get some real clients and stop hanging out with fucking charity cases like this bloke.

Delroy had gone quiet. No one around. The flat would be locked up. As they got closer, he wondered if everything would be all right. He hoped there wouldn't be yellow tape out front or some such. No, that would come later. He listened to the sound of her boots clacking over the wet uneven concrete.

He stopped at the door and offered her another cig. She hesitated, then took one. Delroy slapped his pockets.

"Oh, fuck! My keys. Oh...fuck!"

She took a drag and blew smoke off to the side. She wasn't buying it.

"Shit. Sorry. I've done this before. No big deal."

He grabbed the handle and pushed against the door as hard as he could. He felt pain rocket into his back. He bared his teeth and smiled. *No more. No more of this crap ever again.* The dry rot around the lock snapped and crumbled, and the door came open easily.

"Four hundred quid for this shit hole," he said under his breath.

The place looked different. Someone had tidied it up, vacuumed, washed, scrubbed. They'd left the few pieces of crappy furniture and the mattress. He wondered if that was temporary, if Bill would get better furniture for a *real* tenant, for a *real* person. But he was glad it wasn't filthy, for Denise's sake. She was only a whore, but still, she deserved better than that. It had the look and smell of a place cleaned up after someone died. They were right, he thought, just a little premature is all.

Delroy watched her shuffling around uncomfortably. She didn't want to sit down, not on the chair, not on the mattress.

"Delroy, love, this was a mistake. I'm too tired. I gotta go home."

"Just stay for ten minutes. Please. I got the money." He could tell by the way she looked at him that she knew he didn't.

"Ten minutes. Where's your toilet? I'm about peeing myself."

He pointed to the tiny makeshift toilet. She looked at it for several seconds, then went in and closed the door, pulling and pulling again to make sure it shut properly.

Okay, do it, Delroy. Now is the time. He walked back up the steps, opened the door and stood outside. He'd take one last look at the moon and the stars, then he'd walk back down, ignore whether or not she was in or out of the bathroom, stroll over to the mattress he'd spent so many sleepless nights on, put the gun to his head and pull the trigger. Just like that. No fucking around. He gently touched the gun in his pocket, and took out the bottle of pills he'd gotten that morning from Weaz. He'd take a handful of those, and then...

CHAPTER 23

Klickitat, Washington

Terror cut through the woods at the speed of light and slammed into Rachel with a physical jolt.

She couldn't unwrap it.

A part of her, the part that had raised its head in warning, urged her now to throw the thing back in the hole. Bury it quickly and get the hell out of this place, and make a point of never coming back. Don't give in to it.

Give in to it, she asked herself. Surely that's ridiculous.

Oh, yes? Then how did you know it was here? How? Even as she was thinking this, a slight vibration was running up her arms, calming her, a gentle tickling sensation that seemed to suggest everything would be just fine.

She turned the object over in the palms of her hands. As she did, a night bird called out through the forest. A two-syllable cry that sounded like "*Ra--chel!*" She glanced down at the tree stump and the shovel leaning against it. The spindly flowers surrounding the stump were tightly closed. They looked pale and slick, like tubes being made ready for surgery.

How had she known? She breathed in the pine air, which made her think of seasons, times passed, the hanging of ornaments and opening of presents. She held the package tighter. Some things can't be explained, she thought. It's a privilege to be part of something bigger than the known. Yes. She smiled and listened to squirrels bustling in the trees surrounding her. *A part of the big picture.* The vibration tickled her wrists in a certain sensual way.

She unwrapped the plastic and held the object, still concealed by the fabric, in her hands. The handkerchief was only slightly yellowed; otherwise, it had been well preserved inside the bag.

She pulled one side of the handkerchief away and took her first look at the dagger. She stared at it, overwhelmed by the sense of connection, as if it were something she had pulled out of an old family trunk--not familiar exactly, but stirring emotions that might be memories or dreams, or maybe it was the cold air reminding her of Christmases long gone. But she knew it was hers, and she was scared to touch it. *Tempting and repulsive, like an unnatural desire... It's Unclean.*

"It's just dirt," she said. The unexpected sound of her voice echoed around the clearing.

She would take it down to the river and wash it. *Yes! Touch it, touch it.*

Stop, something told her. *It's taking you over.* And something else whispered, *Don't listen, Rachel. It's yours.*

* * *

Dusk was falling by the time she reached the river. As she walked, she'd begun murmuring lightly with a child's quiet excitement, *"Finders keepers, finders keepers..."* over and over in time with her footsteps, until she reached the muddy bank. Now, she was silent. Parts of the sky were still dirty pink, blue seeping through like bruises on a baby's skin. Night was almost here. She stood beside the river and stared at her silvery reflection. *We've been down below a very long time, Rachel. Time to come home.*

The dagger seemed heavier than possible--than before. It seemed to weigh almost as much as the shovel she'd left in the clearing. She stood in between two clumps of bulrushes and slid it out of the handkerchief, which sailed to the ground as her fingers touched the dagger's pockmarked surface.

The vibration buzzed through her fingertips and hands, instantly warming them, numbing them. Not just the surface now, but deep, spreading up through her arms, through her blood somehow. The dagger joined with her, taking her over like an auxiliary heart. She was horribly aware of the sensation but couldn't react. Unable to let go, she felt no pain, just a dark understanding that pain waits its turn. She felt the very cells in her body flutter and shift, as though aligning themselves in some new and impossible direction.

Her hair stood straight out around her head. She felt it lift from her shoulders and a strange weightlessness about her scalp. The truth was evident in her reflection, but she didn't see it because her eyes were squeezed shut, as if she were on the steep part of a roller coaster ride. She was a cosmic time bomb, her body tick-tick-ticking. Finally, she opened her eyes. Not the forest, or her own reflection in the river greeted her, but something quite different.

Her mind could only observe, as an animal might.

What she saw was a small brown bottle and two hands, one holding the bottle around the middle, the other poised at the lid. The hands were dirty, scabby and unkempt, and, for a few seconds, seemed frozen as in a picture. Now, she was looking at another sky; it was dark, the moon and stars bright. Back down, she watched the bottle drop to the ground and bounce away. The lid too. Small white pills rolled on what looked like filthy concrete. The hands came up close, and she saw they were shaking.

They knew they were being watched.

* * *

That's when he saw the vision. At first, he thought it was an angel, a gently undulating angel. And she was holding something. Something he had seen before.

It couldn't be.

She couldn't be.

He looked up at the sky, still seeing the angel, and caught his breath. Something was happening. Something that had been destined to happen all along. His hands began to shake, and the bottle of pills fell to the ground. He could see the outline of trees moving behind her, and the dagger oddly warped and fluid, as if alive in her hand.

A reflection. Her hair looked as if it were spread out on a pillow, and she floated before him. For this brief moment, he knew that a connection was being made. He was inside his sister, looking out through her eyes.

* * *

A little piece of Rachel still resisted, forced its way to the surface one last time and screamed, "Drop it!" The voice was so loud in her ears that she did drop it.

She found herself back in the woods once again--where she had been the whole time--between the two clumps of bulrushes that stood either side, like dead lion tails sticking out of the ground.

She could see the cabin on the other side of the river. A dark gingerbread house. Her eyes traveled down to the dagger lying in the dirt at her feet. *Had that really happened? What a rush!* She found herself kneeling down to pick it up. She took the dagger from the dirt and slid it into the water. The sensation began again. Quickly, she removed it and laid it on the handkerchief, wrapped the edges around the metal surface, and touched it through the material. The feeling was gone. She breathed out a sigh of relief, and disappointment.

It's not natural. Unclean, Rachel, unclean. But also strangely evocative.

She slung her purse over her head and across one shoulder, slipped the dagger inside, carefully touching only the handkerchief, and started back to the cabin.

As she walked, the sound of the river tried to ease her doubts. Yet a deep dark part of her knew something had been started, and that it was too late to stop. *That's okay, Rachel, relax,* the river seemed to whisper. *Redemption, redemption, redemption,* as the water raced over thousand year old rocks, slowly, slowly, wearing them down into sand.

By the time she reached the cabin, she was sure she must have imagined it. She must have been mistaken.

Of course, there would be only one way to know for sure.

* * *

Delroy had watched the image ripple and disappear. He was reeling, as if taken by the shoulders and spun around in circles. Everything was about to change. He needed to prepare. His body was light and alive, adrenaline masking his usual discomfort. What had happened? He didn't know much, but he felt that would come, and he knew this. He needed to be ready. And he knew something else. He wasn't alone. He had family...and something bigger. Someone out there needed him for something very important. A mission. And it damned well wasn't God. God had used him as a joke, played him for a fool, but that didn't matter anymore. Every molecule in his body was alive with the news. This ugly duckling was about to become a swan.

He heard the whore coming up the steps to let herself out. He pulled the gun from his pocket. She was a stroke of fucking luck; he'd be needing her for a different reason now.

"Get back down." He pointed the gun in Denise's face.

Once in the flat, he pulled his knife from the backpack. "You scream. I cut."

Ten minutes later, the x-rated contents of her bag were spread out on the floor, and he had her naked on the mattress, cuffed to the TV stand. He sat in the recliner watching her.

CHAPTER 24

Klickitat, Washington

Almost dusk, and Magdalena was sure now. The feeling was growing stronger, not going away as she'd hoped. Was time running out? She thought so. But she didn't realize just how quickly. In little more than an hour, it would be too late.

The ratchet would be turned.

She couldn't stop thinking about Rachel. What kind of trouble was she in? Or about to be in. The hairs stood up on her arms.

Yesterday afternoon, she'd gone over to the cabin, but Rachel had been out. Her boyfriend Gavin seemed agitated and nervous. Magdalena didn't know if it was due to his girlfriend being gone or something else. He had been quick with her, eager to get back to his own thoughts. She asked him to have Rachel call. He'd nodded and said he would, he would. But Rachel hadn't called.

This morning, Magdalena had pulled her dusty old car out of the drive for the first time in three weeks, cleaned off the leaves and cobwebs and gone to Father Liebermann's Sunday service.

The church was packed. Magdalena spotted Bertha and asked her about the old nursery rhyme, and if she knew the history of the protection spell. Bertha didn't know anything. But she seemed disturbed, distant, muttering that something was in the air.

She was right, of course.

Moments later a horrible scream filled the air. Poor Father Liebermann. The man must be seventy if he was a day, and to fall like that.

The accident didn't seem like an accident, even though Jimmy Deacon found the rabbit's-foot key ring at the bottom of the box. The flies had used it to lay maggots in. Father Liebermann had gone looking for Bibles at the wrong time.

His congregation was, quite understandably, very upset. Especially Bertha. Magdalena tried to reassure her that it was just a little fall and a few flies, but it was hard to pull off when she felt so affected by it herself.

Magdalena had gone home and spent the rest of the day tinkering around, trying to think, trying not to think.

As tired as she was now, the incident had taken on a surreal quality, as if she might have dreamed the whole thing. So many flies. It hardly seemed possible. They had filled the entire basement with a buzzing black cloud.

The whole reason she had gone to church this morning was to ask Father Liebermann what he knew about evil. True, it sounded dramatic, especially coming from her, but she knew little of such things. She wasn't religious. Her career had always been about ordinary people. Sometimes badly damaged ones, like Peter Denning and the Clamberty case. And she'd had some intense psychic feelings over the years. But the one she was experiencing now...*nothing* felt like this.

If it's indeed real, she reminded herself. *And it might not be, old girl. Look at the facts. What do you have? Nothing.* What about the melody of the spell coming to her while she slept? *But haven't you heard that same melody a hundred times before? Doesn't everyone around here know it?* And what could Father Liebermann do? The most evil he'd probably experienced was the recent vandalizing of his church. So it had been a shot-in-the-dark question she'd gone to ask, and on some metaphysical plane she felt it had been answered.

Magdalena yawned. She hadn't slept at all last night, stayed up waiting for a call that never came, knowing that once she fully committed and allowed herself to open the door, there would be no closing it. Not this time. She couldn't sleep because that is when it was likely to happen, when her mind gave up the reins and her soul did its calculations, unbiased by fears and foes. She pictured it as a dam bursting at its weak point, the water pulling her down into the cold drowning depths. Finally, she'd taken a sleeping pill, knowing she couldn't hide forever. The pill did nothing. Was her fear that great? This morning, she had attended church for the first time in ten years--and only the third time ever that she remembered--to talk to a priest. Yes, she thought perhaps her fear was that great.

And the church had been packed. She knew from talking to Bertha that this wasn't normal. Something was going on, and she wasn't the only one to sense it. But tonight she would sleep. Eventually, she would have to. And then it would be out of her hands.

Her mind was on Rachel again. The spell...why had it been handed to her like a loaded gun? Was she supposed to perform it on Rachel? But what would she think? Rachel wasn't from around these parts.

She would think Magdalena crazy, and the spell needed to be taken to heart, not laughed at. It wouldn't work. But the feeling was urging her. *Go, go now.*

Perhaps she should check on Father Liebermann first. Maybe he could tell her something--anything. *You're putting it off, Mag. The time is here. You must go to Rachel, now!*

Yes, yes, she would. But first, Poor Father Liebermann.

She would take him some of her special tea. See if he was doing all right. If he was, she would ask him what he knew about the old nursery rhyme. *The Fly King, the Fly King, come to take another...*

And if he seemed to be in good spirits, she might just ask him what he knew about evil.

* * *

Father Liebermann lay half propped up on his sofa while Magdalena Baum fussed around in his kitchen making some witch drink. What a day this had been. Perhaps he should tell her to quit with the tea and fetch him his whiskey from the second cupboard above the sink. That's what he wanted, and it would be the honest thing to do. But he kept his mouth shut.

His cheek was cut. Initially, he'd thought that was it, but he'd evidently hit his head quite badly too. Now, he was the proud owner of a painful blue-yellow lump that Bertha had carefully bandaged. Other than that, he felt just dandy. And Magdalena was fussing in his kitchen, with obviously more on her mind than helping an invalid old man of the church. He hadn't asked her yet what had prompted her to attend service.

THE FLY KING

He hoped to God that young Jimmy had gotten rid of the flies. There must have been thousands of them. Not something he'd soon forget.

"Here, Father, drink this."

He looked up and smiled at her. She was an attractive woman, even at her age. He blew the steam and sipped at the witches brew.

"Father, do you know anything about the old nursery rhyme the kids around here sing? It's called 'The Fly King'"

He shrugged. What on earth was she thinking? He'd had enough of flies for one day, thank you very much.

"Not really, Mag, just that it came over with the immigrants." He moved a cushion behind his back. "If you want facts, go to the library. Or research it on the school computer." He turned to look at her. "Why do you want to know about it?"

"Just curious." She went silent for a moment. "Father?"

Here it comes, he thought. "Yes?"

"This might sound odd, but what do you know about evil?"

He took a big breath and proceeded to tell her what he knew. He said that man made his own evil, and that much of the Bible was interpreted this way nowadays. Times change, he told her, and the Church changes with it. Not as quickly as it should maybe, but we realize that evil is in the heart of man, and much of the Bible is symbolic of this. She listened and nodded, but didn't seem wholly satisfied with his answer.

The drink she made him tasted bitter, but he did feel some benefits after it went down. He asked her why she wanted to know about such a thing. He also said he thought she was special. The drink had quite relaxed his tongue at that point. Then suddenly, for no apparent reason, Magdalena jumped up from the couch, placed her hands on her face, and let out a horrible sound. Like someone's last breath. She didn't appear to be hurt. It was almost as if she'd seen something. He followed her gaze to the wall. Nothing but wallpaper. He looked back at her face and saw it was flushed.

"Too late," she whispered, still staring at the wall.

"Too late for what?" he asked. "What's wrong, Mag?" He was standing now, approaching her.

"Don't, Father. It's okay, it's okay." She urged him to sit back down. "It's nothing, I just missed an appointment, that's all." *I missed it. I missed it.* "I'd better go."

She insisted he stay put when she left. She looked very troubled. She looked worse than he felt, and that was quite badly.

* * *

After a while, Father Liebermann pulled himself off the sofa and began to get ready for an early night. As he passed the telephone, which sat on a small round table by the stairs, it rang. He felt anxious, as if this couldn't possibly be good news. He picked up the phone.

"Hello, this is Father Liebermann."

"Father, this is Bertha. Are you okay, Father?"

"Yes, yes, my dear."

"Father, I know this might sound strange, and I know you changed the policy since the vandalism and all, but would you consider leaving the church doors unlocked this evening?"

There was a long silence, and Father Liebermann swallowed a lump in his throat as big as a potato. When he spoke, he felt as though the words had come from the mouth of another.

"Yes, Bertha, I'll see to it.

CHAPTER 25

Gavin cooked the veggie burgers and mushrooms he'd bought in town, and fumed. Rachel had sent him to the Dalles to get Dramamine and some other stuff she'd written down, said she'd taken these things as a kid to help prevent sleepwalking. But why hadn't she gone with him, or at least have been there when he got home, checking to make sure he'd gotten it right, asking about the trip and the strange little town that neither of them had ever been to before? But no, she was out doing *secret* things. And it was going to stop. Right now. He could barely wait for her to get home. Jack had come over earlier, all smug and familiar. He'd only met the man once, for God's sake. The guy was holding Rachel's sweater.

"Uh, yeah, is Rachel here?" he'd asked. Gavin told him he didn't know where she was, then Jack had laughed, handed him the sweater and said, "She left this over at my house."

Gavin was going to tell her they were getting out of this place. He didn't care that they had paid up front. He didn't care about the album, either. She could tell them to stick it where the sun don't shine. He wanted no part of it. He'd made his final decision and he was not going to be swayed. He'd gone along with enough of her harebrained plans, but this one stunk the worst ever. They hadn't even been here three whole days, and he'd already had to climb a fucking pine tree to get the cat, couldn't sleep worth shit, and had become obsessed by some godawful fucking tune that had come to him in the night. Not to mention Rachel acting totally weird and sleepwalking again after seventeen years. He wanted to leave. Tomorrow. He flipped the burgers over and poked at them. Where the fuck was she?

Twenty minutes later, he heard the back door open.

"Rachel, where the hell have you been?" She was filthy, glassy-eyed, and her jeans were black up to the knees. "Planting *vegetables, huh?*"

Jack had informed him--Jack evidently knowing more about their business than he did--that she needed a shovel, that she was going to dig a vegetable patch.

She looked at him and frowned. "What?"

Vegetable patch, my ass. She'd been in that damned clearing again, where she'd gotten those godawful flowers. They still sat on the kitchen counter, all waxy and sick looking. The way *she* looked right now.

He threw the sweater on the bed. "Jack brought this over. What were you doing at his house?"

Rachel glared at him. "I was fucking him, of course. What do you think?"

Gavin sighed. "What's going on, Rachel? Why did you go over there? We don't even know him. Goddamn, he could be a fucking rapist. And why a *shovel?*"

Slow and cool, Rachel took her bag off her shoulder and placed it carefully on the bed, sat down beside it. Only then did she speak. "Really, Gavin, you're acting like a child. I don't have to explain myself.

I'll do whatever I want whenever I want, and if you don't like it..." She paused, stared right at him. "Tough shit!"

"What the hell's gotten into you?"

"Mind your own business!"

Gavin jumped up from the bed and flew into the kitchen. He turned off the stove, grabbed the pan, and scraped its contents into the trashcan.

"Well, that was stupid, wasn't it." Rachel said sarcastically, watching from her position on the edge of the bed.

He stared at her dumbfounded. She was cold, a stranger who had walked into the cabin with Rachel's body and voice.

He was trembling with anger. "What the hell is going on?"

"I dug something up."

"*What?*" Even though the kitchen was filled with heat from the stove, a chill was spreading across his skin.

He came into the bedroom and sat down beside her, just her purse between them. He saw something poking out of it and went to grab it.

"No, not yet!" She pushed his hand away.

"What do you mean, not yet?"

"I'll show you, but not yet."

He was starting to lose it.

"We're leaving tomorrow, Rachel. I'm going to start packing the bus tonight."

A smile spread across her face. "No, Gavin, we're not."

His tongue turned sour and dry. How dare she talk to him that way? After all he'd done for her. Disregarding him with such cold ease. He tried to calm himself, took in a deep breath.

"Okay, Rachel, let's start over. *I* want to leave. And you can't stay if I decide we're going."

She looked at him, her eyes reflecting the yellow glow of the overhead light, and smiled slowly, the way a snake seems to smile before swallowing a rat. "I'm not leaving, Gavin. You can go, but I'm staying."

"What the fuck is wrong with you?" He was raising his voice. Pretty soon, he would be shouting. She was doing it deliberately. He knew it.

"In fact," she went on, still smiling in a way that wasn't a smile, "it might be better if you *do* leave. Why don't you take the shuttle bus into Portland? I bet Jack would even take you, if I ask him to. You can catch a flight back to Chicago. I can probably mix the album better than you, anyway."

"What?" You ungrateful...bitch."

"Bitch?" She laughed sadistically. "I'm not a bitch. You're just lazy, that's all. And I know you've been wasting time on something other than the songs."

"*Lazy? Lazy?* I come out here to--"

She jumped up from the bed, picked up her purse, and started toward the back door.

"Don't you dare leave." He grabbed her arm.

"Get your hands off me, loser. You should take up teaching. You don't have enough talent for anything else." Her voice was cold, spitting the words out like bitter seeds.

He did something inexcusable next, but it was exhilarating and impossible to resist. He slapped her. He looked into her twinkling eyes and slapped her again.

Her eyes never left his as she slipped her hand into her purse and pulled out the dagger. As she pointed it at him, he noticed its dull surface, and a strange oily smell, like something alive yet rotting.

"What the hell is--" He reached out to take it from her.

Surprisingly, she let him.

He held the dagger in both hands. It was heavy, warm, about body temperature. A warmth he could feel in his wrists. He stared at its coarse surface, then his eyes drifted up to Rachel and he watched dreamily as her shadow changed shape, extending up the wall, arms reaching out. Long, long fingers, almost as long as her arms, and dark shapes on her back, like wings. He blinked, looked down at the carpet and back up at the wall. Her shadow had returned to normal.

"Feel anything?" she asked, her face serious now.

He looked at her, quite sure he didn't know her at all, which stirred an excitement in him. He pushed it away. Wasn't he supposed to tell her that tomorrow they... He could see her chest moving as she breathed. Could he hear her breathing, *feel* her breathing? His groin was tingling, purring. He was getting an erection. As if she were stroking him.

He couldn't be sure, but it seemed as though the awful yellow light had dimmed, an opium glow now shimmering over the room.

He couldn't take his eyes off her chest.

In, out. In, out.

"Feel anything?"

God, her voice, it reached right in him, making every nerve alive with desire. He couldn't speak. He felt his mouth hanging open.

"Gavin? Feel anything?"

Slowly in, slowly, agonizingly out. The light dimmed more, to the color of a mustard field. Strong. Heady.

In, out.

All at once his hand reached out and grabbed a handful of her hair. Violently, he pulled her backwards onto the bed.

Her T-shirt was off, and then she was naked. He was watching her creamy skin.

In, out. In, out. Slowly, agonizingly.

He was faintly aware of the dagger in his hand. It *was* his hand, wasn't it? Couldn't tell. *Shhh, Gavin, you can go now.* That skin-- creamy, hungry. He was. But... *Shhh, go now, go. Yes.* He had been waiting for so long. So long.

* * *

Delroy pulled her head to the side by her hair, and sucked hard at the curve of her sweet neck, murmuring noises into her skin. The angel...so beautiful. *Only one sister left. The other had been weaker, and she was gone.*

He smacked her hard around the face, suddenly angry for making him wait all this time. They should always be together. He smacked her again, furious now. Leaving him, letting him be alone. His blood boiled through his flesh, and he felt he must be red all over, like raw meat. He wanted to put himself in her, punish her and love her. He pushed her legs apart and groped between them. She was moist, ready. She had been waiting too. He kissed her hard, pressing his tongue down her throat. He wanted to climb inside her, hide in her, make her suffer.

And he would.

* * *

Rachel looked up at the face. She wanted to look away. So ugly-- it must be wrong. *Shhh, it's your nature Rachel, shhh*. But...

She looked again. No, not a stranger. Familiar, as if she had known him a long, long time ago--a forgotten part of her. His body so ugly, it was almost inhuman. It didn't matter, though. Her own body buzzed with energy. She wanted him inside her, the urge uncontrollable, *Shhh...yesss, Rachel, out of your hands now. Not your fault, go with it.*

As her fingers slipped from the dagger to wipe sweat from her face, she realized it was *Gavin* on top of her. Of course it was. Gavin was making love to her, nuzzling her neck. Vaguely, she remembered the argument, like morning-after fragments. But a second later she slid her fingers up to the pillow, where Gavin's hand lay on the dagger, and touched it again.

In, out. The creature was back again. The terrible ravishing hands, the vile yellow teeth that bit into her tender skin as if he wanted to consume her. And she felt every ounce of fluid, heavy in her.

He was inside, joined. *Bad, bad, bad...*

* * *

The angel wrapped her slender legs around his back. There were no thoughts of pain. He wasn't even here. He was somewhere else, somewhere in-between. He wanted to stay forever, but he couldn't hold on any more. It was all too much, her warm breath heaving against his chest, her long legs, her soft neck, his tongue pushing inside her kiss. His sister, his wife. Then, in a timeless explosive second, he was free inside her. He cried out as a feeling more intense than any he had ever known surged through him, took him, held him suspended in exquisite bliss. A burst of colors, metallic green, red, orange, and blue exploded behind his closed lids. He remained above himself for what seemed like forever. Finally, it ebbed, his breath slowed. The colors turned to maroon and floated away, like amoeba, sluggish, crawling. He opened his eyes. She was fading from him, turning to gray, then black.

Delroy finally looked at Denise lying next to him. She was still breathing, but he'd bitten deep into her neck, fucked her up pretty good. He stared at her. What had he done? What had he become? Just before the pain arrived to take him away, he noticed a drop of fluid glistening at the top of her thigh. *It couldn't be. Impossible.*

Here we go now.

A thunderous pain knocked him to the ground. The mattress, the whore, they became distant, spotty, turned to newspaper print.

And he was unconscious.

CHAPTER 26

Klickitat, Washington

Magdalena was driving way too fast. She had bolted out of Father Liebermann's cottage hoping she could turn back time. But it was too late. Something had changed. Something had happened. She'd failed. What was she to do? Maybe she should just pack her things and leave. *No, no, you silly old fool. Just relax. It's just sleep deprivation-- take it easy. Go home, get some rest. It can't be that bad. It* can't *be.*

But her palms were slick, and her car kept veering too close to the edge of the road. Back home, she almost crashed into the oak tree trying to park. *First, calm down, have some tea.*

She took her tea into the shop, sat down and began fiddling with the lock on the display case. *Can't be that bad. What could be that bad?*

Okay, time to...open up. She made herself take deep breaths. *Breathe deep, circular breaths, stay calm, relax. No, I can't do it. I can't go there. Big, circular breaths, nothing to be afraid of. No, please...scared! Circular breaths. In, hold...no, no, don't! Out, in...out.* Finally, she leaned back in the chair and closed her eyes.

Thirty seconds later, she was out. Had someone knocked, she wouldn't have awakened. Had someone called her on the telephone, which they did--Father Liebermann rang to tell her of Bertha Klaus's request to leave the church doors unlocked--she wouldn't have heard it.

* * *

"Mutter?" With a child's eyes, Magdalena stared up at the tall woman. The air felt different, sweet, younger--as was she.

"Mutter. *Soll ich wirklich gehen?*" Am I really to go?

Her mother's hair was brown. Light brown, with fine neat curls that looked as if they had been stuck on with glue, just at the roots, it was fading into its future white. They stood at the foot of a small airplane. No other passengers were around, although she could see faces when she turned to look: motionless cut-outs, staring unblinking out of the small round windows in the plane.

"Es ist nicht sicher hier, Maggie."

Not safe? Why? This is my home.

In the distance, she could see the Black Forest smothering the mountain range. A warm summer breeze caressed her brown shoulders. Her skin felt pleasant under the gentle heat, but her insides where knotted and sore. She'd been crying.

Mother looked so tall standing in front of the sun.

"Am I really to go?"

"Ja, Maggie." Her mother's eyes were full of tears, and her hands trembled. Even though she was a strong woman, she looked weak.

They stood on the runway, and a hostess beckoned, smiling sweetly.

"*Ja, müssen Sie gehen,*" Mother said again. She dropped Magdalena's hand and hugged her. Magdalena felt she could have stayed forever in that hug--so safe in there. Then the arms were abruptly released, and Mother turned away.

Magdalena reeled for a moment and then walked toward the airplane steps, her shoes clanking on the metal as she began climbing. She turned, Mother was looking back.

Magdalena examined the modular strangeness of the airplane.

She spotted her seat, sat down with the rest of the passengers and looked out the window. She saw Mother slap her hands onto her face, and even from way inside the airplane, Magdalena could hear her howling. All of a sudden, the sky behind Mother turned red, and now Mother was red--red and black, like an imprint behind eyelids.

Now the sky turned completely black, and Mother was gone. The sun was gone, leaving only a strange white luminance in the cabin. The door closed abruptly, and all at once she was pushed back in her chair by a tremendous force. She heard the squeal of engines; the sound became louder and louder, until she had to place her hands over her ears.

They were already in the sky. Higher, higher, out of control. She looked at the passengers across from her. They were not alive. None of them. Only her. Higher and higher. As stars raced by like squealing silver bullets, the dim light faltered, and the cabin began to shake. Magdalena held onto her arm rests, her heart beating so fast, it was barely discernible as a rhythm. *So this is where they go. This is where they go.*

She looked at the cream walls of the cabin. The light faltered again, flickered, and she saw the fuselage begin to come apart. Before she could scream, it was in pieces, floating down out of sight.

She began spinning, unable to tell if she hurtled up and away, spiraled downward, or stayed in one place.

A silent pressure in her ears, a maddening deafening silence.

She wasn't breathing, couldn't tell if she was still alive. Her thoughts were non-forming. She'd died perhaps, passed into the realm of the spirit.

All around was blackness. Was it sky? Couldn't tell. Deep in the earth? Didn't know. She couldn't think, but without needing to, she sensed the black was not a void, not a *blank*; it had depth, desire, consciousness. It was the unknown, the living black that children see behind their closet door. It mauled her...for days. Paralysis of weeks, months, years. It kept her hanging there a very, very long time, and time was no longer ticking; it had slowed to a maddening nothing. It held her suspended for an eternity. And then the spinning ceased. Surely this was the end of her. She would die now, if she hadn't already.

Without warning, her arms flew open. Not voluntarily, but reflexively. She burst out from the blackness, arms spread wide like a shooting star. Alive again. Her lungs wheezed full of air, and she realized she could breathe.

Before Magdalena had time to make sense of her surroundings, she was assaulted by a blinding flash of light, so intense, it turned metallic. Her mouth fell open and filled with the freezing silver brightness, stuffed so full that she thought her jaw might break. It lasted several seconds, then began to disintegrate, the pressure slipping from her mouth like sand.

She could hear singing, unaffected and innocent, like the voice of a child serenading herself while picking berries in the woods. The voice was familiar, as was the melody, but the words? A sweet, plain lullaby. But something else too. She could now hear an underbelly to the singing, a sinister *whispering*.

"...Sleep my baby sleep

Never more shall weep

Time to rest your little head..."

Her eyes finally adapted. She was somewhere dark.

God, that smell. What is that smell? Rotten and cloying sweet. She sniffed and coughed, gagging on it.

Instantly, the voice was close, almost in her ear. She snapped her head around to look. It was gone, distant again. But a light was coming from this direction. She realized she'd been facing a dark wall. Ten feet away was the bright outdoors. She was in a cave.

Why was she sitting in a cave? She stood. *Must get away from that stench.*

The singing was coming from outside.

"...Oh sleep my baby sleep

Say not another peep!

Time to close thy tired eyes..."

Magdalena found herself walking, but not out toward the light, back farther into the cave, where the foul odor was thickest. She didn't want to, but she had to. She took several cautious steps deeper in.

The thing was closer than she thought. She could see it. Dark, but unmistakably a pile of human limbs. It stood five-feet high and was wide at the bottom, narrow at the top. She could hear flies buzzing around the pile, could make out limp flesh hanging from bone. Fingers stretched open like sun-scorched starfish. Arms, legs and feet pointed in hideous contradictions. Around the base of the pile she guessed would be blood, dried into the blackness, treacly and thick.

Almost instantly, she found herself standing in the opening at the front of the cave, her heart pinching fast little beats in her chest. *Jesus Christ Almighty!*

No good calling him, Mag. He doesn't hang around these parts.

She looked down, and wasn't surprised to see the spruce pines below. She was up high, on the ledge of a cliff overlooking a forest.

Something to the right of her. *Go on, Mag, take a look.* She felt her head turn on its own. She didn't try to stop it; resisting wouldn't get her out of this place any quicker. Get it over with, see what she'd been brought here to see.

A young woman. She was sitting cross-legged, dressed in a beige sack-like tunic, and had something on her head, a hat...no, a crown, made from...from pine needles. She seemed quite unaware of Magdalena's presence. It was Rachel. No, Magdalena thought, it looked like her but it wasn't. The girl kept singing. *Is the whispering coming from her to?*

> *"...Time to rest your little head*
> *So softly in thy safe warm bed*
> *Sleep my baby sleep..."*

The girl's hair was different than Rachel's, lighter. Same features but younger, and the eyes just a little farther apart. Her hair was tied at the nape of her neck with a string of daisies. Still singing softly, she threw her head back and looked up at the sun.

Magdalena followed her gaze.

This sun was strange, clearer and brighter than the sun Magdalena was used to. She looked back at the girl, and wondered if she knew about the bodies stacked in the back of the cave.

> *"...Time to close thy tired eyes*
> *And Mother bring a sweet surprise*
> *Come morning, if thee sleep..."*

Her voice was so clear, eerily childlike. A moment later, a disturbing chill wrapped itself in the air.

Magdalena looked up at the sky again. It was in some type of chaotic changeover now, clouds moving in swiftly from both directions. One, larger than the rest, slid in front of the sun, blocking it out. The wind began to whistle and bite at Magdalena's arms.

The large cloud was rimmed with red and cast a strange pink glow over the girl and the forest. A moldy rotten pinkness. The clouds began moving very fast, casting merry-go-round shadows over everything. It made Magdalena queasy, off-balance. She could picture herself tumbling over the edge of the cliff and onto the skewering pine trees below.

Most frightening of all, she looked down at the girl again and saw that she was looking directly back. Magdalena felt her blood go thin with fear.

The girl had stopped singing on seeing her visitor, but now, staring right into Magdalena's eyes, she continued. The dark whispers were becoming louder, taking over, her voice was fading back, disappearing, until all that was left was a small scream, lost in a chorus of snarls and hushed demonic laughter.

Magdalena backed away, closer to the edge.

The quiet laughter turned to chanting, nothing Magdalena could understand. Yet she understood perfectly. It was an incantation. *A curse.*

The young woman grinned at her, and Magdalena saw what looked like tiny black pebbles spilling from her mouth onto her dress. Her mouth was no longer moving, stuck in a grimace, although the voices--*the curse*--continued out of her. That, and the faint, distant screaming behind it.

More pebbles spilled from the girl's mouth.

As her grin widened, impossibly wide, a torrent of them spewed out. They were flies, most of them dead, but some still buzzing.

Then, the girl's eyes turned black as they filled up and overflowed with the insects. Flying out in loud horizontal streams. Now, they came from her ears, too, like black particle streams. A hideous buzzing cloud surrounded her. The buzzing became one with the demonic incantations, giving them a pulse, a life.

The swarm grew. All Magdalena could see now were little scraps of the girl's beige dress behind the ever thickening black. And there was an odor, a vile sickening stench, as if something right next to her was rotting incredibly fast.

As the cloud of flies grew closer, Magdalena was struck with a tremendous fear of even one of those flies touching her. She screamed, her lungs snatching the last piece of unoccupied air before they overcame her, drowning her in a black sea of pestilence.

She couldn't help it, the horror was too much. Magdalena screamed again.

The flies found their way inside.

The scream woke her. Her eyes connected with the blank stare of the plaster wizard in the corner of the shop while the sound of her cry ricocheted, still trapped inside her head.

CHAPTER 27

Wapping, East London

To say Delroy had been asleep, or even simply unconscious, wasn't enough. He had barely moved, barely breathed. A doctor might have diagnosed it as a short-term coma or, more probably, been too confounded to commit.

Delroy's eyes opened.

He was lying naked on his side in a fetal position, his body shaking uncontrollably, like a man rescued from icy water.

I fell in the Wapping Park pond, he thought wildly. Rolled right off the bench in my sleep. His teeth chattered, but his temperature was high fever point. Dirty old pike had nibbled away at him till there was nothing left but bone and pain--eternal pain.

The room was swimming, waving, undulating. He suddenly felt nauseous and vomited on the carpet. He lay there afterwards, vaguely sensing blood trickling from his left ear down the side of his neck, pooling in the hollow of his collarbone.

The agony was paralyzing. Delroy tried to lift his head but it was a giant boulder, impossible to move. The mattress was about a foot away from his face. He could see Denise lying there, only a step above him, but how high a step it was in his condition. She looked so mighty; her black hair splayed out, her thin arms above her head, hands still securely cuffed around the leg of the TV stand. Looked as though the whore was still alive, nose buckling as it pulled in air. He must have broken it for her. He closed his eyes for a moment, then opened them again, resting his cheek against the threadbare carpet. Even through the pain, which was so bad it made thinking impossible, he knew he had acquired vital information. Things were different; *he* was different--*just this pain*--he couldn't hold the pieces together. *A puzzle--like the broken mirror in the bathroom. Something I need to do.*

What is it?

He moved his head down a careful millimeter so he could focus on his upper arm. The muscle there was pulsating, a hideous gnawing sensation. He could almost believe that a rat had found its way in from the alley and was eating him alive, its sharp rodent teeth, wet with saliva, tearing at his flesh. In his delirium, he even pictured it pausing to wipe blood from its whiskers with filthy claws before gnawing on his muscle again.

Delroy bent his neck to look closer, and his face responded with a grotesque contortion. The skin there was blistered. A patch on his arm about four inches long and two inches wide was puffed up, almost *bubbling*. Alarmed, he endured the pain of reaching his other hand to it. His fingers touched the center of the area. It was numb and sticky. He moved his hand to the outer region, and found the pain. He yelped as bolts of agony lit through his entire arm. Catching his breath, he hovered in the white light of faintness.

What was it he needed to do? *Very important.*

There was a similar patch on his leg; he could feel it blistering and moving. *Damned rats.* The white light continued to hold him suspended.

What was it he...

Something he needed to...

Yes! Yes, of course!

It had been there all the time.

The knife lay on the carpet between him and the whore.

Gasping, Delroy grabbed it and, like a half-dried worm on hot cement, flipped and wriggled his way closer to the mattress.

Denise lay motionless. *Fucking cunt. Oh, this pain, Jesus Christ.* Even if he wanted to, how could he ever find a way to make someone suffer this much? He heaved himself up, whimpering like a beaten dog the whole time, and looked at her.

She had been unconscious, but on hearing him again after hours of silence, feeling him breathing on her face, she opened her eyes and screamed. As he threw his hand over her mouth, she bit it. Didn't even register. She couldn't throw a pebble at this mountain of pain. He pulled his bleeding hand away, grabbed her hair close to the scalp, and wrenched her head back. The other hand--the hand with the knife in it--raised up and came down again, carefully slicing through skin and veins one side of her neck to the other.

Delroy dropped the knife onto her chest and watched as her eyes bulged, the whites clear, the irises suddenly so very small. Brown eyes. He'd never noticed that. Imagine how intimate they had been, and he'd never even noticed the color of her eyes. She began to gurgle.

He reached a hand under the flow of blood, wiped some on his chest, and smiled for the first time in what seemed like an eternity.

There it was. There it fucking was.

He began sobbing, overcome with joy.

"God? God?" he cried, his voice strangled with tears. "You're a fucking wanker, God, and I'll *never* take it back again. *Never, never, never!* You never cared about me, but '*he*' does! 'He' really does!"

Delroy smeared blood all over his chest and neck. The pain melted away, leaving him in euphoric bliss. This was a gift, a gift from *his* Lord. And if *his* Lord wasn't everyone's idea of a good time, well then fuck them all to hell!

"Thank you, my Lord. Thank you, thank you, thank you!

"And fuck you, God!" Delroy raised his hand and shot God the bird.

The pale, crippling mounds that stuck out from his back no longer hurt. Neither did his head, his knees, nor that pathetic highway of frayed nerves that passed itself off as his spinal chord. He bathed in the life-flow of 42-year-old Denise Pinkerton, and nothing hurt at all. As he splashed blood all over his body, rubbing it in, playing and laughing, he thought of the collectible plate called *Sparrows in the Birdbath* that had hung in Aunt Gracy's hallway. Uncle Ross had violated him once in that hallway, and Delroy had escaped into the shiny picture. A spring garden, warm sun on his back. Delroy laughed harder than ever. No more pain, no more guilt, just a heart filled with joy. And something else, of course. Oh yes, much more than this, even.

He, Delroy Günter, was on a mission. He was an important motherfucker. No shit. This ugly duckling might still *look* like a freakin' waste of space, but he wasn't; he was here to serve a purpose, and now he knew what it was. Holy fucking shit, he was about to change the world.

"Did you get that, bitch? 'Change the *fucking world*,' I said!" He shouted excitedly at Denise, whose blood-starved heart had slowed to a weak sporadic *tap*. He kicked her in the ribs. "How about Rachel then...that's my sister. Didn't know I had family, did ya?"

CHAPTER 28

Klickitat, Washington

Magdalena looked at the Black Forest cuckoo clock hanging on the wall. She wouldn't sleep again tonight. The dream was still clear and as real as the cold sweat that had beaded up above her lip.

Flies. The nursery rhyme, the protection spell, the lullaby the girl had been singing in her vision...they all had the same droning melody. The lullaby was the *root*; she knew it. The lullaby had started innocently, as just that, and had been molded into other forms over the years, perhaps centuries. And the protection spell. What was it for--to guard against pregnancy? And the nursery rhyme. *The Fly King, the Fly King come to take another, his son is his father, his daughter is his mother--better watch out or you'll be his lover.* Jesus, she didn't know what that meant. Okay. Flies. That didn't take brain surgery--nothing pleasant was ever connected to them. Poor Father Liebermann would attest to that. But she didn't know the specifics. She should look through her mother's old books; perhaps she'd find something in those. Yes, that's what she would do. The wind whipped at the bedroom window. It would be chilly in the attic. She'd better grab a sweater.

The attic was crammed full of boxes. Old books, damp wood and the wind. Listen to it, she thought. *As if it's alive, and angry that I'm here.* The roof of the cottage was steeply sloped, making the attic small and uncomfortable. The books and the rest of Mother's stuff had been boxed up shortly after the funeral, piled up here and shut away.

The first thing she'd seen after climbing the stepladder and pushing aside the heavy wooden cover was an antique tailor's dummy standing at the far wall in front of the triangular eave. Its black stitched eyes appeared to have been added on by someone-- Mother, probably. One hung down in a sleepy line where the thread had rotted, and its mummified skin peeled around the cheekbones and ribs. She would have to pass it again going down.

The wind continued to batter the eaves, and Magdalena wondered if this couldn't possibly have waited till morning. *That's right, old girl. Chicken out again.* She sighed and began, pulled down a box of old postcards and photographs. The light was bad, just a single bulb jutting out from behind the tailor's dummy, so weak that it didn't illuminate the corners at all.

She inspected the first photo her hand had grabbed. There was Mother, accurate to the dream. A working woman in an apron, tall and brusque, tiny curls on her forehead, arm around a small slender child with light hair. She wore flat shoes, the shoes of a hard working midwife, the kind of woman who makes apple pie and whacks you with the wooden spoon if you don't take your nonsense outside. She's smiling, but the little girl isn't. She's holding a teddy bear close to her chest and wearing a dark beret that Magdalena remembers as being purple. Her eyes are sullen, her mouth turned downward. She looks frail, as if in a constant state of anxiety. *Had* she been? She doesn't recall, but the black-and-white photo tells her something. It speaks in more than memories, it speaks moments that were true to them at the time. She had been a scared little child. Even though Mother was robust and safe, something was making the little girl in the purple hat very ill at ease.

The photo had peeled at the edges. She turned it over and looked at the smudged writing on the back, Mother's scrawl, in blue ink from her fountain pen. Magdalena remembered *that*, too.

Me and little Maggie. Iddlesvein Petting Zoo.

The wind slammed at the roof and rattled something that had come loose. Cracks up here, Magdalena thought, weaknesses that are bound to be discovered. She could feel the blasts of chilly air searching for her skin and finding it, especially on the back of her neck.

She returned to the box. At one time she'd considered holding a yard sale to clear herself of all this old rubbish, but now she felt an odd knowledge that this would never happen, that her stuff would be added to Mother's and sit up here in boxes and piles, suffering the wind through the cracks in the eaves.

So many books, their pages yellow and dusty under her fingers. Some were already old when Mother first acquired them. Books on cooking, on flowers, on midwifery--all outdated. She examined the contents of one box after another, carefully putting the ones she'd checked in a new pile to her right.

Then she found a volume on dream interpretation.

It wasn't exactly a dream she'd had. More of a vision--an awful one. After waking--*coming to*--she had staggered from the shop chair up to her bedroom. She'd sat down at the old dresser and studied herself in the mirror, her eyes still blurry. For a moment, she looked exactly like Mother.

She flicked through the book, freeing dust, rubbing her nose to keep herself from sneezing.

Underneath the index, in small type, she read, "Copyright 1946." She read a little of the antiquated language, flipped back to the front page, finger scanning the alphabetically organized index, and stopped at the entry "The Fly, Page 108."

> *The fly symbolizes the immaterial or the restlessly wandering soul. The fly is primarily associated with illness, death, and the Devil. Since the middle ages, there has been a widespread belief that demons of plagues and pestilence threaten people in the form of flies.*

As she read the words, her body began to tingle with adrenaline, the same way it had on the trail when she'd heard Rachel singing. She must be crazy to be considering this. Magdalena continued to read, her fingers shaking.

> *The principal devil mentioned in the Bible is Beelzebub (from Hebrew Ba'al zebhubh, lord of the flies, a perversion of the original Canaanite deity Baalzbul), often represented as a fly. He plays a role in folk belief, especially in magic spells. In Persian mythology, the principle of opposition, Ahriman, slips into the world as a fly. (The Herder Symbol Dictionary, Herder, Freiburg,* Chiron Publications)

Well, there it is then, just as she'd expected. *Flies? No damned good!*

Slowly, she started piling the books back in the box. As she did, her eye caught on an oddly familiar red-and-yellow cover. She pulled it out. Its worn paper spine was broken with use.

Kindergarten Rhymes.

It had been hers.

The book fell open to an ear-marked page. No surprise, it was The Fly King. She began to read, carefully.

> *The Fly King, The Fly King*
> *Come to take another*
> *His son is his father*
> *His daughter is his mother--better watch out*
> *Better hide beneath the cover.*

It had changed over the years, or been altered to fit the purpose of a children's book. *"Or--you'll be his lover,"* was the last line, the way the kids had sung it. She flashed on Bertha's youngest, pointing at her and saying in a way that only a child can, "Not you! You're too old."

She felt reality slipping from her grasp, hanging on by fingernails now, over the edge, down the mountainside. *Look out treetops, here I come.*

She'd sung the nursery rhyme many times as a child, but what did it mean? The hairs on her neck told her it meant something bad. Either that, or the real world was almost gone. She'd soon be drugged up in a state mental hospital, singing nursery rhymes, casting shoddy spells on the wardens, and crooning bedtime lullabies to her fellow inmates. All with the same melody, of course.

Underneath the prose, she noticed a line of tiny print and strained to read it.

"This nursery rhyme is based on the medieval legend of the Fly King."

So, it was a legend? Magdalena remained in the attic till 5:00 A.M. rechecking every box, searching for anything she could find on it. She found nothing.

As she climbed wearily down the ladder back into the false warmth of her house, the phone started ringing, and she heard a siren. An ambulance. The sound changed pitch in an unpleasant Doppler effect as the vehicle sped past her house and up Klickitat Road into town.

CHAPTER 29

Klickitat, Washington

Gavin's eyes opened slowly, like the crusty eyes of a tortoise after hibernation. His throat felt tight and closed, with no spit to break it apart. He swung his feet out of bed, his aching head in his hands, and tried to recall what had happened. Had he drunk a bottle of tequila? He didn't think so, his stomach wasn't sour, even though it felt as if every ounce of moisture had been sucked out of it. He looked toward the window. The pale gray light suggested dawn.

God, what had he done? He couldn't think straight, as if his brain had shrunk to the size of a raisin. *Need water, fast.* He stood up, bent at the waist like an old man. He walked the greasy carpet over to the cool linoleum of the kitchen floor, disturbing the cricket; it immediately began *whirring*, drilling into his papier-mâché head. Once in the kitchen, Gavin closed the door. Still he couldn't remember anything. *What's causing this?* Trying to recount his day, he fumbled for a glass and nearly dropped it. Finally, he got himself a glass of tap water. There was filtered water in the fridge, but room temperature was better; he needed to drink a gallon right now. He gulped down the first glass and filled it again. He could feel his

THE FLY KING

dehydrated cells greedily fighting over it. He gulped only twice and the glass was empty again. What was going on? Had he eaten rat poison? The thought triggered something, and he went over to the trashcan. He looked inside and saw the discarded burgers and mushrooms.

Then he remembered something else, disjointed and strangely dream-like: He had been angry with Rachel for going over to Jack's. Why had she gone?

It was as if yesterday's events had happened ten years ago. One memory triggered the next but none came easy. *Oh, yes, that's right. She borrowed a shovel. Hmm, but why did she need a shovel? She was making a garden.* He turned on the tap and filled his glass again. *No, she dug something up. Yes, yes, and they had gotten into an awful fight, and she had called him lazy.* Finally, it was coming back.

Then his stomach knotted. Something bad had happened. He'd done something...what was it? Something he'd rather not remember. He ripped the knowledge from his gut and threw it on the table before him kicking and screaming.

He'd hit her.

Jesus! Then what? She'd pointed something at him, something that made him feel peculiar. *The bread knife.* She'd threatened him with it. He deserved it, and worse. Hitting her, for chrissakes! *Not a bread knife, it was...it was...what? Yes! She pointed a cleaver! No, a dagger.* But she was showing it to him, not threatening him, and...that was the thing she had dug up.

He was suddenly struck with a thought that made perfect sense, a real thought brought on by the re-hydration of vital brain cells.

Drugs. Only drugs could cause this type of inexplicable behavior.

Gavin didn't do drugs. He had experimented when he was younger, but that all stopped a long time ago. He had just turned fifteen; Mom and Dad were fighting a lot around that time. Gavin would spend hour after hour in his room listening to music.

As he left the house that day, the two of them were shouting, as usual. They didn't even hear him when he said he was heading down to the lake with the gang. It was winter and icy. The cold nipped his ears raw in less than a second. Reluctantly, he pulled his hat from his pocket and jammed it on his head.

He met up with Petronsky and Greg at the mini-mart. As planned, Petronsky had brought along the booty: three tabs of acid stolen from his brother's wallet. None of them had dropped acid before and, though trying to maintain face, were scared as shit.

They sat down by the iced-over lake underneath the Martin Luther Freeway. It was almost dark before they finally got the nerve to pop the little pieces of paper into their mouths.

Petronsky went first. Greg wanted to go home, but Petronsky was adamant, and Gavin had no real desire to go back and watch Mom tiptoeing around Dad, adapting herself to the new, post-fight rules.

All at once the acid hit. Greg began tripping first, started skidding around on the iced-over lake. Then Gavin and Petronsky joined in. They were from Russia, at the Olympics, competing ferociously for the gold medal. A color-fueled, face-morphing hour went by before the ice cracked and Greg fell through.

None of them, except perhaps Greg, realized the seriousness of the situation. He came up, went down. Then Petronsky shouted, "Shark!" and Greg seemed to jump out of the water a good three feet. But then he went down again. He stayed down, his hair floating like mellow-brown octopus legs.

Gavin grabbed his head and pulled it out of the water; somehow, he thought it had come off in his hands, but Petronsky had grabbed Greg under the armpits at the same time. They pulled him out, the ice cracking around them.

Greg was dead. They were sure of it. His face was white, his lips blue, and he wasn't moving. A nightmare in living, drugged-up color.

In a voice that had become a slowed down 45-rpm record, Petronsky said, "I'm going to get help for the fish...I think a lifeboat."

Gavin just blinked, still staring at Greg's violet lips. Evidently, Petronsky scrambled up the bank and onto the Martin Luther Freeway, looking for a lifeboat. There was a dreadful shrieking noise as the truck braked, skidded, and crushed him flat as the aluminum Coke cans they ran over with their bicycles.

Gavin didn't recall what happened next, except that some days later, he and Greg, who ended up being okay, were standing in uncomfortable black suits around a hole in the ground, and their best friend, trapped forever inside a crazy looking box, was being lowered into the earth.

Rachel. Gotta check on Rachel. Jesus Christ, what if she's dead?

In the instant it took him to run from the kitchen to the bedroom light switch, he had already imagined her dying two horrible deaths: In one, she was lying there unable to speak or move, organs frazzled on some unnamable drug, silently pleading for water while he was in the kitchen drinking his. In the other, he turned on the light and saw her with her back toward him, he shook her shoulders, and nothing. He pulled her over. Sticking out of her stomach, her nightshirt soaked in blood, was that oily, stinking dagger.

His hands trembled as he switched on the light. She was lying on her side, away from him. He shook her, and she didn't move. He pulled her toward him and there it was--the dagger sticking out of her stomach. But it was only her hands. She had her *hands* cupped over her stomach.

"Rachel, wake up!" She didn't move. "Rachel!" His voice cracked. "Rachel, please." Tears sprang to his eyes. He hadn't remembered her arms being covered in bruises. She was hurt pretty badly, and he had done it to her.

"Rachel!" Kiki jumped up beside him to see what was going on.

"Uh...wha...?" Her voice was a dry clicking in her throat that he could barely hear.

"Jesus. Wake up, Rachel. I'm getting you water." He ran into the kitchen, dropped the glass. It smashed on the floor and he cursed, grabbed another and filled it. Then he ran back to the bedroom without bothering to turn off the tap and crouched down beside the bed.

Rachel opened her eyes with difficulty, as Gavin had, but the *look* in her eyes was as if she had awakened to the sight of an ax-murderer, or the grim reaper himself. It lasted only an instant, then she smiled, but it kept replaying in Gavin's mind with comic-book clarity. He supposed he was still drugged.

"Gavin, I'm so..."

He held the mug out to her, and she heaved herself up against a pillow and drank it empty. He took the mug back to the kitchen and filled it again. She drank it down just as eagerly.

"Are you okay, Rachel?"

"Yes, I think so. I feel like--"

"I know," he interrupted. "I think we somehow got drugged, ate something, or--"

"Ate something? Gavin, I'm starving."

How can she be thinking about food? "Sure, of course. I'll get you something." It was four o'clock in the morning; she hadn't had any lunch or dinner, he supposed. *Thank Jesus Christ she's okay. Thank you, God. But those bruises. Jesus.*

He went into the kitchen, looking through the doorway every few seconds to make sure she was really all right. She was petting Kiki's head, lost in thought, trying to make sense of it, he guessed. But she seemed to be okay. *Thank you, Jesus.*

He grabbed some eggs from the refrigerator and started to make her an omelet.

Maybe that woman who owned the magic shop, Magdalena, the supposed psychic, had done something to them. Maybe he'd offended her; maybe Rachel had. Maybe she didn't like other people living in her forest, who the fuck knew. But she had come over here twice, both times uninvited, and she had let Kiki out. He thought about the clearing, where Rachel had first started acting strange. Maybe Magdalena had wanted Rachel to find the clearing-- whispered magic into Kiki's ear. His mind conjured images of sacrifices, covens, men in gowns holding up daggers. *Jesus. Witches, cats, daggers.* He turned the omelet over and sprinkled some cheese onto it. Then he took the package of mushrooms out of the fridge.

Mushrooms. That was it! The clearing was full of them. All those ugly tree stumps, covered in that nasty looking fungus. They contained some type of hallucinatory drug. Now *that* made sense. Rachel had gotten some spores on her, breathed them in. It also explained why he'd been feeling peculiar, why he'd been inventing

14th-century sing-alongs in his head. Rachel had found the dagger, which had been covered in the stuff. She'd been hallucinating, thinking it was buried, when it was likely lying on one of the stumps. She'd been on a type of high since the first night, poor kid.

Whatever kind of drug it was, it was most definitely an aphrodisiac. Gavin recalled, in a surreal but not unpleasant way, that he and Rachel had tripped into some type of strange sexual behavior, which is when he must have bruised her. He was getting that thing out of the cabin a.s.a.p. He wouldn't dispose of it; he'd hide it somewhere. If he remembered correctly, it looked old--might be worth something.

They would shower, wash their hair and clothes, air out the cabin, decontaminate themselves. He didn't recall seeing the fungus anywhere but the clearing. Still, they would need to be careful.

He carried the plate in to Rachel, happy with his conclusion. "Here, sweetheart. Anything else?" He watched her swallow the food. Jesus, he loved her. How could he have doubted her, even for a second? Poor baby. He wanted to hug her, but he'd let her eat first, then he'd try and do something about the bruises--kiss them, cover them in ointment, anything he could to make up for it.

* * *

Rachel ate the food as if she'd been starving for days. She didn't remember being this hungry ever before. Thirsty too, but mostly hungry, her belly practically reached out and grabbed the food off the plate. After she ate the omelet, she had Gavin make her another. "Hurry," she called out to him several times. "Is it done yet?"

Some of the bruises were really quite bad, already ochre-yellow. She hadn't been bruised this way since Granger Elementary, when Janice Inkerton and her bullies beat her up. They had pummeled Rachel's soft skin with their bony fists, pulled her hair till it came out in handfuls, and kicked her hard as she lay on the wet concrete. They were the girls that spat and smoked, and swore like boys. She had drawn their attention like hot water draws puss. Joining school late in term, along with the history of her recent metamorphosis from circus freak to pretty, smart new pupil, was more than they could handle.

Gavin was right, of course. It made perfect sense. They had been exposed to some mind-altering drug. She was relieved. The last few days seemed disjointed and blurred in her mind, as if she hadn't been completely in possession of herself. It might take a while to come down, they both concluded, because neither of them felt quite *right* yet.

And they agreed that there would be no more rambling in the woods, even in the places that appeared fungi free. They'd stay in the immediate area of the cabin and the trail, get the album finished, and then get the hell out of Dodge. She could easily find something to occupy her--learn to play guitar, maybe. The clearing was most definitely off limits.

But something else was bothering her. She hadn't mentioned it to Gavin, although if it didn't clear up she would need to get treatment. Not in a doctor's office--no way. She would go into town and visit a chemist, buy the strongest over-the-counter medication she could find. She must have scratched the scar uncontrollably while under the influence of whatever it was and gotten an infection. At the very upper and lower ends, it was starting to blister. It didn't hurt badly, but she could feel it puffing up, itching, possibly spreading.

She put tea-tree oil on it and went back to bed, telling herself it could be a reaction to the drug, or the spores, or whatever it was Gavin had said. But still, something stopped her from telling him about the blisters.

* * *

Rachel was still so tired, exhausted. Even though it was morning now and birds were chirping loudly in the trees--strange echoing chirps to a fatigued, drugged brain--she wanted nothing more than to close her eyes and sleep. As she started to drift off, she realized something had changed. The sleepy fingers of her mind probed around, trying to touch on the answer. *Something deep, something fundamental,* they reported back. Her hands laid themselves gently over her stomach, the same position in which Gavin had found her earlier.

Sleep took her quickly now, and her last thought was, *the hole, silly...can't you tell? It's gone. It's been filled. See?* Her hands gently rubbed her belly and she was dreaming before the realization could settle in.

CHAPTER 30

The phone was ringing. Magdalena waited for the siren to become a distant whine before she picked up the phone.

Some things don't need words to be said, the story is told in other subtler ways: a shake in the voice, a hesitation too long for comfort. Bertha had barely begun to speak, but Magdalena already knew Father Liebermann was dead.

"Good God, Bertha, how did you find him?"

"He said he would leave the church doors open. But even though I couldn't sleep, I couldn't go up *there* either, not until it was almost light. I kept thinking of the dark graveyard and....oh, Mag, if I'd gone earlier, I would have found him, and he might still be alive."

"No, no, Bertha. You mustn't think that. The poor man, it was just his time. *And yours is coming soon, too, isn't it, Mag?* It was nobody's fault."

Oh, yeah, maybe it was yours, Mag. Maybe he got to thinking about what you said. Maybe you scared poor old Father Liebermann into a coronary. The man suffers a terrible fall, and you go over there and start stirring up trouble. Shame on you.

"But Magdalena, if I'd only gone sooner. I was the one who asked him to open the church doors. That's where he was going when he had the heart attack. Opening the doors for me, but he didn't even make it. The church was still closed. Oh, God..." She began sobbing again.

Magdalena waited for a pause, so she could further reassure her. She imagined poor Father Liebermann out there in the cold graveyard, still shaken up from the fall, his confusion over the whole incident now compounded by a visit from the old witch at the edge of town.

"What do you know about evil?" she had asked, then started muttering about scary old nursery rhymes and acting strange, finally rushing off with barely an explanation.

She pictured him leaving his cottage shortly after Bertha called, just enough time to phone Magdalena and inform her that the church doors would be open that night. But they hadn't been, had they? No, because he had walked out, probably holding his aching head and wondering what exactly she had meant by that--evil. And he'd walked to the front of the church in the dark, but tonight he was jumpy; the noise of an owl landing in a tree scared him, and he caught his breath. He continued to walk because Bertha had asked for the doors to be open, and Magdalena had asked him about evil. So he walked, and perhaps a raccoon turned over the trash can by the side of the church. That would have jarred his nerves, maybe even sent a strange arrow of pain down his left arm. But he would have continued on.

At the front of the church now, quite a distance from his cottage. *Look at the gravestones standing dead in the moonlight.* He would have noticed how they laid there, the never-moving, never-breathing dead. Surrounded by it, he would have thought; as he flexed his hand a couple of times to rid himself of that annoying pain. *Must have hurt my shoulder in the fall.* Then he would have turned his attention to the steps leading up to the church, his back now against the gravestones. *Look at those steps. My, that seems like a long way.* But he would have started to climb, out of breath before he even began. Then he would have grabbed his chest and stopped for a moment. *Really not feeling too well. I'll unlock the doors and get back, lie down. Just a few more steps. But what's this now? Something behind me. Who's behind me?*

Only the dead.

Then God's hand stretches down from the sky, reaches inside his chest, grabs his heart as if it were a warm dinner roll, and tears it apart.

On the floor, he looks up at the moonlight. A star winks at him. He turns his head and sees the gravestones from an angle he's never seen before. Welcome home, they seem to say, and then he would have laid there until the stars winked out, and the pain in his chest finally came to an end.

Bertha was still sobbing. "I feel so badly about it."

"Don't Bertha, it wasn't anyone's fault." Magdalena said it sincerely, as if she meant it.

CHAPTER 31

Wapping, East London

He sat on a bench outside Wild Panic. He would never have thought of such a plan on his own, but he wasn't on his own anymore. *Lonely days, lonely nights, where would I be without my woman.* He smiled, almost laughed, but looked down and covered his mouth just in time to avoid drawing attention to himself.

Ringsouth Mall. Never been here before in his life. Why would a man like him need to be around so many goddamn fucking mirrors? Mirrors, mirrors everywhere, big columns of them stretching three stories high, so all the pretty bitches could check themselves out as they strutted past.

He'd cleaned the blood off his arms and face, left it on his chest because that's where it seemed most effective. Denise was still on the mattress; there was more urgent work to attend to than cleaning up her mess. He'd check the flat out later, before Bill got out of jail, he hoped. He'd like a word with that motherfucker, anyway.

It had been several hours since everything changed, and he was feeling pretty darn good. But the euphoria was beginning to pass, and he could feel a pressure starting to build just around the edges of his nerves. He got the message: The blood wasn't a one-time thing. Fine by him, he'd do whatever it took.

He could think a lot straighter, too. All this time, he'd thought he was a waste of space. He wasn't. Those fuckers out there were the waste of space, and he was an integral part of the clean-up crew. Just a few more days, and then nothing would be able to turn back the clock. God would be slapping His forehead and crying in His beer.

Can't even have a cig in this friggin' place. Might smoke up their bloody mirrors. He turned to check out the bird in the floor-length black coat as she went inside Wild Panic. She was cute, all right, but wrong facial structure. Had to get someone who looked like Rachel for the photo. *Love it. What can I say?* He looked down again to hide the smirk that had spread across his face.

Wild Panic was a trendy boutique, not uptown ritzy like the West End, but trendy in a hip young way. Just like Rachel. He'd find a girl of the same ilk here eventually, sometime today. He'd have to go outside for a cig in a minute, though, past the bleedin' mirrors and out the giant reflective doors--vain bitches. He thought briefly of Denise lying on his mattress. What an ugly cunt. She'd only been a vessel, though. It wasn't as if it'd been *her* he'd mated with. *Lord forbid he get one go at it and end up with an old whore like that.* No, unbelievable as it might be, he was beyond all that crap; he was in the realm of the saints, the gifted, the chosen few. And Denise had been useful in very many ways, he shouldn't put her down.

After the *change*, he'd searched her purse. He'd only found a measly five quid stuffed in a zipper. Then he'd searched again and found the false bottom, and the two grand tucked nicely in the lining. *Sneaky old whore.* Two thousand pounds, about how much it would take to get him where he needed to go.

Two hours and four cig breaks later, he finally spotted the perfect match. She was wearing a white fluffy jacket, her black hair spread out over the back of it in striking contrast, like Rachel's against her white pillow.

The face was most important, and she had it. Cute little thing. Bet she had no idea what was in store for her today. Bet she wouldn't have hurried on down to check out the end-of-summer sales--and herself, in the three-story mirrors--if she had. He laughed again and lowered his head. She was inside Wild Panic. He wouldn't go into the shop; that would be a mistake. He already looked like a bad penny in a pot of gold, and the security guards were eyeballing him. He'd seen them whispering into their radios and pacing by every fifteen minutes or so. Fucking wankers.

Ten minutes after she went in, he got up and started moving around, looked at his watch--which wasn't there because he didn't have one--and acting as if he was preparing to leave. Looks like his date is a no-show, they'd think. Poor bastard. Must happen all the time. Then, when she came out and he sauntered casually off in the same direction, they wouldn't suspect a thing. He couldn't risk fucking this up. It was vital, and time she was a-ticking.

A little while after he started pacing, she came out carrying two new bags. He let her get quite a distance ahead, then started to follow. She had other shops to check out. She went in and out of the same one three times before finally convincing herself to buy whatever the fuck it was she had a hard-on for. Don't bother darlin', he thought, don't need to dress up where you're goin'. He hovered by the fountain, pretending to admire it. It made him need to piss, but he couldn't risk taking a leak and losing her.

Finally, she headed for the lift that went down to the car park. Thank fucking God. High maintenance cunt, she was. The door was starting to close, but he jammed his hand in and it wheezed back open. There she stood, along with an old couple. He tried to smile and look normal. The old gal frowned and snuggled in closer to her rickety old bloke. The Rachel look-alike stood in the other corner, staring up at the ceiling. *La de fucking da.*

He'd show her.

Delroy snuck up as she was unlocking her car and jabbed his gun in her back, ordered her to take him to Wapping Bus Station. If he remembered right, there was a photo booth just outside the main entrance.

He was right. He forced the bitch into it. 'Bout pissed her pants, but he kept the gun rammed into her ribs so she didn't scream or make a scene. Then he had her drive them out to the Heathford dump. The name on her driver's license said Pauline Baxter, but she wasn't no Pauline Baxter. She was just another one of *them*.

It was fun driving around in a car. After he killed her, he'd keep it, he had errands to run, and taking the bus seemed below him now. He'd only ever driven briefly, and that was as a teenager, before he snuffed out Uncle Ross. And to think he'd spent so many years feeling guilty about killing that wanker. What a waste.

Delroy had to drive because Uncle Ross, silly fucker, had gotten himself a DUI. Their car was an old banger that stalled at every light, and Delroy couldn't drive worth shit. He supposed he'd be considered handicapped in the real world. Every Saturday, he would chauffeur Uncle Ross's sorry arse down to the bookies, and if Sweet Susie or whatever old nag lost, it would be a helluva drive back home. The old man would beat the crap out of him.

The rubbish dump was a stinky, horrible place. No one hung out here except the rats and the tosspot who sat inside the kiosk at the gate and weighed dump trucks. The entrance for cars was off to the side and unmanned.

Pauline Baxter wouldn't stop sniveling and begging him not to hurt her. He supposed she thought he was after her body. Vain bitch. He only cared about Rachel, and his time with her would come. Soon, they would be together forever. He remembered the initials scratched into the park bench, so deep they'd bled into one. He gently touched the blister on the top of his arm, which was beginning to hurt. His mind was starting to fog up again too, and he'd felt a twinge at the base of his neck as they drove in through the dump gates. This was perfect timing. With any luck, he could nip it before it started. He could feel the blister on his leg. It didn't hurt badly, but it was throbbing. He could imagine it underneath the fabric of his jeans, swelling and bubbling like skin held to a flat iron. The blisters were good, though. They proved it was really happening.

The Fly King cometh.

He made Pauline strip. He supposed it wasn't really necessary, but he hadn't seen many naked women, at least not in real life. She was on the rag. He pulled the tampon out with fascination and threw it, like a small bloodied mouse, out the window. "That's for the rats," he told her, smiling. "They'll think it's a long lost relative." She didn't smile back. He guessed that she didn't realize he was doing her a favor. The smell of blood made him antsy for it, but this was old discarded stuff; he needed fresh, from her veins.

The gun was pointed at Pauline's head, which was shoved against the driver's side window. She looked like a cheap whore with her legs

THE FLY KING

spread like that. "Close your legs, for Christ's sake." And what a fucking noise she made. "Shut up, just shut the fuck up. You don't get it..." He went to touch her cheek, and she pulled away. "Suit yourself."

His eyes glassed over as he watched the flies hovering around the pile of garbage he'd picked out for her. *Flies. Who'd ever have thought they'd end up being so important?*

He refocused, and brought his fist down onto the bridge of her nose, felt it crunch under his knuckles. Like punching into a bowl of dry Rice Krispies, he thought. She screamed, but his other hand was already over her mouth.

"Shhhh Pauline. You should be thanking me."

He laid her down at the base of the stinking garbage pile.

As he took his knife out of the back of his jeans, he felt rain spitting on him again. The sky was gray, as usual, and a few dirty-looking seagulls squawked above.

"Wait your bloody turn," he hissed, looking up at them. A heavy raindrop splattered and dripped down his forehead like bird shit. He took the knife, held it at her throat. "Tell me honest now, Pauline, do you believe God is merciful?"

She looked at him, eyes bulging from their sockets. "Yes, yes, He is. He is."

He shook his head, sighed, and slit her throat.

Ten minutes later he was sitting in Pauline's 1998 Honda Civic, his chest smeared with fresh warm blood. *Shit, what a fucking rush!*

"God is dead, long live the Fly King."

The blood had seeped through his T-shirt almost immediately. But it didn't matter; Weaz, his asshole fence down on Ramsey Street, wouldn't care. And he was closed for lunch, so this was the perfect time to conduct some private business.

He opened the glove box and pulled out the photos of himself and the lovely Pauline.

Perfect.

CHAPTER 32

Klickitat, Washington

Magdalena's eyelids were gritty and burning from lack of sleep. She'd forced herself to eat a little breakfast before walking into town.

The sky was a different kind of gray than yesterday, a sad gray rather than an angry one, and the sun wasn't exactly hidden behind the clouds, it more hazed out from behind them, as if the whole sky had melted into a single thing. The river slid alongside down the hill, off to the ocean to be cleansed.

Bertha had told Magdalena she was going into the Dalles this morning to visit her sister, to chew her ear off about how she'd caused Father Liebermann's coronary. Magdalena wanted to question her about the Fly King nursery rhyme, ask her if she'd heard of the legend, but the woman was practically incoherent. And Father Liebermann himself had stressed, "If you want facts, go to the school library, use their computer and check the Internet." She wasn't up on that stuff and would probably need help. She sighed, so tired.

First, she would buy milk from Jack's, use it as an excuse for being close by, and go see if Rachel was home.

Finally, she reached the store and was actually comforted to see Jack's face, a shot of reality if ever there was one.

"Ah, how's it hangin', Mag?" He smiled and slapped his hands on the counter. "Did ya hear about Father Liebermann?"

"Yes. Yes, I did. Most unfortunate. Awful."

"Ah, yeah. I heard you were at Mass. How come? Thought you were an...atheist."

She was in no mood. This was so typical of him. Even though Bertha would adamantly claim responsibility, he'd soon have the whole town thinking *she'd* killed Father Liebermann.

Had she? Had she in some way brought it on? Left things too late, shirked her responsibilities?

"Yes, I did attend Mass. And yes, I'm an atheist. But I've always held Father Liebermann in high regard, and--"

"Ah, yeah," he interrupted, "but what about those flies? Did you see 'em?" He smiled again, thoroughly enjoying himself. "What do ya think caused that, then?" He waited for a reply as she walked over to the one tiny fridge dedicated to food items and took out a gallon of milk.

"I suppose...just bad timing."

Jack laughed knowingly. "Yeah, I guess you could call it that." He laughed again, and it turned into a cough. He was hacking uncontrollably now, bent over the counter. He looked up at her. She saw doubt in his eyes, and a look that said, *Don't kill me, too, you fucking old witch.*

He coughed some more, cleared his throat, and gained his composure.

Magdalena's smile was half lazy with lack of sleep. "You better watch that cough, Jack. You wouldn't want it to take hold."

He stared at her for a nervous second and laughed. "Ah, yeah, gotta cut down on the cigarettes. Planning on giving up soon, anyway." He got a distant, wistful look in his eyes.

"Have you met the people who rented the Jenkins cabin?"

He looked startled for a moment, as if she had read his thoughts. "Yeah. Yeah, nice people. Especially Rachel. She's a singer, you know."

"Yes, I know," Magdalena said. I've heard it. *I've heard it in the woods, and I've heard it in my dreams.*

"You wanna see the picture she gave me?"

...And the flies. I can see the flies. Hundreds of them, millions of them. Only flies, and piles of... Huge Christmas tree-shaped piles that reach up to the moon.

"Mag?"

"Oh, sure. I'd love to." She smiled, but her cheeks quivered under the strain of it.

Jack had already started fumbling under the counter. The picture was easier to get to than he made out. But he didn't want the old witch seeing he had a thing for Rachel. Not that he cared what she thought, but still, he and Rachel needed to be discreet. He pulled out the promo photo and handed it to her proudly. The old witch didn't know he'd masturbated to it four times in the last two days, that he took it back and forth to work with him. At least he hoped she didn't know.

Magdalena's face had suddenly gone pale. She studied it longer than he felt comfortable with.

"Yeah, I think Zak's been lookin' at it too, that old horn dog." He grabbed the corner of the photo, but she wasn't giving it up. Damn, she looked pale.

"You all right, Mag?"

She didn't answer. She was looking off now, toward Main Street. He thought she might be going into one of those witch trances. Not in his shop, she wasn't. He snapped his fingers by the side of her head. "Hey! Hey, Mag! You all right?"

She finally looked back at him, her mouth slightly open. "Oh, oh, yes. Yes, I'm fine." She handed the picture back, but her eyes were distant.

"What--did ya see something? Something in the future?" He grinned again. Maybe she saw Rachel and him shacked up together.

"No, I'm just tired. How much for the milk?"

Have it your way, he thought. "Two-eighty-seven."

She paid him in silence and left the store.

CHAPTER 33

Wapping, East London

Weaz was sitting in the back room eating pie and mash from Doreen's when he heard the door buzzer.

"Ah, fuckin' 'ell, never fuckin' fails, does it? Sit down to 'ave a little nosh, and the whole fuckin' town shows up."

Weaz balanced his plate on the edge of a bench stacked with stolen TVs and microwaves and went out front.

"Oh, fuck me. Not Roadkill." He stuck his hand underneath the front desk and buzzed him in. "Holy shit, what happened to you?" Weaz was smiling; he didn't give a rat's ass.

"Never mind that," Delroy said. "I've got a job for ya."

Weaz had always disliked Delroy. He called him Roadkill behind his back, but today the fucker really did look like something scraped off the motorway.

Weaz's pawnshop appeared pretty respectable; he kept most of the hot merch out back and sold it only to known customers. He had quite a few sidelines too: forgery, credit cards, a lot of stuff. He was quite the entrepreneur.

The shop's musty smell was due to the old fur coats that hung on a clothes rack by the window, and the stuffed animal heads on the walls. It was Wapping's landmark pawnshop, respectable to those who didn't know any better.

"So what happened to you, Delroy?"

In this line of work he met all the fuckin' loonies around town, even handled goods for asswipes as far south as Stepney. But Roadkill? He was a real wanker. A retard. Today he was different, though. Weaz had to wonder for a minute if he'd really been hurt and was in some kind of shock, but he saw quickly that Roadkill wasn't hurting. And there was something very disturbing about the look in his eyes, as if this wasn't really the silly fucker Weaz knew at all. And what the fuck was all that blood? Paint, maybe. No, it was blood. He could smell it.

Twenty minutes later, and a deal was struck. Roadkill hadn't brought in a bunch of crap the way he normally did. This was a whole different ball of wax, well worth leaving his pie and mash for.

"So, Del, me man, what's this all about 'en?" Weaz was just dying to know what Roadkill was up to.

"None of your business. How soon can you get it done?"

See, that was the thing. Normally, Roadkill was in here trying to fob him off with some crap he'd nicked: bit of cheap jewelry, cell phone, lady's wristwatch. He was a real creepy bastard, although the other day he'd been in here and bought some painkillers and a gun. Weaz suspected he was about to call it quits. Even then, Weaz got himself the best end of the deal. But today, Roadkill was here to employ some of his more specialized services, and he even had cash up-front.

It would be hard to get the job done on such short notice, but there was something in Roadkill's eyes that was making Weaz want to get it figured out by this time tomorrow morning. Boy, that would be pushing it. "All right, I'll get 'em for ya."

"You better." Delroy handed him half the money and glared.

Jesus fucking Christ! It *wasn't* Roadkill. Weaz knew it sounded crazy, and anyone could see it was--of course it was--but he would have bet on anything, even his own life, that those eyes did *not* belong to Roadkill.

"Don't worry, Del, I won't let ya down." He meant it.

Delroy left Weaz's pawnshop happy. He'd parked directly outside. He didn't want to risk walking around like this. It was time to get back to the flat. He had laid Pauline's fluffy jacket over him while he was driving, so he wouldn't get reported by some dogooder.

Shit, did he feel fine. Real fine. He touched his arm after he got in the Honda. The skin broke under even the slightest pressure. He'd have to bandage the areas as they blistered up. The fluid should be kept inside as much as possible--wasn't to be wasted. He licked the watery puss from his fingers. "Nutrition, daddy-o," he said, and started the car.

CHAPTER 34

Klickitat, Washington

Rachel headed down the trail to Jack's Shack. She was starving. She'd thrown up earlier this morning, but the bitter taste of bile in her sinuses hadn't kept her from the fridge. She'd gone ahead and eaten everything in there. *Eating for two now.* She felt a trill of excitement run through her. It was a miracle, an absolute miracle. Yes, she had doubts and fears, of course, but that was to be expected.

Last night, she'd slept soundly when she returned to bed, after Gavin cooked her two omelets and the mystery of their strange behavior was explained away. At about nine o'clock this morning, a fly buzzed past her face, waking her. She turned to snuggle Gavin, but he was gone, already up and at 'em.

Immediately, the knowledge started to nag. Something exciting...what was it? She got out of bed.

"I'm pregnant."

In the bathroom, she stood back far enough to see her body in the mirror. She was *showing*.

The flies were incessantly bad this morning. The cabin was full of them. She hurried to the back door and opened it, perhaps they'd leave.

It's a miracle. She went back in the bathroom to examine her belly again. Swiped at the flies. "Get away, get away." *How dare they?* The blisters were still there at either end of the scar. She touched one; it felt numb and itchy. She'd really have to get those fixed up. She daubed tea-tree on them; the need to take care of herself was paramount.

But I haven't missed a period. I had one only last week. It's already impossible for me to get pregnant...that makes it doubly impossible.

She frowned at her reflection. She'd heard stories of pregnant women not knowing right up until the day of the birth. She remembered hearing of one lady who thought she was going to the bathroom and gave birth to twins.

How could she expect everything to be normal? It was a friggin' *miracle*. The baby was alive, and that's what counted. It had grown enough to displace the area of her lower abdomen. Boy or girl, boy or girl. *Conjoined twins?* No, not twins. A boy or a girl for her to love and care for. A healthy little boy or girl. "It's a rare disease, very rare, almost unheard of in this day and age, and it skips generations." That was a doctor speaking, not her.

Doctor also said you'd never have children. Miracle, or freak of nature?

Paranoia. Understandable. Not every day a miracle happens. And listen, *voice*, if it's alive, then I'm happy. And I'll care for it no matter what.

You'll have to seek medical care. Hospitals, tests...

Oh sure, but not yet.

Not yet? You haven't missed a period, but you're all of a sudden--like 'in one day' kinda sudden--a few months along. Not to mention the fact that you can't have children because you're as barren as the Sahara.

Doctors are always mistaken, and they were in my case, thank God. She felt a slight nip directly below her belly button. She held her breath until it passed. *We'll read up on it. Gavin and I will take a trip into Portland and do some research.*

What about the drugs you've been high on?

She frowned into the mirror and let her nightshirt fall back over her belly. *If it's a girl, I'll call it Ani. If it's a boy, Gavin can choose.*

She put on slippers and went out to the bus. Gavin looked up startled. "You okay, Rachel?" It was the same as before. He quickly pressed the stop button on the machine and pulled his headphones off.

"Yes. Actually, I'm better than okay, Gavin."

"Really? You look a little tired still. Did you get enough sleep?"

"Yes, I just said I feel great." She sat down carefully on the edge of his desk. She moved slowly, carrying precious cargo. "Gavin, I know they say it's impossible, but...but I'm pregnant."

He shifted around to get a straight look at her. He gently touched the bruise around her eye, shook his head remorsefully. "Rachel, you know that's not possible...I wish it were. I--"

She interrupted him. "I am Gavin. I am." She raised her nightshirt and showed him their baby, a small but firm bulge in her stomach. He looked at it, put his hand on it.

"Don't you get bloated when you have a period? Maybe that's

what this is."

"No, I just had my period last week. You know that."

"Yes, I know, but it makes more sense than you being pregnant. And anyway, if you had a period last week, you couldn't be this..." he nodded toward the bulge, "pregnant already."

She pulled the nightshirt down and got up off the side of his desk. "I said I'm pregnant. A woman knows these things..." Tears were starting to spring up in her eyes, and her bottom lip was quivering.

"I'm sorry, I'm sorry." He stood, put his arm around her shoulder. She shrugged it off. "Maybe you are pregnant. Maybe you are, Rachel." Now he was pacifying her.

"Well, I...I am." Then she burst into tears. She cried for five minutes and straightened up.

"Listen, Rachel, I think you should see a doctor. I know how you feel about doctors, but just hear me out. Let's take the day off, catch the shuttle bus into Portland, and see what we can do. Get it confirmed, at least. How does that sound? We could look around town, too."

"Maybe. But what about these bruises, Gavin? You know what they'll think."

She placed her hands over her belly and stretched her back as if it were aching, it wasn't, but it would be soon, she supposed. She'd be just like the pregnant women who shopped at Mothercare on Paddock Lane. Starbucks was opposite. She'd sip her coffee and watch them heaving their huge beautiful bellies around as they picked out cute blue and pink cribs, colorful washbasins, tiny little dresses and pant suits, mobiles, playpens, toys, toys, toys.

"Listen, Gavin, I feel great. I'm going up to the store to get some groceries. You keep working. I'll call around and make an appointment to see a doctor. Any good one will be busy, so it probably won't be today. Realistically, tomorrow or the next day at the earliest. Okay?"

He looked at her doubtfully. "Okay, if you're sure. Ask, though. Ask if they can see you today."

"I will," she lied.

The time for a quack would come eventually, but not just yet. She wanted to make sure little Ani, or little whatever--*Daniel* would be nice--had a good firm hold, that he or she knew it was welcome, that he or she knew it was loved. That he or she knew it was a miracle.

He called after her as she walked back into the cabin. "Rachel?"

She turned, smiling what she thought was a glowing-cheeked-mother-to-be smile.

"You don't look too good, Rachel. Let's catch the shuttle into Portland, take a chance at getting seen by someone."

She frowned. "No!" Then she stormed into the cabin and slammed the door. "Fuck him." She got dressed, choosing the loosest of T-shirts.

Imagine how it would be when her wardrobe was full of maternity clothes. She wouldn't do the L.A. thing: tight sweatpants and midriff-baring tops. She admired their boldness, but she preferred to be traditional where her baby was concerned.

* * *

THE FLY KING

It felt refreshing to be outside. She could barely wait to get to Jack's. She'd buy him out of candy bars. No, she wouldn't. She'd get whatever was healthiest. Gavin should have brought more stuff back with him from the Dalles.

"Get away!" She shook the fly off her hand. "Stupid thing!"

Oh, no. Magdalena. She saw the woman's shape coming down the trail. She hadn't called her. That's where I'm going now, she thought. Yes, that's right.

Two lone cowboys on a narrow trail walking toward each other, fine dirt puffing around them in a knee-high cloud. Like two gunslingers, Rachel thought. She smiled, despite herself.

Rachel hadn't acknowledged Magdalena yet--still too much distance between them--but she was acutely aware of the sound their footsteps made--crunching down, almost speaking to each other.

She's the only one in this town that could possibly help with any of my problems. Maybe I should ask her about the sleepwalking. I don't want to be out there rambling through the woods at night, now that I'm expecting. Maybe she knows about the fungus in the clearing, or an ointment that clears up blisters. She's older, wiser. Should I tell her I'm pregnant?

This time a tickle on the knuckle of her left thumb. She shook the fly off. Since first thing this morning, the damned things had been buzzing around her. Not her head and face so much as her midsection.

Oh crap, the bruises. She knew what that would look like. She pulled her sunglasses from her pocket and slipped them on her face. Her cardigan covered the ones on her arms.

Too close--time to speak.

"Hello, Magdalena. I was just going to call..."

"Rachel, lovely to see you again."

Rachel's right hand extended out for the greeting, while her left hand reached underneath the bottom of her cardigan and began, ever so lightly and ever so discreetly, scratching at the blisters through her T-shirt.

Magdalena shook a fly off her elbow. "Lot of flies around today," she said.

"Yes, I know. They won't stop bugging me, either. Horrible things. Is it the change in the weather?"

"Maybe," Magdalena said. "Something like that." She looked at Rachel. "Why the sunglasses? Are you in hiding?"

Rachel sighed, took them off. "It's not what it looks like. And no, I'm not going to tell you I slipped against the cupboard door." She smiled, and even though the lady looked very tired and pale, she smiled warmly back.

They walked toward town making small talk. Rachel asked Magdalena about her years as a psychic, deciding if she should bring up the sleepwalking or not and, if so, how much she needed to tell her. She hated talking about Ani. She really hated it. Rachel grew morose. *Ani, I know my baby can't replace you. I know it can't make up for what I did, but bless it for me, Ani, bless it...* She felt another nipping pain, harder this time. She put her hand on her stomach. It's bigger, she thought. It's already bigger.

"Perhaps we could go over to my house," Magdalena suggested, nervously. Her smile hung there, drying her lips like two pillars of salt.

"Yes, Magdalena. I'd like that."

"Should we walk along the river?"

Rachel nodded. "If you don't mind, I'd like to stop by the store and get something to eat."

"Why don't I cook you something at my house? It's risky buying food from Jack." Magdalena held up the bag containing the carton of milk. "Out of date!" It swung from her hand like a man from the gallows.

CHAPTER 35

Wapping, East London

Delroy walked through the aisles, sweating. The parka he'd bought was great for outside, but not inside, and they always kept these places so fucking hot. The lights were too bright, as well.

One of Tesco's fine female employees hurried past him. It was 6:30 P.M. The store was about to close.

"Hey, you...where's the Saran Wrap?"

She stopped, sighed, turned and sneered, all in one well rehearsed sequence. Fucking cunt, lucky for her he was in a good mood, or he'd take her out, right here, right now.

"Aisle 3." She pointed to the left with her pricing gun.

He walked over to Aisle 3, and did something he'd never done before: checked himself out in the mirror--a big round security mirror. Nice coat. Yep, today had been a good one, and tonight he would treat himself to a grand finale. He couldn't resist giving a certain bunch of arseholes a little taste before the real curtain fell.

After getting out of Weaz's Pawnshop around 1:30 P.M., he'd

started back to the flat. Along the way, he'd bought the coat and a couple of shirts from Salvation Army. And on the off chance that Bill was out of jail, he'd called his number.

"Yeah, Bill here."

"It's Delroy."

"Hey, man, I can tell by your voice. What'd ya want?"

"I've got a really nice man's gold chain. It's heavy, gotta stamp on it and everything. Wanna swap it for a couple nights rent?"

"Maybe. Where'd ya get it?"

Delroy left quiet space.

"All right, Del, tell you what...I'll meet ya at the flat in twenty. Just takin' a look. Can't make ya no promises."

It took Delroy ten minutes to get there. He pulled the Honda down the alley, parked by the dumpster, and pushed open the door to his flat.

He went over to the mattress and looked down at Denise. Her mouth was strained open in a long oval, the hollow of her cheeks sunken in, the bones sticking out through white skin like chicken wings. Boy, she was a dog. He glanced at the pile of clothes lying beside her, picked up her boots--*nice*--and set them aside.

He took the knife out of his rucksack, tucked it into the back of his jeans, and waited outside for Bill to arrive.

Pretty soon, Delroy heard the familiar *vrrroom* of Bill's BMW speeding down the alley as if he owned it. Which he did, at least for a few more seconds, anyway.

"Hey, Del. What's cookin'? Wanna go inside?"

Stabbing Bill as he was standing at the top of the stairs looking down at the corpse on the mattress had been one of the sweetest moments for Delroy so far--feeling the knife squeeze through muscle, pulling away as the weight of Bill's body tumbled forward and down the stairs. He'd done some really nasty things to Bill. He felt no guilt, either. No guilt was the best ever. And the only reason he felt a tinge of remorse was because he shouldn't have given Bill such an easy way out. He should have left him to experience the full dynamic of the Fly King's revenge. That would have been more fitting. "Fuck it." What did it matter? After suffering through all those years of misery, he damned well deserved some fun. He hollered, hooted, shot his hands up in the air and did a decent impersonation of Zorba the Greek. "Yeah, yeah, yeah." He danced around the flat, whooping and kicking out at the two bodies.

"See ya, Denise. See ya, Bill...you always were a cocksucker." Pumped and ready, he ran up the stairs to the car, leaving Bill a moment from death, fingers scattered around the flat, gagging on his own freshly dismembered cock.

Sitting in the Honda, Delroy took a minute to look around. He pulled Pauline's purse from under the seat and rifled through it again. He looked at her driver's license. *So much like Rachel.*

"Fuck me. Today's her birthday!" Delroy smiled. That had to be fate. Had to be. He pictured how she'd pleaded for mercy, how she'd snubbed him in the carpark elevator. He'd liked her, though. He liked girls. He looked in the back seat and saw a stack of unopened birthday cards. He did her the favor of opening them, since she was currently visiting with some rats down at the Hartford dump. Some from buddies, one from her mum and dad, one from Carol--her sister; these two didn't have stamps, which meant they were given to her by hand, probably this morning. Which meant...*I wonder...I fucking wonder.*

He pulled a map from the glove box, checked the address on the license, and started the car. Pauline was a real helper, like Denise. Maybe he could return the favor.

Benson Street was lined with oak trees. It was an old, quiet neighborhood. Money. Not super rich, but nothing like the slums he'd been brought up in. Number 30. He passed it at regular speed, didn't want anyone recognizing the car. There was a van parked in the street, on the side of it. *Julie's Flowers and Balloons.* And here came fucking Julie, out the front door, counting a bunch of money and sticking it in her pocket. *Fucking bingo! We got ourselves a genuine birthday party. Hot doggy. How fucking appropriate.*

He turned on Pullman Avenue and pulled up across from the school. He'd walk back to Number 30 Benson. This one was to make up for all the birthday parties he never had, to celebrate his new beginning--he went somber for a second--and the coming of the new Lord. "Praise the Fly King."

Number 30 was a nice brick detached with a side gate-entrance that took you into the back garden. He walked close to the far hedge, up to the gate, unlatched it, and walked back behind the house, careful to tread on all the plants. God's stinking plants. What the fuck *were* those anyway--water lilies? That's what they looked like...the things that float in fishponds. Bloody weirdos.

A large bay window with red velvet curtains looked out over their back lawn. He got on his hands and knees. The grass was short and wet, and he felt it through his jeans--was a time his bones wouldn't have liked this, but today he felt healthy as a horse. He crawled over to the bay window and carefully peeked in. What he saw was a hot-looking piece of arse, obviously Miss Pauline's younger sister Carol, standing on a chair in front of the fireplace, adding the last piece of tape to a large banner that said, "HAPPY BIRTHDAY". "Arrr, thanks love. Isn't that sweet."

She had dark hair, a little shorter than Pauline's, and a cute arse. He watched as she climbed down off the chair and stood back, admiring her work. This was the family room. In the alcove by the window stood a large party-ready table and six chairs with helium balloons tied to their backs.

Delroy rose up a little higher. That's when the stupid white poodle came from under the party table, jumped like a fucking schizoid onto one of the chairs, and started barking in his face. Delroy slipped down from the window. "Shit." Little cocksucker. He crawled away from the window and over to a neatly trimmed bush. He sat crouched behind it, still hearing the muted yap of the dog and its paws scratching at the glass.

A few seconds later, the back door opened.

"Go on, Benny, out you go." The door closed, and the dog moved cautiously toward Delroy, growling, teeth exposed.

"Here, Benny. Here, Benny." Delroy's hand shot out from behind the bush, grabbed Benny by the scruff, and held him close to his face. He stared at the dog real hard, didn't have to say another word. When Delroy released him, the dog whimpered and slunk off behind the trashcan on the other side of the lawn.

Delroy crawled out from behind the bush and crouched next to the back door. Element of surprise: No one leaves a poofter dog like that out in the cold for long. Little crybabies.

Carol opened the door a few minutes later. "Come on in now, Benny. Benny?"

Delroy leapt at her, grabbing her lovely Rachel hair and slamming his hand over her mouth. "Come on in now, Carol." He laughed. "In we go. Let's have us a little birthday cel-ee-bray-shon."

Twenty minutes later, he was removing his parka and gazing down at her body. She looked so elegant. Not like that old whore Denise; God, she had made his skin crawl--ugly fucker.

Next came his shirt.

He slit her throat with his knife, held his hands over the thick red flow, and went to the stars. *Beyond the stars, beyond Heaven--way beyond that shithole.* It was getting better each time--stronger. His mind was clear as...as white snow on an ancient forest.

He watched Carol bleeding on the rug, one of those oriental deals. He wandered around the room. There were pictures on the mantelpiece. He picked them up one at a time. Oh yes, there was Pauline, looked to be a few years ago. She had braces over her teeth. This one was Carol, more recent, trying to look sexy in a tight blue T-shirt. "'Cuz baby, look at me now." He sang it, then laughed. *Feelin' fine.* The other one was of the two girls and their parents. The dad was sitting in a chair, pipe in his mouth, his wife on one side and Delroy's two fillies on the other. Nice family. Glad to have been of service. *Fuck, I'm hungry.*

He walked into the kitchen and opened the refrigerator. There were plates of finger sandwiches, cheese and pineapple on sticks, two bowls of jelly--red and orange--and a large white box right in the middle. He pulled it out, slammed a few drawers open and closed until he found a fork, then went back into the family room. He set the box on the table and opened it.

The icing was white with pink lettering and pink flowers splayed in one corner. *Happy Birthday, Pauline.*

He scraped her name off, took the fork and cut a large piece off the side. It was vanilla sponge with strawberry filling. Pretty tasty. "Here, Carol. Wanna piece?"

He balanced a large forkful down to the floor and shoved it in her open mouth.

Which gave him an idea.

Delroy rifled through the cutlery draw. He supposed *this* was the knife they used for carving turkey at Christmastime. He held it up, running a finger down the serrated edge. His guess was, they wouldn't be celebrating Christmas this year.

Decapitation was a lot fucking harder than a person might think. The bone was pretty thick. He had to give it several mighty whacks before her head actually came off. He smoothed down her hair, and sat Pauline's head on top of the cake. Blood drained across the white icing, over the sides and onto the pink paper tablecloth.

Delroy whistled. The perfect center piece. *Happy fucking birthday, world.*

Then his eyes were drawn to the party favors lying on the table. Paper hats and blowers. He became serious for a moment. There was only one green hat. He took it and unfolded it very carefully. He held it up to the light, then to his face, and breathed deeply. He thought he smelled pine and cold white snow. He placed the green crown on Carol's head, bent down, wiped away the cake, and kissed her sweetened lips.

He pulled her hair to the side and whispered softly in her ear, "Don't worry, my darling. The Fly King Cometh."

CHAPTER 36

Klickitat, Washington

The sky was thick with clouds, making it seem earlier than it was, and as they walked along the riverbank, the dullness began weighing on Magdalena; the trees, the reeds, the trail, all flattened with the same bland light. Everything was too clear, too cold. Especially the river.

Neither spoke much as they walked, only fragments of chitchat. They were still complete strangers in most ways, although she did sense a type of silent bonding, an understanding that both were in some kind of trouble.

Look at her face, so pale, and the energy coming from her...

Magdalena wished she could excuse herself from this, drop it from her mind, retire peacefully back to Connecticut. But it wasn't working that way. She dared not continue, and she dared not stop. After being delivered the terrible shocking news about Father Liebermann, what had she done? She'd gone into her storefront with a pen and paper and started work on deciphering the nursery rhyme. Digging herself deeper. She'd spent hours thinking, taking notes, and watching the sky turn from dark gray to light gray, where it eventually stalled.

His son is his father, his daughter is his mother. She'd thought about it long and hard. *His son is his father, his daughter is his mother.* What sense did it make? Simply a nonsensical play on words; kids do it all the time. But she was convinced there must be a meaning. *All nursery rhymes have a meaning.* Maybe at the library she could find information on the legend itself.

His son is his father, his daughter is his mother. It was a loop, a circle, an unbreakable...cycle. Like the chicken and egg scenario. *Unless...* That's when she found an entry point. *Unless* it was referring to a form of rebirth--reincarnation.

She'd stroked her chin and scribbled notes on a pad of paper. If, through incubus or magic, the Fly King spirit fathered a son and daughter, and if the siblings then produced a child, and if this child were a vessel for the Fly King to reincarnate--his son would be his father, and his daughter his mother.

That was it! It made sense. Possible, of course, only in the mind of a raving lunatic, but it did make sense of the words. What didn't was that she was buying into it.

She'd watched the clock until it was a decent enough hour to start calling. First, she tried the publisher of the nursery rhyme book, but they were long out of business. She'd called Hatty, Annie Kaufman, Myrtle Drenich, Paula Heinlich--all of them were familiar with the nursery rhyme--but Hatty, the oldest, was the only one who had heard of the legend, and she knew no details. None were aware of any connection between the rhyme and the protection spell.

They walked single file through a patch of brittle reeds that had grown across the path. One caught and bent on Magdalena's

THE FLY KING

sweater. It pulled taut, then flicked backwards, striking Rachel on the arm.

"Oh, sorry, Rachel...Are you okay?"

"Yes," she laughed, but Magdalena wished it hadn't happened. She didn't want to hurt the girl, even superficially.

She'd perform the protection spell on her. She'd convince her to give it a try. Magdalena had panicked last night, sensing some catastrophic change, something that couldn't be righted. But maybe she'd been mistaken, maybe there was still time. It wouldn't hurt to do the spell on Rachel; Magdalena knew the melody--boy, did she ever.

Jesus, she was tired. Her arms were so heavy, they pulled at the sockets of her shoulders.

"Do you have any brothers or sisters?" Magdalena glanced at Rachel's face. Her complexion resembled the belly of a washed-up fish. The black sunglasses emphasized it.

"I had a sister...but she died twenty years ago. She was only seven." Rachel kept her head lowered and her feet moving. "No other sisters, no brothers."

"I'm sorry. I'm so sorry to hear that." Best news she'd had all day. *Good, good, good.* She managed a secret smile.

They were reaching the wider part of the river. Rachel walked closest to the water, until Magdalena insisted they swap places, like a mother protecting her child from a busy street.

It was then, by an old cedar that leaned precariously out over the river, its exposed roots clinging to the bank for dear life, that they saw the dead beavers. An adult and an infant, crawled up among the roots. Both animals were dark with blood and covered in flies. The adult, presumably the mother, lay straight and the baby lay curled at her belly.

"Oh, how terrible. Don't look." Magdalena knew immediately that this was the work of Albert Crutch. He had been complaining to Bertha about beavers gnawing at the tree across from his house; if it fell, it would crash right through his roof.

By the looks of it, he'd shot them with his rifle, then smashed their heads in out of spite.

* * *

Rachel heard a cold CLANK in the very front of her mind, followed by an explosive yellow light. Her eyes closed behind her shades as the memory, the nightmare Dr. Johansson had never been able to uncover, finally played for her.

They're standing on grass.

The Sunday school bus has just pulled away, leaving them in a thick haze of unburned gas. The smell is strong in Rachel's nostrils, and she feels a sneeze coming, but it passes.

The sun is too hot on her shoulders. She looks up at the sky, a blue frame around the back of Ani's head; she is looking up, too. Ani's dark hair is pulled into two pigtails at either side. Rachel stares at the crooked line of skin where Mother had hurriedly made the part. Hers is probably the same.

They are wearing their crisp white dresses. One dress. Hideous on the hanger. Uncomfortable, but pretty on them.

THE FLY KING

Mom and Dad are not back from church, the driveway is empty.

They walk to the front door and bend in unison. Rachel rolls the stone aside, and Ani gets the key.

Once inside, they hurry straight for the refrigerator. They stare in at a big jug of strawberry Kool-Aid.

Ani pulls down two glasses from the cupboard, and Rachel fills them. The ice clinks as it falls into the glasses.

"What's the time? Maybe we can catch the end of *Kid's Nation*," Ani says.

They begin moving toward the living room, the television and the brown suede couch, when suddenly there's a scream.

It comes in agonized bursts. They look at each other--identical faces mirroring fear.

"God, what is it?" Ani asks in a scared whisper.

Something is happening outside. The scream comes again through the partially open kitchen window.

They stand, wedged in the back doorway. Their green lawn looks impossibly long. The screams keep coming. Louder, desperate.

Rachel snaps her head toward Ani and sees the glass of Kool-Aid fall from her hand, red liquid sloshing out. It lands, spilling a weak red river onto the grass.

Ani is looking straight ahead. Rachel follows her gaze.

At the very end of the garden is the rabbit hutch. The door is swinging open. Bunny, their rabbit, is gone.

They run without thinking toward the hutch. Ani's weight is heavy. Even though she is running as fast as Rachel, it feels as if her very soul is holding her back.

The screaming has turned to a screech. Rachel's heart is beating like Bunny's must be. She can feel that Ani's is, too.

The rabbit must be close, but they can't see it.

They hear a scuffling from behind the shed.

Ani picks up the shovel that's leaning against the shed door, and they look around the corner.

A wiry brown animal is pinning Bunny down with its paw. The animal looks up startled. It's the fox the McMurphys have been complaining about. Last night in bed, she and Ani had talked about it, how they'd like to catch it and make it into a pet.

His teeth have ripped the belly out of Bunny. Loose, stringy red is hanging out. More of the same red is hanging from the fox's mouth.

Bunny screams again. His ears, normally white, are reddish pink, the fur clumped together wetly.

Ani pushes the spade toward the fox. "Get out! Get out!" She yells. Rachel doesn't need to look to know that tears are flushing Ani's eyes out of focus. "Get out!" Ani cries.

The fox scurries into the corner, trapped. But then he slinks off to the right and suddenly darts behind the narrow gap alongside the shed.

Ani and Rachel scramble to look. They see his tail disappearing though a basketball-sized rip in the chicken wire separating the McMurphys' property from theirs.

The rabbit screams again, only weaker. The sound is pitiful. They go over to it. Bunny is trying to crawl away, pulling its guts along beside it, like morbid red streamers.

"Oh, my God," Ani says, the shovel still in her hand. "What should we do? What should we do, Rachel?"

Without thinking, Rachel takes the shovel from Ani. She catches her sister's eye.

"You can't."

"We have to, Ani. We have to."

"Thou shalt not kill. Thou shalt not kill." The bangs on Ani's forehead shoot up as her eyes double in size.

Rachel looks at the rabbit and brings the spade high above her head. It's heavy. The same way Ani had felt heavy as they ran down the lawn. In Rachel's mind, she sees Mrs. Brody, their Sunday school teacher, hovering over their desk. "Rachel, the sixth commandment is?"

Ani screams. She sounds like Bunny.

CLANK!

Everything is black.

Now they are in the living room, hunched in the corner of the sofa. Rachel opens her eyes; her half of the dress is splattered in blood. Ani's is clean.

Something is different.

Something has changed.

Ani is crying on Rachel's shoulder. "I could never do it, Rachel. I'm not strong enough." The words are resigned. Apologetic, yet final.

Something has changed. Rachel can feel it.

Now, she remembers. Remembers the spade coming down, the instant it struck.

CLANK! That terrible, cold dead thud. The moment, the inception, the microsecond in which everything turned.

The moment Ani had begun to die.

"Are you okay?" Magdalena asked. Rachel was standing terribly still, those damn flies buzzing around her. "Rachel?"

"Yes?"

"Are you okay?"

"Yes, I'm fine. Sorry."

Magdalena looked at her. "I'll come back later and bury them."

CHAPTER 37

Wapping, East London

Harold picked up Claudia from the hairdressers at 6:30 P.M.

"What do you think, Harry?" She touched the back of her new hairdo with her hand.

"It looks lovely, Claudia." He thought it looked like pale blue candyfloss.

"We need to stop by the off-license now and get two bottles of red wine."

"I thought Pauline liked white."

"No...red, Harry. Don't you remember anything?"

He smiled. He loved his wife and his two lovely girls. He was a lucky man.

They grabbed the wine from the Queen Ann off-license, then took the back way home down Maynard Avenue to avoid traffic. They didn't want to be late and miss the look on Pauline's face when she got home from work.

"Carol should have everything ready and...oh, no!" Claudia's eyes widened, her hand went over her mouth. "Harry, we forgot the paper plates!"

"It's all right, Claudia, relax. Regular plates will be just fine."

They pulled up the drive of Number 30 Benson Street, got out of their Volkswagen Estate, and opened the front door.

* * *

Delroy paid the Tescos checkout girl and got the fuck out of that place. Like a fucking sauna in there.

Okay, then, three industrial-size rolls of Saran Wrap and a quart of lighter fluid. That should do the trick.

He'd had a lot of fun today with the girls, but the best was yet to come. Tonight would be the icing on the cake, so to speak. He laughed and shouted, "Boo!" in the face of an old biddy as she hurried by.

CHAPTER 38

Klickitat, Washington

Magdalena watched Rachel shoveling down her food. But she sipped timidly on the herbal tea, pulling a face, enduring it for the medicinal benefits Magdalena had promised.

Casually, Magdalena pulled the nursery-rhyme book out of the kitchen drawer. Even after so many years, its red and yellow cover was still shiny. She sat down and flicked through it until Rachel was finished eating.

"Do you know this nursery rhyme? Magdalena asked. "It's called 'The Fly King.'" She held the book out.

Rachel looked at the page without taking the book, shook her head, and wiped her mouth on a napkin. "No, don't think so. Thank you so much for the breakfast."

"You're welcome. Are you sure you don't know it?" She cleared her throat and began to sing it, hating herself, feeling like an idiot, but knowing it didn't matter. She must find out whatever she could.

Rachel stopped wiping her mouth and looked at Magdalena, a little surprised. "Maybe I *do* know it. Well, I know the tune, anyway."

"You know the tune but not the words?" Magdalena stood and began pacing the kitchen.

"Yes, that's right. Why?"

Magdalena stopped pacing and sat down opposite her again. "I've been studying it. I get these...well, I call them *feelings*. Psychic feelings. And I have one about *this*." She stabbed her finger at the page. And about you, she thought, mostly about you. "I deciphered its meaning yesterday." She told Rachel what she'd deduced and waited for her response.

Rachel seemed bewildered. "Well, that's interesting. I hope you find something at the library. Old nursery rhymes sure can be sinister, can't they?" she laughed.

She knows nothing, Magdalena thought. She knows nothing at all. "May I ask you a personal question, Rachel?"

"Go ahead."

"How did you get those bruises?"

Rachel sighed, picked up the one crust she'd left on her plate and started breaking it up.

"Gavin did it. He didn't mean to."

Magdalena raised her eyebrows.

"See," Rachel continued, "he's never, ever done anything like that before. Never. And..." She paused, searching for words. "Can I ask *you* a question?

Magdalena nodded. "Yes, of course."

"Are you aware of a hallucinogenic fungus that grows in the clearing about half a mile from our cabin?"

Magdalena shook her head, still listening.

"It's our theory that we somehow ingested some type of drug. Neither of us has been acting normal, and this..." She pointed under her sunglasses.

"Please, dear, take them off."

Rachel did. "This is *not* the way he normally acts."

"Child, I've never heard of any such fungus, and I've been here ten years."

Rachel continued. "I found something out there in the clearing..."

Magdalena waited, sensing this was important.

"I found a knife...well, more of a dagger, really. I think it's old, and Gavin believes--*we* believe--it's covered with spores from the fungus." Rachel paused, the quiet disturbed only by birds squabbling somewhere up on the roof. "It sounds strange, I know." She lowered her head and looked into her lap.

"May I see this dagger?" Magdalena asked.

"Yes, I guess so, after Gavin gets it cleaned up. He has it under house arrest at the moment." She laughed, limply.

"Maybe it has something to do with all this..." Magdalena pointed at the nursery rhyme.

Rachel looked at her, puzzled. "Why?"

"Oh, I don't know. Just trying to piece it together, I suppose."

"What do you mean? Piece *what* together? Why would they be related--these *feelings*? What, exactly..."

You're *spooking* her. Magdalena quickly backtracked. "Oh, it's nothing, Rachel, It's probably nothing. I'm just being foolish."

Rachel remained tense. Stared at Magdalena for a moment, then dropped it.

Almost lost her there. Better be more careful, you big-mouthed old woman.

"Magdalena?"

"Yes, dear?"

"When I was younger, I used to sleepwalk. It stopped about seventeen years ago, but the night before last it happened again. Have you any idea--being a psychic and all--how to find out why, or how to prevent it?"

Magdalena reached over and touched Rachel's shoulder. "Have you ever seen a psychic before?"

"No. I was hypnotized a few times, but it didn't help."

"Well, perhaps we can try something--a mini séance, if you will. Don't worry, it's not nearly as scary as it sounds." She smiled as warmly and convincingly as she could.

Rachel thought for a minute and nodded.

"Okay, good. Let's go into the shop area."

Magdalena showed her the crystals and the silver fairy necklaces.

* * *

Rachel tried not to keep touching her stomach. *Just pray that mushroom dust didn't do anything to the baby. Magdalena's been here ten years, but she's never heard of any strange fungi in the clearing. Yes, but her cottage is on this side of the forest. How many times could she possibly have been over there?*

A fly buzzed by Rachel's face. She slapped around at it.

"You okay?" Magdalena was fetching a collapsible table from behind the counter.

"Yes, I'm fine." She watched the lady set the table up in the center of the room and place a black cloth over it.

"For ambiance," Magdalena said. She placed a lit candle in the middle of the table and pulled the curtains closed. Rachel felt awkward standing there, while Magdalena fussed around.

"Oh, chairs. Yes, of course." She pulled one from behind the counter and motioned Rachel to sit. She grabbed herself a stool; it was too low, so she ran into the living room and brought back a cushion for it.

She took a deep breath, smiled at Rachel across the table, and instructed her to keep her eyes open if she could and to take hold of her hands.

Nervously, Rachel placed her hands in Magdalena's; Magdalena took them without hesitation. *She's done this a lot*, Rachel thought, *and she's good at it.*

Magdalena began rubbing Rachel's hands with her thumb and index finger. She closed her eyes and began to breathe very deeply. The sound was relaxing, but the intimacy made Rachel somewhat uncomfortable. Magdalena suffered no such coyness; her touch was firm, not in the least self-conscious. "Relax," she told Rachel, and Rachel found herself relaxing. Her shoulders slumped; she had no idea she'd been holding them so tense. Not once did she want to laugh, as she'd thought she might. The pressure of Magdalena's fingers soothed her; making her feel somehow pliable, like a spoon in the hand of a spoon-bender. *The way it was with the dagger.* The thought drifted away, and Rachel felt air released that she hadn't known was there. She watched the candle flicker but sensed no draft; the room was warm--warm and cozy. Still, the candle flickered again. She watched Magdalena's face. It appeared inanimate, as if no life were there.

Suddenly, the room was cold.

Magdalena's eyes began moving erratically behind their lids.

Rachel caught her breath, and the flame went out. At some point, Magdalena had stopped rubbing her hands. Rachel hadn't noticed, as if they were joined together now. She knew that feeling well. It was second nature--first even--to be joined.

Magdalena's eyes opened. Only the whites were showing. Rachel stared at them; it was awful, but she'd seen worse from her other half, much worse. Then Magdalena let out air, foul and old-smelling. Her lips began to quiver, and then a voice came. A child's voice--Ani's voice.

"Rachel? Rachel, are you there?"

Rachel squeezed Magdalena's hands tightly.

"Ani, is that you?"

"Yes, it's me, Rachel." Only Magdalena's mouth moved, nothing else. Her white eyes continued to stare at Rachel, and slowly, she leaned in over the table. Shockingly loud, the voice of Ani screamed at Rachel, "Kill the baby. Kill the baby with the dagger. Kill it, Kill it, Kill it!"

Rachel let go of Magdalena, and her hands flew to her ears. "Nooooo!"

She jumped up and ripped the curtains open. Ani was screaming at her, just the way she had when Rachel killed Bunny, only worse, telling her to... Rachel made to leave--*this is insane, insane*--but Magdalena had slumped over motionless, her head on the table.

Rachel steadied herself and went to her.

"Magdalena, you okay?" She pulled the woman upright and gently patted her cheeks. Nothing. "Magdalena?" She went into the kitchen and brought back a wet cloth, laid it on her forehead, and patted her cheeks again, harder this time. She felt her pulse. It was slow but regular. The room was becoming warm again. *It had been so cold.* Maybe she should call an ambulance. Just then, Magdalena stirred, coughed. A few seconds later, she was rubbing her eyes and apologizing for nodding off. "I'm sorry, Rachel. I haven't slept in days. I'm so--"

"You didn't fall asleep." Rachel interrupted.

"I didn't? That's strange...I usually retain memory. What happened?"

Rachel's voice was cold. Either that, or cry, she thought. She told Magdalena what had just happened, how she and Ani had been conjoined twins, how Ani had died. She told Magdalena she was pregnant, and that it was a miracle, but she didn't mention that the baby was growing too fast. She was wrong about that, anyway. Her mind had been playing tricks the past few days; that's what Gavin had said, and he was right. But what about Ani screaming at her? Had that been real? It couldn't have been, yet in her heart she knew that voice so well.

Magdalena had gone even paler than before. She looked as if she might faint again. "Can I get you something, Magdalena?"

"No, no, child. I'm fine, thank you. Rachel, I know you've probably had enough hocus-pocus for one day, but would you do me a favor? Allow me to cast a spell over you...a protection spell."

"Protection?" Rachel's hands flew to her stomach. "You think it was *real?* Ani wants to kill my baby? As revenge? She can't, can she? Could she? Oh, dear *God.*" Rachel bent at the waist as the nipping pain flared in her belly. It passed, and she straightened. "She wants to kill my baby. She wants *me* to kill my baby!"

"No, no. Calm down, Rachel. That's not true. A spirit can see things out of context. I've seen it happen many times. They say things they don't mean, just like us." She patted Rachel's arm. "They can become confused. I'm sure your sister loved you very dearly and still does."

Rachel thought about it. No one would touch her baby, confused or not. Dead or not. She'd let Magdalena do the spell, then she'd get out of this creepy little town, back to the bright lights of Chicago. Gavin was right, fuck the album. She had more important things to consider now.

"Okay, do the spell."

"Follow me." Magdalena stood. She was shaky, as if she were suddenly twenty years older.

Rachel put an arm around her shoulder. "Are you sure you're okay?"

"Yes, thank you, dear. Let's go outside. I have a special place out there."

Too late, Magdalena, you had your chance. No, maybe the protection spell will kill it, if it's really what I think it is, maybe it will kill it. But there was something Magdalena was missing. She tried to sense what it was, but nothing came to her. *Kill it. Yes, yes, it's worth a try. What's there to lose? If you're insane, all you've done is waste a few minutes of her time.*

Rachel followed Magdalena out of the door and into her back garden.

"Would you mind kneeling down over here by the rose bushes? And bend your head toward the ground."

Rachel did as she was asked. She lowered her head and looked at the fallen petals underneath the bushes, shriveled brown swatches crumbling into the dirt. Nothing more than a memory of summer.

She could see Magdalena's legs from the knees down. They looked peculiar--detached, like a pair of strange new animals God had invented as a joke.

She also noticed that Magdalena was uncomfortable and nervous, hadn't the same self-confidence as before. *And my stomach is bigger, no doubt about it*. In just a few hours, it had grown a good month. Rachel felt a sudden urge to laugh at the absurdity of it all, at the dead petals on the ground, Magdalena and her strange animal legs, at God and the unnatural thing He'd allowed to happen. But what did it matter? The joke was on her, as always, and she deserved it. Once a freak, always a freak. And why shouldn't she pay? Ani had.

But her baby shouldn't have to pay.

Why, Ani? I just don't understand. I've said I'm sorry. I've said it a million times. I never stop saying it. Isn't that enough?

"Are you ready, Rachel?"

"Yes."

"Okay." Magdalena cleared her throat several times, and then began by humming the melody.

Rachel stiffened. That same melody. *What is this? Is this some kind of trick, some kind of obsession this woman has?*

Magdalena began.

> *Safe...safe...safe...*
>
> *The blood that fills her veins*
>
> *Keep it safe...keep it safe...keep it safe*

Her voice entered Rachel's stomach rather than her ears, coming in not as words, but as hands. Probing, examining, beginning to take hold, beginning to...harm.

> *The blood that spills away*
>
> *Keep it safe...keep it safe...keep it safe*
>
> *Let no baby fill this space*
>
> *When'st out of time and...*

Rachel's stomach suddenly burst into white flames of agony, searing through her flesh like a forest fire. So realistic was the burning, she could almost smell it; skin and muscle scorched on her ribcage, blood and veins popping under the heat. She doubled over, hands clutching at her stomach as she tried to squeeze out the flames. From the corner of her eye, she saw her hair smoldering. "Stop, stop!" she managed, then coughed and gagged, choking on invisible smoke.

Magdalena, whose eyes had been closed, stopped at once. She grabbed the smoldering tendril of hair, slapping it between the palms of her hands.

"Oh, my God, Rachel, I'm sorry. I'm so..."

The pain ended the moment the incantation stopped. Rachel hung her head down, trying to catch her breath. As she did, her sunglasses slid from her face onto the grass. *Now I see it. How green, how real. Bold, bright,* real. This woman was trying to kill her baby. Not Ani, Ani was *dead. This* crazy bitch.

Magdalena put her hands on either side of Rachel's head. She held it hard, scared, praying to God that this wasn't happening. Rachel screamed and pulled away. But before she did, Magdalena was knocked back by a vision so clear that she could taste it.

Rachel bolted off into the woods. Magdalena ran after her shouting, "Rachel, you *do* have a brother! You *do! Roy*...or...*Leroy.* He's deformed. He's not like you Rachel, he's turned against God."

"Shut up! Shut up!" Rachel screamed back. "Leave me alone."

"He's with the dark side. He's coming from far away..." Magdalena tripped and stumbled. From the ground, she continued to yell, "He's coming for you, Rachel! You and the baby!" She could hear Rachel crashing through the forest like an animal running for its life.

* * *

Gavin stared at the sandwich. He'd lost his appetite.

Rachel had just come in, looking like hell--looking *really* like hell--babbling something about a spell, and Magdalena being a witch and trying to hurt her baby, for chrissakes. Jesus. He bet she'd been in the clearing, he should've known it. Now, she was hallucinating, tripping again. Maybe she was hooked. Maybe he was, too. After all, today hadn't been any different from yesterday; he'd played that damn horrible tune over and over and over. And now Rachel was convinced she was pregnant, for chrissakes.

He'd shouted at her again. Of course, he immediately regretted it. But she had scared him with all that talk. Now, she was in the bathroom with the door locked. Obviously, if she *had* been over at Magdalena's house, it hadn't helped any.

"Rachel, can I come in? Please?"

"No!"

He could hear the water splashing lightly, and he pictured her soaking down her imaginary baby with the sponge. When she'd first started running the bath, he'd pressed his ear to the door and heard her throwing up.

"Please, Rachel?"

"Leave me alone."

"Were you in the clearing?"

"Leave me alone, Gavin. I'm thinking."

At least she seemed calmer. "Can't I come in just for a minute?"

She didn't reply. He listened for a while to the sound of water being sponged, then sighed, moved away from the door and back to his half-eaten sandwich. He held it up, then dropped it back on the plate.

Just then, he heard a loud knocking at the door.

As he rushed past the bathroom, Rachel called out, "Don't let her in here! Don't you dare let her in." Oh, he wouldn't let her in. He wanted no more of this nonsense.

"Magdalena!"

"Gavin, did Rachel make it back safely? I know this sounds impossible, but listen, she's in danger--serious danger. Her sister Ani tried to warn her today--"

"That's enough. Don't come around here again. Leave Rachel alone, or I'll call the police."

"But please, just listen. That dagger...I think--"

He slammed the door on her. She knocked again and again. He waited until he saw her walking down the trail, then went back to the bathroom.

"She's gone, Rachel. *Now* will you let me in?"

CHAPTER 39

Wapping, East London, U.K.

Smoke billowed out from under the door of the King Edward Inn. The screams were shockingly loud. Blondie, whose real name Delroy had discovered was Fran Ingles--was in there too, but she was already dead before the fire; he was wearing her blood right now. He could get used to this. Yes, indeed.

As he jimmied the lock on the Mercedes, he noticed the scratch. It defaced the whole door panel.

"I'll be a motherfucker." He smiled, completed his hotwiring trick, and backed his new silver car out of the King Edward parking lot. He'd keyed this one the other night. He recognized his handiwork. It wasn't so strange, he supposed. The motherfucker was probably a regular. Only this time would be the last time, for him and every other cocksucking, beer-spilling, happy motherfucker in the place.

He had arrived at the King Edward at 8:00 P.M., looking somewhat respectable in his new shirt and clean jeans. Judging from the looks he got, though, all they saw was a polished turd. *Fuck them.*

The faggot barman had some crappy happy-hour going on and

the place was packed.

He'd spotted pretty blonde Fran Ingles at the bar, in the exact same place she was before. She was wearing office clothes. Probably came straight from work, with big old plans to meet up with her flat-tittied girlfriend and score a wanker from the barstool brigade. *Look at them laughing it up, hogging the heat from the fire. He'd give them a fire, all right.*

He'd formulated his plan earlier in the day, although he hadn't known pretty blonde Fran would be there. That was an added bonus.

Delroy had smiled and drained the last mouthful of beer. His bottom lip, usually limp, had feeling in it now. Funniest motherfucking thing ever.

He bought another Guinness, making a deliberate attempt to be nice to the bartender. The faggot recognized him, but since Delroy wasn't acting hostile, he let it pass. *Oh, yeah, he'll think that one over again--when the skin is roasting off his faggot bones.* Delroy smiled at the man and quickly scanned the back of the bar. He spotted the bunch of keys hanging next to the cash register. *Bingo.*

It was easy. Faggot-boy was working solo, and kept disappearing now and then to take a leak. The sheep didn't even notice. They just stood there, hands full of money, bleating at each other. So when the faggot took a leak, Delroy took the keys.

He walked to the side of the bar, which the faggot had considerately left up for him, and knelt down on the rubber mats. Not one fucker even noticed, although some wanker stood on his hand and quickly moved off, thinking it was someone's shoe. Delroy crawled back behind the bar, over to the cash register, then reached up and grabbed the keys. Piece of cake.

Getting down on the floor with all the Saran Wrap he was bound up in had been a little tricky. He'd wrapped layers and layers around his chest to keep the blood from staining his clothes, and to keep it moist and fresh. It worked great but was uncomfortable, hot and sweaty.

He'd also wound it around his arms and legs to cushion the blisters. It restricted his movements somewhat, but he could save the puss if any of the blisters broke, scrape it off the wrap and into a Tupperware container.

After scoring the keys, he set about scoring Fran. Again, it was easy. Next to the back exit and the bathrooms was another door. Delroy had seen the bartender open it and go up a flight of narrow stairs. His flat, probably, or some type of storage place the faggot used to exchange beer for blowjobs. Who the fuck knew. But that's where Delroy was going to take his pretty Fran.

He'd waited by the back entrance till she came to fix her make-up, which she did regularly. The first time, she'd come with flat-tits, but she came alone the second time. He slammed his arm around her throat, his hand over her mouth, and edged her up the stairs, pulling the door closed with his foot. Basically, it was as simple as that.

The stairs led to the bartender's flat. After he got her up there, he messed around with her a bit. He talked to her some: asked what her name was, what she did, what she *wished* she did, if she was glad they'd finally gotten the chance to meet. He'd also asked her if she believed God was merciful. Then he'd gone, "Brrrrrrrrr...wrong answer. Show her what she's won, Jay!"

He gave her a lovely ruby-red slit throat, which was a great consolation prize. He took off his shirt, wiped two big handfuls of her blood over his chest, and held his arms up above his head while the euphoria hit. *To the stars--beyond the stars. Beyond heaven.*

"Thank you. Oh, thank you."

Fran was still doing a strange wriggle on the carpet, so he bound himself up in Saran Wrap, put his shirt back on, and started wandering in and out of the rooms, checking the place out.

The flat was nice, better than any place he'd ever lived. All white plush carpet and sticks in giant white pots. Had a huge TV too, and a red velvet couch, which was probably the favored arse-fucking area. Delroy thought of Uncle Ross, sneered at the piece of furniture, and pulled the lighter fluid out of his backpack.

He doused it liberally over the whole faggot den, especially the couch. Took a broom from the spotless kitchen and knocked out the fire alarms in the ceiling. Then he lit a few matches and said farewell.

He'd already figured out which key locked the back entrance, so his next move was just as simple. He strolled down the stairs. In less than ten seconds, he was outside in the rain, closing them all in and locking the door. It would be a while before they smelled death above their own cigarette smoke.

Delroy walked over to Pauline's Honda. He got in, started it, and pulled around to the front entrance, straight over God's stinkin' flower beds.

The front door was already closed, of course; faggots, wankers, and poodles named Benny are fussy about keeping their sissy arses warm. Arses to ashes, he'd thought, then laughed.

He took the large copper key and locked them in from the front, like beautiful butterflies in a killing jar. Then he got back in the Honda and wedged it up snugly in front of the door as an added barrier.

The windows in the King Edward were leaded, the small-paned

Tudor kind. It would take these wankers forever to get out of those.

He walked around the parking lot, choosing a new vehicle. That's when he'd found the silver Mercedes and noticed the scratch on its side. That had been a warm fuzzy moment.

He knew that tonight he would sleep like a baby, because even though the Saran Wrap made him sweat and the blisters were bubbling up faster than an unwatched kettle, the Fly King takes care of his own.

CHAPTER 40

Klickitat, Washington

Magdalena hurried down the trail away from the cabin. It would take ten minutes to get to St Joseph's Middle School. She might just get there before lunch break was over. She was still shaken by the events of this morning: the séance, the spell and, most recently, the confrontation with Gavin. She needed facts. How could she expect to be taken seriously when all she had was a feeling? And if she couldn't find facts, no proof that something was wrong, then she might as well drive down to the Washington State Mental Institution and sign herself in.

From two blocks away, she could already hear the kids yelling and screaming. She was so tired, and their tight little voices jarred her frazzled nerves. She passed Jack's Shack. He was standing hunched over his counter. Zak was nowhere to be seen.

She walked through the wrought-iron gates and into the play area of gray concrete, uniforms, and sky. The school had taken the church's name, St. Joseph's, but was newer, built from cinder block instead of wood. It, too, loomed gray.

The kids flew around the concrete, full of random noise and confusing energy. A bunch of girls were skipping rope. As Magdalena drew near, she heard what they were singing: *The Fly King come to take another...* Magdalena felt herself fall into slow motion. She felt weighted, blood sludging through her veins like muddy river water.

One of the girls was Bertha's daughter, head-to-foot drab in the gray uniform, her blotchy pink cheeks the only inkling of color. Magdalena thought of the cloud in her vision--the dirty gray cloud with the rotten pink edge--then of Rachel and the way the flies had buzzed around her, as if something had turned.

A sudden commotion came from the corner of the playground. The children immediately dropped their games and ran over. A fat boy was being pinned by three other boys against the old brick wall, the other side of which was the parking lot. Beyond that was the forest.

"Kick his ass. Fucking nerd." One of the bullies started kicking the fat boy, while the other two kept his arms pinned. He was the prey, and his weakness repulsed them all. The other kids crowded around excitedly, shouting and yelping like coyotes around an injured deer.

Bertha's girl picked up a stone and threw it at the fat boy. It struck him square on the forehead, and the crowd whooped their approval. Several others started picking up stones and taking aim.

"Stop it! Stop it right now." Magdalena ran to intervene, horrified. Before she reached them, the teacher on duty took control of the situation, pointing hard and taking names.

She walked through the open doors of St. Joseph's Middle School and along the echoing corridors. A sign to the library pointed toward the spiraling stairs. She looked up and sighed. *Might as well be Mount Everest.* She climbed, holding on to the banister. She was exhausted,

THE FLY KING

more tired than she could ever remember being. A kid came from nowhere and bolted up the stairs past her.

How time disappears, she thought. Life erased one day at a time. Before you know it, look in the mirror, and it's your mother staring back at you.

She pushed open the library door. No students were there, just huge bookcases loaded with books and an old man sitting by the window staring out at the playground.

"Excuse me..."

He looked her way, startled. "Lord Jesus, you scared me. Magdalena, isn't it?" He spoke with a thick German accent.

"I'm sorry, do I know you?" Magdalena thought she might have seen his face around. Sadly, the old folks were hard to tell apart. Same thing with babies.

"*Ja*, I'm Henry Bowsteiger. I see you all the time. We have your book. Had to take it off the shelf, though. Too *wacky* for the kids." He smiled. "Saw you at church. So sad...I assume you heard about Father Liebermann?"

She breathed in the stale air of old books. "Yes, I did. Very sad." A respectful silence fell between them, long enough for both to reflect on just how terribly sad it was.

Then she continued. "I'm doing research on the legend of the Fly King for a paper I'm compiling." She cleared her throat. "Know anything about it? Any books that might reference it?" She tried to sound casual and sane.

"No, I don't know any of that old rubbish. There are a few books over there," he said pointing a shaking yellow finger toward the back of the library, "but nothing obscure. Only Hansel and Gretel, stuff you'd already know."

"Do you have Internet?"

"Yes..." he phrased it as a question.

"Well, would you mind if I did a quick search?"

He went to the computer station situated in a homemade Formica cubicle.

"Is it difficult?" she asked.

He peered down his glasses at her, huffed an exaggerated, "Noooo...not at all."

They searched for twenty minutes and came up with a rock band called King Fly out of Minnesota, several fishing and tackle stores, a courier service out of Denver, and dozens of other strange variations on the term.

"Magdalena? You know...I knew your mother quite well."

"You did?"

"Ja, she became obsessed by all that legend rubbish. I hope you're not getting like her?"

Magdalena squeezed out a false little laugh. "Goodness no. Not at all."

"Good, good. I just wanted to check. You know, now I think of it, I remember her mentioning the Fly King legend one time." He shook his head slowly. "She was a lovely woman. It was sad...went cuckoo in the end." He waved his index finger around his temple. "I guess you've already checked her books?"

Magdalena nodded.

"And her diaries?"

The diaries. "No." She spoke calmly but her mind kept repeating his words: *Your mother was obsessed by it, went cuckoo in the end.* A faintness drifted over her, making the library seem suddenly very big.

"Are you okay?" He looked over his glasses at her. "I didn't mean to--"

"No, I'm okay. Thanks for your help. I'd better get going." *Obsessed by it. Cuckoo in the end.*

She felt herself swaying to the words like a seasick sailor, as she walked to the door.

Magdalena got back home without noticing. *Check her diaries.* She should never have stayed in this town, should never have stayed in Mother's house. She'd inherited the obsession. And now both sides of the coin were ugly; either something really bad was happening, or she was going...cuckoo in the end.

CHAPTER 41

Wapping, East London

Even as Weaz hung up the phone, bad thoughts were surfacing in his mind. Perhaps it had been a mistake to do it that way. He had the money; he should've taken the trip and paid cash. He lit a cigarette and stared across the road at the blue and red lights winking cheaply outside Canter's Peep Show.

He'd driven to a pay phone eight miles out of his way to make the call. The credit card he'd used to purchase Roadkill's tickets was a stolen one.

It'll be fine, he told himself. The card was fresh, had never been in anyone else's hands but his. And shit, this would all be over tomorrow. Everything would be a-okay.

But Roadkill would be pissed off if he found out. Weaz hoped he wouldn't ask about it. But what if he did? What then?

Weaz shook his head and kicked the wet curb. Why the fuck was he nervous about lying to Delroy? How crazy was that? He'd ripped the retard off a million times before, and all of a sudden he was scared to tell him a little white lie? Something was very wrong with this whole story. Something was creeping him out in a very bad way.

He wondered if he should take a few minutes and check out some pussy at Canters. Might calm his nerves to see a few boobies, spend a few quid; he had a little extra to spare. *Nah, better get back to the shop, get back on Delroy's job.* He'd like to get it done before dawn if he could, even if it meant no sleep. He took a drag on his cig, noticed how his hand was shaking. How was he going to work on Delroy's documents with shaking fucking hands?

Weaz's bench lamp sat on top of the cash register. It shone down in a narrow white spotlight, illuminating only his work area.

He made busy: cutting, pasting, aligning. This was the most intricate job he'd done in ages, maybe ever. He'd had to call in several favors through the evening, had to pay for some others, and totally missed his pie and mash. By the time this was done--taking into account the hours he'd spent, the money he'd have to put out, the risks associated with this kind of job--it wouldn't have been worth his effort. But that didn't concern him now. His only concern was that everything went smooth as a baby's arse, that Delroy would come in here tomorrow, pick up his stuff, smile with those dead eyes and leave, never to be seen again.

Weaz looked up from his bench, startled at the gloom that had snuck in around him; last time he'd raised his head was around dusk. Now, the Victorian street lights were on, and the rain was slapping at the window; he'd been so engrossed, he hadn't noticed.

The glow from the street light directly outside brought to life the pawnshop shadows--improbable shadows. Antlers on the antique deer head, high up on the wall above the old uniforms, cast gnarly long fingers over the ceiling. They stretched out in his direction.

But then there was another shadow, the one that almost had him pissing his pants. He'd only gotten a glimpse of the hideous shape--a creature. It moved unnaturally; nothing in his store could have made a shadow like that. And then it was gone. A second later, the street light flickered and died.

Except for the work light, Weaz was now in total darkness. He shot out of his chair and slapped on the overheads. The room immediately filled with artificial brightness--no shadows, no monsters. But he kept thinking, what if it's still there, waiting for the lights to go out.

Holy shit, was he ever a yellow belly! He puffed himself up, walked into the back room, and flicked on the TV. The scatterbrained sound of the commercials was welcome relief. Buy Arial, and all your whites will stay white. He doubted if that was true, especially *his* whites, but he was glad to hear about it anyway. He turned to the BBC1 local news.

Peter Jackson, with his stifled cockney accent and Saville Row suit, stood clutching a microphone to his face. His excitement was thinly masked by a somber frown, but he wasn't kidding anyone; the little cocksucker loved a good crisis. The camera pulled away for a wide angle.

Of the fucking King Edward Inn.

"Drivers are asked to please be aware that Crow Street and the surrounding dockland area will be closed to traffic until further notice," Peter began. "So far, no survivors have been reported. But it's been confirmed that tonight's terrible tragedy, claiming the lives of at least forty-nine innocent people, is an act of...arson. The police are looking for clues as to who, and why."

Peter paused for tension and extra airtime. "We've been

requested to ask our viewers at home to please call the number on your screen if you have any information regarding the driver of this vehicle, which is currently being investigated as stolen."

The camera pulled in for a close-up of Delroy's Honda Civic. It had been moved away from the door and parked over by the row of fire engines.

Weaz stared at it. He hadn't noted Delroy's license plate number, but it was definitely the car Delroy had been driving.

CHAPTER 42

Klickitat, Washington

Magdalena looked down at the book in her hand, one of her mother's ruined diaries. The preserves shed stood on a downward slope from the river. It had suffered a good six inches of water damage during the flood.

Mother's photographs, clothes, and books were in the attic. But Magdalena hadn't wanted her diaries or personal writings in the house, so she had thrown them in a cardboard box and put it in the preserves shed, way back behind the old chest of drawers she used for her gardening tools.

During the big storm the rain knocked down the power lines, and the river swelled over the bank, flooding most of the town. Huntington's was closed for two weeks due to damaged upholstery, and the quarry down on Ballfork Road had been so badly hit that mounds of gravel blocked the road for days.

She propped open the shed door to let in the weak, late afternoon light, reached behind the chest of drawers and heaved out the box; the bottom was green with mildew, its sides warped and waterlogged.

She placed it just outside the door and sat down on her potting stool. Must be twenty or more diaries in there. If only she could learn something from them, something helpful. Something she could tell Rachel to convince her to...what? Murder her baby? It was too late for the spell. She had been reckless doing it, had come close to really harming, maybe even killing, the poor girl. The way her hair had started to smolder... Magdalena doubted that either Rachel or Gavin would be welcoming her with open arms any time soon.

All of the books were at least partially wrecked. Magdalena picked up another, ran her fingers over the metal spiral and the wrinkly dull cover, and then opened it up.

She began reading, the German coming back to her almost instantly. Book after book, passing over ruined pages, scanning for a few salvageable entries. This one from ten years ago, right before she had died.

She's coming. I feel it. She's coming soon. She'll not stay away much longer. I can't be trusted. CRAZY. My head. She's coming. What now? I must give it back. Yes, yes, yes, of course. No. I could throw it in the river Yes! No. No. No! I'll take it to the woods. SHUT UP! SHUT UP! SHUT UP! God, please help me. BURY IT. BURY IT BURY BURY BUR

The writing scrawled wildly across the page, its madness striking home. Magdalena shivered as if ice-cold hands--river cold--had been placed on her spine. She spun around on her stool, half expecting Mother to be standing there, soaking wet in her night gown, hair sticking to her face in white strings, smiling childlike and humming so sweetly, eyes fixed straight ahead.

Nothing was there but the damp mustiness of the preserves shed.

She turned back to the book.

So that's what Mother had been doing her final night, the night Magdalena had stroked her soft hair for the first time in fifty-two years and covered her with a blanket to hide the ripped nightgown and dirty, muck-streaked legs. She'd been in the woods, burying something.

"The dagger," Magdalena said softly.

Still no proof.

But *she* believed it.

Another entry, from a diary she'd brought over from Germany. Written in Mother's hand over 30 years ago.

> I feel something very bad today. The Black Forest has been my home for 55 years, and I've performed the protection spell on all the local women. Since Mama died, I've begun to take the matter seriously. Mama always said in order for the spell to work, the woman must participate and take it into her heart.
>
> Frau Günter is not originally from here--she's an American woman. When I visited her at the Chief lumberman's cottage and performed the protection spell on her, she all but laughed at me. She did laugh at me. I thought her rude but also understood her reservations. I'd become sloppy, and felt that I had done my duty by reciting the spell, regardless of her non-

participation. This was a year ago.

The child she gave birth to today is a hideous creature. I don't want to be a cruel person, but this boy is more than physically deformed. I saw something in his eyes. I don't like to say any child is evil.

Magdalena took a breath. And here was an entry from a few years before that.

Mama insisted today that I learn the protection spell. She seems to be getting worse, complains about the pains in her legs. I don't think she'll be walking much longer. I've seen her do the spell a million times. She says that once a girl comes of age, she must be protected by it. I don't fully understand, but I know it has something to do with the legend.

Magdalena looked up from the book and over at the rose bushes, where she'd performed the spell. She chuckled humorlessly. Was she crazy? Was her whole family nuts? Or was it something else, something they knew, talked of in roundabout ways, a skeleton of massive proportions lurking in their collective closet?

Her mother and her grandmother had taken it all so seriously. And today she felt eerily connected to them, as if fifty-two years had been just the blink of an eye.

And here was an entry from fifty one years ago. A year before Mother banished her.

I picked Magdalena up from school today. I got there early so she wouldn't have to be alone, not even for a second. We walked the perimeter back to the cottage. She knows not to go into the forest. I don't need to tell her. The poor little girl is petrified enough without me talking about it more. The dreams don't get any better.

I asked Mama what I should do, and she said I should send her away before she comes of age. She's gifted with the eye.

Perhaps I could go with her?

But what of Mama's ailing health--who would look after her? I cannot think anymore. I must fix Maggie her supper and get her to bed. I hope she sleeps soundly tonight.

Magdalena reached into the box and pulled out a bundle of letters--over half were ruined. She pulled the top one free from the faded pink ribbon wrapped around the center. She rubbed the ribbon between her weary fingers, recognizing it as her own; Mother had always tied her hair in bows. The letters were addressed to Magdalena, unsent. She opened one.

Dear Maggie,

I miss you, darling. I hope one day I'll be able to explain. Every night I ask the Lord to watch over you and keep you safe for me. Nana's not doing well. Maybe the warm spring weather will bring some improvement. But she's old, Maggie, and God forgive me for saying it, but if the worst comes to pass, then perhaps I can finally get out of here.

What fun we could have together, Maggie. How I'd love to

be there with you.

I don't know if I should be writing this, dredging up your feelings about us and your old home, but I need to let you know I've always loved you, my sweetheart. Mama has always loved you, and she always will. You have to understand it's for your own good that I sent you away. I cannot explain it to you. Even if I could, you wouldn't believe me.

Maggie, I hope you're doing well at school. Your cousin sends me reports, and I get your letters, sweetheart. I cherish every one. You must stop talking about coming back here. Your home is America. It's a beautiful country, far better than the dismal Black Forest. Remember how much you hated it? Remember the dreams, Maggie? Your cousin says that you sleep just fine now. Is that true, my love?

God, I hope this letter doesn't make you homesick. Nana says not to write, to let you be free and start a new life over there. It's hard for me to know the right thing to do, my little one. I hope you understand. I love you, Maggie.

Mother.

XXXXXXXXX

The pile of unsent letters slipped from Magdalena's fingers onto the dirty stone floor of the preserves shed. She buried her face in her hands and wept.

CHAPTER 43

Klickitat, Washington

Main Street was empty and silent. Klickitat was asleep. It was past 1:00 A.M. when she sneaked out of bed, leaving Gavin snoring into his pillow.

Rachel hung up the phone.

Her crying was tearless, painfully contracting every muscle in her body. She leaned back against the brick wall of Jack's Shack and let herself slide down to the ground. She sat there huddled, the phone ringing off the hook. *Mom--I mean, Aunt--how could you have deceived me like this. My whole life is a lie?* Finally, she stood and picked up the receiver.

Her voice was a hopeless whisper. "I'll be okay. I just need some time. I have to go... Yes, I will. I'll come home. Yes, I promise." She hung up again, slid back down the wall and cried into her knees.

Her belly was huge. There would be no hiding it anymore. When she'd gone to bed at nine o'clock, it was still possible to make excuses. But when she woke at around 1:00 A.M., it wasn't. She was too big--six months pregnant, if she was a day--and at this rate, well...

Her dreaming had been fitful, tense, filled with strange colors and lights, voices chanting and droning to the melody that Magdalena used with the spell. And the words Magdalena had yelled as Rachel ran through the woods--fragmented sentences, part real, part morphed by her own fears--had plagued her sleep, left her more exhausted than before she'd gone to bed.

It seemed like months ago that she had awakened to the glorious realization that she was pregnant, but not even twenty-four hours had passed. The day had steadily fallen apart, and now it had broken open to reveal some diabolical nightmare.

After waking soaked in sweat, she swung her legs out of bed, stunned at how large her stomach had become. That's when she decided to call her mother.

She wrote a note for Gavin, just in case he should wake and find her gone. Grabbing a flashlight and some quarters, she let herself out the front door and walked down the trail.

On the first try, she got Mom's answering machine. Second try, Mom picked up. Mom became almost hysterical on learning that Rachel had sleepwalked again. When she told her she'd seen a psychic, Mom went into a disapproving rage, declaring, "These people are crackpots, and you should know better, Rachel. See a professional."

Rachel interrupted her tirade. "Mom, this lady thinks I have a brother."

"Well, that just proves what a phony she is. These people prey off others misfortunes. They're like vultures...they--"

"Mom, she said he's not like me--he's deformed. He's far away, but he's coming for me." She hadn't even mentioned the part about Ani, or the baby; Mom would have a heart attack, the way she was acting. But then Rachel realized that Mom had gone quiet. So quiet, she almost believed they'd lost their connection.

"Mom? Mom? You still there?"

Finally, "Yes. What else did she say?" Her voice sounded small.

"She said his name was Roy, or Leroy..."

She heard her mother sigh, a sad, 27-year-long sigh.

"*Delroy*. His name is Delroy. It's true, Rachel, you do have a brother."

Now, Rachel went silent. Mom was speaking in an alien tongue. Her words made no sense. No sense at all.

"He's in England. I don't know how this woman knows, or even if she really does know. But it's time to tell you. I just wanted to protect you from the truth, darling. I'm so very, very sorry."

And so Mother had told her. Their real mother, Mom's *sister*, died giving birth to Rachel and Ani. They had been separated from their brother.

"Please, Rachel," Mom cried pitifully, "be careful. Come back home. Your brother...he isn't...right. He did something very bad. He killed his--*your*--uncle. A long time ago, when he was still a boy." She began sobbing.

Rachel had stood there, stunned, holding the phone to her ear, waiting for the rest of Mom's alien words.

"No one knows what happened to Delroy. He disappeared. But if he's coming after you, Rachel, we need to call the police. We need to hide, or--"

That's when Rachel hung up. She couldn't bear anymore. *Too much, too much, too much.*

When Mom called back, Rachel heard herself promising to come home, but her own words were alien, too.

She walked down the trail, not once startled or scared by the strange sounds coming from back in the trees. The fear inside was far greater than anything out there. All the way, she kept one hand on her baby, every so often feeling it move. *Little Ani, or Daniel, what's wrong with you? Why are you growing so fast? Why?* The ugly man she'd seen when she and Gavin made love...it couldn't have been...her brother. She tried to sort through the pieces, one hand pointing the flashlight ahead, the other stroking her baby. Her mind kept wandering back to an incident long ago, when Mom was really Mom. With strange and vivid clarity, she remembered the butterflies.

She was ten years old, and sleepwalking sometimes as often as three nights a week.

She held the jar up to the window and admired the bright powdery colored wings. It was a King George. She could see the broken chrysalis lying discarded in the bottom of the jar--another success. Its spindly legs explored its limited habitat. Soon, though, it would be free. It would discover that those barely dry paper-thin kites would stretch out, catch the breeze, and take it away to the depths of the garden, where all the best bushes and flowers were waiting.

She hadn't experienced any losses with the butterflies. She knew what they were--baby fairies.

Shortly after the release of the George, she found another chrysalis. It was hanging right out in the open, on the privet bush between the church and the traffic light. It was bigger, brighter. She'd never seen one quite like it before. Her young heart was excited at the possibilities. It could be a Red Admiral, or even a Peacock. She hoped it was a Peacock; they were the prettiest and rarest.

Her little fingers gently plucked the twig off the bush. She carried it cupped in her hands back home, where she placed it in her birthing jar.

The chrysalis hung lankily from its branch, and for the duration of a young girl's week, which is longer than an adult's, she was obsessed with it. She had visions of her butterfly. This one would be even more special than the rest. She held a hope that this butterfly would recognize her, maybe even decide to stay.

Every day, she fantasized about its release. She would take it down to the lilac bushes and put her hand into the jar. The butterfly would crawl onto her warm skin, and she would bring it out. Holding her arm straight, she would wait for the inevitable moment when it flapped its wings and took off deep into the purple lilac bushes. But it wouldn't. She would shake her hand a little to give some indication that movement was required, but the butterfly would close its wings resolutely and crawl down her hand onto her wrist. It didn't want to leave her.

She'd already named it "Ani." And it would be the longest living butterfly in history.

It was 7:00 A.M. Outside, the sky hung undecided. Inside, she watched as the shell started to break apart. First at the top, then in the middle, as its wings pushed the restricting encasement away.

So long it had been in there, waiting to be born. So long it had been growing, never seen by anyone. Hers would be the first eyes in the whole world to see it.

Then it came. The sides of the chrysalis fell away, and there it was: a hideous, brown segmented insect, its shiny slick body hardening by the moment, its bulbous eyes quickly scanning its surroundings; its pinchers, the color of dead spider legs, flexed out in front as it began to search its world. Rachel screamed and dropped the jar. The jar broke, and the thing--the fly, the whatever-it-was--buzzed a clumsy dirty sound as it looked for a way out.

She realized that it was only a harmless insect, but there for a second she'd heard a prophetic whisper, an unspeakable understanding that even bad things must be born of someone.

Rachel cradled her stomach, scratched the scar. The blisters were getting worse.

Almost back to the cabin. Still weeping, silently now. She realized that she'd been fooled, by *everyone* it seemed. She knew where Gavin had put the dagger--on the front wheel of the bus. He'd wrapped it in two plastic shopping bags and tucked it under the mudguard. She'd watched him do it from the window.

* * *

The last time Delroy had been called Delroy Günter, he was five years old. He inspected all the documents carefully, gloating over his passport, which was full of fake stamps. Shi-it, he was a world fucking traveler!

It was 10:30 A.M. in the morning, still dark where Rachel was. He hoped she was okay. Soon, he'd be there to take care of her. He'd dreamed last night about the cave, and the three of them. Back where it all started, so long, so very long ago. And there it would be completed. *Good-night to all you fucking wankers.* Such a brilliant plan it was. What a fucking honor to be related to *Him*.

Weaz watched from behind the counter. Delroy hated that fucker, hadn't realized just how much until today.

"What will ya give me for these?" He slapped Denise's boots down next to the cash register.

Weaz looked nervous. "I dunno. How much are they worth?"

Delroy snorted a laugh. "You're a chickenshit, Weaz, you know that?"

Weaz smiled uncomfortably, trying to maintain the illusion of authority. "Well, let's see...you still owe me another grand for the job, and--"

"How's your sister, Weaz?"

"What...Denise? She's all right, I suppose. Haven't talked to her in a while."

Delroy grinned. "Oh. Well, when you do, give her my regards." Then he whipped his gun from the back of his waistband and pointed it in Weaz's face. "Let's see what you've got in the safe, motherfucker."

Weaz didn't resist, didn't try and talk his way out of it, didn't mumble anything about not keeping cash in the store or things having been slow lately. It's almost as if he knew it was coming, Delroy thought.

Wonder if he knows what else is coming.

Delroy moved his gun to the back of Weaz's head and instructed him to walk slowly, hands by his ears, into the back room where he kept the safe.

Five thousand pounds, a man's Rolex watch, and a one-carat lady's engagement ring...for Rachel. Delroy used his free hand to shake open the brown paper bag he'd picked up off the table, then ordered Weaz to scrape the contents into it.

"By the way, Weaz, in your grand estimation, would you consider God a merciful fucker?"

"Wh...what?"

"Yeah, that's what I thought. Don't forget to say hello to Denise for me." Delroy watched Weaz's expression turn hopeful for a second, then pathetic as he realized what Delroy meant.

With the gun lodged firmly in Weaz's temple, Delroy stepped away from the trail of piss streaming from the dirty fucker's trouser leg and pulled the trigger.

He took a couple of mouthfuls of the cold pie and mash Weaz had left on the bench and walked to the door.

He'd made a point of avoiding the spray of blood and bone from Weaz's head. Male blood was no good. Only girl's. He'd have to score one soon. But he *had* enjoyed watching Weaz's brains shoot out the back of his head and into the empty safe. Delroy had closed it and twirled the lock. *Greedy old Weaz ends up with his brains in the safe. What do they say...more money than brains? Guess the opposite was true for Weaz. Now* that's *poetic justice.*

The bell above the door tinkled in agreement as he walked out into the street.

Delroy stopped for a second and checked the contents of his brown paper bag. Five grand, his fake docs, info on the tickets, which he'd pick up at the airport, a Rolex, a diamond ring, and a Partridge in a fucking Pear Tree.

Soon he'd be there to protect his little boy. He smiled as he walked to his car. Roll on, six o'clock. He could hardly wait.

* * *

From the tree closest to the cabin, a white owl swooped down upon its prey like a deadly angel. But all Rachel heard was the choirboys, singing their song from below the river. The moon was full, and the air cold and still--still as dead beavers, or the bones of a rabbit buried next to an apple tree.

With both hands, she held the dagger up at the sky. The whispering of river and trees, the voices inside her, joined together in a dark hypnotic hymn--so beautiful, perfectly in time with her heartbeat.

Her hair became light on her shoulders, charged with strange life, as if some lover had lifted it in his hands. And the whites of her eyes stared blindly at the moon.

* * *

Delroy was sitting in his new Mercedes, examining the passports, when the vision came: a large silver moon, cut in half by something dark and gray. He smiled. The three of them. Rachel on the left, him on the right, the Fly King straight down the middle holding it together--or breaking it apart, depending on your perspective.

He and Rachel had bonded; they were in love. Rules didn't apply to them. They were different. And now he could prove himself, let her see how powerful he had become. How worthy he was of her now.

Together, they will finish what was started. *The Fly King cometh.*

His eyes looked though hers at her stomach. One hand, badly shaking, had moved down to the baby, caressing it through a baggy T-shirt. It was growing fast, just as it should be. He fingered her thoughts. She knew about him. She was confused.

But what is this? Delroy started breathing hard through his nose, like a bull, as he began patching it together. Someone was trying to stop them. Some interfering bitch. No, *witch*.

* * *

As she looked through his eyes, she felt a strength in him that hadn't been there before. Her pulse began slamming hard in her temples, as if her blood was being pumped by a heart too strong for her body.

She stared at the ugly man's face in the small passport photograph. The writing was foreign--German. *Yes, of course.* Underneath the photo, she read the words, *Delroy Günter. It was him, her brother.*

Something else. A red cover. It opened--another passport. A photograph of a woman. She looked a lot like...

Underneath the photo, the name, *her* name--*Rachel Günter*.

The dagger dropped from her fingers and onto the ground with a sick and finalizing thud.

CHAPTER 44

Klickitat, Washington

THE LEGEND

A candle flickered on the kitchen table. Magdalena picked it up on passing, opened the back door and proceeded out into the night. The chilly air nipped the skin on her arms, but she couldn't go back in for a coat. It was now or never.

By the time she had finished crying over Mother's unsent letters, the light had faded, and the sun had sunk behind the trees and the edge of the earth. She walked around the house, thinking nothing--allowing her mind to become an empty receptacle--preparing herself to receive that which needed to be known. *Such a long time, so much misunderstanding.* Ten years she'd held it back, kept Mother at bay. Finally, she was ready.

Now, she sat cross-legged by the rosebushes, hands resting palms up on her knees, staring up at the huge silver moon.

She stared, and she stared.

Her eyes stayed on the moon's flat face for an hour, unmoving, unblinking.

As time passed, it became less flat. At first, it seemed as if her concentration had brought definition to the craters and the gullies of the moon's surface, but it was not so; the features were human. She watched in calm wonder as they became more prominent, as if her eyes themselves had sculpted the moon a nose, a mouth--a face.

Her mother's face.

Magdalena's breath quickened slightly as the features animated.

Unconsciously, she steadied her respiration by breathing in a slow circular motion.

Deeper and deeper became the trance. Still, her eyes were fixed upon the vision as it began breathing life. Her mother's eyelids slowly opened and closed, cheeks moved subtly. Then the lips parted, and the image spoke to her.

"Magdalena." Her mother smiled in just the way she always had. "I've missed you, sweetheart." By the time the smile was fully extended, and the warmth of it conveyed, Mother's face was beginning to change again. Smoothly and naturally, the eyes widened their distance from each other, the nose grew longer, the chin became a little less heart-shaped. It was Nanna. Nanna smiled, in a way Magdalena could barely remember but felt very deeply, and then her face, too, began to change.

Magdalena watched passively as face after face came and went, lives chained together by blood and time. These were her ancestors. Without these women, she would not be.

Her eyes remained fixed on the moon, as she went deeper than ever, back even further. Face after face, life after life, link after link, and then...

This last woman stayed. This face did not change because this is where it had all begun.

She couldn't see the woman's hair, for she had a black scarf covering her head. She seemed old, her skin in poor condition. She began to utter words in a foreign tongue. Magdalena didn't feel she was being spoken to directly, although the woman's voice deepened her trance to a point where breath was almost nonexistent.

Suddenly, she was there. Looking into a large bubbling pot, flames leaping up around the sides. Magdalena herself was muttering these strange words. At first, they remained foreign to her, some form of ancient Germanic, but as the words continued to leave her mouth, she found she did understand.

The pot was a large rugged cauldron full of bubbling liquid. The odor was at once sweet, with a sour after-smell. Small pieces of bone stuck out from the liquid, along with leaves, soggy black sticks, and steam. Much steam.

She turned away from the pot, still muttering the words.

Over in the corner, on the windowsill, was a shiny black bird. A raven. She called its name and charged toward it, shouting now the ancient Germanic words. All of a sudden, she was slammed against an invisible barrier. Then, momentarily disorientated, she realized her perspective had changed once more. She was now looking out from the eyes of the raven.

The bird crowed once, took to wing, and flew out the open door.

She flew through dark sky, over the village, high above primitively thatched roofs, chicken coops, and naked maples. Streams of smoke twisted in the chilly air, and candlelight flickered through poorly shuttered windows. Beyond it all, surrounding the village on three

THE FLY KING

sides, was the Black Forest.

The bird quickly descended. She landed on the edge of an empty wooden barrel in an alley behind a row of shabby, mud-and-straw buildings. She was behind the local tavern. Inside, people sang and laughed to the raucous sound of accordion and fiddle.

Leaning against the back door were three men dressed in earth-colored shirts and muddy pants. Farmers, field workers--coarse men. They laughed, and one of the men pissed upside the wheel of a cart stacked with hay.

Then, from the east side of the alley, soft footsteps patting the dirt, a rustling of material, and a gentle familiar humming. It was a young woman in white farm-style dress, the girl from the cave.

"Looky here. If it ain't Gweneth King, pretty as a picture and bad as an apple." The three men leered at her, and the largest one, whose thin lips seemed to be constantly sneering, spat indiscreetly on the ground as she approached.

"I'm not looking for trouble. Let me pass. I have to take these home to Mama." The girl's arm was curled around a wicker basket full of brown chicken eggs.

"Your mama is a whore, little girl, and we thinks likely you the same way. Give us a little sample, Gweneth."

"Don't you touch me, or--"

The sneering man interrupted her. "Or what? You ain't got no papa around, and what's your brother to do? Slobber us to death?" They hollered and whooped and slammed their beer jugs together.

The girl looked frightened but kept her head high and continued to walk past the jeering men.

It was after she had made it a few steps by and let her shoulders relax slightly that the sneering man came from behind and grabbed her around the waist. "Come on, Gwennie, give the boys a little kiss." He pulled her toward him. The other men cackled and chugged more beer from their crude clay mugs.

She screamed, but it was cut off almost instantly by the man's large calloused hand. She struggled, kicking out, but the men were strong and drunk and unafraid of discovery. They laughed at her efforts. The harder she struggled, the more they laughed.

The three men took turns raping the young woman over the side of the hay cart, crunching the spilled eggs underfoot as they violated her. Finally, they threw her to the ground, left her curled on the dirt and eggs, blood staining her white frock, and went back inside the tavern. The music swelled as the back door opened and Magdalena saw people inside, dancing and merrymaking.

The raven flew from the barrel, up into the sky, away from the village and straight for the forest. It flew in between the pines at an impossible speed, until the branches began to blur, flicking by faster and faster and faster.

All at once they were out of the woods. The sky was blue. The season had changed to spring. Late afternoon. The air was heavy with blossom, honeysuckle, and the smell of fresh bread from the small bakery across the way.

The bird slowed, glided to the left, and began following a weed-lined cart track heading out of town. Several minutes later, a small cottage came into sight. It stood at the very edge of the forest, the towering pines behind it, a small patch of pink-and-white wildflowers in front.

The raven landed on an oak branch shading the cottage and

waited. Momentarily, a girl came running from the same dirt trail, the girl from behind the tavern. Her stomach was swollen with child, and she was crying into her hands. She tripped up the small mud step, in through the open door, then deliberately fell to the ground. Another woman was in the cottage. She turned from her woodstove, wiped her hands quickly on her apron, and knelt down beside the crying girl.

"There, there, Gwennie, Henn will be all right. Please, Gwennie, don't cry. It's not good for the baby." At that, the girl raised her head.

"I hate this baby. Poor Henn, how could they blame him for this?" She banged her fist against her belly. "His heart is pure as gold. It's not right, Mama. The Lord has never been fair to him." She began crying again.

The older woman stroked the girl's back and shook her head. Then she stood, walked over to a rickety little pinewood shelf, and pulled down one of about thirty small green ornaments.

The woman held the green cup-size castle in front of the girl's face. "Look, Gwennie, look at this one. It's much better than the others, isn't it? He made it for you. He made them all for you. Weeks this one took him, remember? Carefully sticking all those pine needles together with sap he'd bled from the trees, taking his sharp stone and cutting each needle to size...he loves you more than words can say, Gwennie. Don't let him come home and see you crying like this. They won't hurt him too badly."

Gwennie took the pine-needle castle from her mother's hands and looked at it. She examined it from every angle, her breath finally beginning to steady. Then she caught her mother's eye and they smiled at each other.

Back to the other side of town. Over the tavern, over the bakery, and into the village square. The raven landed on a wooden bench opposite the stocks. The man held captive there was Henn King. He wore nothing but dirty ripped undergarments. A crowd of fifteen children, dressed in ragged clothes, dirty knees and noses, were hurling stones at him--next to the stocks was a pile of rotten food to throw, too: lettuce so spoiled it had turned to slime, wilted and stinking cabbage leaves and moldy tomatoes. But the children preferred to *stone* him.

A man and woman walked past arm in arm. "You dirty bastard!" the man called out. "May the Lord see an end to the likes of you."

The woman spoke next. "Rot in hell, Henn the Fly King."

It was hard to tell Henn's age, for his face was severely deformed, as was his body. Stooped over, hands and head in the stocks, it was also difficult to know the extent of his disabilities. His shoulder blades were the worst of it, though, and quite plainly the reason for his cruel nickname; they extended quite far out, almost giving the appearance of wings.

The raven hopped closer. Henn seemed to look at it for a second, although his bulbous eyes didn't properly focus after so many long hours of torture.

"Henn the Fly King fathers his own sister's baby," one boy shouted, then he got in close and spat at him.

"Yes," another boy shouted back, "but it shouldn't surprise you, Metherweld, because his own mother and father are brother and sister."

"Didn't know he *had* a father," the other boy said, looking at his friend.

"Oh, yes, my papa says he's in prison."

"I didn't do it, didn't do it..." Henn King's voice was hollow and undefined, suggesting a cleft plate.

"Yes, you did. Yes, you did. The Fly King is an animal. A beast...a--"

"He's lower than an animal, he's an...an *insect!*" shouted a skinny girl of about fourteen. "God makes humans...the devil makes the likes of him. He's only good for one thing. Eating shit." With that, the girl ran to a horse trough at the edge of the village square, scooped up two handfuls of horse manure, ran back over to the stocks and rubbed the excrement into Henn King's face. He screamed in his guttural muted way, and the children fell silent for a few seconds before resuming their torture. The girl, who had apparently been caught up in the moment, scowled at her dirty hands and ran back to the horse trough to wash them.

A boy of perhaps eighteen, dressed in dirty sack-colored pants and suspenders, stepped up close and spat directly into Henn King's eye. The liquid slid down his dirty face like a thick brown tear.

The bird took to wing again, circled the pathetic creature a few times, then flew away from the village square, over to the alley behind the tavern, where it landed and hopped in through the partially open back door.

"We don't need that bad blood. It should stop right now. Before you know it, the whole town will look like monsters."

"Yeah, yeah, he's right."

A group of village men were drinking and smoking through thin white pipes. They gossiped and snickered, their excitement building in perfect ratio to the amount of ale consumed.

"Yeah, we should get rid of 'em. It's only right. Let's kick the whole family out of the village--Henn the Fly King, his whore sister, and the unholy bastard in her belly. The whore Mother, too. Throw 'em all out and--"

"No." The room went quiet. When this man spoke, the others listened. He was the strongest, the meanest, the ringleader, and Magdalena recognized him as the man who had instigated the rape.

"More than that. We need to...get *rid* of them."

The rabble remained quite for a moment as they digested the idea.

"Karl is right!" piped in another man Magdalena also recognized from behind the tavern. "They's witches, the lot of 'em. Better off dead, I say. Better off being done with that bad blood. God would want it so. 'Tis up to us to clean the Lord's house."

Another moment passed.

"'Tis true, them women is wicked temptresses. I seen the way that Gwennie looks at my boy. And whatever monster be that in her belly? Eh? And we all know what the whore mother did! That alone say *she* should be punished. And then Henn, well any fool can see the devil lives in *his* bones. Witches, the whole lot of 'em." Otto the fat man nodded at his own speech and looked over at Karl for a pat on the back. Then the other men started whooping and hitting their mugs together, agreeing that it was the only right thing to do.

They each downed several more pints of ale quickly, for courage, and started out the tavern door. The landlord grabbed several jars of whiskey, threw them in a sack, and locked his establishment up for the evening. The few people present who were not part of the mob complained bitterly--not at their terrible plan, but at the terrible inconsideration the landlord showed by turning them out unquenched.

Dusk was falling as the mob journeyed through the village, a few more men joining them. No one interfered. Some of the men picked up weapons as they passed their homes, several picked up torches to light the way.

Otto the fat man stopped to grab the large iron dagger his father had forged as a wedding gift for him and his late wife. The baker stood on his doorstep and shouted to his daughter to bring him the wood axe. "It's out the back, Anna, by the woodpile."

The raven flew above them as they made their way over to the cottage at the edge of the forest. They walked briskly, cursing and laughing and telling one another what strong men they were for taking action. They shared a jar of whiskey, which fed the fire raging in their hearts and groins, and told stories of how God would reward them.

When they arrived, Karl Brun heaved his large foot at the cottage door, kicking till it broke open. The men charged inside, still holding their smoking torches.

"What do you want?" the mother screamed, running over to Gwennie's side, who had been readying for bed and was dressed only in her nightshirt. Her breasts were large and virtually exposed under the thin material.

"You women are whores...witches!" Karl Brun sneered and spat on the floor. "I saw ye, singing that monster to sleep, praying out loud to the devil that he be released come morning." He came in close to the older woman's face, his eyes burning with hatred and passion.

"I demand that you get out of here!" the mother shouted. "Right now!" But it was the sound of a sparrow barking at a hawk. Already, the other men were eyeing Gwennie, chuckling and edging in closer. Just waiting for the word.

The three men from behind the tavern avoided eye contact with Gwennie, perhaps wondering if the bastard child in her belly was their own. Instead, they concentrated on the whore mother. They used their fists and their feet, and a heavy wood table leg that Seth the carpenter had brought along. Finally, she was still.

"That's enough. The whore is dead."

Otto the fat man unbuttoned his pants and began pissing out the night's ale over her body. He swore curses at her as he did, although his eyes were not as brave.

"You deserve every last drop, you dirty harlot. Your brother Serge was a fine man. Bewitched him, you did. Flaunting yourself at him like that. Then what do you do? Blame him for your own pact with the devil. Now he sits rotting in Grunsich prison. He was my friend, you dirty whore. Serge was a good man."

Gwennie was unconscious. All had taken a turn with her, except the three who couldn't stand to see the belly up close. One had tried to take her from behind, but couldn't finish the job.

"Cut it out of her," the landlord said, taking yet another swig of whiskey. "Isn't that what God would want?" The men fell silent for a moment, then each took another hit of whiskey and agreed that it was God's will.

"Here, take this." Otto the fat man handed his iron dagger to Karl, who finished half a jug of whiskey before performing the bloody task.

Afterwards, the men bundled out of the cottage, not bothering to hide the corpses or the evidence. They were their own law, and besides, the man of the house was locked away forever in Grunsich Castle prison.

"Now let's get the evil little bastard himself."

THE FLY KING

"Yeah, to the town square."

The smell of rotten cabbages hung heavy in the air. Henn King was sleeping. Drool trailed from his slack mouth in long streams onto the dirt and debris below.

He woke as he heard the sound of men coming, lifted his head the small amount allowed in the wooden fixture, and saw approaching lights. He grunted in fear.

"Get him out of the stocks. Get me some rope."

In minutes, Henn was released from the stocks and hogtied.

"Let's drag him back to his cottage, let him say hello to his family, shall we?"

"Yeah." The men jeered and kicked at him as he lay helpless on the ground. "Let's take him home."

"Hey, isn't it a little far to go?" the landlord interjected. "I mean, all the way back there? It's getting late, boys."

"Shut it, you *woman*. Give us some more of that whiskey."

The landlord looked hesitant for a moment, then laughed, pulled another jug out of his sack, took a large swig for himself and passed it around.

They dragged Henn through the village. The mob was noisy, impossible to sleep through, yet no one came to a window or a door, no one called out to them, "Stop this!" The village turned a blind eye. Most would have been glad to be rid of the King family anyway. The wives did not like a free woman out there on the edge of town, and Henn the Fly King was a demon for sure. Made it unsafe for their own children to walk around unattended, especially the girls; look what he'd done to his own sister. No, it was better to keep quiet and mind one's own business. The men knew best.

Soon, they were back at the cottage. The fire was still burning a little in the hearth, and white smoke puffed up into the night.

They had dragged Henn all the way. Beating him, kicking him, cursing, accusing, and torturing.

When they finally reached the door, they untied his legs and pulled him to his feet. He stood, stooped over, bleeding and bruised, several bones already broken. But nothing would be as painful as what they did next. The ringleader kept hold of the ropes behind his back and kicked him in the buttocks to move forward. Henn walked through the door and howled.

All the men stood silent, listening to the sound of his misery. Otto the fat man gulped, and his mouth dropped open. His eyes fell to the ground, where he saw his iron dagger lying next to the girl's mutilated body, covered in her blood. Shame rushed though him. His whole face turned crimson.

"What's the matter, Otto?"

"I...I don't know. I..."

"For God's sake, man. Don't forget, this is a mission. You cannot see these people as human. Look at him...he's a devil. And those whores...it's the likes of him, springs from the bellies of whores like that. Landlord, fetch this man another jug of whiskey from your sack."

After the jug of whiskey was shared, and another after that, when finally the sound of Henn King's sobbing was dulled by the fresh intake of alcohol, the mob was ready to go again. There was no turning back now, and those that felt the guiltiest showed the most bravado. In the end, it would be about *believing* it was right. And the only way to believe it was to *feel* it--wholeheartedly.

"Let's kill him now, rid the world of this monster."

"No, let's make him lie on top of her one more time, so he can die knowing why, and knowing that the devil comes for him. That God's punishment will be far worse than our efforts."

Karl Brun pushed Henn on top of Gwennie's body, slamming his foot down into the small of his back, watching in disgust at the huge pointed shoulder blades that stuck up, red and raw from the beatings.

Finally, they pulled him off, and Otto the fat man, who felt much better about the whole thing now, wiped his hands slowly and deliberately in Gwennie's blood and then smeared them over Henn's chest. It was symbolic of nothing, only the passing fancy of a drunken man who was possibly trying to justify something to himself.

Henn's chest, face, and body were already covered in his sister's blood. But it was this--*wiping it on him,* the overt cruelty of it, that made Henn cry out one last time before they bludgeoned him into silence.

At last, his eyes stopped flickering beneath the lids as he crawled up to death's door, his sister's blood now comforting him, freeing him from the pain.

"He's not quite dead," the landlord said, as he bent down, swaying over Henn's broken body.

"Then that is a sign from the Lord. We bury him alive."

"Wait a minute, man. Are you sure?"

"More whiskey," Karl Brun shouted. His voice was slurred, and he had already vomited twice.

"How are we to do this? Should we not come back in the light?"

Otto the fat man asked.

The men mumbled amongst themselves; the thought was sobering.

"Arh, to hell with ya all. We do it now. That's what I say. Now...while God is strong in us. Tomorrow we may fall prey to mortal weakness."

"I agree...better get it done."

They shared another jug of whiskey and decided they would take Henn and Gwennie out first. Take them into the woods, way back there where no one goes. Dig two holes, bury them, then come back for the whore mother.

The Black Forest was alive with strange sounds. And the whiskey had run out. The men were starting to complain of dull throbbing heads and sour stomachs, and the sounds of the night set an anxious backdrop around them.

They dug the first hole; the work was hard, real labor, and the more they dug the more they sobered. The girl, and the child they tore from her womb were slung into the hole along with the murder weapon and quickly covered, each shovel of dirt mercifully burying it all from their sight.

After resting for a few minutes, the shovel was passed off to Boris, whose job was to begin digging the second hole.

"I have to tell you something." Boris, the village smithy, who had been quiet most of the night, enjoying the kills in silence and never actually participating--except for taking his turn with the girl--was now suddenly ready to talk. "If this spawn of the devil we call Henn the Fly King, along with his wretched family, are truly kin to

THE FLY KING

Beelzebub, then think ye not that the demon will lend his hand in vengeance against us?"

The men looked at one another, their own faces demonic under the orange glow of the torches.

"Do ye not hear that?" Boris continued. He lifted his arm and pointed out into the darkness toward the unknown sounds that seemed to be creeping in around them. They all listened, and did hear. "For all we know, that might be the devil coming up from Hell, moving like a shadow through the forest on his horse, come to find out who it is has killed his unholy children."

"I say it's wolves," Karl Brun said, but his voice was uncertain, and lent only to the ever increasing nervousness that had spread among the men. "We better get on with it."

"Why not let the wolves get Henn?" Otto the fat man spoke up. His high-pitched voice sounded oddly feminine; normally, the men would have mocked him for it, but tonight it was the last thing on their minds. "And since the boy ain't completely dead, then it would be the wolves that killed him. Let the devil talk to the wolves about it, that's what I say."

"What about the girl and the whore mother? We killed them true enough," piped in Boris, the new voice of reason.

"This is so, but all of us know the boy. *He's* the evil one...it takes only a look at him to know it." Otto pointed his torch at Henn King lying in a grotesquely inhuman curl at the foot of a giant spruce. The torch cast his shadow on the trunk, and the wings of his deformed shoulder blades stretched up high.

"Right, then..." Karl spoke. "Let's leave him for the wolves. Tomorrow we come back to the cottage for the whore mother. Let's go." And the men started walking out of the forest.

By the time they had gone twenty paces, most of them were running.

By the time they got home to their beds, they were praying for God to keep the demons at bay.

It was almost dawn when the raven flew back to the witch's cottage. The woman was outside, muttering and scrambling around, harnessing up her donkey to a cart.

"Come on, you old nag." The donkey *hee-hawed* at her, bent his head and scratched in the dirt. She had no torch, which implied that her journey was a secret one.

She trucked around the back of the houses slowly, whispering to the donkey to keep his mouth quiet. At the edge of town she turned down the weed-lined trail that led to the King's cottage, slapping the donkey's neck. "Come on, you old nag. Hurry up."

The witch stood over the mother's body, the moonlight revealing the severity of the wounds on her head. "Let's get you out of here, Helena." She dragged the woman by the legs and, with much effort, heaved her onto the back of the cart.

Once back home, the witch hurriedly pulled the woman into the house and laid her on the bed, then lit candles and started a fire under her cauldron. She ripped a piece of the woman's nightgown and wiped some of her blood onto it, then threw it into the cauldron along with a strand of the woman's hair. Next she began taking small bottles from the shelf.

The raven flew from the forest.

Winter had arrived. Snow sat heavily on branches, covered the ground and the rooftops.

Past the village they went. Past the cottage where the Kings once lived, farther back, over the forest, climbing higher and higher toward the mountain.

Finally, they reached a cave halfway up the side of Mount Breech. The raven landed on a ledge directly above the cave opening, knocking loose a few flutters of snow with his claws.

The bird sensed a movement on the flat surface in front of the cave, and saw that it was Henn King. He was maimed almost beyond recognition; his body was deeply scarred, and the broken bones in his legs and arms had fused together at disjointed angles. Then, to the left of the opening, not far from the four-hundred-foot drop, were the skeletal remains of his sister. On her decaying head was a jagged green crown made from pine needles that Henn must have placed there. He wore a similar adornment on his own head.

Henn's face, which had always been hideous and caused him much pain and exclusion, was now even worse. His cheek bones, which had been shattered, had mended lumpy and irregular; his lips were flattened and smeared with deep scar tissue. His nose wasn't much more than two irregularly shaped holes in his face; and his eyes, which had always been bulbous and weak, now looked off in opposite directions. And, perhaps partially due to his emaciated condition, his wing-shaped shoulder blades seemed to protrude considerably farther than they had before.

Henn had escaped the wolves, suffered unknown horrors of pain-

-both physical and emotional but had managed to survive. At some point, he had returned to the place in the woods to dig up his sister's remains.

He still wore the tattered undergarments he had been beaten and left for dead in, and his chest was smeared with blood. He didn't appear to be cut, and the blood was too new to be his sister's.

The stench of turned meat wafted from the mouth of the cave. The snow in front of it had been carefully swept away, and a large pentagram had been scratched deeply into the dirt. In its center lay the iron dagger and a small dried animal, red and hairless. The raven looked closer, saw that the dried creature was Gwennie's unborn baby.

Night was drawing in; the sky had begun darkening to a deep blue. Henn seemed to be waiting for something. He sat very still beside the pentagram, looking alternately at his sister and the moon.

Suddenly, as if he'd received a silent message, Henn took the dagger in his misshapen hands and pointed it up at the sky, his arms shaking with some incredible force. Energy lit his entire body, and the dagger glowed a brilliant silver, the same color as the moon.

Then he spoke, but not in a human voice, and the language was unintelligible. It came *through* him--powerful whispering voices, many of them, edging their way in from some other world and stilling the forest.

The raven did not move. Through all the things it had shown Magdalena, it had remained confident in its disguise and purpose, but at this moment it seemed in mortal fear of discovery.

The whispering ceased, and the true Henn spoke, in a way that was his own:

"Yes, Lord of the dark, I give you my soul in return for vengeance. When I breathe my last breath, take it, do with it as ye wish. God wants it not. Where thou leadeth, I shall follow, for I am your servant, and so shall I always remain. This I promise you."

Henn lowered the dagger to his side. He looked at his sister one more time, disappeared into the stench of the cave, then returned with something dangling in his hand--a piece of blood-stained nightshirt. He tied the dagger to it, then hung it around his neck.

Silently, he began climbing down the side of the mountain. His crippled hands were miraculously strong and flexible as he lowered himself easily down the snow-covered mountainside. Periodically, he would stop to check his surroundings, peering over his own shoulder blades, which pointed up in hideous bony arcs. His bulbous eyes had suddenly righted and glistened with the light of the snow reflecting into their blackness.

Only when Henn King was fully out of sight did the Raven fly off for the village tavern.

"More ale, Petir." The landlord slapped down fresh jugs for the men. No one was laughing, but much talking was being done. The conversation was quiet and somber, respectful of the circumstances at hand. The tavern had closed early; only the men who had been there on *that* night, now a full six months ago, were allowed to remain. Several of the men were dressed in black over-tunics and pants.

"What are we to do? We cannot wait for the Freiburg Law. Twelve days, and still they do not come." The men nodded and muttered.

"Six women stolen, six women dead. Twelve women in as many

nights. 'Tis like the devil is upon us. We must tell the wives and daughters to take leave. Boris, you must escort them into Freiburg. What say you?"

Boris nodded eagerly. He had no complaints about leaving this cursed village.

"'Tis the Fly King," said Otto the fat man.

"Horseshit," Karl Brun replied, and spat on Petir's floor. "The King boy is dead where we left him, or dragged off by wolves. Go check, see if I'm wrong."

The room fell quiet.

None had gone back the day after to remove the King boy's mother as they had planned. Nor the next day. For weeks afterwards, they hadn't even talked about it. Finally, Otto had mentioned that he was getting nervous about "you know what." Surely someone was soon to wonder where the King family had gone.

And so they started a rumor that the Kings had left the village for Grunsich, where the mother's incestuous brother was kept prisoner in the castle. It stirred up gossip about a possible reunion between the siblings and soon became too sordid a topic for the women to discuss, at least openly. "Good riddance to bad blood," they would say to any man who brought the subject up over ale.

Karl and his two accomplices went up to the Kings' cottage a month later. They found the door open, and a trail of blood indicating that the woman had been dragged off by wolves.

"Should we go back in the forest, see if Henn's body is there, check on the girl's grave?" one of the men asked.

They quickly agreed that the wolves would have long since taken Henn, and that the sister was hidden well under the dirt. Why go out there? Why venture deep into the forest to revisit the place where they'd felt the devil on their backs? They had gone home to their families instead.

"We must get the women out quickly. They're scared enough, they'll put up no fuss about it. In the morning. What say ye all?"

All the men agreed. The morning it would be. Then Otto began to cry, his face crumpling in large red folds as he wept over the bar.

One of the men patted him on the shoulder. The others were quiet and uncomfortable.

"Why Frannie, my only little girl? Her throat sliced like a pig at market. 'Tis the Fly King, I tell you. 'Tis the Fly King come for his revenge."

"Stop it now, Otto. 'Tis no such thing. 'Tis most likely an escaped murderer and--"

"Then why is he not spotted?" Otto said, his voice thick with tears. "Twelve women, including my poor little Frannie. Twelve. And no sign of the murdering beast who did it."

"'Tis not true," Boris said, eager to relay what he'd heard. "Old Frau Becker swears she seen a beast all covered in blood, running away with the body of young Mary Fluss night afore last. She say it went through Jon Weily's cabbages, that way..." he pointed, "and yonder back into the forest. She do swear on it."

Karl scowled at him. "Shut it, you fool. Old Frau Becker has no more sense than my chickens."

Otto began weeping louder than ever, believing for sure now that he had caused his own daughter's death. Had he known the instrument that slit her throat was the dagger his father had given him and his wife as a wedding present, he would have run himself and the rest of the gang off the Heidelrein Bridge.

They had been talking for an hour when they heard a loud pounding at the door. Petir glanced nervously at the men as he went over to unbolt it. There in the snow stood Hubert Freindlich, dressed in his bedclothes and shaking all over.

"Is Karl Brun here?"

Karl turned.

"It be your mother, Karl," Hubert said quietly, remembering the screams he had heard coming from next door. Remembering how he hadn't the courage to check on her until the screams were long done. "She's dead."

The flies arrived at midnight, covering the entire town in a thick black cloud. From above, it looked as though the village had disappeared into a giant black hole.

The screams of the villagers were muffled by the sound of the flies and soon disappeared altogether. The buzzing was terrifyingly loud, a morbid, almost hypnotic drone that could be heard far up on the mountainside.

Where the Fly King was working his spell.

The cloud of flies hung just inches from the roof of the cottage but came no closer.

The witch stared at the squirrel bones as they fell to the ground from a small leather pouch. "There is much evil at work here. 'Tis far worse than Henn himself could manage."

THE FLY KING

Helena King stood sweating over the cauldron, stirring frantically as she had been instructed.

"More wormwood, Helena!" the witch shouted, "and keep the fire hot. Must keep it hot. Make it boil!"

In between orders to Helena, the witch muttered and mumbled spells to keep the flies from their door.

"I cannot believe this is his doing. My boy Henn has a heart of gold."

"He is not your boy any longer, Helena," the witch said. "You must accept it. Like Karl Brun and his mob, Henn believes you and his beloved sister are dead...it's more than the boy could take. In his pain, he has turned to the dark forces, the spirits of the underworld. He has asked for their allegiance, and they have given it."

She stopped talking for a moment, hurried to her shelves and threw the contents of several small bottles into the cauldron. There was a loud "*Phooof*," as the steam turned the color of spring violets.

"Once a man has turned, there is no coming back. You must put him to rest, Helena, put him to rest. Tonight is our only chance. If we leave soon, we will be there by early morning. And if the heavens are with us, we shall find him sleeping."

They left with the donkey and cart in the dead of night, taking the rig as far as they could before abandoning it by the roadside to travel the forest by foot.

The two tired, frightened old women climbed the side of the snow-covered mountain, moving slow and slipping often. Helena prayed to God, and the witch muttered spells to save them from the treacherous fall. By the time they reached the mouth of the cave, dawn was breaking.

Both women gasped at the sight of the crowned corpse leaning against the outer side of the cave. The old witch sniffed at the sweet meaty odor wafting from the opening.

"'Tis the ones he stole," she whispered. Helena had begun shaking now, on the verge of hysteria. The witch took her by the shoulders, forcing her to look into her wise old eyes. "Calm now. Calm. Calm thyself, woman."

Helena King broke free from the witch's hold and began weeping into her frostbitten hands. "Oh, my poor Gwennie, my poor Henn. I cannot do it. I cannot kill my boy."

"*Shhh,* you'll wake him. You *must* do it, woman. Everything depends on it. I have seen it in the bones. I've seen it in the stars. For godsakes woman, you've seen it with your own eyes. The whole village is dead. He is not your son."

Helena King dropped her hands from her face and looked deeply into her friend's eyes, knowing those eyes didn't lie. "God forgive me," she said, and started into the darkness of the cave on hands and knees.

"Remember," the witch whispered to the Helena, "the dagger will be by the left side of his head."

A few moments passed, and no sounds came from within the cave. Still more passed. The witch wrapped her arms around herself, sat shuddering by the entrance.

Then came a voice she recognized as Henn King's.

"Mother? Mother? Is it really you? Is this a dream?

"Shhhhh, my baby, 'tis no dream. 'Tis your mother."

"Oh, Mother, I think thee dead. Mother, Mother, I have done bad." He was weeping now. "Worse than thee know, Mother. I'm so afraid, so afraid..."

"Shhh now, Henn. Go thee back to sleep."

"I dare not, Mother. I be too scared."

"Close your eyes, my child," she said, and began to sing to him.

"Sleep, my baby, sleep

Never more shall weep

Time to rest thy little head..."

The witch hummed along quietly to the melody, but then her eyes widened with realization. Something wasn't right. She had missed something. Why was Henn so scared?

"...Oh sleep, my baby, sleep

Now not another peep!

Time to close thy tired eyes

And Mother bring a sweet surprise

Come morning, if thee sleep."

In a voice almost lulled into slumber, Henn whispered, "Mother, promise...you must help me, get me back to God, for if not I fear a terrible thing--"

"Shh, my boy."

The witch sprang to her feet shouting, *"No!"*

It was too late.

Henn cried out at the same instant, *"No, Mother! No!"*

Helena stabbed him through the heart.

Henn's scream filled the entirety of the Black Forest and even beyond. It wasn't the sound of his mortal body dying, but worse, his soul being seized by the darkness. The agony of his struggle woke every animal, shook every tree to the root, echoed for an eternity though the hearts of all who heard it.

The witch collapsed on the ground, faint with dread. What had she done?

She waited for that which she feared, and it came.

With Henn's last breath, in a language she'd heard of but never heard, came the curse of the Fly King. Her heart deciphered the serpent's tongue as it unleashed its venom.

"You fools, you fools, now I have passage to this place." There was a horrible hiss of laughter. "Thank you, witch." More, whispering, hissing, laughter. "I speak to the heavens, and now they must hear. Though, wait I must, to your world I shall father a boy and a girl, siblings who, against your law, will come together in unholy hand." The voice paused. Nothing in the forest moved or breathed. "The Fly King be their bastard child, come back to see God's children die." The hissing laughter returned, louder, and the witch felt warm blood trickling from her ears.

"And whenst I come, I shall again call forth the flies. This time 'twill be the final end."

The voice fell silent.

Not a sound came from inside the cave now.

After much time had passed, the witch called out weakly to her friend. "Helena?" Her heart knew there would be no response.

She crawled into the cave.

In the moonlight, she saw the two bodies. Henn King, with the iron dagger sticking from his chest, and his mother lying beside him, clutching her son.

The old witch sighed. She moved to Henn, and pulled the bloody dagger from his heart. Once in her hands, she understood the full meaning of the curse. Henn would never know God's mercy now; his wretched soul had become one with the demon of the Dark Side. How could she have been so stupid.

"And this is where he waits to work his poison, inside the very dagger that has slain both his sister and himself."

She would guard it, watch over it. She would spend her days devising a spell to stop the conception of the siblings. It would become her life's duty.

The raven flew off into the cold night sky, having conveyed to Magdalena all that had taken place.

It took her into the forest now, one last time.

Out again. Only this time, more than just the season had changed. The village itself was different, now four times its previous size, its cottages timber-framed and larger, more sophisticatedly constructed.

The witch's cottage still stood at the far edge of town, although it had been converted into a storage barn, and a newer cottage sat twenty feet off to the east.

Behind it all, the Black Forest remained unchanged.

Summer hollyhocks lined the pathway up to the cottage door, and small spotted curtains blew gently in the mild warm breeze.

The raven peeked in from the windowsill.

A middle-age woman fussed around sweeping the floor with a crude straw broom. Her face held much resemblance to the old witch, perhaps her great-granddaughter, or other kin. As she swept she muttered to herself. "Oh Agnes, why did ye take the dagger? Why? Now you be dead. I did the damned spell too late...that cursed child already be in ye belly. Oh, what a fool I be." She swept harder, angrily. "'Twas the charmed blood flowing through your veins, killed both you and the unspeakable one. I didn't know it be that way Agnes, I swear.". She seemed flustered, even a little insane.

Quite suddenly she stopped sweeping, listened, her face frozen in an expression of fear.

Horses were coming up the trail.

The sound grew louder, and now she could hear men's voices as well.

"Come on, lads, let's get her!" someone shouted. "Witch, we know you be in there! You killed young Agnes and her unborn child."

Someone else yelled, "Did it with witchcraft, she did!"

The woman let her broom fall and dropped to the floor. Hurriedly, she removed one of the wooden floorboards, pulling out the loose

THE FLY KING

nail with her bare fingers.

"You accuse her of stealin', then fix the matter with ye own hands, huh? The devil's hands," the men jeered, off their horses now and coming toward the door. "Well, now ye must stand trial, witch. Ye shall burn. Come on, lads. Let's get her."

She quickly removed the plank, reached in and brought out a burlap sack, then she sprang to her feet and headed out the back door into the forest.

As she disappeared behind the first layer of trees, a few of the men began torching her cottage. The others, anticipating her escape, were soon close behind her, searching. She ran like a fox, nimbly jumping over broken branches and tree stumps, holding the dagger tightly with both hands.

After gaining a small distance, she stopped among the mighty pines and hastily scanned the area. She spotted a hollow, ten feet up in one of the trees. She tried three times to throw the dagger into the hollow but failed. And the voices were getting louder.

"I saw her go that way!"

The sound of breaking underbrush signaled that she had only seconds before discovery. She looked up at the hollow, then tried one last time. This time the burlap bag disappeared into the hole.

As they dragged her off, the woman shouted up at the sky, "I have failed. May the gods have mercy and protect us."

The raven sat motionless for a while, then closed its eyes.

It would be another 271 years before Jakob Günter and his crew from the Badenklein Lumber Corporation chopped down the tree.

CHAPTER 45

Klickitat, Washington

THE FLY KING COMETH

The river was swollen over the bank, and the wind had arrived, thrusting the downpour this way and that, whipping the trees.

Delroy Günter stepped out into the storm. He closed the door to the old Jenkins cabin, held his hands toward the silver moon, and let the rain wash the blood from his fingers.

Over at the store, the beer sign buzzed in the window, but the front half of the lights were off, and the cardboard plaque in the door read, "Closed."

Jack sat behind the counter studying Rachel's photo. For once he didn't feel the least bit horny.

Jack smiled, admiring the way Rachel's hair fell on her bare shoulders. So pretty, that's for sure. But after last night?

At 3:00 A.M., he'd gotten a call. Had taken him a moment to wake up. It was Rachel. He'd cleared his throat and pretended not to have been sleeping. She was at the payphone outside his store.

"Me? Nah, I hardly ever sleep. Don't need it. Pick you up?" He'd countered the surprise in his voice by quickly adding, "That's so weird, 'cuz I was just getting ready to come down and grab myself a couple of six-packs. Fucking coincidence, huh?"

So he got in his truck and headed down to the Shack.

"You all right?" Fuck, she looked bad. Her skin was almost pale blue in the moonlight, and she had a huge black raccoon eye.

"Did your loser-boy Gavin do that?"

She said no, but that didn't mean shit, any chick would've said the same thing.

And her gut. She was wearing a very unsexy long-ass T-shirt, the kind fat girls wear with spandex pants, with a big Mickey Mouse on the front. It looked as though she had a cushion up there, or was pregnant. She couldn't be, of course; he'd seen her just the day before yesterday. She said it was some type of stomach complaint. Boy, ya never know, he'd thought, every chick on the fucking planet comes with baggage.

He'd gotten her to the house. As she walked in the door and he saw her in the light, well, it was even worse than he'd thought. There were a couple of big blisters on her face that she kept scratching. Looked fucking nasty. Turned his stomach, actually.

Jack held the photo in his hand and stared out at the torrential downpour. The wind had started thumping the glass. He'd wait it out in here for a while before heading home.

Then there was the way the dogs acted toward Rachel. Rufus, who's a real love pup, wouldn't even come in the same room as her. It was like she had this...air about her. He didn't believe in all that crap

Mag spouted off, but if he did, then he would have said that Rachel's vibration was all fucked up. *Hey! Maybe Mag put a curse on her. That would explain her charging in here just a little while ago.*

Mag had banged on the door, so hard that she nearly broke the glass.

"Hold it, hold it," he'd said, as he let her in.

"Have you seen Rachel?" Her eyes were all fiery and darting around, like she was scared--real scared.

"Uh, yea, as a matter of fact I have."

"Where is she, Jack? It's important."

"I dunno. She spent the night with me, then I dropped her off at the church this morning. Her boyfriend beat her up. Guess she went to pray for him or something." He rolled his eyes at the thought. "She's probably back with him by now."

Mag hadn't even wanted to stay and chat; she ran right back out into the storm, got in her little car and took off.

It had been like one of them soap operas in here today. Earlier, around 2:00 P.M., Gavin had been in.

"Have you seen Rachel?" he'd asked.

Rachel had made Jack promise--silly girl's stuff--that if Gavin, Magdalena, or anyone else came around asking, he'd say he hadn't seen her. He'd told Mag, though. He didn't want to get on her bad side, not after what she did to Father Liebermann.

"Nah, haven't seen her since the other day when she borrowed the shovel," he'd told Gavin.

Gavin looked anxious. "When I woke up this morning, I found a note saying she was going into town."

Jack laughed. "Well what do ya expect? You can't knock a chick around like that without gettin' her pissed at ya!"

"I thought you said you hadn't seen her."

"Well...I mean...I haven't. Well, only for a minute. Yeah, she was gettin' the bus into town."

Gavin glared at him, shook his head like he was real disgusted, sighed and said, "Gimme a bottle of tequila. *If* you see Rachel, tell her she and I need to talk. Would you do that, please?" He was being sarcastic, but Jack just nodded and Gavin took his brown paper bag and left.

Jack didn't feel sorry for the dude. He deserved it. Last night, sitting on his couch, Rachel had been in a sorry state, she really had.

This morning she was already up. He'd slept like shit for some reason. He had lain there in the dark for the longest time, scared to close his eyes.

"Jack, would you drop me off at the church?"

"Church? There's no service today. Father Liebermann...he just croaked. I heard he's up there on display in his coffin. See...I don't get that. When my mother died I--"

"Will you?" she interrupted.

"Fuck. I suppose so. But why? I mean...how you gonna get back? I have to be at the store all day."

"I just need to go."

"Suit yourself." He didn't want to pry; you shouldn't let a chick think you're too interested in their crap. And quite honestly, he wasn't sure if he was. She smelled bad, like rotten eggs, and the flies that usually hung around the dog food were buzzing around her like she had shit in her pockets.

Staring at the promo picture, Jack sighed. She looked so hot and sexy there. But still, for a million bucks, he couldn't get a boner over Rachel anymore.

Startled, he looked up. Someone was pounding on the door. He walked over and yelled loudly, "We're closed. Closed at six. It's ten o'clock!" *What is this? Grand Central Station?* Again the pounding. "I said..." Fuck it. The rain was loud as machine gun fire, who ever it was couldn't hear him. Better not be that little red-ass river-rat Zak.

He peered through the glass.

Delroy stood waiting.

Jack unlocked the door and pulled it open.

"Uh, sorry we're closed."

CHAPTER 46

Three candelabras lit the small church, one either side of the coffin and one in the very back. Father Liebermann's face appeared waxy in the candle light, the flickering flame creating shadows that made his face seem strangely alive. The sight of him and the rain slashing angrily on the roof made Magdalena shudder.

She had scoured every nook and cranny for Rachel. She wasn't here, and she couldn't be in the cellar because it was locked. The keys were on the altar next to the coffin, the gleaming black coffin with brass hinges.

She'd checked under each row of pews. She had to find Rachel before it was too late. Jack was right, she could have left hours ago. But she wasn't with Gavin, that much was certain. Magdalena put a hand to her forehead, noting a slight fever. That was to be expected after what had happened last night.

Sometime in the early hours of the morning, the vision had ended, although she didn't recall it ending. The rain had finally awakened her, thrashing on her face. She stirred and turned on her side, suddenly aware of the musty smell of wet earth. She opened her eyes, startled to find that she was not in her bed. She sat upright, shaking her hair and wringing out her skirt. Dark rolling clouds filled the sky, and she heard the distant rumble of thunder.

As she pulled herself to her feet, she was reminded of Mother, how she had found her that night, wet and covered in dirt. *Just like this.* Disorientated, Magdalena started slowly toward the cottage, as if she had just stepped out of the grave.

Once inside, she checked the clock: 8:00 P.M. *Impossible.* She'd slept the whole day away! All that time lying asleep next to the dead rosebushes.

But there was no time to wonder. Quickly, she readied herself. Showering, drying, putting on fresh warm clothes. All the while she prayed she wasn't too late, even as her instincts reassured her that the timing would somehow be right. But deciphering her feelings incorrectly could easily lead to a fatal mistake. Like not casting the spell on Rachel while there was still time. *We witches sure can screw things up.* She pulled on a sweater and scowled at herself in the mirror.

It was time to go to Rachel, tell her what she'd seen, convince her somehow that Ani had been right.

The car started after two tries. She turned on the windshield wipers and the heater, and headed out into the storm for the old Jenkins cabin.

Gavin was in the bus, but no Rachel.

Magdalena peeked her head in through the door. "Gavin, please, I need to talk to you."

"Come on in, Magdalena," he called, beckoning her in an exaggerated way. "Come on aboard!"

His warm, dry studio-on-wheels was welcoming. He seemed happy, a little *too* happy. She climbed into the bus and saw he was drunk.

"Here, wanna shot?" He held out a glass. She shook her head; he knocked his back in one go.

"Gavin, where's Rachel? I need to speak to her. I swear to you, she's in danger."

Gavin's expression turned serious, but his eyes couldn't quite focus. "She's not here. Look at this..." With much effort, and nearly falling over twice, he managed to pull a piece of paper out of his front pocket. "When I got up this morning, I had no Rachel, only this." He waved the note and handed it to her.

Gavin,

I didn't want to wake you. I've gone into town to buy a pregnancy test, and I'll check out the doctors while I'm there. Won't be back till late. Love you,

Rachel

Magdalena handed the letter back. "She's not home yet?"

He winked and took a big swig from the bottle. "*If* she ever went. Ah, ha! See? The plot thickens..."

"What do you mean? It's urgent that I find her."

"Oh, well...yeah, me too. But methinks I know where she is." He smiled slyly, took another swig. "I think, and don't ask me where or why she acquired this sudden taste for rednecks, pardon the expression, but I believe she's with Jack." He swayed, and finally slumped down into his chair.

He turned toward his computer. "Wanna hear what I'm working on?"

"I'm sorry, I don't have time. Look, I need to ask you--"

"Wait, I think you'll like it. I think it might have something to do with all this," he made a sweeping gesture with his hands, "madness."

He pressed play, and the bus filled with the dark melody, which was complete with all kinds of instrumentation. Magdalena went lightheaded. She quickly sat down and breathed deeply, filling her lungs with wet pine air.

"Ah, ha! Just as I suspected. All I need now is a vocalist to add the words."

He's not completely unaware of what's going on, she thought. *He's probably scared as hell.*

"Gavin, I need the dagger."

"*Oh, ho, ho!* The dagger, eh?" He bent forward, and she thought he was going to vomit, but he came back up with a grin on his face.

"Tell ya what...you record me a vocal. First take'll do, since you're in such a goddamn rush, and *then* we can talk about the goddamn dagger." He was slurring badly.

Reluctantly, she agreed. "Which version?" she asked. *There's several.*

"The one that..." he started, then paused to swallow a belch, "that protects the blood, of course."

He's picked up knowledge, being around it. He's a receptive channel for certain energies--frequencies--that's where his talent for music comes from. He's confused though, who wouldn't be.

"You mean the protection spell?"

"Whatever you call it. Just sing it into the microphone. Come on, let's go." He did a sloppy clap, handed her a microphone.

She sang the spell, her voice quivering and nervous. After it was done, she handed the microphone back to him. "Now please, Gavin, tell me where the dagger is."

"Don't rightly know. Why you in such a rush?" He took another long swig of tequila.

"Please, stop, Gavin. Don't." She grabbed at the bottle, but he swung it out of her reach. "Gavin, I need you to be straight with me."

He smiled at her and hit the play button. Instantly, Magdalena was mesmerized. The words actually *entered* her. By listening, she realized after it was finished, the spell had been cast on herself. Oddly, the idea made her want to laugh. Lot of good that would do! If they'd done it to Rachel little more than a day ago, then things would be different right now. But it was too late. The old witch in the vision had spent the remainder of her days composing a spell that, in the end, would fail to stop the coming of the Fly King. Had her ancestors any back-up plan, she wondered. Any late-in-the-day spell she didn't know of? She looked up toward the metal roof and sighed.

Standing now, she turned to Gavin. His eyes were closed.

"Gavin? Gavin?" *Shit, he's unconscious.* She shook him hard, slapped his cheeks--no response. Damn him. What was she to do? It was possible, she supposed, that Rachel had taken the dagger with her. Time was running out, the dagger would have to wait. She had to find Rachel before the brother beat her to it. And Magdalena sensed he was close.

She jumped in her car and sped down the muddy trail toward

Main Street, hoping Jack was still there.

Now here she was, staring down at Father Liebermann's pale dead face.

She would search the graveyard next.

* * *

Rachel needed no more proof, yet she tried it again. In *God's name--"* The painful ripping in her stomach cut her words off. It felt like teeth. Her life had become a sordid crippled nightmare, a dream in dark miserable colors that never ended, slow, feet-stuck-in-tar-with-the-monster-at-your-heels nightmare. Maybe this had always been her destiny. She'd prayed to God for the hole to be filled, and her prayer had been answered, but not by God. *"Fuck, the pain..."* The creature in her belly, little Daniel--it was a boy, she *knew* it--did not belong to God. "Jesu--stop, please, stop!"

From the moment it had started growing inside her, the mention of *Him, God,* would bring on this sharp, stabbing pain. She recognized this fact later, when it became too obvious to ignore.

She had been up here on this hilltop all day long, out in the wind and rain, groping around this graveyard like the living dead, excommunicated. She couldn't think straight, cold, shivering, drenched to the bone. You deserve it, she told herself. *I'm so frightened.* You should be, she thought. But what bad deeds had she done *purposefully*? What crimes had she committed that were awful enough to warrant this punishment?

THE FLY KING

It had started the day she and Ani were born. Her mother died in childbirth; her father had been so distraught, he'd taken his own life, which is what she must do, too. Yes, it was a sin to take your own life, but surely God would want her to end this unholy abomination.

Her stomach was smooth and huge. She could feel her baby moving, shifting. It wouldn't be long now. She must act fast or it would be too late and she'd be forced to gaze upon whatever monstrosity she and her brother had created. How could it have happened? Yet it had, and her brother was coming.

She had come to the church this morning with still a glimmer of hope. Maybe she could pray for forgiveness--for guidance. But she hadn't been able to get into the church without keeling over in agony. Eventually, after several attempts, she resisted the pain and went inside. She forced herself to sit in a pew until she almost fainted, then staggered out again, banished to the graveyard and the treacherous storm. No room at the inn, she thought and laughed madly up at the shadowed moon. She wouldn't be able to kill her baby so there was only one way.

They both had to die.

Rachel took the rope and swung it over the beam.

***

The rain pelted Magdalena as she reached into the backseat to pull out the flashlight.

She began moving along the path toward the graveyard. The wind was even crueler up here. It whistled and howled, groaning through the eaves of the church. She could see the town below, twinkling fractured lights.

Heart hammering in her chest, Magdalena began moving between the grave stones, pointing the light behind each one, praying, *dreading* that she would find Rachel crouching there.

"Rachel?" She kept calling out and sweeping the area with her flashlight. She needed to move faster, but her shoes were sticking in the mud. "Rachel?"

No way could Rachel hear her over the storm. Even if she did, would she trust her? It could well be *her* she was running from. The wicked witch who wants her to stab her own baby to death with a dagger.

Magdalena paused for a moment, exhausted. *Mother, I'm so sorry. For everything.*

Move. No time to rest. She pointed the flashlight toward the tombs and the row of oak trees behind them.

The tombs loomed up like sentries along the back edge of the graveyard, gothic and somehow unfinal. Tonight, the moon cast them the blackest shadows. Someone could easily be hiding there. Just then, she noticed something. The door to the Adeshek family tomb was slightly open.

"Jesus!" she whispered.

She turned the flashlight off. The moon was plenty bright to see a shadowy reality, albeit distorted by rain and wind like a silvery half world. *Tread carefully, for the truth is not always as we wish, is it, Mother?*

She walked slowly toward the door, her heart beating frantically, her wet hair clinging to her cheeks like dead fingers. She glanced once over her shoulder, then peered in through the gap.

A tall black figure, almost as tall as the ceiling. Motionless, huge, with wings and...

"Rachel?"

Startled, Rachel raised her head from her chest. The moonlight glowing through the small stained-glass window cast colored shapes on her face. She was standing on the wooden viewing bench, her head in the noose of a rope thrown over the roof beam, preparing to step off.

"No, Rachel, don't!" Magdalena pushed her way in and grabbed her around the waist. "Rachel, please. This isn't the way." *I can feel it,* she thought, *I can feel it in there.*

Magdalena stood on the bench and carefully slipped the noose from Rachel's neck. Only then did she let her breath out in a sigh of relief. Rachel began sobbing into Magdalena's shoulder, colored moonlight cutting harlequin shapes onto their faces.

"Come, come, child. There, there." Magdalena gradually eased them down off the bench. She held her for a moment longer, although there was nothing comforting she could think to say.

"Rachel, you know what has to be done. Ani was right. Only you can stop this now."

Rachel looked up. Slowly, hopelessly, she nodded. Magdalena noticed the terrible state of her face, blistered and sore, and the smell was rotten flesh.

"You must be strong, Rachel. It's the only way."

Magdalena pulled herself free. They had to move fast, they probably wouldn't be alone much longer. They needed to get this over before the brother arrived. *God help us then.*

"Rachel, this needs to be done in the church."

"No! No! I can't. I can't!"

"I understand. It hurts, but you must endure it. We'll be safer there, and the...child..." She could barely bring herself to call it that. "Will be weaker."

"The spell..." Rachel said in a low voice. "Kill us both. It'll be better that way, Magdalena. It really will."

"No, Rachel, I'm not going to let you die. This isn't your fault. You must believe me. Come." She grabbed Rachel by the arm and dragged her out into the rain.

Magdalena turned the key, and the cellar door creaked open. Jesus, she didn't want to go down there. Rachel stood behind her, soaking wet, doubled over in pain.

She started down the unfinished wooden steps. *Wasn't there a light? Please, God, let there be a...what was that?* She thrashed wildly at the darkness as something brushed across her face. *Shit, shit, it's the light cord! Holy Mother of God.* She reached up and pulled it. The weak bulb swung, its dim light touching the dark corners then moving away, leaving them dark again.

Magdalena paced around the cellar, inspecting, with Rachel shadowing her closely. "Dear, find a place to sit. I'll close the door." She walked back up the stairs, pulled it shut and bolted it.

Look at her, poor girl. The weak light did nothing to warm the color of her skin. *And those blisters...sweet Jesus!* "Do you have blisters anywhere else, Rachel?"

Rachel nodded. "Around the scar that separated me and Ani,

and..." She hesitated, then whispered, "Around my nipples."

Dear God. Magdalena's eyes dropped to the floor and saw that it was littered with dead flies. She looked at her muddy shoes, crusted with tiny corpses. *Holy Mother of...* "Don't sit on the floor."

Rachel stood there clutching her stomach, flinching every few seconds. Her eyes were worn, defeated, as dead and black as the flies on the ground.

"Let me find something for you to lie on." Magdalena pulled a box from a stack leaning against the wall and opened it. Red curtains. Those would work, red was good. For soaking up the blood, if its blood *was* red. And the dagger. She hadn't asked Rachel yet. Either she had it hidden somewhere, or it was at the cabin. As long as they kept the baby in the church, it would be weak. But Magdalena would have to go for the dagger. First things first. The time was at hand, she must concentrate, and pray.

She spread the curtains in layers on the floor and instructed Rachel to lie down. Rachel screamed out as she crouched down but her pain was deep, no amount of screaming could ease it.

Magdalena reached into the pocket of her skirt and pulled out two small bottles, one containing regular castor oil, the other a potent mixture of black and blue cohosh, cotton-root bark and angelica. "Drink these down. It'll help." Rachel did as instructed. She wanted the thing out of her, desperately.

Desperately enough to take her own life.

Three minutes later, Rachel went into labor.

The dreaded birth had begun.

* * *

Thunder rolled across the sky. Little Becca Klaus looked out the bedroom window, covering her ears, and watched as lightning struck the forest, the night cracking open like a giant black egg.

She began humming the nursery rhyme as she flopped back down on her bed and grabbed Mr. Snuggles, her favorite bear. She stared up at the ceiling. Was the buzzing in her head or coming from outside? She closed her eyes and saw Harry Click's fat face, how it had crinkled up when she hit him with the stone. Everyone picked on fat Harry, it wasn't her fault.

* * *

Zak kicked the TV.

Cousin Bello was fast asleep, slouched in his recliner, mouth wide open. "What are ya tryin' to do...catch a friggin' fly?" Bello was too drunk to wake. The sound of the thunder only made him smack his lips and roll over a little.

"Fucking thing." Zak whacked the side of the TV with the palm of his hand. "Stop it. Stop it." Then he gave it a good shake. The broken clock and the ashtray sitting on top fell to the carpet. "Stop it, goddamn it!" He turned the TV off and shook his head. He could swear the fucking thing was still humming.

* * *

THE FLY KING

Delroy pulled over to the side of the road. The tires skidded in the thick mud, and the sky flashed awake a bunch of cottonwoods.

It's happening.

Soon, the three of them would be together, just like before, tucked away nice and safe in the cave. He had all the documents to get them there, courtesy of his no-good buddy Weaz.

He sat still for a moment, smiling, breaking open a blister. He licked his lips. *"Sweets for my sweet, sugar for my honey."* He laughed, but it was tight; he'd hoped to be there at the birth, but the baby was a few minutes early. *Relax. Nervous dad, son, husband, and all the rest.* He slapped the steering wheel and yelled, "Yeehaaaa! The Fly King has come!"

And soon it would begin. On the flight from Heathrow to Portland PDX, he'd seen it all in a vivid waking dream, the clearest one yet. A vision, he supposed. He'd had several since it all started. What a brilliant plan. What an honor to be related to such a genius. He smiled. For the first time ever, he belonged. He was the friggin' Father, the Son, might as well be the Holy-friggin'-Ghost, too. The three of them would finish the curse from the cave. There, the Fly King would call upon the flies. Delroy knew what to do, and Rachel couldn't deny her nature. Even if she did at first, she'd come around. He didn't want to be forced to kill her.

The new *King of the World* would be practically a toddler by the time they got to the cave, even though it could be as soon as tomorrow; he would grow at an incredible pace. The end of God's children. *Let's get that party on the road.* He laughed again and adjusted the cellophane on his upper arm. It would be poetic justice. Delroy knew all about poetic justice, yes sirree. As soon as the Fly King called the flies, they would come in droves. They'd land on his hands, his little outstretched fingers. Delroy had pictured it a hundred times or more. It would be beautiful. The flies, each one of those dirty little fuckers--begging your pardon...those sublime little deities--would be touched with the curse. *Fuck me, it's brilliant!* No one could get away from the flies. They would spread it to everything they came in contact with. Fucking-A, the whole world would eventually be infected. Fast, but not *too* fast. The Fly King wanted to relish the panic, the chaos, savor God's lands wrought with disease, rebellion and anarchy.

And the Fly King would rule the Remainers, those who renounced that fucker--God. Not the bad motherfuckers, like Weaz and Bill. Shit, that would get the whole friggin' world off. No, only those who had denounced the Almighty. They knew who they were. He sensed some of them were even anticipating this event.

And he believed the Lord would also let a few God-lovers survive, too. Let them multiply a bit, get a type of New World order going; because everyone knows the power of Good cannot be demonstrated without some Evil in the picture. Well, vice versa is true, too. Oh, and shit, would the God-lovers suffer. Oh man, big time. He thought he'd suffered, well, his pain had been a friggin' picnic compared to what they were gonna get. He sat solemn for a minute, almost regretting burning down the pub. Ah, fuck it. He guessed it was okay; he'd gotten a lot of satisfaction out of killing those fucks, even if it wasn't the worst they could've gotten.

The streets would soon be changing. A horn honking rudely here and there, where some wanker had keeled over at the wheel. He'd seen it in the vision, right before the air hostess brought around the peanuts--he didn't want her faggy peanuts, but he'd helped himself to something else later, after he'd followed her out of the airport. In the vision, he'd looked in at the guy behind the wheel and recognized him as Uncle James. *Can ya fly, Del? Bark for me!* Uncle James was almost, but not quite, dead. The window was down, and the poor old bastard was covered in flies. They were feeding on him, his face one massive blister. Delroy wondered what that must feel like. His own blisters were small in comparison, and temporary; Uncle James' were deep bubbling lesions that had erupted on the skin while his organs were being liquefied. Yellow stuff was running out the side of Uncle James' mouth.

"Hey, remember me?"

The man couldn't see and probably couldn't hear either, but Delroy continued to talk to him, telling him the best part: that his soul wasn't going anywhere. It would remain right there in his rotting body, and he'd be forever held in his current state of agony. Delroy took out a cig and blew smoke at him. "Fuckin' racket!" He shifted the old bastard's head off the horn. It didn't make much difference, there were several others going off in the same street. The flies looked like pimples, except they moved from spot to spot, sucking the putrefied flesh. Del noticed an area of clean white in the crook of Uncle James' neck, little pearly seeds about an inch long and wide. *Ah, yes. Eggs, of course.* Uncle James had turned into a hatching ground. His back was probably wriggling with maggots. Delroy moved away at that point. *Dirty fucker.*

"Take a bath, Uncle James. You always were a dirty fucker. Hope your cock rots off!"

And back in the cave, or wherever, he supposed the Fly King moved freely now as a grown man--more flies were sent with the antidote to God's filthy infection: mankind.

In his vision, the sky was no longer blue, but almost black. The flies were everywhere, naturally, creating a type of gray haze. Sometimes they swarmed an area, sometimes they played alone--deadly stealth bombers. In the beginning, it would be a massacre, no one would know what was going on. After they lost a few hundred thousand idiots and finally started wising up, when the world was gripped in fear, that's when the fun would really start. The Fly King's little missionaries would be sneaking in through holes in screen doors, finding their way into cutlery drawers and air vents; landing on any exposed skin. No one would be safe. *Too bad...let the fun begin.*

And the food that no one really knows for sure is okay to eat? Feel that ungodly pain firing up in your stomach? Whoops, looks like that sandwich took a little too long getting from the fridge to your face. Too bad...here come the blisters.

No one was safe, and they knew it. You can't hide from the flies. Sure, the government had pumped gallons of poison into the air, but it was too late; the light was going out. They might as well lie back and enjoy the ride.

The real kicker was the idea of them being stuck here afterwards. Brilliant plan. Their souls prisoners to the pain. He wondered if perhaps the Fly King had an even bigger plan, if maybe he was trying to tempt God to show His almighty ugly face.

"If you want it, here it is. Come and get it." He sang the line and cracked up. Was that Bad Finger, or the Beatles? Pretty friggin' close, either way. Lucky for, you Mr. Lennon, your skinny white arse escaped while it still could.

And if you're up there listening, John, old buddy, I've got a few words I'd like you to pass on to your God: "Fuck You!"

CHAPTER 47

It wasn't what Magdalena had expected. In her mind, she'd seen a hideous demon that would *invite* slaying through the heart, but this was real, a flesh-and-blood baby. The cellar's pale ocher light slicked across the baby's naked body. A monster, not a baby, she told herself. It kicked its little legs and wriggled. Full of life--*unspeakable life.* Human or not, it would be difficult for Rachel to kill this thing, Magdalena realized that now. There would be the resistance of flesh giving slightly under the pressure of the dagger; blood, whatever color, being released from the wound; eyes staring, pleading. Rachel was its mother, and if she were to do this, she *must* believe. It would have to be done quickly, an act of faith. Until that moment, she mustn't look at it. Ungodly as it is, it's still alive, still *hers.*

"Rest, Rachel. Just you rest for a while." Rachel lay on the curtain, moaning slightly. But Magdalena knew she'd soon come around, recover her senses.

The birth had been surprisingly quick and easy. The castor oil and herbs had helped, *or it was simply supposed to be that way.* Magdalena took in a deep breath. The cellar air was rank and thick as a Louisiana swamp. The stench was coming from the thing in her arms, as if it was rotten inside.

Its skin was cool under her touch, and slightly translucent. Its eyes were large, oval, and bugged out beneath strained pinkish eyelids; they were widely spaced and completely black--no pupil or iris, just a touch of bloodshot cornea showing at the far sides. As Magdalena held it in her arms, she noted it was heavy for a newborn. When it yawned and gurgled, she saw tiny pointed teeth, like sharp little fish teeth, spread far apart.

As she cradled it with one arm, it seemed to be staring at her, but the blackness of its eyes made it appear blind. She carried it away to the darkened corner of the cellar, where several other curtains lay by the empty box. Its long pointed shoulder blades dug into her arms as it squirmed. For a second, she contemplated wringing its neck, but she knew it wouldn't be as simple as that; the cursed soul was here in this world now. She had no idea what would happen if she killed this baby, but she did know that only Rachel, the mother, could cast it back whence it came.

Rachel struggled into a sitting position. "Can I see it?"

"No, it's better that you don't." Magdalena kept her back to Rachel, quickly wrapping the baby in a curtain and laying it in the empty box. The little hands reached up to her, longish fingernails with blood caked underneath them. As she pulled the flaps over the box, it began to cry. *Sweet Lord, it sounds like a normal baby.*

When Rachel started to stand, Magdalena rushed over to her. "No, sit down. You must rest. It's better that you don't see."

"But it's crying," Rachel pleaded.

Magdalena said nothing. She returned to the box, pulled back the flap, and looked in. The infant stopped crying at once. She sighed and turned to Rachel.

"Where's the dagger? We need to do this before your brother arrives."

Rachel slumped back against the stack of boxes and began to weep into her hands. "Is it a monster? Is it really a monster?"

"Yes, Rachel, it is. And worse...much worse."

They heard scratching from inside the box--those fingernails. *Jesus, can this really be happening?*

She went to Rachel and sat down beside her. Rachel's eyes flicked back and forth from Magdalena to the box.

Magdalena took hold of her shoulders. "Please, Rachel, you must listen to me. I'm going to tell you everything. Listen carefully with your mind and your heart. Okay?" Magdalena took a and breath and began.

After Magdalena finished, Rachel wiped the tears from her eyes and looked at her.

"Please, Rachel, where's the dagger? We must move fast. We've already lost time."

"I hid it in the tomb, underneath the wooden bench. Far back in the corner."

"Rachel, I'll be quick. Don't move, rest. I'll be back in no time at all."

Rachel nodded. With effort, she seemed to be ignoring the scratching sounds coming from the box.

Magdalena walked up the steps and opened the door. The air outside the cellar was icy in comparison, but she relished its cleanliness.

Out in the storm again, she turned the flashlight on and began making her way over to the far end of the graveyard. As she walked between the gravestones, she caught an occasional glimpse of a date, a "Beloved Mother Of..."

Its skin, almost translucent. I could see the blue of its veins. Its little head, practically bald, just a few wisps of fine sandy hair. Those sharp little teeth and dead eyes...

She moved the light onto the approaching tomb. A yellow claw of lightning ripped the sky as she placed her wet fingers around the brass handle. She pulled open the door, plowing mud up behind it, edged herself into the tomb, and quickly knelt down, her back to the open door.

And its legs, did you see those? Bandy little legs. Feet way too long, deformed. A big toe, and then the others joined with a membrane of skin. And the shoulders...

She set the flashlight on the ground and looked under the bench, she reached her hand under and felt around in the far corners.

What was that? For an instant her shoulder had been bathed in light. Not moonlight, and not her flashlight.

Magdalena jumped up. The light was gone.

No, it had moved.

She stood behind the door and peered out. A car was coming up the driveway.

She tuned off her flashlight and squeezed out the half open door, hurrying back over to the church, her heart beating like a rabbit with a fox on its tail. She made it in just before the vehicle pulled up. She pulled the door closed, just leaving a small gap to see through. If it's the brother, there's a chance he might not be able to come in a holy place, she thought. But she was guessing, hoping.

Vaguely, she could hear an engine idling. Its headlights shone through the church window, casting a glint on Father Liebermann's fine black coffin. She waited, her breath small and scared.

When the engine cut off, she inhaled sharply and peeked through the gap. It was a truck--Jack's truck. Lightning forked behind, and she saw the silhouette of his trademark baseball cap. He'd gotten curious after she'd left the store.

Magdalena let out her breath. To hell with him. They'd shut themselves in the cellar until he was satisfied no one was here. He'd seen her car, no doubt, but once he looked around the church and saw it was empty, he'd leave. She'd go back and look for the dagger again as soon as he was gone. *Damn him.*

Magdalena skipped past the gap in the doorway and headed toward the cellar. The door creaked open under her hand. To her dismay she saw that the light was off. The bulb had blown. "Rachel?" she called out in a whisper, loud as she dared. "Rachel?" But she knew that Rachel wouldn't be able to hear, the storm was too loud.

Carefully Magdalena took a few steps down and turned on her flashlight, scanning the cellar floor. "Rachel? Rachel?"

The sound of rain was instantly deadened, as the door slammed shut behind her. All she heard now was the rusty grate of the key, locking her in.

* * *

"Sorry, Magdalena," Rachel whispered as she turned the key. "You should've left us to the noose. The dagger's not in the tomb, it's at the cabin."

Magdalena shouted, banged on the door.

She meant well, Rachel knew, but she must protect her baby, any mother would do the same. There must be a way to avoid its unspeakable fate. A desert island, where the two--three of them, if Gavin came--could live in isolation. If she could escape Magdalena and Delroy, her child might be able to live out its life. It might not be a long one, at the rate he was growing, but at least she could show him love. She could care for him, and if it became obvious that Magdalena was right, then she'd do what she had to do. She looked at his ugly face, his empty black eyes, and her own filled with tears.

From the crack in the doorway, she recognized Jack's truck; he'd come back for her. "Come on, Daniel, let's get out of here."

She kissed the baby on the forehead and placed the keys back on the altar, next to the priest.

Shielding the baby's face with the red curtain, she walked out into the pouring rain. To think she'd almost killed them both. She was exhausted and sore, but she felt nowhere near as awful as she had earlier. Daniel had come out so easily--*eagerly*. As she got closer to Jack's truck, the engine started up.

Rachel peered in at Jack through the window. She could convince him to take her into Portland. She would hide out there until she decided what to do.

Jack seemed mesmerized, staring straight ahead into the rain spiked beams of light. Shifting the baby to one arm, Rachel pulled open the passenger door.

"It's good to see you, Jack," she said, sliding onto the wet passenger seat. "Jack?" She touched his shoulder. He fell forward, his head hitting the horn. As cold hands grabbed the back of her arms, her eyes flew up to the rearview mirror.

"Delroy," she breathed.

"Hello, Rachel."

CHAPTER 48

Rachel was shuddering. Shaking, actually. All over. And his boy, the Fly King, was wrapped in her arms. Delroy's heart could have burst.

"Are you cold?" he asked her. Fucking incredible. She was gorgeous, even though she was pale and scared. No wonder--childbirth--he didn't envy her that. He cracked the window. Phew, that stink would take a little getting used to.

"Here, want my coat?" He wriggled out of it, the Saran Wrap crinkling, his eyes never leaving her. Boy, she looked scared. "It's all right, I ain't gonna bite ya."

Still, she was silent.

She thinks I'm a killer. First time we meet--in person, that is--and I'm shoving dead blokes under her nose.

"I had to kill that man, Rachel. He's the enemy. Don't you get it? People are gonna want to hurt your son. *Our* son. Wouldn't you kill for your own son?"

She didn't move. Maybe she was in shock.

"Can I hold him?"

Now, she moved. Her eyes got real big. She looked at him and hugged the baby tighter to her chest.

"Rachel, I know you're scared. But it's okay. I ain't gonna hurt our baby, am I?" He sighed, popped down the passenger lock, and leaned in over her. She backed against the door.

"Say something, Rachel. Anything." His face was on top of hers now. He could feel her breath, which was a little sour, but that was fine. This was his beloved sister, the love of his life, his flesh and blood. "Let me feed him."

She looked at him, the first sign of anything other than fear. "What do you m...mean?"

"Give him here, Rachel. Stop messin' about. We haven't got all day." He smiled and started rolling up his sleeve. "Come on. Give him here, or I'll have to *take* him." He held his hands out expectantly. "Come on..."

She looked at the baby, looked at him. Tentatively, she handed the baby over.

"Oh, man, oh, man." Delroy cradled the child close, kissed its head. It gurgled back. "Oh, man..." He looked at Rachel, his eyes bleary with tears. This was the best moment of his life. The skin on his cheeks was suddenly warm, and he realized he was crying. He allowed himself to weep, holding his baby close to his heart. He sobbed loudly, unashamedly, with happiness and relief.

Rachel put her hand on his shoulder. He looked up at her, saw six of her through his tears. He tried smiling, but his face was contorted with emotion.

All right, pull yourself together. She ain't gonna want a fuckin' cry baby. Girl like that needs a strong man. He cleared his throat and said, "See, this is how we feed him."

He moved the baby's head toward his bare forearm, and it flew for the blisters. "Owww!" It was fucking painful, but he relaxed, determined not to be weak again in front of his family. He let himself go, listened to the rain spitting a dreamy lullaby on the roof, the wind blowing against the truck, rocking it back and forth like a giant metal crib. And vaguely, he sensed an overall vibration, a hypnotic buzzing in the air.

Rachel watched on in horror. *That's all right, she'll get used to it.* Sure enough, the look of horror in her eyes was soon gone and she was asking if she could try. Delroy handed the bundled baby back to her.

This was the man from her visions, the man who had fathered her child. Rachel had never known about him. All these years, she'd had a brother and hadn't known. But he was bad, a murderer. Poor Jack. Poor, poor, Jack. Would Delroy hurt her son? No, but if she tried to take him away... The whole thing was terribly wrong, just as Magdalena had said. He wanted to use their child for something evil. At all costs, she had to stop that from happening. She didn't care if he *was* her brother and little Daniel's father. She wouldn't let him *use* her child.

Poor little mite needed a bath. She saw an awful shimmering wetness around its mouth, the puss from Delroy's blisters. Her stomach revolted. In one uncontrollable motion, she vomited onto the floor.

Delroy grabbed the baby, sat it in his lap and stroked Rachel's back. "It's all right. Puke, if ya wanna."

She wasn't vomiting now, but she was still bent over, retching. His hand was still on her back. First, it patted, then caressed, and now it was moving around the side of her ribcage, cupping her breast.

She felt an instant warmth in her groin and pushed his hand away. "Get off of me."

He held a hand up in submission. "All right, all right, keep yer hat on," he said, then slipped his coat over her shoulders. Wiping her mouth, she straightened.

"You wanna feed him now?" She nodded, took Daniel and lifted her T-shirt. Delroy watched, riveted. Daniel dove for the sores around her nipple, and she bit her lip hard enough to draw blood, it dribbled down her chin. Before she could push him away, Delroy had leaned in and licked it clean.

She pulled her head back, aware he was admiring the shape of her neck. "Don't touch me, Delroy. It's not right." *I have to get away from him*, she thought. She closed her eyes and let the baby suckle. *Have to keep him away. But he does love the baby. Would he ever harm Daniel? No, he'll protect him with his life. He's right about one thing: other people will want to hurt my child.*

"Guess what? We're leaving this place, Rachel. We're going back to Germany."

She opened her eyes now and looked at him. His poor, ugly face. How painful it must have been growing up with all the jokes and the disgrace. Looking down at the baby, she clearly saw the resemblance. *Somewhere far away. Far away, where no one can judge him.*

"Did you hear me?" He touched her hair.

This time, she didn't pull away. She could imagine how many times people had done that to him. "Yes, I heard."

Daniel's mouth sought out a fresh blister, and his sharp little teeth dug in. Her eyes misted and stung, as if snowflakes were falling in them. She let the pain dissolve into a type of euphoria. Fractured pieces of light glistened through the windscreen, shifted and moved like a lost village emerging from a cloud. Then she began to see it. In her mind, she was standing outside a cave, reaching up to a snowy twilight. And the strange ringing in her ears was getting louder.

"Rachel, you okay? Don't friggin' faint on me." Gently, he touched her brow.

Blinking away the image, she sat up straight, carefully removed Daniel's teeth from her breast. "That's enough now. You're already growing way too fast."

Delroy frowned, his face reddening. "There ain't nothing wrong with that baby. Nothin', you hear?" His voice was even but angry.

"I know," she said, frightened. "I know."

"By the way," he continued, "there's a certain *witch* we need to deal with. She'll do everything in her power to see our boy dead, and she ain't givin' up without a fight. Do you know where she is?"

* * *

Magdalena switched off the flashlight. The door was opening.

CHAPTER 49

The deer stood frozen in the middle of the road facing the truck. Delroy whooped loudly and pushed down harder on the gas.

"Stop it!" Rachel screamed. "The baby!"

Diagonal lightning ripped the sky, backlighting the deer perfectly for a second. Delroy swerved across the road into the mud.

"I wasn't trying to hit it, silly." He stared at her. *Why is she still so friggin' scared?*

This was the same place he'd pulled over on the way to the church, he recognized the cottonwoods. Only this time, he wasn't in the company of some dead redneck, but with Rachel--with his family. She was right, he shouldn't be fucking around. *Such a good mother, she is.*

He leaned in toward her, wanting to breathe her in. She turned away, looked out the window; her black hair shone blue under the moonlight. Gently, Delroy put his fingers under her chin and turned her toward him. "I'm sorry, darlin'. No more foolin' around."

A blister at the corner of her mouth had burst, and watery puss trickled down like a tear. Delroy leaned in, licked it away. Then, knowing he shouldn't, he pushed his lips hard against hers. His mouth muffled her struggling sounds. After a few seconds, she broke free.

"I'm sorry," he said, but he wasn't.

She bowed her head toward the baby. He was sleeping now, belly extended, lips and chin crusty from feeding. Soft little noises were escaping from his mouth and nose. Very slowly, his hands opened and closed; they were getting bigger. Delroy slipped a finger into his grasp, it was surprisingly strong.

"Where's the dagger, Rachel?"

She didn't answer.

"Come on, stop playing games. You know we can't leave without it."

Rachel remained silent. She lifted the bottom of her T-shirt, spat into it, and began wiping the baby's chin and mouth.

"It don't matter," Delroy whispered, getting close to her ear, breathing on her neck. "You don't think I'd let something that important wait, do you? I got it right here. Your ex-boyfriend, though, didn't want to hand it over."

Her head shot up, panic lighting her face.

"What did you do to him? You didn't...you didn't..."

"It doesn't matter what I did to him, Rachel. All God's children are gonna die."

He slipped a hand underneath the driver's seat and pulled out the dagger. He held it up, admiring the way its pockmarked surface seemed to undulate in the moonlight and the black shadow of rainfall. Carefully, he put it back and turned to her.

"I don't know what you saw in him, anyway."

"No...oh, no...oh, my God..." She was whining.

"What? What's wrong?"

He had this terrible feeling in his gut. It made his blood boil thinking of Rachel with someone else. He wasn't all that a man might be, but he could make up for it in other ways. Didn't she know that yet? His whole body began to shake, his eyes closed to slits. *How can she still care about another man?*

Rachel was breathing in short stabbing breaths. "Gavin...oh, no. Gavin...Gavin..."

"Stop it! Stop it!"

But she kept on saying his name, over and over, in short staccato breaths, the kind she'd made when they were making love. Only this time, she was repeating that cocksucker's name.

"Stop!" He swung out, slapping her across the cheek.

"Sorry, Rachel. I'm sorry."

She bent over and wept into her hands.

"Give him here." Delroy took the baby. "I said I'm sorry." What did she expect, for him to be over the moon? No, sirree. She'd have to prove her love, once and for all.

He grabbed Rachel's hair and jerked her head out of her hands. "What about *me*? Don't you love *me*?" His voice was choked. "Who do you love, Rachel? Answer me. *Answer me.*"

Rachel shuddered, her teeth chattering. Tears began streaming down her beautiful blistered face.

Delroy turned away, glaring out at the cottonwoods. He tried to calm himself, but the veins in his neck and temples continued to pulse. "Why should you care, Rachel?" he whispered. "They're all gonna die anyway."

Muttering under his breath, he started the car and pulled back onto the road.

* * *

Bertha peeked in through Magdalena's kitchen window. *Please, God, let Mag be all right.* Why wasn't she home?

Shoot, what's that noise? It had started earlier this evening, an infernal whirring in her head. Maybe some kind of static electricity caused by the storm.

She ran, slipping in the mud, around to the back of the cottage.

Where was Magdalena? She tried the back door, and found that it was unlocked. She pulled it open, stepped inside and shut the door behind her.

"Magdalena?" Bertha was breathing heavy, terrified. She flipped the switch, but no light came on, the storm had taken down the power lines.

CHAPTER 50

THE CURSE OF THE FLY KING

Outside the cabin, next to the old graffiti-stained boulder and closest to the river, Gavin lay curled on the ground. Delroy had tied him up earlier and left him there as collateral.

"Look, Rachel," Delroy shouted, "I didn't even kill him! I left that for you."

He glanced down at the baby. he'd placed the infant on the high roots of an oak tree, which were acting as natural drainage. The Fly King was safe, growing stronger by the minute.

Rachel dropped down on her knees and grabbed Delroy's legs. "Please, please, let him go."

"See, I knew it!" Delroy raged, kicking at her. "No! If you want to keep your baby, then you better kill *him*." He pointed at Gavin. "He's gonna die anyway."

"No, please!"

"Get the fuck off, Rachel. Kill him and be part of the Fly King's World, or don't and I'll kill you both. How's that?"

She threw her head back and cried out; lightning gripped the sound in its claw.

"If you love me, Rachel, if you love your son, your father, then do it."

"Do it!" he yelled, not at her this time, but at the rain filled sky.

Rachel crawled closer, through the mud, looked up at him and pleaded again, "Please. Please, just let him go."

Delroy threw his arms up in the air and screamed, "Kill him, Rachel! Prove your love." He looked up at the sky, fingers spread. "Believe in your father..." Now, his left hand swept toward the roots of the oak tree, toward the baby. "Believe in your son." He then pointed at himself. "Believe in me."

Delroy pulled the dagger out of his coat.

"Take it!"

Rachel looked away, but he saw fear flash across her face.

"Take it, I said." He pulled her off the ground, grabbed her hand and forced the dagger into it.

The change was instant, her eyes suddenly clear, no longer weak with emotion. They glistened, like sticky black pits. A thin, drenched mad woman. She turned to face Gavin.

Her hand warmed on the metal as it fed her blood. Her whole body tingled, alive with its need.

"How come *you* couldn't make me pregnant?"

Gavin stared, helpless.

"I *won't* let you kill my baby," she said, inching toward him.

"Rachel, I don't want to kill your--"

"Oh, you liar," she said, laughing. Then, she looked at him, serious again. This man was the enemy. He meant them harm. She must protect her family. Die for them. *Kill* for them.

"No, Rachel. Drop the dagger."

Delroy's shoulders shook with mad laughter.

"You're a liar. *Murderer.*"

"No, Rachel, I don't want to hurt you. Or the baby." He began to push himself away from her, moving slowly.

"You're a liar," she whispered. She took another step. "You're just like all the others."

"Rachel, you're confused. Just drop the dagger."

Delroy snickered over her shoulder. "Don't listen to him, Rachel. Do it. Prove your love."

Her heart thundered in her chest as she held the dagger to Gavin's throat, pushing it tight against his neck. He swallowed beneath its tip, and she pushed harder. His skin popped, and a bead of blood rose and melted into the rain, spreading like red ink down his neck.

"Rachel, I'm begging...don't do--" His expression changed, and he cried out. The muddy river bank was giving away.

Suddenly Rachel returned to her head, and in a moment of clarity she quickly used the dagger to saw through the rope binding his ankles, but the bank was collapsing fast, and before she could get to his hands, he was disappearing into the river. She fell with him into the raging water. Her head slammed abruptly against waterlogged roots, the tide flipped her over, and she was dragged away by the hungry current. Gavin, was nowhere to be seen. He had been swept away like a scrap of flotsam.

Delroy dropped to the ground and slid across the mud on his belly, snatching the dagger just before it slipped over the edge of the crumbling bank.

"Fuck!" He rose to his knees, shielded his eyes from the rain, and looked downstream. Rachel was barely visible.

Oh, fuck! Fuck. What should I do--let her go? She was no longer necessary to the plan. But maybe this *was* part of the plan. With her gone, no one could send the Fly King back. She was a danger. Besides, they didn't need her anymore. *Don't need her.*

Delroy jumped to his feet, ripped off his coat, and threw it and the dagger alongside the baby.

He needed her.

Delroy raced to the bank and dove into the river. Down, then up, slamming his lungs with air as the cold water bit his skin. Rachel was now even farther away. He'd have to be fast. Delroy took a deep breath and started swimming.

But then he stopped. Looked around. Waited to see her again.

Nothing.

Thunder groaned loudly across the sky, but Delroy's ears were numb from the deafening sound of the rain slapping against the angry river. Up high, lightning flashed. She was gone.

Rachel moved like a ballerina underneath the tide, her hair floating about her like an oil slick. *So calm down here.* A few final bubbles of air slipped up from her nose. *Sorry, Ani. Sorry Daniel, Gavin.* The choirboys wanted her to stay, they sang it in such a sweet way. She knew that song. *Stay,* they whispered. *You're not needed anymore.* Too dangerous up there. *Look after us Mommy. La la la la la la.* Sweet little faces, so pale, so pale. Her body moved as though boneless, her arms and hands dancing gracefully at the bottom of the river. So calm, so still. Just a soothing pressure on her ears and the lullaby. No thoughts now.

Shhhhhhhh.

* * *

Bertha closed the door to Magdalena's cottage. Maybe Mag was walking the trail. She often came home along the river instead of the road. But tonight? On a night like this? She'd have to be insane. Bertha shook her head. She must keep searching. Something was going on, something dreadful. Never, even if she lived to be a thousand years old, would she forget the look on Magdalena's face.

Bertha had spent the early part of the evening cleaning out the rectory, preparing for Father Liebermann's funeral. Finally ready to call it a night, she had run, ducking her head under her coat, from the rectory to the church to blow out the candles and lock the place up. She spoke to Father, told him again how sorry she was. That's when she heard banging and hollering coming from the other side of the cellar door. It about stopped her heart. She'd almost run out to her car and sped away, never looking back. But instead, she put an ear to the old pinewood door and listened. She recognized the voice-- Magdalena's.

She pulled on the handle, but it was locked. *How can it be locked if she's...* Bertha moved quickly to the altar, grabbed the keys and, with clumsy fingers, unlocked the door.

Magdalena shot out, almost knocking her over. "Get home! Get in your house and lock the doors. *Now!*"

Then Mag had charged out into the rain, jumped into her car, and taken off like a bat out of hell. Being locked down there in that cellar must have been hell, all right. But who would do such a thing? And why?

Bertha thought about heeding Magdalena's warning. But Mag was her friend.

* * *

"Fuck!" he shouted at the moon. She had gone down about here, the center of the river. Delroy took a giant breath and dove into the water.

It was quiet and dark, he could see very little, although the moon shed some light--deep blue luminance, like the darkest of twilights.

Delroy surfaced again, took another deep breath, and dove back down.

Something white. Rachel's white T-shirt. It had risen up over her head. He came up one more time, filled his lungs to capacity, and went down again, paddling furiously to get deeper.

He kicked his way to the bottom of the river, reached to the back of his jeans, and pulled out his knife.

Rachel's body was swaying back and forth in the white balloon of her T-shirt. Her breasts were exposed, bluish-white, the blisters pocking them like barnacles--a shrouded figurehead from a sunken galleon.

He grabbed her foot and began hacking at the thick fibrous weeds that had wrapped around it, careful to keep his own feet clear of their deadly grip.

Once he'd freed her, Delroy grabbed Rachel around the waist and took them both up, gasping as they broke the surface. Rachel remained still, her face merely resting on the pillow of water, blank eyes staring at the blank moon.

"Oh, God, no..." He held her neck in the crook of his arm and began swimming to the bank. "Oh, God, no..."

He hauled them both out of the water, laid her on the muddy ground, and began pushing her stomach. Nothing. He held his cheek to her mouth. Nothing. "Oh, God, Pleeeease!"

He pushed again and again, a thin whining noise rising from his throat. "Pleeeease!"

All of a sudden, Rachel's stomach contracted, and water gurgled out of her mouth. As Delroy quickly rolled her onto her side, she began coughing up river water.

"Oh, thank You. Oh, thank You, thank You." He fussed around her, trying to protect her from the rain as she gagged and choked up more and more water.

Delroy yelled, *"Thank You, Lord!"* and lightning struck the forest on the other side of the river.

But then he stopped.

Delroy stood, turned slowly looking back toward the baby.

There, kneeling in a puddle of splattering mud with the dagger at the child's throat, was the witch.

Delroy moved toward Magdalena, glaring at her through the rain. "You can't kill it!" he shouted, then held his hands up in submission.

"Don't come any closer. I've cast a spell, and I can kill it!" Her voice rang with the lie, but it was enough to stop him. "Send over Rachel," Magdalena shouted.

Rachel was up on her knees now, head bent, still coughing.

"Send her over here." The moon glinted on the dagger as Magdalena held it to the baby's throat. Jesus, it's grown, she thought. Its buggy eyes remained closed beneath the thin pink lids. It sensed no danger from her.

Delroy strode back to Rachel, grabbed her arm and pulled her up, pushing her toward Magdalena. "Go. Get the dagger."

Rachel was still bent over at the waist and coughing as she started toward Magdalena. The rain was so heavy, Magdalena could barely see her face, let alone her expression. Rachel approached slowly, the wind blowing her T-shirt like a sodden wet sail.

Watching her, Magdalena's heart flapped weakly in her chest. She looked up at Rachel, close enough now that she could see her eyes. Weak, scared, cold. Poor child was shaking all over.

Rachel stopped, held her hand out toward Magdalena.

"Rachel, please. You must end it, stop the curse. Kill the baby. Put its wretched soul back in the dagger, or it will kill us all...it's not human. It's Evil. You must believe me. Do you understand?" She searched Rachel's eyes, but they were flat, unreadable. Magdalena could only pray to God that there was a miracle inside Rachel's heart.

"Do you understand?" she repeated.

Rachel nodded. Magdalena had no choice, she had to believe it.

She moved the dagger away from the baby and handed it to her.

The instant she did, Rachel changed. Her eyes became bright and vicious.

Delroy strode over confidently and stood at his sister's side. He stared at Magdalena as he held his hand out. Rachel placed the dagger in it.

"Whoops, you lose." Delroy smiled and pointed the dagger toward Magdalena's head.

But then Rachel began acting confused. "Leave her," she said, grabbing his arm. "Let her go."

Delroy pulled easily out of her weak grip and hooked the dagger under Magdalena's chin. Magdalena backed up a few muddy steps, and Delroy followed. Now, she had no place to go, her back was against a giant boulder.

"Oh, dear, looks like you...*still* lose."

"Just let her go."

Delroy sneered at the pleading in Rachel's voice. "Just let her go," he mimicked. "Off you go then, witch." He moved the dagger from under her chin to behind her left ear. Magdalena closed her eyes. He laughed. "Yeah, you'd like that, wouldn't ya? You'd like to take the easy way out you coward. I don't think so." Magdalena opened her eyes, his face was next to hers and he was smiling at her, his misshapen nose dripping rainwater.

Delroy moved the dagger from her neck and held it to her stomach.

"You're gonna die, all right, but you're gonna suffer first," he said. His eyes began shining black and he thrust the dagger hard and deep into her belly.

The dirty blade ripped through Magdalena's clothes and into her flesh. She gasped in air as the pain uncurled inside her. Delroy's lips were stretched in a wide, cruel sneer. He twisted the knife once, then inched it slowly out.

"How's 'bout a front-row seat to witness how well you and your God failed?" He pressed hard on Magdalena's shoulder.

Grabbing at the wound, Magdalena's back slipped down the rock. She landed on the ground in a sitting position, a red pool already filling her skirt. She had failed. It didn't seem possible, didn't seem right, but she had.

"Oh, and as a special bonus, *you* get to be the first one to sample the Fly King's plague." He was grinning down at her excitedly. "They only have to touch ya, ya know. Don't matter if you die a second later, you'll be damned like all the rest! Fucking clever, huh?"

Without turning, Delroy addressed his sister in a flat, menacing growl. "Drop it, Rachel." She'd come up behind him with a rock in her hand. Now, he twisted in her direction and shook his head slowly, pointing the dagger to a place about twelve feet away. "Sit. Don't ya know I've got eyes in the back of my head?" He returned his attention to Magdalena.

Instead of looking at him, Magdalena stared out into the black, rain-scarred night. She could see the moon, large and vacant. She'd failed. Failed. And she could hear them. Even above the pelting rain and the furious river that sounded like stampeding buffalo, she could hear the deadly curse of the flies. They were coming.

"You sit still and wait. Oh...one more thing. Nearly forgot." He crouched down to watch her face. "I've heard from good authority that you're all psychic and shit so guess what, *You* get to be the official *greeter*. That's your job, isn't it? So who better to welcome all them pissed off little souls into eternal damnation. Better start coming up with a speech." He laughed and slapped his thigh. "Feels right, don't it? Feels *righteous*." His eyes had fixed upon the red stain seeping through her sweater and the pool of blood in her skirt. "Hmmm, I could use me some of that."

Delroy quickly stripped off his sodden shirt. He threatened Rachel with the dagger, grabbed his coat from beside the baby and formed a rudimentary umbrella over Magdalena and himself. She could smell his sweat and breath as he cupped big handfuls of her blood. She tried to push him away, but it was useless. In the dark cave of his coat, she could sense him wiping it over his chest.

"Ahh." His air filled the space. "I needed this."

Could it be? Could it? She waited for answers, and sensed that maybe it could. She smiled thinly in the darkness.

Delroy let the coat fall around him, slipped his arms in, and zipped it up.

Standing, he grinned down at her. "Much obliged, witch." With great effort, she raised her head up, caught him in the eye and smiled back. "You're welcome."

Suddenly, Delroy began to stagger; he fell toward the boulder, regained his balance, then blinked a few times then fell backwards, into Rachel, almost knocking her back into the river. "What the fuck--"

What was happening to him? What the--

The ground came up and hit him. He rolled, then struggled to his feet. Panting, he grabbed his chest. "Rachel?" The world faded in and out, he heard loud sounds, then silence, then loud sounds again. And then...

Magdalena watched as the man's hands flew over his ears, and he began to scream. He cried up at the moon. "Noooooooo!" His fingers ripped at the flesh on the sides of his face, and blood spilled down his hands. He fell to the ground, inches away from Magdalena.

The two of us will die here. She smiled weakly, realizing the protection spell Gavin had drunkenly helped her cast upon herself, had poisoned her blood to Delroy. Those clever old witches, she thought, laughing silently to herself.

But Delroy wasn't dead.

Neither was the Fly King baby.

Rachel looked down at them. Magdalena was leaning against the rock, clutching her fatal wound. Delroy was laying beside her. His limbs were spasming, *thwacking* in the mud.

She clapped her hands over her mouth. "Oh, dear God."

She could hear the flies, an electrically charged undercurrent of sound. There had to be millions for her to hear them over the storm.

"Finish...the...curse." Delroy's voice was choked by invisible, strangulating hands.

Magdalena lifted her head from her chest, eyes still shockingly alive. "Kill it," she whispered, blood trickling from the side of her mouth.

So close. Delroy could see the dagger lying just inches away from him. If he could touch it, he'd have a little more time; it would give him strength. He stretched out his arm, pain rocketing through his entire body.

"Fuck." His world was spinning out of control. He could taste death rising in his throat. His fingers worked toward the dagger, crabbing through the mud. Just as he touched the handle, Rachel began coming toward him.

No, not toward him, *past* him. Over to the baby.

Its energy tingled through his fingers, and as she ran by, he curled his leg up toward his chest and swiftly booted her. He heard the air knocked from her stomach as she went flying toward a tree. She whacked against it, brought down a torrent of pine needles and cones, and fell onto her side.

"Sorry, Rachel. Gonna have to do this alone."

She lay there unconscious.

He held the dagger in his hand, the rain washing it clean. It would keep him alive--temporarily. Just long enough to see this through. The witch had poisoned him, fucking cunt. He hoped she'd live long enough to get what was coming to her. But he needed to move fast. The curse of the Fly King would be complete, and then none of this petty shit would matter. He pulled himself through the mud over to the high roots, where the Fly King waited.

"Here I come. Daddy's on his way." He groaned. What waited for him beyond this life, he wondered. Too late anyhow. It had always been too late for him, he understood that now.

The curtain was pulled up over the baby's face, and for a horrible second, Delroy thought Rachel had killed the child when he wasn't looking. *You're delirious, Delroy, get on with it.* The material was heavy with water, he pulled it down, and there was his boy, his little eyes closed. Bigger, quite noticeably, and that wasn't delirium talkin'.

He pulled the Fly King baby from the tall roots to the ground. It woke up and started crying, shrill yells that cut through the roar of the wind.

"Shhh, shhh, Daddy's here," Delroy whispered.

The flies responded to the sound of the baby. They began edging in, buzzing louder. This moment had been long anticipated, its pattern tattooed into their collective psyche.

Thunder yawned through the heavens as Delroy dragged himself clear of the two women, carefully hauling his boy along in the sacked-up red curtain.

Like Santa, a paralyzed Santa. He giggled manically. *Satan's Santa, Satan's Santa.*

Six feet from the river's edge, where the moon and the sky were unobstructed by tree branches, he stopped.

"Shhh, shhh, don't cry. It's time, my little man. It's time." Delroy could feel the very air around him changing. Beasts squealed in the woods, wild with excitement. Every creature could sense it.

Unable to stand, Delroy heaved himself up onto his elbows and unwrapped the baby. It wriggled heavily in his arms.

"It's all right, it's all right, you'll see."

He pushed the blanket aside and sat his naked son up in the mud, packing wet earth around his lower back to create a support. The creature waved his arms and kicked his legs, flipping up clods of dirt with his strange long feet, wailing loudly.

"Don't cry. It's okay, it's okay. Here we go. Here we go."

Delroy stopped packing mud and slid around to face the baby. The time was *now*.

He put the dagger into the Fly King's hands, holding the weight while his pale fingers touched it. As soon as they did, something happened. The baby stopped bawling, looked down at the dagger, gurgled and smiled. He took it out of Delroy's hand, wielding it as though it were weightless--a feather. It was as if it was connected to him. It began glowing at the tip, and the energy moved downwards.

Delroy, no longer protected by the dagger was thrown into a seizure. He lunged backwards, legs kicking at the air, arms slapping at the ground. The buzzing grew louder, drilling into his mind, filling his head.

Delroy's eyes, though white and blind now, were frightened by something they saw beyond. He began to whimper, muttering rapid verse that might even have been a prayer.

The baby pointed the dagger toward the moon, his black eyes shining. He was quiet, changing, becoming that which he was.

The night went still. The thunder hushed and the wind stopped, commanded into silence. The rain turned magically to snow, floating down like the ash of a million souls. The beasts in the forest went silent. The only sound remaining was the buzz of the flies.

Close now.

The change had come. The Fly King sat in readiness, the dagger glowing silver in his hands.

Then, a terrible snapping. The baby stiffened as if rigor mortis had struck him. His chest thrust forward, pushing his back into an unnatural arch. He was merely a vessel for the curse now, mindlessly preparing for the final stage.

The dagger fell from his uplifted hands and stabbed the mud between his knees. His fingers flicked out in a terrible expectancy.

Magdalena *pushed, pushed, pushed* her thoughts toward Rachel. If she allowed herself to slip away now, she would be free. But she couldn't do that, not while there was still a chance.

Rachel's eyes snapped open, as if someone had shaken her. "What? Why?" She raised a hand to the bloody wound on her head. She caught her breath, and tried to recall. She looked over and saw Delroy laying there, her baby sitting in the mud, arms reaching out. "Oh, God. God, no..."

She heaved herself to her feet and ran, slipping, to her boy.

But it was too late. The voice of the Fly King came forth from him. Rachel could only look on, stricken with dread.

The child wasn't forming the sounds, rather letting them out. An incredible hissing came first, like sour air being released from a casket, then faraway screams. She'd never heard such a sound but there was no mistaking it--the cry of souls pleading for salvation. The flies grew excited and louder, wrapping themselves around the sound as if feasting upon it. And then the words came. Rachel dropped to her knees. "Stop, stop, stop!" she cried.

"I have returned. Now I call to the flies. Come touch my hand, take with thee my gift to mankind."

Diabolical laughter followed. Then, in one startling *snap*, the baby's shoulder blades shot out from behind him. Beneath the remaining translucent layer, black fibrous wings and their delicate bones were now visible.

The baby remained rigid, fingers stretched wide, readying for the first of many. They were incredibly loud now, no longer just a dark whisper in the minds of fools and prophets.

Up in the sky, powdering the night, they began to swarm, a black cloud shadowing the white. Swirling together, they massed in front of the moon like a dark kaleidoscope. More appeared. The cloud became darker, grew louder and louder as they assembled.

Magdalena watched. Her strength was quickly fading, but she had to try and gather the last of her power to call upon her past, her people. She closed her eyes and mouthed the words silently, over and over and over. She couldn't speak them, didn't know them, but they emerged from her just as the words had emerged from the child.

The flies began moving in, a dark army eager to be led. Rachel's skin crawled, as if they were already upon her. She looked down at her baby. He was reaching out, beckoning them in. Just one touch, she knew, would be the end. She grabbed him, picked him up off the ground and cradled him. He didn't move. He lay on his arched back, wings shifting beneath the skin, arms stretched out tautly toward the sky.

Her heart breaking, Rachel cried, tried to push them down. "Please, Daniel...please don't."

But his eyes remained fixed, staring straight up as if he had turned to stone. She pulled and pulled at his arms, but he wouldn't, or couldn't, move them. He seemed dead.

She considered running, but every cell in her body told her that running would be useless. They had come. *He* had called them. So she simply wept, hot tears that melted the snowflakes as they fell on her face, cold-hearted snowflakes, with their lying promise of Christmases and happy families. And then she felt something on her side, on the scar. The blisters were gone, and the scar was beginning to warm. She felt life there.

The flies had gathered into two twister-like cones, one for each of her boy's hands, and the moon shone clear again. As Rachel stared transfixed, as still as the child in her arms, the dark shape of a raven flew across its silver surface.

There was a face on the moon--Ani's face. She could see Ani's long dark hair, her pale features. *Oh, God, it's Ani.*

"I'm sorry, Ani," she breathed. "I'm so sorry. What have I done?" Rachel cried out, as she rocked her baby.

Only one thing could stop it, and Rachel didn't have the strength.

Louder and louder, two deadly black arms reaching down from the sky.

Ani spoke, but the words came from within Rachel's own heart.

"Be strong, my sister. Darkness lies at the doorstep. Your heart is true. Look into it. You were always the one, Rachel. Always the strongest. I would've failed where you will not. Something inside me spoke, told me to leave this world, and I did, Rachel. It was my way of being strong, too. I let you go, so you could do that which must be done. But I'm here now, and I never really left you. Feel me?"

Rachel put her hand to her side, over the scar. "Yes. Yes, I do." The warmth, the love that had been a part of her, was back.

Ani smiled and raised her hand, as if stroking Rachel's face, and Rachel felt it, the tender touch of her sister's love. She covered Ani's hand with her own and cried, huge teardrops that fell down on the angry metal of the dagger and hissed away into steam.

"You must do it, Rachel. You're the strong one. You must do it. You must, you must, you must..." The voice faded.

Rachel looked up, and Ani was gone. The raven flew back across the moon, away from the funneling flies and into the darkness. The funnels were closer now, their tips hovering just over the tree tops, unnatural shadows in the night.

Nothing could fight such numbers, such force. And yet even more were gathering. The first of them came closer, then closer still, smelling him out. Come to find his precious fingers, to be infected with the curse he had laid hundreds and hundreds of years before, a curse that had perhaps lain dormant in the bowels of the underworld since the beginning of time.

Rachel dropped to her knees and began to rock in the mud, her cries barely audible over the ever increasing noise. The air was different, she could feel the warm toxic breeze from their wings. In her arms, she cradled the stiffened body of her child, the child that would never grow up to be normal, to know the sounds of the playground or the laughter of a family. Whose destiny was not to be a musician like her and Gavin, or even an accountant, but a king. The Fly King. As she rocked him, accompanied by the maddening drone of his followers, she began to sing. Somehow, she'd known it all along. Through dreams, through genes, through Ani, it had always been there waiting for her. Her voice was calm against the frantic *buzz*.

"Sleep my baby sleep

Never more shall weep

Time to rest your little head

So softly in thy safe warm bed..."

Rachel looked now to Delroy. His eyes were staring blindly at a horrible nothingness, a tiny squeezing of breath faintly audible above the din. With a shaking hand, she brushed away the snowflakes on his face, kissed his cold lumpy cheek and whispered, "You saved my life, brother. Thank you. God forgive us."

"Sleep my baby sleep

Zzzzzzzzzzzzzzzzzzzzz

Oh sleep my baby sleep

Now, not another peep!"

As she stared into her child's eyes, they seemed to soften for a second, and she knew that somewhere in there was a part of her. A part of her soul, her disgrace, her redemption, her love. She knew what that part of him wanted, what the prisoner inside needed her to do.

"Time to close thy tired eyes

And Mother bring a sweet surprise

Come morning, if thee sleep."

The sound of the flies was terrible. But even over their diabolical noise, Rachel's song lulled the baby, and he closed his eyes. Gently, she laid him down in front of her. The drone grew even louder, anxious.

She pulled the dagger from the ground. Before she could stop herself, just as the first of them came within only inches of his frozen fingertips, she brought the dagger down into her baby's chest.

His blood splattered across her face. Her hands flew from the dagger to her mouth, and she screamed. The baby didn't move. He remained motionless, as if nothing had happened, but for the two twinkles of moisture that appeared at the corner of his closed lids.

But everything changed a moment later. The eyes flew open, glowing furious red. In the same second, the baby's face turned from pale to crimson, and it began thrashing its legs. It lashed at Rachel, small razor-like fingernails swiping at her skin. It grabbed and pulled at the dagger. An impossible writhing maggot of a creature, it hissed, hellish eyes full of fury. Lightning cracked, and the snow suddenly changed to hail. It pelted Rachel and the baby, but it was warm on her skin. She looked down at her legs, already knowing it wasn't hail falling from the sky, then screamed as the larvae pattered down on her head. She tried to shake them off, but their gray-white bodies clung to her, wriggling on her skin, brushing her cheek, crawling in her hair. They fell heavily on the baby too, pooling around the dagger. Rachel screamed again.

The maggots landed only within a six-foot radius of the Fly King, like rice on a bride. Rachel scrambled away, coughing and gagging, rubbing crazily at her skin.

The child hissed, head craning around on tiny neck, body steaming and spinning in the mud, larvae flying from his chest. Screams from inside, outside, everywhere.

Not my...not my boy, Rachel thought as she watched him thrashing around unnaturally, far too strong for any baby. With a hideous ripping, the skin split open on its shoulder blades, and black slick wings sprung out. They were ribbed like bats wings, and they flapped. But the dagger would not be freed. It began to glow red, and the baby's body glowed red with it. A terrible scream came from some indiscernible place, perhaps from the past, and the baby threw its neck back in agony and rage.

Just as suddenly as it had begun, the maggots stopped falling. The last of them pattered down on the Fly King's smoldering skin and were fried with a series of rapid sizzling sounds.

The flies became confused, lost their direction. They broke apart, buzzing bewildered. The energy, with its promise of dark secrets, had disappeared. Their noise grew less menacing, less urgent, and they began to thin. Finally, with the rising winds, they began to disperse.

The baby's body was smoking. Its wings went first, in a crack of flame, and soon it was blackened and charred. The larvae around it popped and sparked like embers. Then, with a distinct smell of sulfur, they faded into the mud. Rachel stood watching, hands over her mouth. Beyond screaming.

She fell to her knees, collapsing onto her side, and passed out.

Magdalena tried in vain to raise her hands over her ears as the beast screamed, an ancient cry that rose above the snow, the thunder, the clouds.

To the stars--beyond the stars. Beyond heaven.

Then it stopped.

The Fly King was no more.

Magdalena watched motionless as its flesh burned in the snow.

Oh, thank You. Thank You, God. Please, give me just a little longer...just a little.

She pulled her bloodless body away from the rock and dragged herself, inch by inch over to where Rachel was lying. She was no longer in pain, that had passed. The world looked different now, and she believed her spirit was rising. Soon, she would have no more use for this body. The raven would fly her on her final voyage. *Just a little longer...hold on just a little more.*

Magdalena pulled herself up beside Rachel, patted down the sleeve where the flames had caught it. She stroked her head and whispered in her ear. "You did the right thing, Rachel. God knows it. He knows you belong to him."

Magdalena rolled away from her and towards the blackened remains of the Fly King. As she pulled herself closer, she gagged on the sourness of its burnt flesh. In its charred over-large skull, she could see the tiny needled teeth.

The curtain was lying on *her* side of the body, thank God. She heaved herself up on her elbows, much as Delroy had, and wrapped the combusted pieces into it. She dragged the creature to the river's edge and shook its remains from the curtain into the hungry water. She lay for a moment and closed her eyes, the curtain still in her hand. *One more thing, just one more.*

Magdalena didn't know how much time passed, it could have been seconds, minutes, or hours. But Death was here now, waiting by her side. She wasn't scared.

Noises from the trees.

Branches breaking. Voices.

Closer. She recognized them. Bertha and Gavin.

Thank God. Thank God. One more thing, just one more thing.

Bertha appeared out of the darkness, Gavin's arm slung over her shoulder. "Magdalena. Oh, no." She released Gavin and ran over to her friend, pausing only slightly at the sight of Delroy's body. She knelt by her side. Magdalena looked past her at Gavin, who was crouching beside Rachel, and whispered, "She's okay. She'll be okay." Gavin couldn't hear her weak creaking voice.

Bertha turned to him. "She said your girl will be just fine. I pulled him out of the river," she said to Magdalena. "Lucky for him, I'm a big woman." She smiled, her tear-filled eyes silently assessing Magdalena's condition. "Let's get you an ambulance."

Magdalena shook her head. "No, no, it's too late for me."

Gavin came toward them, carrying Rachel in his arms. "I'm taking her to the cabin. I'm getting help."

As he moved by, his eyes caught Magdalena's. "Thank you," she croaked. When he smiled softly, she smiled back and whispered, "Go. Take care of her."

"Is there anything I can do for you, Mag?" Bertha asked, her hands clasping her friend's.

"Yes, there is." Magdalena's voice was now a wisp of air on dead lips. "Come..." She motioned Bertha closer, then handed over the bundle. Magdalena spoke into her ear.

Bertha's eyes widened as she listened.

Magdalena sighed. She had done all she could do. Leaning her head back against the rock, she stared up at the moon. She stared and stared, until her eyes were still. The shadow took her arm.

And here was Mother.

Smiling, just the way she always had.

"I've missed you, sweetheart. Welcome home."

* * *

Rachel opened her eyes to find Gavin looking down at her worriedly, holding her hand.

"You okay?" he asked.

"Yes. Yes, I think I am."

The ambulance took the winding Klickitat Road slowly. Rachel could hear its tires splashing through flood water.

"You're gonna be just fine, Rachel." He bent down and kissed her cheek.

"Magdalena?"

Gavin took a deep breath and shook his head. "She did what she had to do."

"Gavin?" The soft light in the ambulance was comforting. She looked at him. Really looked.

"Yes, Rachel, what is it?"

"I'm going to be okay now. It's gone."

"Shhh, Rachel. Rest."

"No, I mean the hole. It's *gone,* I'm free."

"I know, I know. Sleep a little, if you can."

He didn't understand, but that was okay. She didn't need to explain. He'd see. She was so lucky to have him. Him and Kiki, and wonderful parents back home in Chicago.

EPILOGUE

One week later.

In the trees behind the tombs, birds sat on bare branches, chirping questions at one another. The storm had whipped the leaves away and left them with lumpy skeletal arms to perch on, arms that latticed a now gorgeous blue sky.

Bertha walked up the path to the church. Her gaze moved to the left, toward the short bushes where they had discovered Jack's body. Unwittingly, she found herself searching for remnants--a candy wrapper, a quarter from his pocket.

Shaking her head, she glanced up at the church steeple, its cross dark against the blue sky. Three deaths in one week, not including the...man.

Bertha stepped off the path and on to the grass. She walked over to Father Liebermann's gravesite. The dirt had already begun to crisp. Soon the headstone would be in place and everything would be settled. A done deal.

The flowers, too, were beginning to dry, the petals curling and darker at the edges. Bertha said goodbye to him, and moved on with a groan. She had pulled her back saving the young man, Gavin, from the river. She could put that in her book of good deeds. She took the brown bag in both hands and headed over to the church. One more good deed left to do.

Magdalena's casket stood in the same spot Father Liebermann's had. Hers was a lighter wood, blonde oak. Poor Mag. She looked so peaceful. Bertha's eyes wandered down the casket. "Jesus Chri-- Sorry, Father."

Looming large in the pattern of the wood, quite clearly for anyone to see, was an evil face made up of wood-grain and knots! Two devilish eyes and... Bertha forced a nervous smile. It's just wood, she told herself, just unfortunate patterns in wood. Don't be foolish. She laid the brown bag down on the altar. But really, who could blame her for being a little jumpy after all that had happened?

She had no idea what was inside the bag; well, the red material, of course. But inside that?

She shuddered as she recalled poor Magdalena trying to whisper into her ear. She'd sounded so desperate.

"Bury it...with me. Hide it...in my coffin. Don't look at it. Don't touch it." She'd pulled away and tried to search Bertha's eyes, to make sure she understood. Bertha had nodded. Magdalena had sighed and slumped back against the rock.

Bertha removed the mud-caked material from the bag. She'd recognized it as a piece of the old school curtain. The ones that had, until last year, adorned the assembly stage.

She carefully raised the bottom half of the casket lid. They'd dressed Magdalena in a high-necked lace blouse, and black pants. Poor Mag. Bertha's eyes welled up with tears, and Mag began floating in her white satin lining. They'd put her in pants, but she'd always worn a skirt.

Bertha began sobbing, the sound echoing around the empty

church.

She finally pulled herself together. Better get on with it. Someone could come along at any moment.

Where could she hide it? She slipped her hand under the small of Mag's back. No, that wouldn't work. She tried pushing the bundle up her trouser leg. Good God, no. If Mag had a skirt on, as she usually did, she could have hidden it under that. Damn thing was just too bulky to hide.

She took the bundle and began trying to smooth it, flatten it somehow. The bright sunlight beaming through the church windows suddenly dimmed. A cloud was passing across the sun.

Bertha's nerves pricked awake, and she thought of the face in the wood. So clearly a face--a terrible, glaring, snarling...

And this mysterious bundle. *What's in here anyhow?* She held it up and dragged her hands along it, squeezed it, still trying to make it smaller. Hadn't the mortician seen that face in the wood? Heavens above! She kept trying frantically to smooth out the lumps. Mag would have to lie eternally with that face...that... Bertha's hands were shaking.

The heavy dagger slipped out of the material, striking into the wooden floor with a loud thud.

"Jesus Chri-- Forgive me, Father." She went to grab it, hesitated, covered the handle with the material and pulled it from the floorboard. A dagger?

Her eyes scanned its surface. So beautiful. *So old and beautiful, so... Bury it. Bury it with her.* That's what Mag had said, and that's exactly what she would do. But is that what she said? Her voice had been so weak... *Yes. That's what she said. End of conversation.* Bertha's hands trembled underneath the material. *Perhaps I can pluck some stitches from the satin...hide it in the lining. But is that what she meant? Perhaps she meant for me to look after it.* No, she said, "Don't look at it. Don't look at it, and don't touch it." *Touch it. No, don't touch it. Touch it. Touch it. Touch it.*

Bertha gazed down at the dagger. Without knowing, she had been stroking the metal with her fingers.

She pulled her hand away from the dagger and quickly folded the material around it. *Magdalena trusted me...*

Magdalena was dying, talking crazy. No blood in her head. Bertha searched frantically in the casket for a place to hide the dagger, but she was distracted, not thinking clearly anymore.

Then she stopped.

Just one more look wouldn't hurt.

Truly, it had been hard to hear her friend over the river and the wind, and the strange buzzing in the pine trees...

READER NOTE

Thank you very much for reading the FLY KING. I hope it scared you in all the right places and that you'll be back to read my next novel. If you did enjoy it, I have a favor to ask. Reviews are extremely important to an author. In the world of e-publishing, reviews can make or break a book. If you liked the Fly King, I would really appreciate it if you could take a few minutes to go to your favorite e-book websites and write a short review to let others know that they would enjoy it too.

Thanks for supporting and be sure to watch for my next novel.

Made in the USA
Columbia, SC
31 August 2018